DALE MAYER

CHILLED BY DEATH

BOOK THREE OF BY DEATH SERIES

CHILLED BY DEATH
Beverly Dale Mayer
Valley Publishing Ltd.

This is a work of fiction. Names, characters, places, brands, media, and incidents are either the product of the author's imagination or are used fictitiously. Any resemblance to actual events, locales, or persons, living or dead, is entirely coincidental.

ISBN-13: 978-1-988315-85-0
Print Edition

Books in This Series

By Death Series

Touched by Death

Haunted by Death

Chilled by Death

By Death Books 1–3

About This Book

After losing two close friends three years ago in a snowboarding accident, Stacy Carter has become a loner and can't seem to make peace with this loss, not when Death intrudes upon her personal life again and takes two more people she loves. Meeting new people and trying to make a normal life for herself proves to be harder than anything else she's done. Meanwhile, in her career, being a forensic pathologist puts her in close contact with the dead. While fascinating and never dull, it isn't exactly a cozy conversation starter. When her brother tries to coax her out for a mountain vacation to help her heal, she has reservations, even as she tells herself rationally that she needs to face this. Reservations and rationale, however, were in short supply the last time she saw Royce O'Connell at that mountain …

Royce is floored when Stacy finally returns to the spot where she lost her two best friends, intending to deal with the depression that she's battled for some time. Royce and Stacy have been longtime friends, but Royce wants so much more between them. Yet he's well aware that he blew their last time together. Stacy makes it clear she's not looking for reconciliation. However, he can't help seeing her reappearance in their tight-knit group as a second chance, maybe his *only* chance.

Out in their winter wonderland, the vacation atmosphere shifts from merry to mayhem in a hurry, when they come across a dead man. Then, not long afterward, Stacy's brother goes missing. The nightmare is only just beginning, as the realization settles in that they can't trust anyone.

Maybe not even each other …

Sign up to be notified of all Dale's releases here!
https://geni.us/DaleNews

Chapter 1

Three Years Ago

STACY CARTER SLID across the fresh white powder to come to a rest on the top of the small rise. She smiled up at the stunning blue sky and tall evergreen trees dusted in white.

It was a gorgeous day at Blackcomb Ski Resort in BC. A place she and her brother and their friends considered their home away from home. Their winter and summer play home was close enough to Seattle to make it an easy drive and far enough away to make it a change.

They were staying at her brother's friend's cabin, one they'd come to many times over the years. It was perfect. The day. The mountains. The situation.

Her best friends—they were like sisters really—Francine and Janice were up ahead. Or they should be. They'd been boarding.

However, Stacy hadn't been feeling well and had been in town all morning. Feeling better, she'd come out to meet them at the top of Gorman's Peak. It was a well-known run that could take one farther into the backcountry, and, yes, out-of-bounds if they wanted to—and her friends often wanted to. Stacy wasn't like that. She hated breaking the rules. But so many of the others loved to ski and to board the pure, untouched runs down the backside. They'd been doing it for years, and conforming to the new rules and regulations was difficult. And not appreciated in many cases. Areas that her friends had played in for years were carefully watched now.

Many of the tougher runs had been closed all week due to avalanche hazards. Although that disappointed several of her friends, Stacy didn't mind. She'd been skiing this resort since forever. There were lots of runs to keep her interest.

Then she was calmer, more relaxed, when compared to the other two women. They were the play-hard-and-love-harder variety.

Stacy was much gentler. More safety conscious and much more laid-back. She would have been happy to grab a coffee and to sit at the top of the run to just enjoy the moment. She worked hard at her job and preferred to relax when on vacation. Life was about balance.

Her two friends were both dashing raise-a-little-hell modern women. Stacy had never understood just what drew the three of them together, but something had, and it worked. They were opposites who complemented each other. They'd been friends for close to a decade. They'd changed over the years that they had known each other, with Stacy becoming more laid-back over time, whereas her friends had gotten wilder, becoming even more daredevilish.

The men loved it. Loved them.

Stacy had watched in bemusement, as Janice ate up a lifetime quota of men before she was twenty-nine. With her long black hair, a slightly olive tint to her skin, and massive brown eyes with long lashes and pouty lips, all on top of long and lean physical perfection, yeah, she could have any man anytime. And she did. Often. She also never let her heart get involved.

Francine was a slightly curvier and shorter version, but just as much of a go-getter. She'd been following in Janice's tracks since forever. Not quite as good as Janice in boarding, or with men, but Francine never seemed to care. She was content to take second place. However, she'd never slide to third. No, that was always Stacy's spot.

Not that Stacy cared. She'd always felt slightly out of sync with the other two, but they all loved each other.

It was all good.

Her phone beeped.

She pulled it from her pocket and smiled. *Janice.* She read the text, and her smile fell away.

Damn it. Janice wanted to end the day with a splash on the long back trail and cut to the cabin at the right time. Only that run was out-of-bounds. According to the text, the two would meet Stacy in a few moments.

She quickly texted a reply. **Back runs closed due to avalanche hazard.**

And waited.

She didn't have to wait long. The next text read **Phooey.**

That was it. Stacy stared down at it, chewing on her bottom lip, and wondered. Out loud, she murmured, "Phooey what, Janice? As in phooey that's too bad, or phooey like that'll matter?"

Stacy shifted positions, so she could see her friends ride up the lifts. They'd be about ten minutes, if there wasn't much of a line at the bottom.

She sat back to relax.

Francine texted her next, asking where she was. She answered. Then deciding it was better to ask than worry, she texted Janice and asked, **Which run do you want to take**

down? The face looks great.

She knew her attempt to convince Janice to go down the sheer drop in the front of the mountain wouldn't likely work if she was set on going down the back to the bowl, but the face would be perfect. Usually no one was there, leaving them lots of space to take jumps, to weave through the trees, or to just cut a narrow strip, racing to the bottom.

Her phone beeped again. *Janice.* **I want to take Gopher Run to the bowl.**

Damn it. **The bowl is closed too.** The bowl was an in-bounds area—as long as the weather cooperated. When it didn't, it was a closed area. Like everything connected to the resort and winter sports, safety was paramount. They had a great medical center here, and the search and rescue teams were second to none. Thankfully Stacy hadn't had any reason to use either.

She studied the chairs swinging in the gentle breeze, as the lifts toiled upward, carrying the many groups of happy winter enthusiasts.

"Stacy!"

Stacy turned in the direction of the yell, then smiled at Janice and Francine and waved.

Hearing her name again, she caught sight of her brother and two of his friends, who were also her coworkers, Mark and Stevie, several chairs below the women. "Hey," she yelled back.

Within five minutes, they all stood in a group at the top of the runs, just out of the way of the others getting off the lift.

"We're going for another run. See you in the cabin in an hour or so." With a big wave and lots of hoots and laughter, the three men jumped over the steepest part of the face.

Stacy grinned at their antics. They were all incredibly skilled and a joy to watch. "Awesome! We'll follow." With a big grin still on her face, Stacy turned her skis, planning to follow the guys off the top edge. "Come on, women. Let's go." She slid forward slightly, then twisted to make sure Janice and Francine were following.

They weren't.

Shit.

Awkwardly Stacy flipped her skis around, now facing the direction where the women stood, and Stacy struggled back the short distance to where she'd left them.

And reached only their trails, from where they'd plunged over the back of the mountain to the bowl. "Damn it, Janice. Why don't you ever listen?" she cried out to the vast white expanse in front of her. "That whole area is a bad deal right now."

Then Janice had always done as she pleased. Stacy wished she'd said more in her texts. Had she made it clear how dangerous the area was? It was closed. Avalanche warnings. Surely that spoke volumes about the snow conditions. She studied the pristine area in front of her, looking for their tracks. The women were already halfway down.

"Fine, then I'll catch you on the upside again." Although, as frustrated as she was right now, maybe she'd just head toward the cabin. She was in perfect alignment to cut across to a run that would take her back there.

She hated to see them do this. They were always taking unnecessary risks.

Like wild birds that had to be free to do their own thing.

Sure, Stacy had more understanding of the risks than most people, given her job. So many ended up on her table at the morgue because they made the wrong decision.

Given her experience with accidents and death, was it any wonder she worried about them?

Decision made.

She pushed off and glided along the ridge. She could see the women a long way down the slope. They should be turning right to head to the bowl and connect to several other runs lower down to bring them back around to the bottom of the chair lift they'd just gotten off of. Stacy debated waiting for the two to make their way back up again but decided she had already spent a lot of her time waiting for them.

She carried on for a few more feet, when she glanced down at the women, she saw them cut to the left.

Into the out-of-bounds area. And away from the chair that would bring them back up to where Stacy was. Would they turn left lower down and head toward the cabin? There was a run that cut off and would take them back home.

Her heart damn-near clogged up her throat, as she watched their devil-may-care attitude, while they raced across the mountain face and started the beautiful long zigzag pattern. "Damn it, Janice. Why do you always have to push it?"

She wanted to turn away and to ski her own path down to the cabin, but she couldn't tear her gaze away from the two women. They were incredible boarders, so graceful they looked like birds floating in the sky, crossing the mountain-scape below.

As Stacy watched, she thought she heard something. A muted, deep booming sound. And a gentle rumble. She glanced around, but no one else was close by, and those farther away were busy laughing with their own friends.

Several groups came off the lift and never stopped, skiing right on down again.

She glanced back at her girlfriends. Her gaze struggled to catch sight of them racing far below. They should be wrapping around the mountain to the left to catch the run toward the cabin. Only they were still going straight down the mountain.

And then Stacy saw the reason for the rumble.

One of the hard crusted overhangs of snow at the top of the peak had finally let go of its tenuous hold on the rock and had pounded onto the snow below. The impact started the massive sheet of snow to shift in a slow-motion slide that picked up speed the lower it went.

Within seconds, an avalanche raced downhill.

Down to her friends.

"Janice, move it!" Stacy screamed, her hands cupped around her mouth, but they couldn't hear her. Of course they couldn't. No way her voice could be heard over the noise of the destruction racing toward them.

Neither could she stop screaming at them to move faster.

The women needed to turn left. Now. And, once again, they had to take it to the limit and go down even farther. Finally they started the curve to the left, away from the cliff edge ahead of them.

"Jesus."

Stacy could only watch in terror as the two women suddenly noticed what was bearing down on them. Both women crouched down and raced as fast as they could out of the oncoming path of the avalanche.

"Faster," Stacy screamed. "Faster."

And faster it was.

The avalanche picked up speed ...

And picked up the two women …

And tossed them into the white snowy melee.

As Stacy stood in horror and watched, the massive wall of snow and women slipped off the rock edge and out of her sight.

Forever.

Chapter 2

Three Years Later

STACY STARED AT her brother and repeated, "You want me to go back? To Blackcomb Mountain? Tomorrow?" She shook her head, her long blond hair flying wildly around her head. "No way."

"Yes," George said to her. "It's time."

"It doesn't matter if it's time. I can't go." In a quiet voice, she added instinctively, "I'm not ready."

And yet … she stared across the restaurant, almost blind to the steady stream of customers walking through the popular place. He'd pointed out a truth that Stacy had come to realize lately.

It *was* time. She shuddered. But that didn't mean she was ready to face the grief, … the loss she'd been through. Or face the place where it had all happened. Yet she knew she would remain crippled until she did. "I'd rather go where it's warmer," she muttered.

"You might, but, since you won't go on any vacation at all, that won't happen either." Calm, direct, and gentle, George leaned forward earnestly. "Look. You don't even have to do any skiing. Bring some books and hang out in the cabin. Enjoy the break. Face a few memories and move on. This isn't an all-out crazy sports event. It'll be a gentle go-at-your-own-pace kind of thing. Yes, it's the same cabin, so there will be a few ghosts. Face them." He grinned, adding, "Then grab your camera and do what you do best. Well, besides, dead people …"

Trust him to get her to crack a smile. "Yeah, I do those all the time, so why would I want to go back and see more—at least in my head?"

"I think *because* you deal with bodies and *because* you can't find your friends—to have their bodies to care for, a funeral to arrange—it makes it that much harder for you to find closure."

Very insightful of him. She played with her coffee spoon, turning it over and over again in her hand. "I hadn't considered that." True. She saw death like most people never had a chance to. She was a forensic pathologist, after all. Bodies were her stock in trade. But the bodies on her table were strangers. Not her best friends. It was different when the losses were personal.

"We're cooking the food ourselves—"

"Ha," she broke in teasingly. "Now I know why you want me to come. You want me to be the chief cook and bottle washer."

"No," George protested, but not much heat filled his word. "If you wanted to do it, that would be great, but, no, we are all expected to do our parts."

"*Uh-huh.* Sure." She didn't necessarily believe him, but finding out this tidbit made her feel better about going. She wouldn't be expected to ski every day, like the others. She was an experienced skier and an intermediate snowboarder, but her first love during winter was her camera. The thought tugged at her, going back to some of those indescribably beautiful days with the brilliant icy scenes. She had been getting into it with her earlier travels, and that had stopped as her trips had stopped.

At the same time, she'd turned away from many aspects of her life. It was a move that had surprised many. She had retreated within—from everyone and everything. To heal. To adjust to the new reality of her life. It had changed her. When she'd recently picked up her camera again, she'd done so quietly. Privately. Before, she would have considered herself open and friendly. Now she kept to herself and shared little, even with those closest to her.

Her brother had called her secretive and had considered it part of her depression. Maybe he was right. Yet he didn't know about all the issues—good and bad—in her world.

Life used to be simple. Then, when she was wide open and enjoying her day, fate took scissors and cut away the very steps she was standing on. As if to say, *Comfortable, are you? Well then …* Snip, snip, snip. *How about now?*

She wiped those thoughts from her mind and forced a smile at George's hopeful look. She'd dealt with a lot of her issues. Most of them anyway. She just hadn't shared how far she'd come with him. And that was too bad. He was still worried about her. In many ways, his concern was justified, but it wasn't any longer. She was almost philosophical now.

Life was a bitch, and then you died. Sometimes you died earlier than planned. She'd seen a lot of death. Sometimes it was comforting. Everyone came to the same end. Just the routes people took were different.

It was time to let him know how well she was doing.

"If I can come and go at my own pace, do a couple day trips on nice sunny days, stay home when I want to be alone"—she chuckled at his rolling eyes and his bright, happy grin—"then I'll come. I'll help with the food, but I won't be responsible for all of it."

"No worries. I meant it when I said we're all pitching in." He stood and tossed money on the table to cover their bills. "Besides, Royce is a damn good cook."

With that bombshell, George walked to the front door, as if to leave.

"Hey, you can't just say, *Royce is a good cook*, and walk away," she called out, racing over to stand in front of him. "You didn't say he was coming."

George raised his not-so-innocent gaze in a wide-eyed look of surprise and said, "Oh, didn't I? Well, he's part of the group. He always comes. Not to worry. We're just looking to get away for a week, you know? Just a chance to relax and to hang out."

She glared at him.

"Besides, what difference does it make if he does come?" He gave her a knowing grin. "You don't even like him."

For the life of her, she couldn't hold back the wince or the flood of memories that took over her psyche. She'd known Royce since forever, as he was her brother's best friend. But the hardest part of that history was the carnal knowledge she'd kept to herself. And, wow, had that been good. And hot. And so damn addictive that she'd walked away, afraid she could never let him go. He wasn't long-term material. Certainly not marriageable material, likely not monogamous—whereas she couldn't be anything but. But being with him had made her wonder for a little while if she could do it his way, ... which was not likely, given what little they had.

A wild, crazy, all-out sexual weekend.

A weekend she'd loved. And hated. Because it had changed her. She'd gone to him hurt, in need. She'd taken everything he'd had to give and had wanted more. So much more that she'd been terrified.

And he'd been unaffected.

How fair was that?

Then she'd been grieving. She'd needed to reaffirm life. She'd needed to reaffirm that she wasn't alone. She'd needed to reaffirm that she had a reason to get up in the morning. A reason that didn't involve dealing with loss.

For the duration of that weekend, he'd given her what she needed. That she'd gotten so much more was a shock she hadn't liked. But she'd been a big girl. And she'd known Royce, a bad boy, would never make a partner for life. He'd done the rounds. Even with Janice and Francine. Then that was hard to blame him for, considering the women's own dating habits. Besides, how many wild animals mated for life? They made for a hot, unforgettable mating session, but after that? They were best left to go their own way.

She'd seen him a time or two since then in Seattle. From a distance.

She hadn't spoken to him. Or been in the same room with him. She'd been too afraid. The sparks between them were obvious. And she was essentially private. At least now that she'd locked down her emotions.

That way was easier to deal with the blows that life dealt her.

And she had dealt with them. It just hadn't been easy. There was one she was still working on.

Guilt.

Being a survivor sucked in many ways. She'd had night-mares for months and still wasn't sure why her friends had to die that day. She knew she wasn't responsible, but she couldn't help but think she hadn't done enough to stop her friends from going down that side of the mountain. Surely there'd been more Stacy could have done.

Maybe this trip would help release her from that heavy burden.

She watched her brother race out of the restaurant. He'd just set her up, darn him. She made a face at his retreating back, then shrugged. He was right. It was time. And, at least this way, it would be easier. She wouldn't be alone. She'd be hanging out with people who understood her and what she was going through.

She wondered if several of the guys from work would be invited, Mark and Stevie in particular. They'd been part of her brother's group for a long time. Rock climbing, snow-boarding, hiking—their life was a big party. Stacy had been involved in the group for a long time, at least when her girlfriends had still been alive. They'd been party animals too. Maybe because everyone around Stacy was so extreme, she'd been the opposite. Quiet. Calm. Careful.

Now she was even more so.

Loss did that to someone.

Considering she hadn't planned this trip, she wouldn't mention it to her coworkers, not until she heard back from her brother. Maybe the group was full up. Maybe there was no room for Mark and Stevie to join in this time. A group would often run eight to ten people, cabin capacity. Maybe a couple more, but too many were a hardship to plan meals and activities and to keep track of where everyone was.

Given the hour, she didn't waste any time in getting back to her office. She had no shortage of work ahead of her. It had been great to spend some time with her brother. He was a bit of an oddball himself. He didn't do ... anything. Yet he did everything. Though he had a degree in econom-ics, he'd made it big-time doing sports action videos. He was now working for a large camera company, running around the world, taking videos of crazy stunts. He had a large group of buddies who set up crazy bungee jumps and skydiving formations. He and his buddies loved it.

She had to admit it sounded like a pretty fun way to get through the day. At least while George was young and in his prime. Maybe later he'd find something less dangerous. She couldn't help worry about him. Especially now. They'd lost their parents a long time ago. George had been old enough to live on his own, but Stacy had gone to live with her aunt and uncle. She and George had stayed close. But losing her parents young had made her afraid something would happen to her beloved brother. For that reason, he usually didn't share the details of some of the crazier stunts he was involved in. Thank heavens. She had enough nightmares to keep her awake at night.

Although outdoorsy, she wasn't much of an extreme sports fan. She wasn't into adrenaline. Too hard on the system. And she hated major shocks. Her brother thrived on them. He and his friends played punk-ass jokes on each other all the time. To her, they were horrible, but the group of guys he hung with thought they were hilarious. And, true enough, he played just as many on his friends as they did on him.

You had to be one of them to understand.

The double doors to her lab opened automatically, as she stepped on the entrance mat. She strode through and brought out her security card, sliding it down the key lock and heading inside to the morgue. When working with the dead, she liked to think she'd learned to appreciate life a little bit.

"Enjoy your lunch?" Mark asked, doing wheelies on his

computer chair, when she walked through the lab. Some martial arts schedule was up on his monitor, like that was allowed. And likely why he had it up there. He was quite a pro himself and taught on the side.

"Yeah," she said, grinning at his antics. He was the same age as her but acted a dozen years younger. Then so did her brother. Maybe that's why she got on so well with Mark and Stevie. However, she preferred Mark more as a friend than a coworker, since he didn't necessarily have the same work ethic, preferring to skip out early to meet the guys for the next adventure in progress. Still, he was good people, and that counted. "I had lunch with George."

"Really?" He grabbed the desk to stop his wild ride. He stared up at her, shoving his long hair back off his face. "And?"

She raised an eyebrow at him. So he did know. She had wondered. Chances were good both men—or rather, overgrown boys—she worked with would be going on this weeklong fun adventure. She paused, considering that. How much of a real break would it be, if she went with guys she worked with?

Not by a stretch could she use that as an excuse to get out of this trip. No, she was going. ... If she had a few last-minute qualms, well, that was to be expected. Besides, both men loved these trips and were huge board fanatics. They were also search and rescue volunteers. They deserved their fun on the slopes, like anyone else.

"He wants me to go on this ski trip to the cabin," she tossed over her shoulder, as she carried on down the hallway to her office. "You know. ... Go back and face my memories. A great idea in theory, but ..."

"Wait, he did?"

"Yes." She grinned as she heard his footsteps. She knew he couldn't leave it alone.

"Well"—Mark popped his head around the corner—"what did you say?"

She waited a beat, then looked up at him, still smiling. "I said yes."

GEORGE WALKED QUICKLY away from his sister. He needed to get as far away as soon as he could, before she changed her mind. He half expected his phone to go off so she could do just that.

He walked with purpose. The sooner he could escape the crowd, the faster he could call his buddy. Royce owed him a beer for this one. George had hoped Stacy could be persuaded to come with them, but Royce had bet she wasn't even close.

George didn't understand what had happened between those two. Yet somehow the relationship had gone from the two of them being friendly, with lots of teasing and joking, to a cold silence. It was uncomfortable being in the same room with them. That was the only thing that bothered him about the two of them being together on this trip. Everyone was coming for a vacation—not to partake in a cold war.

He gave the street a quick look, then dashed across to the small park on the other side. He walked to the park bench, sat, and called his best friend. "Royce, you need to find a way to make peace with Stacy before this ski trip happens. I don't want the week ruined with you two fighting."

"What are you talking about?" Royce joked. "It's not like Stacy will go. Besides, should that miracle happen, you'll see.

Nothing's wrong between us."

"Bullshit. You've been pushing for this as much as I have, and God knows Stacy needs to get back out there, but there must be peace between the two of you, *before* we go."

"I promise. If she actually says yes, then I will make a point of speaking with her."

The mocking note in Royce's voice brought a savage grin to George's face. He was so going to enjoy the next few moments.

"Then you'd better get ready to face that because"—he paused for dramatic effect, savoring the moment and his victory—"Stacy said yes!"

"SHE SAID WHAT?" Royce sat back in his home office computer chair and stared blankly at a wall across from him. He didn't dare breathe. He waited, hoping George would repeat his words.

"She said yes."

The breath gushed out of him, and he closed his eyes. *Oh thank God.* He collected his thoughts quickly. George would razz him endlessly, if he understood how rattled the call had made Royce. "Good for you for getting her to finally agree."

"Yeah, I'm hoping she won't back out. She needs this," George agreed.

"She's still so pale," Royce said. "She hasn't fully recovered from that bout of flu a few months ago."

"That's because she didn't take the time to recover." George scowled. "Instead she worked herself to the bone."

Royce nodded. "That completes our numbers then. Three women and five men to start and two more, one of each, coming for the weekend." He stared across his tiny apartment. "I still can't believe she's coming."

"I did have to promise that she could come and just read a book by the fire. Pick a day trip or two to do a couple runs, as she wishes. Along with not having total kitchen duty."

"Good. She needs the rest. We all might take a day or two off and follow her lead. The weather is calling for cold and sunny, but that doesn't mean it won't change in an instant."

"I'm just damn happy she's coming."

"Me too." George rang off, leaving Royce staring at the phone in his hand, only one thought uppermost on his mind. Stacy was coming. He had one week to redeem himself. One week to show her that he deserved another chance.

He groaned. Why had he promised to fix the issue between Stacy and him *before* the weeklong vacation? And in such a manner that she didn't cancel out on the trip? That would be a disaster for everyone involved.

But especially for him.

He knew George didn't understand the problem Royce had with George's sister, and it wasn't exactly something Royce could share. And he had to do something quick, since they were leaving tomorrow. Feeling caught between a rock and a hard place, he realized one thing.

He'd better not screw this up. Or else.

Chapter 3

STACY'S AFTERNOON GAVE her plenty of reason to regret her decision. Sure enough, Mark and Stevie were both going. They'd both been in and out of her office so many times that afternoon that she was ready to scream.

They were so excited she was coming.

She was already sorry she'd said yes.

Still, she felt both chagrin and relief at having agreed. She couldn't stay hidden forever. Besides, she didn't have the heart to cancel on George now. He would be so disappointed—and especially in her. Although she'd cancel on Royce in a heartbeat.

She finally managed to close her office door and to get some work done. By the time she made it home at the end of the day, she was tired and irritable and still pissed. She'd worked herself back into thinking she should cancel the trip, but she felt locked in to her decision.

She unlocked her apartment door, walked inside, and threw her coat and purse on the counter. Her home phone rang, as she wandered into the kitchen. She picked it up. "Hello?"

There was silence on the other end of the phone.

She hung up. The call only pissed her off more. The caller was lucky. If he'd responded and tried to sell her something, she would most likely have given him an earful.

She opened her fridge door and sighed. She hadn't gone shopping yet. The last thing she wanted was takeout. But, if she wanted to eat—and she needed to—that looked to be the best option. She didn't want to do too much shopping, as she was leaving soon. She planned on some major resting time, trying to regain some of her lost pizazz for life.

She stood in her kitchen and stared out the window.

The afternoon was cool and the sun still high, but it was cloudy. Kind of like her mood. Then she remembered the fish and chips on the boardwalk. Now that was a hell of a good idea. And the run there would be good for her. She'd been slacking off on her running lately. Time to pick it up. She was fit but always tired. That bout of pneumonia had damn-near killed her. She'd told George it had been the flu, as he would have worried all the more if he'd known the truth.

From the sheer number of times he'd called to check up on her, maybe he had known.

It only took a quick couple moments to get changed and to tie up her hair. Then she was out the door and running to the boardwalk. Ten minutes later, she found her rhythm. She stretched out her legs, the longer strides eating up the miles. She smiled as she breathed in deep fresh-air-hogging breaths.

It felt good. She ran a couple times a week, but she should do it more often to reduce her stress levels.

Light traffic was on the roads around her, but, with the evening soon upon them, most people were looking to get home. A breeze picked up, making her smile. She ran into the light wind, loving the cool feel on her face and chest.

She watched the birds swoop and dip, as they played in the wind, still hopeful for handouts from the people walking by. Sure enough, an old woman sat on one of the many benches and threw out chunks of bread. The birds were loving it. Stacy laughed, as several fought in the air, and both lost the tidbit to a third bird. Up ahead was the fish-and-chips van. She waved at him, as she jogged by. "I'll catch you on the way back."

"How long will you be?" he called out.

"Fifteen."

"I'll have it ready."

She laughed and waved back at him and kept on running. She'd try to make it faster. She rounded the corner and picked up her pace. She raced around the loop and started running back the way she'd come. After another few moments, she slowed her pace again, until she was just walking. The breeze picked up, and she waved her arms around to cool down and to loosen her limbs. Before she knew it, the smell of fresh fish and chips wafted toward her.

The vendor was waiting for her. "Here it is. Two pieces and a large order of fries."

"Do I look like I need a large order?" she joked, handing the man her money.

"No money required. The guy planning on helping you with those fries already took care of it."

She glanced up at the vendor, startled. He motioned behind her. She turned, tray in hand, and froze. Damn it.

Royce.

Well, there was no help for it. She smiled at the cook, so he knew she was okay and walked over to sit across from the man she'd done her best to avoid for the last couple years. It was all she could do to act cool and composed, when she couldn't stop staring. She wanted to eat him up—he looked so good. Dark wind-blown hair. A snug-fitting sports jacket over jeans that loved his body almost as much as she did. Then that had been part of the problem. The chemistry between them was combustible. Always had been. When she'd been a teen, she'd had no end of wild fantasies about this man.

Then she'd grown up.

"Why?" she asked coolly.

"I figured, if we could get past some of the awkwardness, it would make for a nicer week for everyone."

She picked up a fry and dipped it in the ketchup before biting down. "Awkwardness?" she asked him straight out.

"Is there none?" One corner of his mouth tilted upward. "No? If not, that's great."

She blinked, not sure what to say. "I'm good. Sorry you aren't."

Royce leaned back and stared at her. "So you'll be that way?"

She lowered her lashes. Inside, her stomach churned. Lord, she hadn't expected this. "Be like what?"

"Whatever." He snorted and stood. "I guess we're good then."

And he walked away.

Shit. She stared down at her fish and chips, which had lost their appeal. She felt sick. "Wait," she called out.

He slowed his steps but didn't stop.

"Royce," she called out. "I'm sorry." She hated saying that. Yet he'd caught her by surprise, triggering her defenses.

He continued to walk away.

ROYCE TOOK TWO more steps before coming to a jarring stop. "Damn it."

He wasn't going to do this. The cold war was supposed to stop. That meant he had to stop this behavior too. Besides, he'd promised George. Shit. He stood, his back to her, his hands on his hips, hating this.

"I said I was sorry," she repeated, and her small voice made him feel worse.

He spun around and looked at her, sitting there, her plate of food untouched and going cold. At the motion to the side, Royce noted the cook, encouraging him, gesturing for him to rctakc his seat and to work this out.

Royce felt like an idiot standing here. He walked back. "I'll sit and talk, as long as we *talk*." After her gaze slid away from his, he sat down and added, "And you eat. You're even skinnier now." Even as he said it, he winced. The reference to their history was like shining a spotlight on the big white elephant standing between them.

Still, it had the desired effect, as she picked up a piece of fish and took a bite. She closed her eyes in sheer joy. "Oh, I forgot how good this is."

"All that fat and carbs, you mean?" he asked in a humorous voice, trying to ignore the tightening sensation in his groin at the sheer sensuality in her voice over the simple pleasure of fast food. "You've always been such a health nut."

She shook her head. "Not really, but, in my line of work, nothing like seeing clogged arteries and abdominal fat choking the life out of people to remind me that I could make better food choices."

"Absolutely. But there is a time to make choices for other reasons." He motioned to the meal in front of her. "Like right now."

She polished off the first piece of fish and picked up the second.

The cook showed up and gave her a takeout container full of hot fries and removed the cold ones. "Now you eat. I cook. You eat. That's the way it's supposed to work." Then he returned with an extra piece of fish. "Here. You need one more." Then he disappeared again, leaving them alone.

Royce grinned at the surprise on her face. "See? I'm not the only one who thinks you are too skinny."

She rolled her eyes at him but dug in.

He let her eat, wanting to confirm she got a good meal down. She'd probably only had a few pieces of rabbit food and a yogurt or some such thing for lunch.

When she finally slowed down enough to breathe, she let out a happy sigh. "This is marvelous."

"He does a great job."

She nodded, popped a fry in her mouth, and chewed. Then, out of the blue, she said, "Maybe I should cancel after all. Be easier."

"Oh no. You're not using me as an excuse to get out of this."

She narrowed her eyes at him. "I said yes, didn't I?"

"Sure you did, but second thoughts and all that ..." He grinned. "I'm sure your mind was reaching for excuses the minute your brother walked out of the restaurant." With a knowing eye, he watched the color rush across her cheeks. "I thought so."

"Whatever." She shrugged. "I'm still looking for ways to get out of it. Of course I regret saying I'd go. But George has been working on me since forever. So I finally gave in." She lifted her gaze to him. "Besides, maybe it'll be fine."

"That's the attitude. You can do this."

He hadn't meant to sound patronizing, but obviously she thought he did, as he could see her temper building in those incredibly blue eyes. She'd been the best thing to happen to him, and he hadn't a clue—not until she'd blown out of his life as fast as she'd blown in. She'd been a butterfly before, living life large.

Until that damned avalanche.

Then she'd gone quiet and dark. She'd been in so much pain, so needy that weekend, that he'd had no choice but to be everything she needed. The depths of emotions she'd pulled from him had surprised him as well. He'd always been a lighthearted *love 'em and leave 'em* type of guy.

She'd had a profound effect on him that weekend. Made him want something different for his future. Something he thought might be obtainable, after being with her.

And he'd changed. For the better.

He'd planned to show her that he'd turned over a new leaf, but she'd shut him out of her life. Completely. Now he hoped that his long wait was over. That she'd finally worked through whatever demons terrorized her. He understood to a certain extent. He'd gone a little crazy with his own demons, after he realized he couldn't get around her locked doors. He'd played on an extreme edge of life, sports, drinking, driving race cars … Taking chances he wouldn't normally take. George had pulled him to one side and had asked what the hell had happened that gave him such a death wish.

Now he wished he hadn't said anything to him. In truth, all he'd said was one word, but it was enough. *Stacy.*

George had worked to keep them apart after that.

Now this week was coming.

Royce knew Stacy could handle it. She'd treat him like she treated everyone these days.

She'd just freeze him out.

He didn't want that. He'd been on the receiving end of

her moods already. Now it was time for that deep freeze to warm up—and hopefully let him back in.

After all, that was where he belonged.

INTERESTING. HE STOOD off to one side, trying to stay out of the wind that had suddenly come down with a cutting edge to it. Pedestrians moved around him, as they headed home.

He couldn't remember ever seeing either Stacy or Royce in this part of town. And never together. So what was going on? He almost felt left out. At that, he laughed. Of course he was left out. They didn't know he was here.

And, if they did know, would it make a difference? It was hard to say.

Likely they'd ignore him, as they always did.

Or rather like she'd always ignored him before. Somehow he appeared to be invisible to all women. Until he stopped them in their tracks.

Then they had no choice but to see who he really was.

He smiled. And, if the pedestrians took a close look and scuttled past at top speed, all the better. He preferred his insular existence.

It made it easier to carry out his hobby—his buddy called it art—but one no one ever seemed to appreciate the skills required.

Especially not the women who played key roles in the final pieces—forever.

Chapter 4

STACY FELT LIKE shit. She hadn't meant to start off on the wrong foot. In fact, she'd pushed off the thought of seeing Royce, like a dose of medicine to be taken with a screwed-up face and loud complaining. That he'd caught her off guard with his unexpected presence said much about how he'd affected her already.

"Truce," she said seriously. "I don't know why you get my back up. I know we have a history, but we've both moved on. So no reason we can't be friends." She caught a downward movement of the corner of his mouth and quickly amended, "Or at least cordial enemies." She looked at him hopefully.

He just gave her a flat stare.

"Fine." She threw up her hands. "What do you want from me?"

"Cordial enemies would be at the bottom of the list. Friends would be dragging along down there too." He glared at her and stood. "As to what I really want, I'll leave that to you to figure out. It shouldn't take a smarty pants like you too long."

And he walked away.

Her mouth opened, but no words came out. She watched him leave. Who else could drop a bomb like that and walk away unscathed? He'd scored a direct hit, and she knew she would feel the bruising for days. Not to mention worry on his words.

Had he meant what she thought he'd meant? No, surely not.

She stood and threw away her last few fries in the garbage. The wind had picked up again, giving it a snarky bite, as it brushed past her cheeks. She strolled home, her mind working on what he'd said and on what he deliberately hadn't said. Even an imbecile could work it out. He didn't want to be enemies and neither did he want to be tossed into the friend zone. That left the closer-than-friend arena, and she didn't want to go there.

But heated memories prodded her.

It had been a horrific phase in her life. He'd been there for her, but they'd been animals. Taking what they needed, giving back, but, as it was such a blur, she wasn't sure she'd acquitted herself well in that department. She'd been so lost. Yet, through it all, he'd been there, an anchor in her world.

She'd appreciated it. Yet she couldn't stay. She'd seen a future with him that she couldn't have. Because of who he was. Because of who she was.

Did she really want to open that door again? He'd been the hottest lover she'd ever known. However, sex was no basis for a relationship. Maybe he just wanted an affair. She frowned. She didn't do those, and that's all he did.

Or was she just hoping that's what he wanted?

One thing she did know. She hadn't had a serious relationship since losing her girlfriends. It hurt to lose those you loved. And, damn, she'd loved those two. Everyone had called the three of them a matched set.

Since then, she'd dated a few odd times but hadn't taken any to bed—except Royce. And he would be the last one she would want a relationship with. With his hobbies and extreme sports, not to mention his part-time job photographing these extreme sports, there was a good chance she'd lose him too. Although she knew he was working on a completely different career path, she had to wonder how much of that would stick or would that adrenaline always call to him?

No, that was enough. She would find a nice staid accountant and settle down eventually. A crazy live-life-on-the-edge kind of guy was not the type of man she was looking for.

However, since they were leaving tomorrow for a weeklong vacation, sharing a cabin, she must find a way to get along with him.

For everyone's sake.

REALLY? STACY WAS coming? Finally, after all these years. A dream come true. Something he'd worked for, toiled over, waited anxiously for—and now it was happening. He wasn't sure whether he should be screaming for joy or remorse.

He knew she was ready for this.

Hell, he was ready for this.

But did she realize how important this trip would be?

Chapter 5

THE MORNING OF the trip came too early. They weren't leaving until almost noon, as the journey was only a couple hours long, but crossing the border could hold them up. They also had to grocery shop on the other side, before driving the last hour to the cabin.

Stacy was still trying to gather the necessities of life, remembering at the last moment that her brother had said to bring extra thermals. George had all the sporting gear and equipment. She just needed to bring enough clothing and cold-weather gear for the week. And books. She was looking forward to a few hours of skiing but found that sitting in front of the fire, a book in hand, with the nice rich aroma of a pot of stew simmering beside her, was just as appealing. And maybe spending time with her camera.

Books. Damn, she hadn't packed any books. She raced back to her room and snatched two mysteries she'd picked up last week. She couldn't wait to dive into them. While trying to stuff them into her already-full bag, the doorbell rang. "Shit." She ran out of her bedroom and pulled the front door open, not even looking at her brother. "I'm almost ready. Just need another couple minutes."

"Not a problem. We've got a little leeway."

Royce's voice stopped her, and she turned. "Where's George?"

"Downstairs, reshuffling gear to make room for your

bag." He surveyed the room. "Have you got much more?"

She ran back into her bedroom, checked her list, and realized she had it all. "No, I think I'm done. It's just this bag." She picked it up and groaned. "Damn it. When did this get so heavy?"

"Since we're not flying, weight doesn't matter."

"It does if I have to lug it very far on the other end." She carried it to the front door and dropped it, then took one last look around, while she pulled on her coat. "Okay, I'm good to go."

He picked up the bag easily with one hand and walked out ahead of her.

She locked the door, a pang of fear zinging through her as she did so. This was her first trip away since that avalanche had ripped apart her life.

She could do this. She had done this many times before. *Remember, Stacy. You leave home every day before you go to work.*

But, in the past three years, she'd never left her home overnight. She'd never risked it. She'd lost so much on the last trip that she hadn't been able to.

Not until now.

What if this time, *she* never came home?

As she got into the back seat of the Land Rover her brother favored, Stacy noted Royce had taken the passenger seat up front. Good, it was crowded enough with six of them traveling in this rig, without having to deal with Royce sitting next to her. They still had to pick up Geoffrey. Thankfully Stevie was traveling with Mark in his truck, and they were taking much of the other gear and provisions. They'd stop at a store on the other side of the border for fresh produce for the week.

Stacy smiled at Kathleen, George's current girlfriend, one who'd actually lasted longer than six months. "Good morning, Kathleen."

Kathleen grinned at her. "Can't believe you're here. This will be great."

"I hope so, especially after George hollered so much about me coming." She leaned forward to see another woman on the other side of Kathleen. "Hi, I'm Stacy, and George is my obnoxious brother," she said, by way of an explanation.

"I'm Yvonne," the tall redhead said, with a big smile.

The other two women laughed, while George protested the insult from the driver's seat.

"Who else is coming, George?" Stacy asked.

"You already know about Geoffrey, Stevie, and Mark, plus Kevin and Christine are last-minute additions, but they won't arrive until the end of the week."

"Really?" Stacy asked in delight. "That's great. I haven't seen Geoffrey in such a long time."

"Actually I think he's coming because you are coming," George said, with a big grin. "I've been trying to get him to come along with us forever. He's boarded this region several times a year but rarely with us, and the last time was quite a while ago. We're picking him up on the way out of town."

"He's also a spelunker, isn't he?" Kathleen asked. "This area is hugely popular for ice caves too."

"Yeah, Geoffrey's first love is caves. Some in this area never thaw. There was talk of opening up a few of them to the public in a touristy kind of way."

That elicited groans from everyone in the vehicle. "That

would be horrible," Yvonne said. "If people want to see those caves, they should do it the hard way."

Stacy withheld her comments. She understood both sides. Tourists brought in big bucks to the smaller communities that generally surrounded the wilderness areas, but, at the same time, that type of tourism brought other problems with it. It needed to be managed carefully, so as to not damage the delicate balance of the ecosystem. However, she knew better than to get into a discussion with raised tempers on both sides of the debate.

Feeling eyes on her, she looked up to see Royce staring at her in the rearview mirror. She remembered he'd been on her side on some of those discussions. And his warm gaze invited her to share in those memories.

She flushed and turned her gaze out the window.

What the hell was she doing here? And why did she suddenly feel like she'd made the right decision in coming?

GEORGE KEPT A wary eye on his sister. He loved her dearly, but, like any siblings, they'd done their share of fighting. Both artistic and active, they'd had their problems, but they'd stayed close regardless. She was the brain. He was a jock. Somehow they'd still found enough common ground—maybe just sibling love—to work through all the problems. When her friends had disappeared in that avalanche, she'd gone a little crazy. He'd tried to help. So had the police. Hell, she'd badgered them hourly, then daily, for news, leads, any tidbit to help her sleep at night.

When there'd been nothing to report, she'd died a little bit inside. As time went on, instead of picking up the pieces and getting on with her life, she'd pulled inside—a turtle-like shell growing on her back—in a state of waiting. As if she knew the answers would come. Eventually. And, until then, she couldn't get on with her life.

It had been beyond sad. Depressing and debilitating for everyone around her.

Then something had changed. Now George realized it was due to Royce. Too bad George didn't know what had gone on between them, but Stacy had suddenly turned a corner. She'd started to return to life. More reserved. More afraid. More damaged. But alive and living once again.

For that, he was grateful to Royce.

Stacy was still tottering on the edge. At this point, she could go either way. That's why this week was so important. George didn't want anything to set her back. That she'd come was already a wonderful surprise. He'd been expecting her to cancel every hour since she'd agreed. But she'd stuck it out, and here she was. Now it was just as important that she have a great week. Deal with a few ghosts and move on even more. He'd do everything he could to make that happen.

His sister was special. The work she did was difficult and yet so important for everyone else. And no one was there to make her feel special. To hold her when her world collapsed. He'd hoped Royce would be the man to take that place but apparently not. Royce had always remained in the background, keeping a watchful eye on George's sister.

George sneaked a quick glance at Royce, sitting in the passenger seat beside him. He was busy staring out the window. George looked back at this sister in the rearview mirror and smiled.

Maybe more was there than George thought. She stared at Royce like she didn't know what to do with him. But her gaze was intense. Interested.

That was always a good sign.

Seeing that, George felt much better. He barely hid his grin. It could be a great week after all.

AN HOUR LATER, Royce knew he shouldn't have come. Damn. Behind him, he heard Stacy's laughing response to Geoffrey's teasing comment. Those two had been getting along famously since Geoffrey had joined them not far out of town. Who knew she'd actually tease and play like she was doing right now? And why not with Royce? He held back a shudder, as he suddenly realized that he had no idea whether Stacy had a boyfriend or not. The atmosphere between her and Geoffrey said not. But she was lighter, more playful. So maybe she was open to the concept.

Still, that just pissed him off. He wanted her to be open to a relationship with him. No. One. Else.

"Hey, Royce, what are you frowning at so heavily? Jeez, you look ready to kill someone." Geoffrey called out, his comical tone eliciting laughter all around.

Except from Royce. "Nope, just thinking about life."

"Wow, that's deep, man. Sounds like your last girlfriend ditched you. Sorry. I know how much you loved her."

Again, that overly mocking solicitous voice brought on more laughter and pissed Royce right off. He'd broken it off months ago, and it had been casual at best. Another attempt on his part to fill his life with companionship. What could he say? He'd been lonely. In a casual voice, he said, "Not a biggie."

"That's all right. Lots more where she came from," Stacy

said coolly. "Right, Royce?"

Royce turned to look back at her, caught something hard in her gaze, and felt a pain deep inside. But he'd be damned if he'd show it. He snorted and joked, "There always is." As she turned away, a curl to her lip, he repeated, "There always is."

Chapter 6

THE TWO VEHICLES stopped on the other side of the border for gas and coffee. Stacy had missed breakfast, so she loaded up on muffins to sustain her, until they arrived at the cabin. She ignored the teasing and munched happily away, watching the miles go by. She'd forgotten how beautiful the journey was. They would start climbing up the mountain roads soon. The Land Rover would make it to the cabin just fine. If there'd been other vehicles in and out lately, it would be even easier. The plan was to meet up with the other vehicle at the lunch stop on the other side of the border, then stay convoy-style, in case one or the other got into trouble. With the border crossing and shopping involved, the trip ended up being a longer drive but one well worth the effort. It had been three years since she'd been here. As she looked out at the icy mountains ahead of them, she realized it had been too long. It was desolate. Cold. And incredibly beautiful.

By the time they arrived at the cabin, it was late afternoon, and the evening sky had settled like a cold dark blanket on the region. Being in the mountains, once the sun went down, the night settled in early. If it weren't for the powerful headlights of the Rover leading the way and the expert knowledge of her brother, Stacy didn't think they'd have found the driveway. As this was also a popular climbing area, there had been signposts, but, with the drifting snow and the thick soupy darkness, they'd been hard to see.

George parked in front and left his headlights on, until Royce opened the cabin door and ascertained that it was empty and available for them. They'd booked it for the week, although a few might stay just for the weekend. It was owned by one of George's friends and made available to the group at large for a pittance. They'd all made good use of the owner's generosity over the years.

The cabin had an emergency generator in the back. As the women worked to unload gear, the men set about bringing light and heat to the cabin.

Within minutes, a huge fire blazed in the big heater stove, and a pot of water was put on top for making hot drinks, while the hot water tank was turned on. Food would be needed soon, but, for the moment, everyone was just overjoyed to be here. Stacy wandered through the cabin and chose to claim her bed up in the loft. It would be the warmest place, and she was no fool. This might be a vacation, but there'd be more icicles and thermal underwear here than bikinis and tropical drinks.

She dumped her bag in the loft next to one of the beds, each topped by a thin mattress, and went downstairs to claim a down-filled sleeping bag from the stack her brother and Royce had supplied. They were used as bedcovers.

"Stacy, where are you setting up?" George asked.

"In the loft, if that's all right."

There were a few calls and nods of agreement, as that freed up several private bedrooms within the cabin. She noted that George and Kathleen took one of them, and the two guys she worked with took another—with double bunks on both walls, as did the other bedroom.

Only a few other choices remained for sleeping. Royce had yet to pick one.

And neither had Yvonne or Geoffrey.

GEORGE LAUGHED AT his sister's choice. "Hey, Stacy, how come you have to hide away upstairs, like that?"

"Ha," she said. "I just wanted to make sure you and Kathleen managed to grab a private room for yourselves. And not sure if other couples were happening"—she grinned—"like Stevie and Mark, I'm just being nice."

Everyone cracked up in laughter, as Stevie turned on her. "Hey, it's not like that," he protested, but it was an old joke among the group, as these two guys had been best friends since forever. "There are other beds in our room, if you want to bunk with us."

Stacy laughed and shook her head. "I'm good. Besides, another couple is joining us, so they will need a place to sleep too. Just think. The lot of you can have a foursome!"

A pillow hit her in the chest, as Mark tossed one at her. "That's all right. Go ahead. Hide upstairs. We know when you don't want to spend time with us."

She threw the pillow at Stevie. "I just know where the warmest spot in the house is."

"True enough." Stevie smirked, adding, "But, if you slept with us, you'd be even warmer."

The other males in the group raised their hands. "No problem, you can sleep with me."

"You don't want to sleep with them. I'll keep you warm."

Stacy snickered. "Like that'll happen."

"Hey, what's wrong with us?" Stevie protested in an injured tone.

With an eye roll, Stacy muttered, "Too much to count."

The pillow hit her in the face, amid a howl of laughter.

LOOK AT QUEEN Stacy. Always apart. Always in her perfect little bubble. Not touching anyone. So untouchable. The perfect ice princess.

He narrowed his gaze.

If that was the way she wanted to be treated …

He barely held back the unholy grin threatening to break loose. Not that anyone else would understand. Well, one would. The talk continued around him. He shifted slightly, so he could keep her in his view, as he considered the issue. He'd thought about it before and had discarded it as not possible. Too much trouble. But his years of experience had helped. He might pull it off now. Especially since she was here.

Of course someone else wanted her too. That could be troublesome.

"Hey, Stacy, your turn to make popcorn," George said, nudging his sister. "Come on, lazybones, get up."

"Hey, I'm tired too," she protested, but she got up and headed to the kitchen good-naturedly.

An interesting proposition, he thought, as he watched her stroll forward. No doubt his hobby had become almost too easy. He must up the ante to keep the game interesting.

And it was, but now that something harder, more challenging had come up, his other prey seemed paltry. He wanted to be ready for more. But was he?

Still, this was Stacy. He'd have to fight to get her for himself. An interesting twist to an already challenging concept.

Then again, it was the fear of being caught that gave him

the thrill.

Of course he could do it, if he chose to. He just had to figure out how.

And when.

ROYCE SLID DOWN on his corner of the couch and closed his eyes. He was also tired. He'd barely slept last night. He hoped he would tonight. Yvonne had put her bag in his room though. In a separate bed, thank God. He had no idea if it was a random choice or she was just looking for a place to call her own. Either way, she'd sleep only two feet from him. When he'd seen her bag there, he'd turned to look around, and, sure enough, he'd seen Stacy peering over the loft railings, staring right into his room.

She'd been pissed.

Damn right. He hoped it choked her. And immediately he felt like a heel. He hated feeling this way. Wanting to walk away from someone who obviously didn't want to want him but was angry that she still did.

How could she not want what they'd had together? It had been the best thing in his life. To think he'd been alone feeling that way made it so much worse. He wanted her to be just as involved. To want what they'd had.

He hadn't been able to throw it away. How could she?

Royce tried to ignore Stacy's tired steps to the kitchen to make popcorn for this group. Then couldn't. She'd been outside a lot today and was still recovering from a long illness. Damn it. Frustrated and angry, he hopped to his feet and strode into the kitchen. He ignored the smirks and smiles he knew were evident behind his back. They could laugh. They had no idea what he'd been through—was going through.

A lovesick man who would do anything to get Stacy back in his life again.

All he could do was hope she'd see their relationship in a different light and give him a second chance. And, because he cared, he wouldn't let her work herself to death like this. She should be in bed. Not making popcorn for these goofs.

He stopped at the doorway and opened his mouth to say something—he had no idea what—when he realized she just stood there, head down, shoulders slumped. Eyes closed. Shit. He stepped forward, and, in a voice too low and too harsh for his liking, he snapped, "What's wrong?"

In a sudden jolt, her eyes flew open, and she spun around. She shook her head hard, her hair flying around her shoulders, maybe to clear the sleep that was obviously clouding her brain, and said, "Nothing. I'm just tired."

"*Just?*" He took the few steps to bring him to her side. He reached out and grabbed her shoulders. "Of course you're tired. Go sit down. I'll make this." He turned her in the direction of the others and gave her a gentle push.

He studied the table in front of him, where the cast-iron handheld popper was filled with popcorn but didn't have the butter out or ready to melt. He measured it quickly and dumped it into the popper.

"No," she said, turning back to the table. "I'll be fine."

"You're not fine," he said in a low voice. "Why won't you let me help you?"

The popcorn popper was held tight in her fist, as she turned away, but her gaze lingered on his. He thought she wouldn't answer for a long moment, but then she opened her mouth. He bent his head to hear what she said, his gaze trying to read her gently moving lips. Her voice had been so soft that he wondered if he'd heard her correctly.

She walked back into the main room to pop the corn on the big fireplace. But her words rippled through his mind in wonder and almost broke his heart.

He thought, hoped, she'd said, "Because it hurts too much."

Chapter 7

STACY FORGOT HOW high energy this group of friends was. They worked hard, and they played hard. Such was their life. She watched the men tease the women and bug the other guys. She was in a category altogether different. She knew them all, with the exception of Yvonne, and had been friends forever with some of them. That she worked with two of them, not all the time and not all day, made for an odd relationship there too. Then there was Royce and that bit of history and Geoffrey with their long-term friendship. At one point he'd asked her out, but she'd refused, realizing she liked him as a good friend only. He was a great guy, and she was more than happy to have him along.

And, unlike many of the others here, he wasn't an adrenaline junkie.

Safety was always her prime concern. Even more so now after what had happened to her best friends.

She cozied up by the fire, grateful for the moment. Her brother had brought a huge pasta dish to heat up on the big heater stove for tonight, but it was taking its time warming up. So was the cabin. The conversation went around in a mix of laughter and arguments. The others were already planning their trips out tomorrow. She was still thinking a book by the fire was the right answer.

Royce plunked down beside her. "Are you going out

tomorrow?"

She studied his face, aware that the conversation had died down around them. "I'm not sure. What are the plans?"

"Two groups," he said. "One is heading to the runs beside the waterfall. The other is going to the snowboard park."

"*Hmm.* High winds, freezing cold air, or my camera in the sunshine." She grinned. "I'll go with the sunshine."

There were exclamations at that one.

"I'm good with a camera," George said, "but she's gifted."

That drew a snort from her. "Not likely. Look at the stuff you take pictures of. You have to be gifted to do that."

"And then look at your images. They are surreal. Like you see something no one else can," George countered.

"Hey, I didn't know you were *both* photographers," Kathleen said. "Really? How come I haven't seen any of your work, Stacy?"

Stacy curled her lips but stayed quiet.

"You have," George said. "You just didn't know they were hers."

A surprised pause stopped everyone, as they turned en masse to look from him to her.

She groaned. "It's no secret. I made a little bit of a name for myself way back when, that's all."

"And what name is that?" Royce asked, his gaze narrow, searching.

She shrugged, uncomfortable with having the spotlight turned her way.

Her brother answered. "You guys have the privilege of being in the presence of Eternal."

A shocked silence filled the room. Stacy wanted to laugh.

She didn't know whether the name was bringing that reaction or the fact that they didn't know the name.

It was no big deal. She'd been doing photography since she was in her teens. She had stopped for a long while, after losing her friends. She'd been lost herself back then. After her weekend with Royce, she'd picked it up again. That was when she'd started working on her new project—Faces of Nature.

"Really?" Stevie asked in shock. "And you didn't tell us? We've ranted and raved to you over so many of those photographs over the years. And you never said anything."

"I thought Eternal was dead," Kathleen said, with surprise.

Geoffrey walked to stand in front of Stacy. "Seriously?"

She shrugged. "It's no big deal."

"It's a very big deal." He snorted. Then he stopped, as if considering her words. "You know, in hindsight, that makes a lot of sense. You went through a lot of phases. I remember that series of ice-climbing photos you took. The images in the ice that you managed to capture that even those of us who'd been there with you couldn't see."

"Well, I for one haven't ever seen your work," Yvonne said in a tight voice to go with her tight smile. She tossed her long red hair.

"I didn't expect anyone to. I haven't done much work lately." That was a lie. She'd done a lot recently but under a different name. Another pseudonym. She looked at her work as an artist looked at his. Some of it she hated, and some of it she loved. And some of it she loved but was unsure how anyone else could.

So she'd started a new name. It's not that she'd been a different person, but this new work was different for her. She hadn't shared that name with anyone.

Yvonne popped up and said, "I really like Rebirth's work."

Managing to keep her face bland, inside Stacy jolted at hearing her second name mentioned.

"I don't know that one." Royce made an odd sound. "And what's with the artists putting up their work under these abstract names?"

"I can't answer for everyone," Stacy said, "but, for me, it was about the photos in that series."

Everyone looked at her, confused. She laughed.

Her brother said, "I hadn't thought of that. You're signing by the series."

"On the back is my real signature," she added, with a smile. "In your case, George, you don't own your photographs. You work for the company, who gets the rights to all your work, so it's not an issue."

He nodded thoughtfully. "At the moment. Who knows where I'll be down the road? I hadn't thought about the individualism with my work."

She didn't add that she'd been in a strange space when she'd started doing her professional signature series that way. In truth, they weren't signatures. They were titles. But as there was more than one photograph in the series, the name had stuck. The world loved different. It added mystery to her work.

Considering this was the first time Stevie and the rest were hearing about her work and seeing the slightly injured looks on their faces, she realized that their relationship would be changing again too. Maybe it was time. And maybe that was the real reason for coming on this weeklong adventure. She needed fresh inspiration.

It would center on letting go.

She needed to open up the narrow scope of her world. Her girlfriends were gone. She wasn't responsible for what had happened to them. She couldn't hide away on the off chance that something might happen to her. And, if fate intervened, making it her time, then she needed to come to terms with that. Still, it was time to move forward. Time to move on. Time to say goodbye. Somehow.

She'd been looking for months for some new inspiration. She'd been working on a massive urban portfolio of her local area for some months now. She hadn't shown anyone but the gallery owner. He'd immediately booked her for a showing under her Rebirth name. She knew that, at the release of this next set of photos, the world would understand some part of who she was.

Now she needed to heal the other areas of her life, and coming here was part of that.

She settled back comfortably. For the first time, she felt that spark of need, that spark of creation in her soul. She'd find her inspiration here.

She knew she would.

All she had to do was recognize who or what that was.

Then do everything she could to learn how it ticked.

ROYCE WATCHED GEORGE and his sister interact. Not only was affection and sibling love there, but there was no professional jealousy. At least none that he could see. George was fanatical about his work. Always had been.

Yet his stuff was all action.

George, as if realizing Royce was out of the loop, came over, his phone out in front of him, and he clicked on something, then held it out for Royce to see. In a quiet voice, he said, "This is one she did several years back."

Royce shot him a quick look, then glanced at the image. It was a flower, dying from the outside in. As if in pain, the leaves were curling in on itself.

"Kind of depressing," he muttered. He had to consider that a few years ago meant three. If ever someone had been affected by the loss of her friends, Stacy would be the poster child.

"Look closer."

Frowning, Royce studied the photo. And startled. It was a huge aster type flower, the tips brown and dying, almost hanging like rotten teeth. Yet juxtaposed to those teeth was a series of tiny buds reaching up toward the brown tips as if ready to feed off them. And, sure enough, a single drop of dew hung down, giving the life force to the little ones that they might grow strong. The aster in death was reaching out a hand and helping, offering the gift of life.

Royce stared, hating that he'd read so much into the picture. Surely that wasn't what she'd meant to show. He glanced over at Stacy, speaking quietly with Geoffrey, then let his gaze slide from one person to the next, then on to the next. Finally he came back to his best friend.

"Do you see it?" George asked quietly. "Or tell me what do you see?"

"I see the old and dying reaching out and nurturing the young."

Stevie walked past just then and leaned over and saw the image. "Oh, that one. God, those teeth give me the chills." And he walked away.

"Some people only ever see the teeth."

"I saw those first," Royce said. "Then saw them more as

umbrellas but also directing the gift of water to the buds below."

Stevie walked back. "Yeah, you could see that. Or you could take the teeth concept one step deeper and realize those buds are feeding off the mother plant's decaying flesh." With that, he sauntered away, a beer in hand.

Royce stared down at the image. "Not a nice thought."

"It's why her work's so popular. People see different things with every one of her pictures. Are they innocent and spiritual or dark and devious?"

Royce shot his gaze back over to Stacy. As if sensing his look, she turned to stare at him. He dropped his gaze back to the image and recalled the disturbing interpretation Stevie had mentioned. "Have you ever asked her?" Royce asked George.

"No," George said, putting away his phone. "Not sure I want to know the answer."

WELL, HE DID. He'd been listening in quietly, studying the pictures with interest but from the sidelines. Stacy was a photographer? Like what the fuck? He hadn't pegged her for the artist type. As his daddy would say, she was all book smart and life stupid.

Now he found out she has a hobby. Not just any hobby but one of his hobbies. Well, one he was working on developing. It kind of went along with his other hobby. As he sat here, contemplating the implications, he started to burn inside. Like, how dare she?

If, and that was a big if, she was the artist known as Eternal, then she was considered a leader in her field. One with a perspective like none other. Touted as a fresh look on life.

What bullshit.

She was like every other bitch he'd met on these trips. Only, in Stacy's case, she was too good for anyone—not just him. She wanted to be the queen and have everyone dote on her. Well, he had plans. Plans for her. To put her in her place, like she had him all these years.

She would see the results of her actions then. It might be years late, but revenge was best served cold.

And he would make sure she was damn cold.

A shudder rippled down his spine. Goddammit. He clenched his jaw so hard that he swore he heard his teeth grinding.

He glanced down at his hands. A tremor was already starting. He shifted, tucking them out of sight. No one could know.

No one could suspect.

Or else he'd have to ramp up his agenda. And make Stacy pay—now.

Chapter 8

THE NEXT MORNING, Stacy woke up cold and sore. She had no explanation for the aches. Maybe from the long drive yesterday? Maybe the extra heavy running workout schedule she'd put herself through this last week? As she rolled over, a groan slipped out. Well, there was that answer. She'd earned those aches from sleeping on this uncomfortable bed last night. Maybe she should take another look at her choice of sleeping quarters. Although all the beds were probably topped by the same thin mattresses. After a day out on the snow, she would sleep regardless. She'd gone to bed before the others and had felt self-conscious doing so. She opened her eyes to study the large loft. Was she alone here? Was she so lucky?

It appeared to be so. For some reason, instead of cheering her up, she felt let down. As if finding out no one had wanted to share her space was deliberate. Silly. Everyone was in groups already. And plenty of bedrooms were downstairs. So why would anyone come up here?

And, if she felt a pang of upset over the concept of Royce having paired up with someone else, then she'd stomp on it. She and Royce weren't an item. Never had been, not when the relationship could be measured in a matter of hours and days, not weeks.

Besides, she'd chosen the warmest place in the house. If

that didn't seem to matter to the others, well, it did to her. She'd been out of the loop with this winter playtime, and she was feeling the cold big time. If the fire wasn't lit and coffee not bubbling, she so wasn't getting out of bed.

Of course several in the group were likely to be cuddling up with someone special. That would keep anyone warm. She halted on the image of Royce and Yvonne.

He could do what he wanted.

Hopefully the others had stayed up late drinking. That would mean no early risers.

She smiled and curled up again. She could actually see her breath. And she'd come why?

She closed her eyes again, breathing the cold air deep inside. Wafting upward was the smoke of a fire and the smell of coffee, all combined with the rustling movement from down below. Sliding forward, she looked through the railings to see who was awake.

And damn if her heart didn't jump for joy. Royce. His open sleeping bag was in front of the fire, where he'd obviously slept. Dressed in just long johns, he was poking at the fire, willing it to burst into flame. A pot of coffee sat on the stove. It wouldn't be ready for a while yet, but at least the process had been started. A coffeemaker was here somewhere, but coffee made this way had a special flavor.

She leaned over farther, wanting to confirm that he had slept alone.

He had.

Instantly she felt terrible. Plenty of room up here in the loft. She would have shared. Damn it. Then again, as she studied his bedroll down by the fire, why should she? Likely his had been much warmer than hers, and it was pretty damn smart of him too. Although, as she'd gone to bed early, that place would hardly have done her any good.

"You could come down and warm up," Royce called up softly, not turning around.

She waited, wondering if he was talking to her. When he twisted slightly to stare up at her, she wanted to pull back, like a little kid. Instead she stared down at him casually. "Is it warm enough to venture down?"

He grinned. "If it isn't, you sure won't want to go outdoors."

"Not sure I am anyway." She yawned. "Let me know when the coffee is done."

"Ha. You're not the boss here, sis," George called up from the closest bedroom. "It's first come, first serve on that pot."

"And I'm here on the spot," Royce called back. "Good luck getting any."

There was a mad scramble from all the rooms, as the men left their beds and raced to the pot. In various states of heavy winter underwear, the gang huddled around the heater stove and watched the coffee boil.

"You're all nuts," she called down, sinking lower into her sleeping bag.

"Ha. Look who's out here in the middle of nowhere with us," George called up.

"Don't remind me," she muttered.

"I heard that."

She ignored him. But tucked inside her warm bag, she smiled. Life was good. She lay back peacefully, enjoying the novelty of her surroundings. Below her, the conversation between the groups floated up. Everyone discussed the day ahead. She was thinking that what she was doing was the perfect activity. She yawned. How had she become so worn out? Maybe it was the constant overtime and the heavy workouts. She'd filled her time so she didn't have to think. And now that she had nothing to do, no reason to get up, it was hard to do anything but doze off again.

"Hey, sleepyhead."

The voice woke her from her daydreams. She rolled over to find George standing over her, a mug of coffee in his hand. "Sorry, I guess I fell asleep again."

"You need it," he said, his voice serious. "You're exhausted." He squatted beside her and lowered the cup to the floor beside her head. "I don't think you even see how bad you've gotten. You're completely worn out." He plunked his butt on the floor. "You are working yourself to the bone."

"I'm not that bad," she protested, rising up on one elbow.

Stevie called up from below, "Yes, you are. You're the first one into work and the last one to leave."

Mark added, "And you usually come in on weekends."

"Not to mention," George said, "what are you running now, 5K and 10K?"

"Both," she said. "It depends on the day of the week and how I'm feeling." She smiled and lay back down. "I'm in bed now. I might just stay here today." At the frown forming on his face, she added quickly, "Maybe go out for a couple runs, when it warms up outside."

"Ha." He laughed. "I bet you're still in bed when I return."

"Hey." She kicked him through the sleeping bag. It was a faint effort and hurt her more than him. "That's not fair."

"We'll see." He grinned. "You were always hard to get out of bed."

"What? When I was six?"

"Maybe." He stood, a big smirk on his face. "Stevie and Mark and I are heading out to do a quick check on the snow conditions. Then we can make plans."

"No breakfast?" she asked, not moving and having no intention of moving anytime soon. "Make sure you load the fire to keep it going."

"Maybe you should work on breakfast." He headed to the stairs and called back, "We'll be back in just over an hour. And we'll be hungry."

She groaned. "Listen to you, giving orders already."

"Always, sis. You're the boss at work. I'm the boss here."

No arguing that. She lay on her back and listened with half an ear, as the group discussed the array of runs offered. They wanted to do as much as possible over the next week. She had no such ambition. As it stood now, going downstairs was about all she could manage. She sipped her coffee and relaxed. The more she relaxed, the more she realized how long it had been since she'd let her guard down. The last few years had been very stressful. Too stressful. She'd seen herself how bad she'd gotten. The nights she hadn't been able to sleep. She'd worked herself until she collapsed to the floor, then picked herself up and did it all over again. She hadn't really noticed, until she'd been flattened by pneumonia.

What she hadn't realized was that others had noticed.

Of course one was her brother. If anyone would notice, it would be him. Or maybe not. She worked with Stevie and Mark. They'd seen her day after day, as they worked in the lab. She'd been promoted just after her friends had died. As a way to avoid being overwhelmed with grief, she'd worked her ass off. Staying late, coming in early. She'd picked up extra duties and had kept her own. She still did.

Then she'd spent a weekend with Royce and, after that,

had done everything she could to forget him.

Instead of just missing lunch, she'd also skimped on breakfast, and, when she got home, she often crashed before eating a decent dinner.

The end was a foregone conclusion.

She'd caught herself before completely collapsing. She'd actually gone to a doctor, something she rarely did but knew she couldn't put it off anymore, before she got any worse. If she couldn't work, she didn't think she would have survived.

The doctor had been horrified when she'd seen Stacy. Immediately she had been heavily dosed with vitamins and minerals, put on heavy antibiotics, and weighed and measured, so she could check her progress.

That had been her epiphany.

A massive wake-up call.

She'd only realized as she'd stood on the scale in the doctor's office how dire the situation had gotten. She'd been a hair over 105 pounds. At five foot nine, that meant she was a skin-covered skeleton. And she'd seen more than her fair share of those. The mirror showed her starkly how much she'd let herself fall. How she was only a step away from death. She could just imagine her coworkers performing an autopsy on her young bag of bones and wondering what the hell had happened to her.

The doctor had also ordered her to a psychiatrist for a mental health checkup. Stacy had been just scared enough that she'd gone. It had been difficult to convince the good psychiatrist that she wasn't suicidal or bulimic or anorexic. As she'd tried to explain, she'd seen the decline herself. Her actions were that of a woman trying to forget. To remove herself from the world that had become too painful.

Just not in a suicidal sort of way.

But the psychiatrist hadn't been so easily convinced. Indeed, she'd seen him for over three months, before she realized he'd helped and that her emotions *had* stabilized. If nothing else, she understood what she'd done. And how she'd gotten to this point. With his help, she had picked herself up, made a promise to take better care of herself, and to rejoice in the life she'd been so quick to underappreciate.

It had taken six months to add a layer of flesh under her skin and another six months to get the rounded look back on her face.

Still, it had scared her. It had also shown her how weak she'd become. And how greatly she'd been affected by the loss of those she'd loved.

She'd vowed to never let that happen again.

Only she'd fallen sick again a couple months ago—a relapse—minor, yet scary when she considered how slow her recovery had been. In some ways, still was.

She'd brought her physical health back as far as she could but understood that it was sitting on a delicate balance. And so was her emotional state.

"Are you coming down here or staying up there all day?"

She startled. She'd been so lost in her own musings that she hadn't even realized where she was. Or who she was with. She sat up and looked over the railing.

"Oh, so you are awake." Royce stood in front of the heater stove. "Are you coming down? Or"—his voice deepened—"are you scared to be alone with me?"

"Alone?" she asked. She bounded to her feet and leaned over the railing. Sure enough, no one was down there. "Is everyone else asleep?"

He shook his head. "They're gone." His grin flashed. "George came back and checked on you, but you'd dozed off—again."

"I'll be down in a few minutes." she cried out, unaccountably flustered. She hadn't meant to sleep again.

"Don't worry about it," Royce called up. "Get dressed and come down for a fresh cup of coffee though."

"I'll be right there." She dressed quickly, picked up the cup still full of cold coffee, and carried it down the stairs. He stood in front of the stove, holding the coffeepot, when she made her way around him. She dumped the cold coffee and rinsed out her cup and returned to where he stood, her cup held out in front of her.

He filled it.

"I'm surprised I slept so much," she said, with a smile.

"It goes with the territory. Coming out in the cold like this often tires someone out. Especially someone who isn't used to it."

"I do remember. It's been a while though."

"Three years by any chance?"

She knew he was asking if she'd been skiing since the avalanche. "Not since then," she said. "Everything was before then."

He didn't agree. "Not everything."

That deep dark voice rolled through her, bringing back memories better left forgotten. She glanced at him sideways from under her lashes, but she stayed quiet, not sure what to say. After a little silence, she asked, "When will they be back? I was supposed to have breakfast ready for them."

That brought a healthy laugh from him. "In that case, let's get them something to eat. They're likely to be here in about fifteen to twenty minutes."

He walked over to the coolers of food and opened them. He found what he was looking for in the second cooler and hauled out sausages and eggs. He nodded to one of the boxes on the side. "Several loaves of French bread are over there. And crumpets."

"Oh, now that sounds good." She pulled out the crumpets and one loaf of bread, then spied the wire toaster rack, where she could clamp the bread in between the racks and hold it over a fire. She turned to glance at the open fireplace. "Toast would be good."

"Absolutely. Have a piece now," he suggested. "I'll put a pan of sausages on the stove, and we'll do a big mess of eggs as well."

She quickly cut several slices of French bread and sat in front of the fireplace, making toast. The others might not be here on time, and that was okay with her. She'd eat it all with the appetite she'd worked up.

"I hope you plan on sharing that."

"If they get home in time."

"I'll have a slice, please."

And, with that, they slid into the easy camaraderie they'd had years ago.

THAT HAD HAPPENED easier than expected. Royce hadn't been sure when she'd first come down, but, after a few awkward sideways glances and a weird buffer of space between them, she seemed to settle down with being alone with him.

Good.

He wanted a lot more, but, hell, he'd take baby steps, if that's all he could get right now.

She was so damn skinny still. He wanted to feed her several meals before the others returned. As he watched, she broke off a piece of toast and popped it into her mouth, closing her eyes at the taste.

Christ. She was 100 percent into everything she did. It was damn irritating when she turned that concentration into ignoring him, but, when she'd turned it on him that weekend? … Well, she'd blown every other relationship out of his reality, and he finally found what he'd been missing all his life.

Her.

Now she was here. He wondered, should he bring up their history? Say something about their future—not that they had one together, but, if things went well, they could have something to work toward. He hated the gauche feeling of being a teenager again. Worrying about what to say. Worrying about every nuance on her face when she looked at him. Worrying about making the correct interpretation from everything she said.

But they were alone.

So it was a good time to talk. To ask what he'd done that had sent her in hiding and that, whatever it was, he wished he'd known. Because he was damn sorry about it.

He opened his mouth and said, "I'm so—"

And heard sounds of the crew laughing outside.

Stacy shot him a disconcerted look. "Did you say something?"

"No." He shook his head. "At least nothing important."

Chapter 9

THE GROUP WAS loud and raucous when they came in the front door, bringing freezing cold air and lots of laughter with them. Now in the boot room, George stomped the snow from his feet and took off his boots. Going through an interior door, he stepped into the main room of the cabin and announced, "It's a gorgeous day out there. We will have some awesome runs today."

Royce grinned. "Glad to hear that. Did you go up Robber's Trail or over to Sycamous Trail?"

"Both—well, almost both. We went to the base of Robber's Trail, then took Green Trail to Sycamous. Both were great." He walked over to the fireplace and held out his hands. He was joined by the others, all huddling around the flames.

"Something smells great," Stevie said, his head tilting up for a bigger sniff. "Toast." He sniffed again. "Stacy, did you make breakfast?"

She shot him a look at the disbelief in his voice. "I do cook, you know? But Royce did most of the work." She turned around and grabbed the platter of toast she'd made and held it out. "However, I did make these."

"Yes," he crowed. "Toasted on an open fire."

"That's the best kind."

"Hey, pass it over here."

Within seconds, the platter had been reduced to several of the smallest pieces. She grinned and placed it on the small coffee table.

"Stacy?"

She turned around. Royce motioned her toward him. "I'm serving. Can I get you to deliver?"

And, with that, she had a plate for everyone. Some of them stood in front of the fire, others sat on the couch, and several took their plates to the small dining table.

George motioned to Stacy with his fork. "Where's yours?"

"Ha, I ate first." If she hadn't been looking at him, she'd have missed the narrow-eyed look he tossed at Royce. As she turned away from him, she also caught Royce's nod in response. Really? She wondered about making an issue of it but decided that it was just her brother ensuring she was looking after herself. He would need to see for himself that she was okay.

She couldn't blame him for worrying. If their positions were reversed, she'd do the same thing.

She loved him.

He loved her.

That's what caring was all about.

While the others ate, she and Royce washed the dishes in companionable silence. She put on a second pot of coffee, while the group discussed where they were going. Given it was just day one, several people were determined to make the most of their time. Others were more concerned about overdoing it on the first day.

She knew she'd be asked about her plans soon. She had no idea but heard one group talk of the runs by the frozen waterfall. That was where she wanted to go. With the blue sky and sun, she'd be sure to get some amazing photos.

She walked up to her loft room and dug around for her gear. She put on different socks, her thermals, and her outer layer. That was the easy decision. Now what did she want to take for camera equipment? She pored over her lenses. She didn't want to pack anything unnecessary. However, any camera buff would be in the same boat—they would want to take it all with them. Just in case.

In the end, she cut her choice down to the basics, then headed back downstairs. She caught George's surprised look. She shrugged. "I thought I'd come and see what the light is like."

"Three groups are going out right now," Royce stated, his gaze penetrating. "Where are you planning to go?"

"To the waterfalls," she said lightly. "Unless anyone objects?"

"Glad to hear you're coming," Stevie said, a big smile on his face. "Make sure you catch my good side."

That brought the insults flying, as they teased him. Stacy just smiled and sat down to put on her ski boots. The others were in various states of dress, as they all got ready to go back out. George sat beside Stacy, and she asked him, "Anyone staying here to keep the fire going?"

George shook his head. "No, it will hold fine."

She smiled. "I'll only be out for a few hours."

"Good. Don't overdo it."

"I won't."

"When you're ready," Royce said, "someone will come back with you."

"No need," she said smoothly. "I'm an old hand at this. Remember?"

"Safety first, remember?" Royce repeated. "I'll be making

sure you get there and back." His tone brooked no argument. If anything, he shot her a hard look, as if to remind her who was the boss. Then he grabbed his jacket and walked out.

She made a face. And here she'd thought she'd just have her big brother worrying about her. Still, this wasn't a small resort. It was dense with hundreds of runs, and people were often only found missing when, hours later, they didn't show up. Often no one could say exactly where to look. After the avalanche that had ripped apart this group's lives, they had adopted a few rules. *Never alone. Always let someone know where they would be at all times. Do not do anything stupid.*

ROYCE STOOD ON the closed-in porch dubbed the boot room and breathed deeply. The bite of the cold helped stabilize his mood. It had been a great morning, with just the two of them. Friendly. Companionable even. As if the years of silence between them had never been. He paused to reconsider. It was as if the years *including that weekend* had never existed. He'd been friends with George since Stacy had been in pigtails. He wasn't sure exactly when it happened, but somewhere along the way he started to care for her more than he should for his best friend's kid sister. George hadn't been the one to warn him off. Stacy's father had. And in no uncertain terms. Stacy was going on to university and getting a real education. She didn't need a bad-boy jock giving her the eye.

He'd hated that meeting. But he'd respected the man. And the lecture. He'd backed off and had stayed well back. He'd stepped forward, after she lost her friends, and she'd had these massive walls up, keeping him firmly on the other side. He'd given her space. Then about three months afterward, when he'd tried again, he had been rebuffed in no uncertain terms.

It had surprised the hell out of him when she'd come to him many months later, but he was no fool, and, from the first touch, they'd gone up in flames.

And, damn it, if immediately afterward, she hadn't given him the deep freeze of all deep freezes. He'd backed off, giving her space, thinking to come back in a few months. It hadn't worked out that way. She'd shut and locked that door.

She'd stayed behind that icy wall ever since. He'd hoped she'd drop it one day, but he hadn't waited. He'd gone on with his life. Somewhat.

He had no idea when she would ever warm up enough to let someone join her in her icy prison. Even better, to let her heart open up and let that icy exterior melt forever.

God, he hoped he was there when it happened.

"You okay?" George stood beside him, reading his reactions.

George knew Royce well. And knew how he felt about Stacy. How he'd always felt about her. He shrugged. "I'm fine. It's just weird."

"Yeah, it would be. I'm hoping it's all good."

Shit. This was his garbage. Not George's. "It's all good. It's great to see her here." He grabbed his board. "Now if only we can get her through the week."

He glanced over at Stacy, as she joined the rest of them, satisfaction rippling through him as he watched her settle in. All through the drive yesterday, she'd been an outsider. Although sitting in the vehicle *with* them, she hadn't been one *of* them. Even last night, she'd been uncomfortable with

George bringing up her photography. Particularly the controversial ones. Her Eternal series.

Her room choice for sleeping had also been indicative of how she felt. She'd chosen the loft. Maybe for the reason she had voiced, but also so she didn't have to share a room with anyone, again keeping herself separate.

Yet more than one bed was up there. However, no door for privacy. He'd planned to go up to the loft with her, needing to be close. Not too close, but close enough to keep an eye on her. So she would know she wasn't alone. He'd actually hoped that she'd be waiting and watching to see if he shared a room with Yvonne. Instead, by the time everyone had crashed—well after she'd gone to bed—she'd been sound asleep.

He should know. He'd crept upstairs, intent on putting his bedroll up there as well.

Instead he'd decided, since she was sleeping so well, that he'd stay down by the fire and let her have her space.

That might have been the right thing to do, as she'd slept soundly. He'd shushed the second group as they headed to their bedrooms, to avoid waking her. And it had worked. She'd slept though the ruckus.

Now this morning she was comfortably in the middle of the group, as if she'd never been so separate. A little too comfortable with Geoffrey though.

"*Hmm …*" George said in a low voice. "She's not interested in him, you know?"

Heat washed up Royce's neck. Damn. He'd hoped George hadn't noticed. She was always so relaxed, so playful with Stevie and Mark, that Royce couldn't help but wonder about her closer connection to Geoffrey.

"They're just friends."

Royce pulled on his belt and slammed it home, checking his buckles. "I'm sure they are." He knew that; it's just that he didn't want them to become anything more.

"Good." More clicks and snaps sounded as George put on his helmet. "Are you good?"

"Yeah." And Royce was. He always was. Like he and George had discussed, they'd do everything they could to look after Stacy and to see that she enjoyed her first vacation since that fateful time.

Then maybe they could coax her out of her shell again.

BITCH.

That was the nicest thing he could say about her. She'd slipped into place with the group, and damn if he didn't feel like he'd been ousted to make room for her.

Stupid bitch. There, that was better.

Maybe he'd do a series of portraits too. Her face in stupid positions, so that everyone could see her true colors.

The thoughts only festered in his mind. He'd tried to clear them out. And failed.

She was like mold. Insidious and all-encompassing. Everything she touched succumbed to her will.

Like hell.

If anyone was the ruler in that department, he was it.

And she'd learn that lesson soon enough.

Chapter 10

STACY STOPPED, STABILIZED her breathing, and then climbed up another rise. Ski boots were not made for walking. However, it was an easy climb. Her movements were strong and steady. She'd been more overwhelmed by the extreme beauty of the frozen waterfall than the physical exertion. She'd forgotten the sheer joy of feeling the fresh air fill her lungs and the burn of her muscles, but her heart was full of laughter.

The scenery was spectacular.

She was glad she'd come. She crested the top, and damn if Royce wasn't waiting for her there. She did a quick step and laughed out loud. Life was good. She dropped her skis and clicked her boots in the bindings.

"You aren't as out of shape as I thought you'd be," Stevie crowed at her side, giving her a big hug. Their helmets clanged against each other.

She let him. It went with the day and the scenario. She'd have stomped him if he'd tried that at work.

"You're doing great out here, you know?" He gave her a big grin.

She rolled her eyes at him. "I haven't been that bad."

He gave her a serious look. "Yes, you have."

Startled, she took a closer look and realized from the deep, dark, troubled look in his eyes that he cared, like really cared. And she was touched. "I'm better now."

"*Now*," he muttered. "Finally. It's been a rough couple years, watching you fall apart, then put yourself back together again, as if the new model was made of steel, fortified so you'd never be hurt again."

"Wow, does everyone know about that?" Being a private person, it was disconcerting to think that others knew of her breakdown. "I thought I'd hid it much better."

He rushed to reassure her. "You did a great job, but, for those who knew you and loved you, it was hard to watch." He shrugged sheepishly. "We couldn't help you, besides being friendly and supportive. And hoping you pulled out of it."

She nodded. She tilted her helmet back slightly and rubbed an itch along her forehead. She didn't know what to say. She'd been unaware of so much back then. Now that she was pulling herself back into line, she regretted not knowing. Maybe she wouldn't have fallen into such a downward spiral if she hadn't been alone.

But she had. And here she was today. Realizing she had more friends than ever. "Thanks, Stevie. I hadn't recognized much around me back then. It was a difficult time. Thanks for standing by me."

"Always. We'd tried to get George to do something …"

She shook her head, a startled laugh coming out. "Good try. George loves me dearly, but he's never been able to force me into doing anything I didn't want to do."

"And yet"—Stevie threw his hand wide, pointing to the wide expanse of frozen beauty all around them—"here you are."

With a shout of laughter, she slugged him lightly on the shoulder. "I hate to disappoint you or to knock George off a pedestal, but I'd already decided it was time to face this. I came because George requested that I come, but, if I hadn't come this time, then I'd have asked to come another time."

At Stevie's look of dismayed astonishment, she laughed again. "At the risk of really ruining your mood, I'd also like to find some new inspiration for my photography." She motioned to their surroundings. "I need to heal myself and get back to living life like I used to."

OH, LOOK AT that. The ice princess deigned to come out and play. He hid his smirk and waved at her. Bitch. He smiled brightly. "Hey, nice you came out." He buckled up his belt. "You're just in time to have some fun."

Then I'll have fun with you later. Whore. After Royce, are you? He watched her smile at the man in question, a burning sensation in his gut. They were all whores. Women. The scourge of the earth.

Royce slugged him on the shoulder. "You're next."

"Ha. Race you to the bottom," he responded. "You'll never beat me."

"You're on."

He put all thoughts of Stacy into the back of his mind, as Royce took off. No way would he let Royce win. "Like hell, prepare to get your ass whupped."

That started the laughter, the cheers and jeers from everyone around, as they urged the racers on.

And he laughed. Damn, he was good. He grinned. Soon he'd make sure everyone else knew it too.

Chapter 11

THE REST OF the morning passed in a blur of runs. They skied and boarded and took the lifts to the top. It was fun and bloody cold. Stacy opted out after several runs. She was sore and tired but thrilled to be here.

She pulled to a stop by the frozen waterfall. "Go on," she said, waving her group past. "I'll stay here for a couple runs and rest. See you on the next pass."

And the others whooshed by with hoots and hollers. They'd be gone close to forty minutes, before returning to where she waited.

She laughed, watching them race down in front of her. It was a stunning day. As the silence descended, she tilted her head skyward, letting the warmth of the sun land on her face. She opened her eyes and turned to look up at the frozen waterfall. Such beautiful ice forms. Who said white was white? This was so much more than that.

The sunlight was perfect. It bounced and echoed, a soundless splash of color across the scenery.

And she saw it. That face. A hidden gem of perception. Like when naming one cloud an elephant and another a snail. There. A head, ... mostly a profile, hidden in the crags above her, a play of lights and shadows. Her heart pounded with the excitement of this discovery.

She studied it for a long moment, trying to mark the

spots that defined the nose and eyebrows, the chin, so she could find them again from the other side of her viewfinder. The longer she looked, the more intense the spark grew. This was truly special.

She removed her backpack and dove in, searching for her camera. Her hand closed around it, and she sighed with relief. She'd been sure it was in here, but, in the joy of the moment, there was that fear that she'd somehow forgotten it or worse—had lost it. She pulled it out, pulled off the cap, and lifted it all in one movement. The sun was changing. She needed to grab as many shots as she could.

She peered at the ice wall. Where was it? She studied the area, looking for the markers she'd set in her mind. Where? She took several shots anyway, knowing that, just because her mind might not have seen it right now, it didn't mean she wouldn't find the image markers later, when she had prints of the pictures.

There.

She caught sight of the tip of the nose. From that point, she looked back to find the eyebrows and the jaw. Beautiful. Like seriously beautiful. She started clicking, trying to catch it in its entire splendor. As the light changed, she saw several long waving columns of frozen ice rolling down the cliff, like locks of curly hair. Mesmerized, she quickly became lost in her panic to get her shots before the light changed again.

Click.

Click, click.

There. She shifted. *Click. Click. Click.* She could hardly breathe for fear of missing something. As the sun shifted, the rays brought yet another image into focus. Oh God. Stunning.

"So beautiful," she murmured. The icy beauty locked

into the mountain was something she'd never seen before. *Ice maiden*, she'd instinctively called her. Frozen in time. So appropriate, given her friends' snowy graves were somewhere here too. Maybe she'd do this series as a memorial. What a wonderful way to say goodbye.

Potential titles for the series just rolled off her lips, as her camera never stopped. She walked closer and then stepped to the right. More shots from the left. At one, she swore the sun had picked up a tear on the woman's frozen features. A big fat dewdrop-shaped ice ball hung delicately on her cheek. "So gorgeous."

"What is?" Royce asked quietly behind her.

She gasped in shock. Lost in her world, she hadn't heard anyone else approach.

He reached out an arm to steady her, for the first time making her aware of her body, now cold and tired. She was swaying on her feet.

"I think it's time you came back to the cabin," he said in a harsh voice.

She frowned and then glanced up at the frozen waterfall to see the clouds had moved in. Her frozen lady was barely visible. Now there was a gloomy, sinister look to her.

And just as powerful. She lifted her camera, lost once again.

"That's enough, Stacy." He reached out and grabbed her elbow, forcing her to turn around. Dragging her gaze from his face, she looked back at the waterfall and noted her frozen lady was asleep once again.

She turned to look down at her pack. Only it wasn't here. Her pack was somehow hundreds of yards away from where he found her. Surprised at the distance, she turned to study the path she'd taken in her need to capture her frozen lady and realized she'd, indeed, walked that far away on her own. The path was churned up from the effects of the warming sun and her movements—the twisting, crouching positions she'd used to take her shots.

Bizarre.

As she put away her camera, a sense of having touched something special filtered through her. If she'd caught what she'd hoped to catch, this could be her best series ever. They were simple, yet stunning. At least she hoped they were. The sky darkened even more. She stood and motioned to the cloud cover. "I thought the weather was supposed to be good all week?"

"That's life in the mountains. Storms blow in and out without warning. At least today was great." He smiled and adjusted her pack on her shoulders, having caught the corner of her coat. He had her skis in his other hand. "Now, back to the cabin."

She went without protest, casting one long last look at the lady sleeping in her frozen home.

With the sun completely obliterated, there was no sign of her at all.

Stacy could only hope she'd caught the image she needed to prove to the others that the ice maiden mirage had ever existed in the first place.

ROYCE HAD BEEN watching her for the last hour. Several times he'd moved in to say something, only to realize what he thought was a break in her concentration was actually just a shift. Not enough for her to be aware of her surroundings either. He'd watched the cliff behind her with worried eyes several times. She hadn't seemed as aware of it as he was. And that bothered him. Hell, everything about her concerned him. She was something else. Her focus was so intense, so complete.

Something about the way she perceived the world around her was so at odds with others. Maybe she had a heightened sense of perception. He didn't know. It was just special. The photography she did was unique. He wished he could see what she saw when she looked at the cliff face. He'd looked plenty of times already and had no idea what had necessitated hundreds of shots. If not thousands of shots. He knew if he saw the final piece, he'd recognize the area, but, until she pointed out what was so special, he wouldn't have seen it first.

Then she'd almost fallen. And not by tripping. From fatigue. She didn't even seem to realize her own limits.

Damn that girl. Had she any idea how tired she was?

He'd moved into position soon afterward. He had mentioned leaving within minutes, but she hadn't even registered he was there. He'd waited another twenty minutes before he'd pushed it again. He doubted she'd even noticed the passage of time.

They skied back to the cabin. It was a gentle slope, but he kept a close eye on her, in case she fell.

It was late afternoon, and, with the heavy cloud cover, the winds had picked up. It was getting ugly quickly. "A storm is moving in fast."

"I see that." She slipped down a path through the trees. The trees were dark and cold. The atmosphere gloomy. Dark. And much colder. The wind was gone, which helped, but the darkness fell faster. He was pissed. They should have left a long time ago. It was his fault. He'd seen her. Had known they should have left earlier, but he'd stayed, so she could take her damn photos. Anything for her.

He was a fool. A lovesick fool.

Chapter 12

STACY PULLED HER jacket closer around her neck. The chill was bone deep all of a sudden. There'd been no warning of the change of weather. Or, she winced, she'd ignored them. Typical of her.

"Are you okay?" Royce called out to her into the eerie silence of the woods.

"Very." Knowing he might not be able to hear her as they skied down the slope, she gave a little wave.

The woods appeared to be endless. She knew the cabin was likely only ten minutes farther. She pictured the warm fire ahead. That and a hot rum toddy, together with a hot meal, kept her going. She was not normally nervous in the dark or in the woods, but something about the combination of the two ratcheted up the anxiety factor tenfold. She had to admit to being glad Royce was close by. He was a strong, steady man. And, for all the problems she had with him, he was a good man to watch her back.

They wound their way down the slope to the long flat stretch at the bottom. When the path was wide enough for two, Royce shifted up beside her. She hated to say it, but it was a comfort.

He pointed out a small light in the darkness.

Her heart lightened. That should be the cabin. "Are the others back already?"

"They should be."

She shot him a disbelieving look. "No way. They would've passed me on their way back down."

He nodded. "And, while you were busy taking pictures, they probably did another couple runs, then called it quits. Chances are, they've had at least two drinks and have already eaten most of the dinner."

"They'd better not have," she said. "I'm starving." She took a deep breath and winced, as her lungs filled with icy air. She coughed once, then twice. She felt more than saw Royce's hard look. "I'm fine."

"Good. No more sick days for you."

She grinned. "No. I can't afford any more of those." She could, but, such as life was, it was only because she had a great medical plan where she worked that such a thing was possible. She desperately wanted to cough again but tried to hold it back. She plodded on.

Royce clicked on his helmet's headlight.

A broad beam of light lit up the gloomy sky. Relief filled her. And she hated to realize how nervous she'd really been.

A shout across the pasture was heard clearly.

"Someone is out looking for us," she said, with a smile. "I'm sorry. I didn't want to worry anyone. I really had no idea it was so late."

"No worries." At her sidelong glance, he grinned. "It's not your fault." As she hit a bump with one ski and almost fell, he reached out a hand to steady her, then she righted herself. "Besides, I was keeping watch on the time. We're coming home just when we're supposed to."

There came a second shout.

Now a third. A sense of urgency in the voice.

"What's wrong?" But she knew.

"Someone's missing," Royce replied.

They met up with Stevie and George, rushing toward them. "Mark and Geoffrey are missing."

Royce was immediately all business, his cell phone in his hand. "No reception."

Stacy glanced from one to the other. "A search party?"

Stevie nodded. "Yes, but let's get you back to the cabin."

She shook her head. "No. I'm slowing you down. The cabin's in sight. You'll need Royce."

The three men stared at each other. She said impatiently, "Come on. Let's not be foolish. You need to head back up now. Hopefully they just are having equipment troubles or lost track of time or the storm caught them unaware."

Behind her, came a sudden shout.

Everyone turned. It was Mark and Geoffrey. Everyone cheered.

"Oh, thank God," she murmured.

"Well, that's that then," Royce murmured.

As the other two met up with them, Geoffrey grinned. "It was my fault. I wanted to check out another slope. Sorry for the worry."

"No problem. Let's head back."

As one, they trooped toward the warmth of the cabin.

ROYCE WALKED INTO the cabin to cheers and shouts, as those left in the cabin realized everyone was back, safe and sound. The smell of fresh chili filled his nostrils. Good. He was starving. He caught the look on Stacy's face and almost grinned. She looked ready to steal the bowl from George's hands, and George saw it. He held his bowl to the side. "Get your own."

She grinned. "Will do. Just make sure you save me some."

Royce packed away his boots and gear in the boot room. He came back inside, just behind Stacy, her own footsteps faster and perkier now that they were back. The high energy of the group was contagious.

He headed for the chili pot, happy to see a lot was left. He dished up one bowl, only to have it gently removed from his hands. Stacy flashed a grin at him and said, "Thanks."

He could only grin back. At least she was looking better. He scooped a second bowl full and set it down. And damn if Geoffrey didn't pick it up. "Thanks, man." But an odd tone was in his voice.

Surreptitiously Royce studied Geoffrey's face. He had a sour look as he stirred his chili, adding sour cream and cheddar to the top. "What's the matter?" Royce asked.

"Nothing," Geoffrey said, his tone brusque. "At least nothing more than usual." He turned away at the same time Royce turned, and he watched as Geoffrey caught sight of Stacy standing beside her brother.

And damn if that look on Geoffrey's face wasn't a lot closer to hate than just some sour look.

It chilled Royce to the bone.

GEORGE STUDIED THE undercurrents going on around him. Damn it. Stacy was in the middle of it. Again. Kathleen squeezed his hand. He smiled down at her, loving the reminder of her presence at his side. It was not something he was used to. He'd had dozens of girlfriends, and none had left him feeling like half of him was missing when they were gone.

Not since Kathleen. Besides, he'd hoped that having Kathleen and Yvonne along would help Stacy adjust to being here. The group had been doing these trips together for a long time. They were friends. He trusted them all.

It was a great feeling.

As he glanced over at his sister, then at Kathleen, he realized that, right now, his world was complete.

Chapter 13

T HE ARGUMENT THAT broke out startled Stacy. She hadn't seen it coming. Hadn't even noticed the undercurrents—until they'd turned into a riptide.

"I was being safe," Geoffrey snapped. "Sorry if I didn't meet your expectations."

George glared at him. "You know the rules as well as any of us. Stick to the timeline. If someone has to go out after you, then you're putting them at risk."

"So no one needs to come after me," snapped Geoffrey. "I'm not an amateur."

"Neither was Andrew Corso. He's still missing. And so is Karl Henderson. They were both experienced skiers."

"Well, they couldn't have been that experienced then, could they?" Geoffrey said impatiently. "Come on. I've been coming to these mountains for over a decade. I've never even had a close call."

Stacy hated the raised voices and the dissension. Not good for anyone. Especially not good for a small group like theirs. "We just don't want anything to happen to you," she said in a gentle voice.

He rolled his eyes at her. "Neither do I want anything to happen to you, Stacy, and we were just behind you."

"True. I got lost in my photography," she admitted, with a small smile.

"And what's Royce's excuse?" Stevie asked, with a laugh. "Did he get lost in you, I wonder?"

Raucous laughter filled the air and eased the tension brought on by the earlier sharp words. Trying to hold the tidal wave of heat washing over her cheeks, Stacy smiled good-naturedly. As she slid a cautious gaze at Royce, hoping he realized Stevie's comment was a shot in the dark, she realized he'd gone silent. Grim.

Shit. See? This was why she wasn't into relationships. They were too much work. She stood and collected the many empty chili bowls. "Thanks so much to whoever made the chili. It was delicious."

"I made it," George said, with a grin.

She laughed. "That's why it was so good—it's my recipe."

"Hey, it's Mom's recipe originally," he protested. "Now it's got my own personal touch, thank you very much."

"Yeah, like what?" she challenged him with a grin, happy to feel the others relaxing. It was the way the evening should be.

"It's got elephant garlic in it instead of the regular stuff," he said quickly.

Kathleen laughed, then added, "And that's because the store was out of the regular stuff. You asked them specifically for the little guys."

He gave her a mocking look to shut up, but the rest of the room had already erupted into laughter.

Stacy carried the bowls into the kitchen and called back, "I'll do the dishes if someone wants to carry that kettle of water in here and pour."

Instantly several people hopped to their feet. She busied herself packing away the rest of the chili into a glass bowl.

Chances were good it wouldn't have a chance to get cool before someone would look for seconds. Boiling water splashed into the sink. Instantly soapy bubbles formed.

"Thanks," she said to Stevie.

"No problem. I was hoping there'd be hot water for showers, but it doesn't look like it this time."

She stopped to think about that. They'd had hot showers the last time they were here, but it had to do with the water outside coming in, and the pipes being wrapped around the stovepipe to warm up the water. She turned on the tap, and hot water gushed out. She laughed. "Old habits die hard. I could have just used this hot water."

"Better you didn't." He interpreted her gaze. "There's running water, but, with this many people, no way we could keep the hot water for everyone to shower."

He refilled the kettle and carried it out to the big heater stove. Not only was the steam needed for the air, which would dry out quickly, but this way there'd be hot water for the proverbial teapot. And speaking of hot drinks, she filled the coffeepot and carried it out to heat up as well. Coffee was another staple for her. She'd brought a pound herself, just in case.

Only half listening to the conversation going on around her in the living room, Stacy quickly finished up the dishes. She couldn't help but wonder at the undercurrents of hostility she'd caught earlier. She knew she'd been in a fog for much of the last few years as to what went on within the group, but she'd like to think that, if it had been serious, then someone would have mentioned it to her. She'd definitely pulled the ostrich thing and had buried her head in the sand since losing her friends. Like, why them? She couldn't help asking herself that for the ten millionth time.

Both women were fun-loving and people-loving. They weren't mean or nasty or selfish or stingy. They were wonderful. Why did Stacy deserve to live and not them? She was no better and no nicer than they were.

"Hey, Stacy, what are you thinking about so deeply?"

Startled, she pulled herself back to her surroundings. Now that Stevie had drawn the attention to her, everyone stared at her. She smiled and said, "I just realized that, as I've been out of the loop a fair bit these last couple years, I don't know all of you as well as I'd like to. Some of you I've known for years, and yet others"—she brightened her smile—"I barely know at all."

"Well, you've known me for years," Geoffrey said. "So no mystery there."

"But there is. Whatever happened to …" Stacy frowned, trying to remember who his last girlfriend was. "Karla?" she hazarded a guess.

The group burst out laughing. Geoffrey gave her a mock solute. "Yeah, as if that's so important. My failed love life. She's gone. As in gone years ago. Something about not liking my lifestyle."

She winced. As she remembered, he'd been very much in love with Karla. "Sorry about that."

He shrugged good-naturedly. "It wouldn't be so bad, except for the way she walked out. She just walked. Took her stuff, and, from one day to the next, she never answered my calls or contacted me again."

"Ouch, that's have to hurt," Mark said. "Don't know why women do that. I had that with my last one—Becky." He groaned. "She was the sweetest little thing, with a wonderful chipmunk-cheek ass."

That brought the room into gales of laughter.

Stacy shook her head. "Somehow I don't think she would have appreciated that comparison."

"Oh, I told her that a time or two," he said, with a big grin.

"And you wonder why she walked?" Kathleen hooted. "Maybe leave off the comparisons next time."

"*What* next time? He's been on a long dry run since," Geoffrey said.

"Ha, no longer than yours," Mark teased.

Geoffrey winced. "True enough. It was a rough-enough exit that I didn't exactly want to jump back into the relationship arena." His grin widened. "Now I'm just waiting on Stacy here to get back in, so I can scoop her up."

"Like hell," she teased. "I'd bore you to death with my shoptalk."

"Considering you work on dead bodies all day, *boring* is not quite the right word I would have used." Kathleen gave a tiny shudder. "Thanks for being as sparing with the shoptalk as you appear to be."

"You learn early that it has a tendency to kill a dinner conversation." Stacy had tried to be sensitive to other people's feelings in regard to her profession.

"And why would a beautiful girl like you go into such an oddball career, I don't know," Stevie said, shaking his head. "Yet a lot of women are choosing your career."

"Why is that?" Geoffrey asked.

"I always figured because we already deal in the creation of life, so it makes sense to want to be involved with the other end of the spectrum and learn about death."

"But you're an anthropologist, aren't you? As in very old bones?" Kathleen asked.

"I'm the forensic pathologist for Seattle. However, I also

have a degree in anthropology, so I consult on a wide variety of cases."

"Death. Murder. Suicide." Kathleen shivered. "That's a rough field to work in."

"Comparatively very few people end up on my table because they've been murdered." She withheld saying that usually the worst ones did. She loved the challenge of the unusual. And, to be honest, she loved outwitting the criminal mind. When she could find pivotal evidence in a murder case, she felt a huge sense of satisfaction. That she had an overlarge caseload of unsolved deaths in her files made her angry and sad at the same time. Still, most of her work was of the more normal variety.

"As we convinced Stacy to get out into nature and away from the death that she lives in, I suggest we change the subject," Royce said.

George picked up his GPS and asked, "Anyone used one of these to chart maps on the mountain?" He held it up. "Mark, weren't you the one showing this to me?"

The room erupted at the new topic.

Stacy sat back and let the group run with it. She knew she tended to make people uncomfortable. She didn't always know how to handle that discomfort, but she seemed to have skirted past it tonight.

She waited a little longer, then excused herself.

She was cold, tired, and just a little sick of being around so many people. She could use a few moments to herself—and a good night's sleep.

ROYCE WATCHED AS Stacy made her way to the bathroom. When she came out, she looked tired. Her slow climb up the stairs seemed to take more effort than he expected. Then the cold would have a huge effect on her. When she disappeared from sight, he turned back to the group and caught Geoffrey glaring at him. Royce lifted an eyebrow. What the hell was his problem? Geoffrey got up and went into the kitchen. Royce watched him, wishing he understood what the hell that had been all about. Out of the corner of his eye, he caught sight of George studying him. He faced him and asked quietly, "Do you know what that was?"

George made a tiny motion of his head toward where Stacy had disappeared to.

Royce settled back into his seat. Damn it. Was Geoffrey sweet on Stacy? Not good. Royce contemplated the issue and realized it really didn't matter. Anyone could be sweet on Stacy—they still wouldn't get her.

She was his. She just refused to admit it.

BITCH. SHE WAS his. She just didn't know it. But she would soon. He glanced around the cabin, feeling the sense of connectedness within the group. The group she'd joined and shouldn't have been allowed to.

She didn't belong.

She shouldn't have come this week.

It had been great without her all these years. Without the reminder of her rejection. But her stupid brother just had to bring her back into the fold.

His gaze switched to Royce and hardened. And so had Royce. Without her around, life would be different. It would be back to just them. The way it used to be. The way it was supposed to be.

He was starting to hate all women.

Chapter 14

STACY WOKE SEVERAL times in the night, cold and achy. Not good. She needed to be careful, to stay warm, and to ensure she didn't get sick again. It had been a long, painful year, one she couldn't repeat. She hadn't thought to be out so long or so late yesterday. She still wasn't so sure how that had happened.

Except, when she got lost in her art, she got *lost* in her art.

Was it a coincidence that Royce was with her then, or had he been keeping an eye on her all afternoon? She rolled over and bit back a moan. Her shoulders and arms throbbed. Damn. She should have thought ahead and taken an anti-inflammatory. Then she would likely wake up loose and moving freely. Possibly still with mild pain but not the feeling of having her muscles locked in place, every movement a hard tug to get them going. And it was cold. Damn cold. She snuggled deeper into her sleeping bag and closed her eyes.

"Hey, sleepyhead. Time to get down here, if you're planning on getting any coffee," Stevie called up to her.

She groaned loud enough for him to hear. "You could deliver," she said, without hope, knowing that would make her the butt of the jokes but not caring. They'd all been drinking heavily last night. She, on the other hand, had gone to bed early. Again.

If she were home, she would have made coffee and brought a tray back to bed with her. No such luxury here. Then she heard a welcome sound. The heavy thumps of footsteps. She smiled, "I hope that means coffee is coming."

"It is coffee, but I also wanted to make sure you're okay this morning," Royce said in a quiet no-nonsense voice.

She rolled over in surprise, the sudden movement causing the pain to flare up, and she barely held back the cry. But his knowing gaze said he'd seen it.

Hating not being in as good a shape as the rest of them here, she stuffed her feelings of insecurity down deep inside. No room for that out here. Good health was paramount for her—not self-esteem issues. Should she fail in keeping herself safe, then the others would be required to step in and to rescue her. She couldn't withstand the guilt. Not again.

She hadn't been responsible for her friends' deaths, but she felt that she was. And that made all the difference. She couldn't help but feel that she should have known what they were planning to do. That she should have done more to warn them about the snow conditions. Warn them about how their behavior had gotten them into trouble before and to play it safe this time.

And maybe she was just overwhelmed with survivor's guilt. She couldn't sort through her feelings, as she couldn't step back. She needed to get closure on their deaths, so she could analyze it better. She couldn't help but feel they were around every corner on that damn mountain, and, if she would just look a little harder, she would find them.

To bring them home.

Royce squatted and placed the steaming mug of coffee beside her bed. He held his other hand out for her. She frowned at the two reddish-brown pills in his palm. "For your muscles."

Her gaze flew up to his, seeing that knowing look in his eyes. She sighed and plucked them from his hand. She swallowed them quickly. Knowing she wasn't acting gracious, she forced out a "Thank you."

"Look at that? It didn't choke you," he sneered, standing back up.

She closed her eyes. This wasn't her. She was generally a polite, easy-to-get-along-with type of person. But something about Royce just got to her. Or maybe it was because, although she was feeling cruddy, she'd like nothing better than to have him lie down beside her and take her in his arms.

"I am thankful," she muttered.

"Just can't show it, can you?" he mocked. But something else was in his tone. Frustration maybe?

Her gaze flew up to his, and damn if heat didn't flare between them.

Her breath caught in the back of her throat. His gaze was an overwhelming warmth that slid through her, warming up all the cold places inside.

She desperately wanted to tear away her focus, but he held her captive. Then, as if he cut a string, he broke eye contact to stare over the loft railing, down at the group below, a muscle in his jaw throbbing out his aggravation.

She shuddered, hating the lassitude inside her, now that he'd given her that magical invisible stroke of his touch. She didn't know how he did it, or what exactly he'd done, but it always felt like a soothing stroke of his hands—only without physical contact. Then she realized that he was as affected as she was. He was having trouble controlling his breathing. It came out in short raspy breaths.

She hated this. This awkwardness between them. "It can't go anywhere, you know? That's the problem."

He stared at her in astonishment. "What are you talking about?"

She flushed. She'd completely misread the situation. Shit. Shit. Shit. She was a complete idiot. "Nothing," she mumbled, sliding down into her sleeping bag and rolling away from him.

Please just leave, she whispered in her head, as she lay still.

"I'm leaving, for the moment," he snapped, "but we'll talk about this again."

"Nothing to talk about," she whispered, mortified.

"Yes, there is. What you just said is garbage. Nothing's stopping us from having a relationship—but you."

And he turned and stomped down the stairs, leaving her stunned into complete silence.

There wasn't?

ROYCE SHOVED HIS sadness and frustration deep inside, as he rejoined the others, but, from the look on George's face, Royce knew he'd failed there. Whatever. He glanced over at Yvonne. She appeared to be deep in discussion with Geoffrey. She'd been sending out signals all last evening that she wasn't averse to spending the week with someone. For a brief moment he'd contemplated it, more to pay back Stacy for all the pain she'd given him and then realized that it likely wouldn't have hurt Stacy in the first place. But he had no wish to find that out for sure.

It was also a step forward that he could never reverse.

Not to mention it was hardly fair to Yvonne. She might want a weeklong fling, but that didn't mean she wanted to be used as a pawn in a broken relationship. Who would? Ashamed for even considering the thought, he'd quickly tossed it from his mind.

"Plans for the day?"

Royce listened, while George laid out the day's runs he wanted to hit. He called out to his sister, "Stacy, are you skiing today?"

"I'm coming with the group but bringing my camera," she called down.

George smiled. "Sounds great. Then get that skinny butt of yours down here and eat. We'll be pulling out in thirty."

ANOTHER PERFECT OPPORTUNITY wasted. George needed to shut the hell up. Royce needed to leave Stacy the hell alone. What was wrong with these people? She was nothing. A whore. That was it.

He stomped out to the boot room part of the cabin, where all the gear was stowed. He needed to get his boots on. Not to mention a whole mess of other gear. At least his new gloves were holding up.

Now if only Stacy would leave her camera behind. That would also make his day.

The others would follow soon enough. If he were lucky, one group would follow his lead, and they could get up the mountain early. That's what they were here for, after all.

Something they'd all do well to remember.

Instead of fawning over the bitch.

Making sure she had her coffee when she woke up.

That she had a group to ski with all the time.

What the hell was this? Babysitting?

They were all so damn predictable. And so was she. Always late, always making the others wait for her. Always quiet, so the others spoke up for her. Jesus. Enough already. He opened the door to the outside and smiled. Clear skies and fresh snow. Absolutely the best conditions.

Now if only they could get there before the damn snow melted and winter was over.

Chapter 15

STACY MADE IT on time. Barely. She'd dressed, raced down to the bathroom, then inhaled breakfast and coffee, before gearing up for the morning outside. She wasn't skiing today, so she wore winter hiking boots. Should make it easier to walk in the snow. That was about all she could plan for right now. At least her body shifted and moved with grace at this point. A few twinges and squeaky joints but essentially she was doing well.

She packed up her travel mug, sorted through her camera lenses, and quickly grabbed a bigger memory card. Last night she hadn't taken a look at how full her storage was. Big mistake. She didn't dare not have enough while she was out there. The last thing she wanted to do was come back because she couldn't take any more images.

Not that she planned on being out for long. She was making dinner for everyone today, since she had agreed to take a turn. She hadn't brought anything preplanned though, so someone needed to give her the menu for the week, so she didn't accidently use up ingredients needed for other meals.

As she strode out the door, she cast a last look behind her at the cabin. She wasn't the last one out. Royce locked the cabin and placed the key on the top of the doorframe. The lock was more to stop the elements from opening the door than to keep anyone out. They'd all been briefed on the location of the key on the first day. Basic safety.

The early morning light hit the side of the cabin, bounced off the window, and split into a wide band. Colors rippled on the rays. It was beautiful. And it almost blinded her. She lifted her hand to shade her gaze from the glare. Like so much light work, a bit of information was helpful. Too much and it was a killer.

"Let's go." Royce walked past her, reminding her that the rest of the group was striding out strongly in two directions. She had to stop and think. Who was she going with today?

"This way." Royce stepped in behind the first group. "We're going back to the same place, but it's relatively easy terrain. Maybe you can find something to photograph there."

"I'm sure I will," she said in subdued tones. It was the first thing she'd said to him after his earlier comment.

"Are you okay?" he asked.

She nodded but stayed silent. In fact, speech would have been difficult. What did she want to say? At the moment, she had no idea. Did he really want to have a relationship with her? As in a real one or just another weekend fling? God, she wished she knew her own mind.

Or maybe she wished she knew her own heart.

Something she hadn't known for a long time.

They continued to hike in companionable silence, when the group stopped. There were shouts ahead. Royce picked up his pace.

"What's up?" she asked, when they reached the other three.

George said, "One of the other group fell into a ravine of

some kind."

Immediately their group headed in the direction of the other group. With the sunny day and no cloud cover, the cell phone reception was strong and clear. Good thing. George continued to talk to Mark, as they moved across the plateau to where the second group currently stood.

They'd been heading to a different run that day. No one had been along that path in days. Crossing as they were now was hard going. The leader had to break a path in the deep snow. Stacy was smart enough to stay in the middle of the pack. Of course, Royce pulled up last place to ensure there were no stragglers.

"Was anyone hurt?" Stacy asked.

"No. Not at all. He slid down more than anything."

She nodded. "Good."

George's phone rang again. "Apparently the fault line goes a fair bit in our direction, so approach carefully," George said, after he put away his phone.

He pulled out the long stick he'd found earlier and stabbed the ground with each step. The others held back and waited. In deep snow, anything could be waiting below. Most of this area was popular with skiers and climbers from all over the world, but, like everyone, her group wanted to play where others hadn't gone before. *Figures.* Still, even the popular runs ran into trouble sometimes.

Snow that appeared to be more solid than it was often hid a small gulley.

Up ahead, more shouts could be heard. With the others in front, Stacy couldn't see who was shouting.

Royce said, "That's them. We're almost there."

Stacy had her camera around her neck. She wanted to break rank and take pictures as they approached but wasn't sure where she was in relation to the fault line they were talking about. So she stayed in place.

George changed direction, stepping into the trail their other group had already made. The walking got a little bit easier yet again.

And suddenly she could see them. Her group spread out, so she could step closer. Sure enough, a bit of the ground had given way, and Stevie appeared to have slid, rather than falling down. He waved up at her. "Hey, Stacy. Glad you came to see."

She laughed. "I'm just wondering why you're still there. With all the help around, I'd have thought you'd be back up on top already."

"Ha. I actually tried to climb up by myself, but the bank keeps coming down."

"Of course." They always did. She stepped back and pulled out her camera. Within seconds, she had Stevie's predicament captured for posterity. Then she took another and another. When Stevie understood what she was doing, he called out a mocking protest. The others all laughed. Stacy kept clicking, as they worked to get Stevie up from the fifteen-foot-deep hole. She made sure to document where it started and stopped, if for no other reason than to mark it on the maps for other people.

A few more depressions were on one side. She carefully followed the light, so she could see the full scope of the depression, faint until she saw it in the shadows, and where it ended. "It stops here," she called out.

"Which means that it likely goes underground for another twenty plus yards. Such is the way of faults," Royce said, as he walked toward her, so he could see the magnitude of the fault line himself. She watched the narrow edge in his gaze, as he studied the ground. She couldn't resist. She pulled out her camera. The look of intensity on his face, the knowledge in his eyes. He knew his stuff. And that sense of authority was damn sexy.

And she sure as hell needed to stop thinking like that.

She stepped back again.

And felt the snow give way.

She cried out in surprise.

And fell.

GEORGE HEARD STACY call out. He spun around to see her disappear from sight. "Stacy!"

The others raced toward her.

Royce held out his arms. "Wait. We don't know how far the fault goes."

George took a cautious step forward. "Stacy, are you okay?"

"Yeah, I am."

The sound of her voice hit Royce so hard that he had to stop his headlong plunge and close his eyes. *Oh thank God.* All business now, he called out, "Are you hurt?"

"No, I'm fine," she called back. "Just pissed at myself."

"No need to be," he called down to her, carefully walking forward and poking the ground with long sticks, making sure it was solid enough to stand on. They stepped forward as a wall and the poking continued. They'd almost reached her when the wall of snow caved in front of them.

And there she was. With the bank down and the crevasse widened, it was easy to see her now. She stood on her own two feet—staring up at them. She studied the space and turned to the left. The group was walking down the path and poking into the ground to make sure it was solid, but they had seemingly opened up the crevasse as far as they could see. They had quickly opened up the space between Stevie and Stacy. Stacy walked toward Stevie with every new step that opened up until she could see him.

She laughed and ran over to give him a big hug. He picked her up and twirled her around, only the ground was full of snow and ice chunks, and they both fell down to the amusement of everyone watching.

It took another twenty minutes before the two of them were standing on solid ground. The group had continued to collapse the snow along the fault line, so it would be visible to others.

"Well now, that was a fun trip, but let's move on," Stevie said.

"Nope. We're not going anywhere," George called out. "Royce, come here, please."

Royce walked closer. "What's up?"

George glanced behind at the others, slowly making their way over. In a low voice, he said, "This." He pointed into the crevasse.

To the boot attached to a man's leg, partially buried under the fresh snow.

ROYCE STARED AT the cowboy boot. "What the hell?"

He skidded down the loose snow and managed to stay on his feet. He walked over and scooped the snow off the body. The way the snow had fallen had buried the top half of the body. "George, you start making the calls."

"Yep, on it."

Royce heard the others talking up top and the sounds of

several other people making their way down the slope toward him. He hoped it wasn't Stacy. She had had enough death in her world.

The snow kept sliding down the slope and constantly filled in the space he had cleared. He glared at the snow bank. There really was no help for it. He bent and grabbed the man's ankle and tugged. And it didn't move. Shit.

"I'm here. Hang on," Stevie said. He approached with a tiny shovel. With the two of them, they made short work of spreading the loose snow around the side and out of their way. Before he realized it, they had the bulk of the snow off the man. And he used the word *man* loosely, as the head and face were still buried. Stevie dropped his shovel beside the body and fell to his knees, then carefully brushed the rest off the man's face.

Royce studied the solid marble-looking body and had to wonder. How long had it been here? That didn't change the fact that the dead man didn't look in any way like a winter sports enthusiast. Neither was he dressed for cold weather.

But, if he wasn't either of the missing men he knew about, who was he? Why the hell was he out here in the middle of nowhere?

"I'm here," Stacy said, from behind. "Let me see."

Chapter 16

ROYCE STOOD WITH his hand out, saying, "You shouldn't see this."

Stacy choked back a laugh. "Really? And why is that?"

He groaned and smacked his forehead. "Somehow, for one moment there, I completely forgot who and what you were."

"I didn't," Stevie said, with a grin. He motioned his hand toward the body. "After you."

She rolled her eyes and walked closer to the unexpected gravesite, as others made the necessary phone calls. She'd seen more death than most, but this hadn't been on her plans for the day. Still, death was never on one's plans.

Royce and Stevie had started cutting stairs in a solid slope behind her. It was a faster and more effective answer than using ropes and hauling the dead weight up that way.

Squatting beside the dead man, she studied his features. She didn't recognize him. Thankfully. Young, between his late twenties and late thirties most likely. She studied his posture, the angle of his body, the look on his face. She stood and walked around the young man. Only silence came from the others, as they watched her work.

She hadn't seen too many who came in from a deep freeze like this. The temperatures always played havoc in looking at time of death. She motioned to Stevie to roll over the body. No blood was anywhere. No visible injuries. She checked his fingernails and the tips of his fingers. His eyes. Death had been fast.

Then she pulled up his sleeve as far as the stiff material would go and found raw marks on the guy's wrist. She quickly checked his other wrist. Both showed signs of having been restrained. No blood showed, no broken skin, but the angry redness spoke volumes.

She never said anything to the others. A quick search of his pockets turned up no ID. Curious and curiouser.

"Another climber, do you think?" George asked. "There are a few missing."

"Potentially." She frowned. "But, considering he's not deep enough for the fall to have killed him, no blood shows from an injury, and he was within walking distance to the cabin—why?"

"Drunk?" asked George. "Going for a walk often makes sense at the worst times after a few drinks."

"True enough." She stood back and stared at the man's boots—cowboy boots. "He's certainly not dressed for the weather. Even his footwear is more suitable for a stroll than a winter hike."

She glanced off in the distance, trying to mentally place the road, wondering if he'd had a car accident and had wandered off, looking for assistance. If he'd been in shock, he could easily have gotten lost and disoriented. But this area wasn't well-known, and those who frequented it were better prepared as to what to expect. And where would his vehicle be, if he'd driven here? The police would have reports on abandoned vehicles in the area, but it often took days for such vehicles to be reported in a resort like this—particularly if he'd gone off the road.

She sat back on her haunches, puzzled. For all intents and purposes, at first glance, it appeared as if he had succumbed to the elements. The real question was, what was he doing out here in the first place?

And how did the marks on his wrists relate?

She checked her watch. "The police will still be an hour or two, I suspect."

"Head back to the cabin, and we'll stay here and keep an eye on him," George told her.

She shook her head. "No, I'll stay." She'd seen worse. Had waited in worse conditions. The body was her responsibility now. She would not leave.

The group split up, half choosing to carry on and to get in a few runs, whereas the rest of the group, with the exception of Stevie, headed back to the cabin to wait for the coroner's office.

Stevie pulled his thermos from his pack and offered her a cup.

"Thanks," she said, with a smile.

"I'm surprised everyone left," Stevie said, with a grin. "Royce has become your watchdog. Why don't you give the poor guy a break and go out with the man?"

She let out a startled laugh. "I don't think you're reading the situation correctly," she said, shaking her head.

"I don't think you're seeing the situation for what it is. He's always watching you. As you climb the stairs for the night. As you come down in the morning. As you leave the room." Stevie smirked. "He's got it bad."

"You're exaggerating," she said comfortably, knowing she was being teased.

He hooted. "Like hell I am."

"Really?" She studied him curiously. "He's not that bad surely?"

"Hell yes, he is. And I tell you, Geoffrey does the same. Maybe a little less often."

"Now I know you're having me on."

He shook his head. "No, I'm not. I'm warning you. Those two might come to blows over you."

The seriousness of his tone had her staring open-mouthed at him. "No way." She shook it off and took a sip of the coffee. Standing over a dead body and listening to Stevie's wild talk, she would take comfort where she could.

"Are you okay for a moment here?" Stevie asked. "I saw another depression a little farther over. I just want to make sure it's solid."

"Go for it." She motioned to the stairs. "I'll stand on top and watch, so I can make sure you're safe too."

He laughed. "You know me. I'm always good."

"True enough. But life happens to everyone."

"You're a worrywart now. You didn't use to be. You used to love life. Laugh at life."

"I did." She knew that. "But, after losing our friends, and then getting so sick …" She let her voice trail off.

"I know, but as you just said," Stevie added, almost running up the stairs behind her, "life happens. So why worry?"

"That seems to be the problem now," she muttered. "I can't stop worrying."

"No point in worrying about what you can't control." He grabbed his stick and headed to the other side.

"And the stuff I can control?" she called after him. "What about that?"

"You have to let life happen."

"Maybe," she said in a low voice, "but that doesn't mean I have to like the results."

*

BY THE TIME the body was removed, questions answered, and photos taken, Stacy had to decide whether to head back to the waterfall or go back to the cabin. She cast a wary eye at the cloudy skies. "Back to the cabin for me."

"Good." Royce, who'd returned with fresh coffee just ahead of the cops, turned to Stevie. "What about you?"

"I'll meet up with the other group and see if I can get in a couple runs."

Stacy started to walk back to the cabin. "Royce, go with Stevie. No way I can get lost now." There was almost a highway back to the cabin. Snowmobiles had taken the body out on a rescue sled. She could still hear the engines droning their way down to the waiting ambulance.

"I still don't think you should go alone," Royce said, coming up behind her. He reached out and grabbed her shoulder to stop her. "Stacy."

"Look. Stevie is likely to run into more trouble than I will. I'm following tracks the whole way back. I'm fine."

He watched her stride away, her body relaxed and moving easily.

Stevie stepped closer beside him. "I'm also fine. You go on with her."

"Ha," Royce said. "She's right. The track to the cabin is easy to follow. Finding the group of boarders for you to join them is a whole different story."

"Nah. I know the runs they're on, and Geoffrey just sent me the GPS coordinates." Stevie smacked him on the shoulder. "I'm good. Go on after her. You know you want to."

At that last part, Royce shot him a dark look, which rolled off Stevie's back.

"Hey, I'm just saying …"

"Saying what?"

"Saying you're wearing your heart on your sleeve for the

world to see."

"Damn it." That was the last thing he wanted to hear. His misery should be private.

"Don't worry about it."

Except George already knew. That meant Kathleen knew. So who else?

He started to turn away, when Stevie added, "Of course, with the competition, I'd watch your back."

Royce stopped and stared at him. "What competition?"

Stevie tossed his pack on his shoulders and headed in the direction of the group. "Geoffrey. That guy is mad about Stacy."

"What?"

"Yeah," Stevie called back. "He watches her almost as much as you do."

NOT BLOODY LIKELY. No one watched her as much as Royce did. Of course he'd kept it from everyone else. That was part of the game. They were all so damn stupid. Simple. They couldn't see the viper in their midst. He laughed out loud, uncaring if they heard him. He'd been doing this for a while now. He was good at it. The others weren't stupid. They were actually very smart. It was just that he was so good that he made them look like fools.

Stacy was the smartest of the lot. Only she'd not been around for a long time, so she would have missed the subtle nuances of the group dynamics over the last few years. It would be interesting if he could fool her as easily as he had the others.

Obviously he still could. But would her multiple degrees make any difference when the chips were down?

He doubted it.

Chapter 17

BACK AT THE cabin, the atmosphere was slightly louder than normal, as those who had elected to return hashed over the identity of the man. And why'd he'd be there of all places.

Stacy knew that too often people did a lot of stupid things for even stupider reasons. There wasn't much that humans did that could surprise her anymore. Of course what they did to each other was often worse.

As she entered, leaving her gear and outer clothing in the boot room, an awkward silence followed, as if they'd been caught gossiping. She smiled at everyone. "Stevie and Royce have gone to meet up with the other group."

Silence.

"I didn't think he'd leave her alone," muttered Yvonne.

Stacy stiffened slightly, pretending to not hear. What she'd heard just confirmed Stevie's earlier words. So it was more than just Stevie who had noticed.

"The coffeepot is full, if you're looking for hot coffee," Kathleen said quietly.

"Thanks." Stacy filled the teakettle and put it on the stove too. She actually would love a mocha but wasn't sure if anyone had brought hot chocolate. She certainly hadn't thought that far ahead.

She realized as she'd stared at the kitchen that she'd

planned on doing dinner. "Do we have a menu planned for the week?" she asked.

"Sure do. Today is pasta."

Another awkward silence passed. "And your name was penciled in beside it," Kathleen added.

"If that's okay?" someone else asked awkwardly.

Stacy wondered at the constant treading on eggshells around her. Was she really considered so delicate that she might break down at being asked to make pasta? Really? She knew her name was there. She'd put it there. "I volunteered for tonight," she said lightly.

And damn if there wasn't a perceptible softening of the air. Weird.

She studied the ingredients. "I do wonder about what I have to work with though. I don't want to use up any ingredients that were planned for other meals."

"No worries there," Kathleen said. "We have this sheet here." And she wandered over to Stacy, paper in hand. "It shows what we bought for each meal."

"Oh good. That will certainly make it easier."

"There's no leftover chili from yesterday, I presume," she asked, glancing around the table. "I could use a bite to eat."

There were several guilty looks.

She laughed. "No worries. I'll make a sandwich."

That was one thing she knew they had plenty of. George often scarfed them down as snacks. Bread was a very important food item for her brother. She found a loaf of French bread and decided that would be garlic bread for the spaghetti. Then she started in on the onions and garlic. She was tired, but not wanting to sit with the others or to lie down, she chose instead to make the sauce while she still had the energy.

She'd forgotten how the cold seeped into her bones and zapped away her energy. She'd been out there, standing around and waiting for hours. The others had been better off, as they had gone snowboarding, and the other half had come back into the heat. Grabbing a couple slices of ham and cheese, she made a simple sandwich to eat, as she worked on the sauce. With any luck, it wouldn't take too long, and she might catch a nap before the others came in.

As she worked, she wondered at the lowered voices. Were they trying to have a secret conversation? And, if so, why?

She hated it, but she couldn't help listening in.

"You know he's been crazy about her forever."

"What happened between them?"

"The fact that there was no 'them.'" And the snickers started.

Stacy froze, her head down. Really? Had everyone always known? Although they didn't appear to know about the weekend she'd spent with Royce. Thank heavens. But that he'd been crazy about her? Had she had her head so buried in the sand for these last few years that she had no clue? She tried to think back to what their relationship was like before that weekend. It had been casual. Teasing. She'd never considered him relationship material.

He was a playboy. He made a great toy to play with for a weekend, and that was it.

That he'd been anything but that during their weekend together made no sense.

She'd shoved that discrepancy to the far corners of her mind for a long time. But now the issue rose to consume her thoughts again.

Had Royce cared more than she'd suspected? But if he

had—for how long? Had he been just hiding his feelings for her all along? No, surely not. She remembered the long string of women he'd flaunted through those years. He'd been enjoying every moment. That was one reason she'd never taken that walk on the wild side. Then, when she did, he'd been so caring and compassionate; it had been the opposite of what she'd expected. And maybe that's what had thrown her off yet again. As he wasn't the man she'd expected to find in her bed.

But she'd needed him. As she'd never needed anyone before.

What she couldn't understand—even today—was why had she chosen him?

And why had he accepted?

ROYCE STAYED AWAY from the cabin, happy to spend a couple hours on the mountain. He'd chosen to go with Stevie after all. Especially after realizing that following Stacy to the cabin would only confirm everyone's suspicions.

It had been the right decision. He texted George to say they were on the way back. As he confirmed the message was sent, he smiled. At least something was working today.

Stevie stepped up beside him. "Hey, see? That was worth it, wasn't it?"

"It was. Nice to get up there, even if only for a short time."

"We did get a couple hours, but, of course, it went by too damn quick." His stomach grumbled. "And now I feel like I have to eat." He held up his hand, pulled off his glove, and tried to hold it steady.

"Low blood sugar?"

Stevie sighed. "It's getting worse every year."

"And you're looking after it carefully, right?"

Stevie laughed, pulling an energy bar from his pocket. "Absolutely." He held up the bar and took a big bite.

Royce eyed it. "Don't have a second one, do you?"

Stevie drove his empty hand into his pocket and pulled out a second bar. Royce accepted it, with a big smile. He ripped open the package and took a big bite. "Pasta for dinner."

"Great," Stevie said. "I won't have any problem eating my share." He waited a beat, then added. "And yours."

"Ha. I'll be eating mine. I do hope we brought enough food. I'm starved."

"George arranged the food, so hopefully that's not an issue." But he did look a little worried. Stevie was tall and scrawny, with whipcord strength, and performed all sports like the athlete he was. He could climb the most difficult of all climbs like a monkey. He had a great sense of humor and loved women, as Royce used to love women, only Stevie didn't have quite so many options as Royce.

Then Royce had tired of it. Of them. He'd gotten in too deep emotionally over Stacy many years ago and had gone a little crazy for a while, trying to get over her. She'd been too young. She'd been George's little sister.

She hadn't been for him.

He'd bedded every willing woman he could find. The more he did, the more he loathed himself. And the more he hated himself and thought he was not worth Stacy's time, the more he fell into the same damaging cycle, proving his point over and over again. The women rolled through and blurred his mind, as the names and places mixed with the never-ending video of faces.

He looked back on that stage of his life and cringed. He wasn't proud of it. In fact, he was pretty damn ashamed. Still, during those years, Stacy hadn't seemed to give a damn what he did. Although she'd been friendly, she'd never shown any interest in him. In fact, she'd ignored him.

When she'd come to him without warning, he'd figured he'd found heaven. Instead he'd learned what purgatory was. He'd been trying to find his way back home ever since.

In the days, weeks, months afterward, he'd done a lot of self-examination and had seen his life through her eyes, and he'd been ashamed all over again. So he'd straightened up and had tried hard to show her his different side. And she never noticed.

It damn-near broke him.

She was so close and yet so damn far away.

He didn't know how to cross the impasse. He knew it was there. He knew it needed to be crossed. He also knew that Stacy wouldn't even acknowledge that it ever existed.

And, if she didn't know it was there, she wouldn't know to cross it. And he desperately needed her to take those steps across the bridge. He would be waiting for her at the end of that bridge. Hell, he'd hold her hand and help her across that bridge, if she'd just take the first step.

He needed her to take that step. And to save him.

WOW, NOW THINGS were getting interesting. He'd wanted to laugh when he'd seen the body. Like really? The guy never made it anywhere. Too bad. He would have liked to tell the asshole that his sneaky escape was useless. And that he'd almost made it out alive. But almost didn't count. The dead guy never knew how close he'd made it to surviving.

Stupid idiot. Look at the way he was dressed. Besides, it wasn't his fault the guy had taken off at a dead run into the storm. Like, what an idiot.

Still, he almost made it, so he'd award him a few brownie points for that. After all, the guy was dead. He could afford to be generous.

Chapter 18

STACY WOKE IN the middle of the night, chilled, her heart racing in a panic, her nightmare still clinging like wet cobwebs to her brain. She shuddered at the clamminess of her skin. What was that all about? She rarely got nightmares. And didn't appreciate the odd occurrence. There wasn't a sound in the cabin but for the odd crackle of the fire in the big heater. She snuggled lower in the bed, hating the darkness. She wondered if finding the body today had set off her nightmare. Anyone normally would get a nightmare from something like that. But she wasn't just anyone. Bodies were her business.

But something was beyond odd about this one. Her mind had already cataloged the case, even though she wouldn't be the one working on him. She had an urge to send a text message to the coroner, asking about drug tests on the victim. Although they wouldn't be back fast enough to satisfy her.

There was also no guarantee the case would be worked on anytime soon. If the local office was as overworked as Stacy's, the coroner would be overwhelmed. And, not to forget, she wasn't even in her own country.

She closed her eyes, determined to get some more sleep. She needed it. She was feeling the cold more than she had expected. Her body should be snapping back faster than this.

That it wasn't made her look for the stressors inhibiting her healing.

Royce was at the top of that list. Then there was the poor man they'd found today. Too many suspicious elements were in that case. Poorly dressed for the weather, missing ID. No sign of where or how he'd gotten there. It could have been a body dump, but why there and when? The police had confirmed no abandoned vehicles reported in the last month. It could be spring before his vehicle was found, after all the snow had melted away.

Had someone else found him and stripped the wallet from the man's pockets?

People did the damnedest things. Especially when stressed. So the man could have quite easily removed everything from his own pockets. As soon as hypothermia set in, confusion was the rule. Victims lost their way, and what seemed to make sense at the time made no sense under normal circumstances.

Nothing was normal about his situation. If there'd been a car close by, then maybe it would make sense, but no roads were anywhere near there, except the one to the cabin.

She yawned.

And that's when she heard it.

A door opening. She grabbed her cell phone and checked the time. It was two in the morning. Who the hell was going outside?

Or were they coming in?

If so, why?

She peered over the edge carefully. Maybe it was monkey business. She could see Yvonne sleeping beside Royce. She slept in her own bedroll but close enough for him to reach out and touch her, if need be.

The person who'd been outside had on a heavy pullover with the hood pulled up. She tried to look outside, but the darkness was absolute. There was a shine from outside due to the snow on the ground, but she had no way of knowing if it was snowing. But it would be cold regardless. She would have likely pulled her hoodie up over her ears too. She shifted cautiously to see his head turning away from her. Shit. Had he seen her? She wasn't doing anything wrong, but it seemed that she was spying, and she didn't want anyone to think that.

Only then did she hear the heavy rasping breath below her. Waiting.

She felt the first stirrings of fear. And she realized that, for all her casual attitude about choosing the warmest place in the house, she'd also chosen the one where she was alone. The most unprotected. And worse, she was trapped here. If someone came up the stairs, she had no place to go to escape. She could scream, but what if they came up while she was asleep?

She'd never know until it was too late.

ROYCE JERKED AWAKE. Shocked into awareness, he sat up and studied the quiet room. Yvonne slept in the bedroll beside him. She was a quiet sleeper, no snoring or restless shifting in the night. Made for an easy bedfellow. At least he thought it was her. With the covers pulled over her head, who could tell? And they'd all been plenty drunk last night, so it could be anyone. These trips were like that.

As he sat in the dark, the chill worked its way into his bones. He wasn't a light sleeper normally, but he'd had a hard time getting to sleep these last few nights, so he had several drinks last night, hoping it would help.

Now a sense of something wrong washed over him. As if he'd missed something important.

There was an odd noise in the main part of the cabin, but it was hard to decipher over the heavy winds beating against the cabin walls. As he lay back down, his ears intent, his mind wondered why it mattered. So what if he'd heard something? People got up in the night all the time. He would often get up to go to the washroom, get a drink, and walk around because he couldn't sleep.

No biggie.

Then he realized it had been the outside door he'd heard. That latch made a loud heavy *thunk* when it shut securely. Someone had gone outside. He sat up again slowly. Walking around outside in the middle of the storm was an easy way to get lost. The group had a general rule of no smoking indoors, so maybe someone had gone out for a smoke. He went through the list of people here, trying to figure out who might have gone out and whether he had to worry about them. He hoped not.

But he never heard the door open again. He waited. And waited. Then he had to consider that what he'd heard was the person coming back in. No way to know until everyone got up in the morning. Determined to put it out of his mind, he rolled over and tried to go back to sleep.

HE LOVED THE night. It was his time. So was winter. The darkness and cold were a perfect marriage for him. He never felt the chill the way other people did, and this resort was his playground—and hunting ground. Maybe he was more reptile than human. He'd long ago understood his nature. Had been a

problem accepting it. But after that? ... Well, it was who he was. And what he was—it was pretty damn unique. He'd always wanted to be different.

Interesting that he was that *different.*

He sat comfortably in the back corner of the cabin. Out of sight of everyone and under the loft.

Where she was.

He watched as Royce slept. He'd been awake earlier but had fallen back into the deep sleep too much alcohol created.

It was great for a temporary buzz, just not so good if you needed to do something—or wanted to do something. But for him, watching the others imbibe too much made for great entertainment. He learned a lot from watching them. Who they really were on the inside. Who they chose to cuddle up with for the night.

It amused him. People were fake. Then so was he, and that just proved his statement. Picking through the layers to find the person inside made for a great hobby. It also allowed him to assess them as potential subjects.

Most failed his examination.

A few excelled, but, for this trip, one person was perfect. He knew her name was up for a special piece already—even if it wasn't his piece—but he wouldn't let her stay as part of that homage. In fact, it might be time to take care of his friend too. He pretended to be an artist for his buddy's sake, but he had no doubts about what he really was. And why he did what he did.

Still, knowing that Stacy was here and available for the taking was something he couldn't let go of. Although, in a way, his friend had a prior claim. She would complete his trio. He'd wanted to finish that one for a long time. So maybe he'd let her be part of that exhibit for a little while. Then move her to his.

He could make a move tonight. Or maybe wait until the end of the week. They were all a little more on edge, after finding Brian today. He wanted to laugh out loud at that one. Talk about perfect timing.

And he hadn't even planned it.

Chapter 19

S PIRITS WERE HIGH the next morning. To Stacy's ear, it was almost artificially high. They'd brushed up against death again yesterday. It was sad and difficult, but everyone knew the risks of their fun-filled sport. And, of course, everyone pushed off the risks, until it was in their face again. Last night they'd had a chance to deal with the gloominess and the sadness, but, after a good night's sleep, everyone looked more rested. Or at least they were trying to look that way.

It didn't appear to have affected her coworkers' moods. Then they had an edge, as they were in a line of work to hers. There was a reverence for life among the three of them. And a very healthy respect for death.

At a distance.

But, over the years, as she had lost various family members and then her two best friends, death then became so upfront and personal. She'd had no idea how to deal with the growing accumulation of her personal losses.

The others had experienced this too. Kathleen had lost a boyfriend to a car accident years ago. George had lost a few friends in a hang gliding accident. He'd grieved for months, then had dealt with it per his usual aplomb. For Stacy, she'd cared so much—or had carried so much guilt—that the loss of her two best friends had stopped much of her ability to function. And losing Janice and Francine seemed to remind Stacy that the bodies on her lab table had grieving family and friends too. That all had made every new one in the morgue even more difficult. Hence, her damn slow-ass recovery.

Royce stepped in front of her, with a big plate of eggs and toast.

"Hey, where did you get that?"

He nodded to the kitchen, his mouth chewing through a large bite of sausage.

"Damn." She really didn't want to miss another meal. She couldn't believe how hungry she was today.

"Are you coming skiing with us?" George asked.

"I'm bringing my camera and will do a little skiing, but I saw something the other day, and I want to see if I can find it again."

He nodded. "We're going in two groups again."

"I'll be in the last one then," she said. "I need food. As I'll be taking pictures, I don't need to race." Skiers and snowboarders alike were notorious for wanting to be the first ones on runs.

"The first group is leaving soon."

"I'll meet up with you in a couple hours," she said, as she filled her plate.

"That works."

There was a flurry of activity, as the first group grabbed their gear. She snuck around behind the stove and headed to an empty seat beside the fire. The first bite was so good that she almost moaned. "Oh, wow, not sure who made break-fast, but these eggs are lovely."

"Royce did."

"Nice job, Royce."

She glanced up to find him walking out to the boot

room. Maybe he hadn't heard her. As the door slammed shut, she figured he definitely had. "What's his problem?" she muttered to no one in particular.

Stevie just laughed at her.

She forked up another bite and ignored the rest of them. She hadn't slept well. Maybe that was the cause of her appetite. Or maybe she was just starting to heal. She certainly felt better. Stronger.

"Hey, did you leave anything for the rest of us?" Stevie asked, sitting down beside her.

She shook her head. "Hope not. If I did, it was a mistake."

"Wow, aren't you nice."

She popped a big bite of sausage into her mouth and stood up. "I'm about to get seconds. Did you get any?"

He held up a cup of coffee. "I'll drink this first."

"Your loss."

"Whoa, you weren't kidding about extras, were you? *Geesh*." He bounded to his feet and raced around, until he was ahead of her. He was busy scooping up eggs, when she snagged a piece of toast and returned with a cup of coffee. He sat down beside her. "Did you ever notice the effect of death on the others?" He said it in a low voice, as several other people were still getting dressed in their outerwear.

She nodded. "Just because we're used to it doesn't mean anyone else is."

"It's as if their fear of mortality kicks in. Really weird."

"Everyone likes to think we're invincible. Instead we're an organic system that is way too delicate."

"Soft-shelled with no defense system against Mother Nature," he mumbled around his food. "Such easy prey."

The way he said that last bit had her studying his face

with a sharp look. He was right. But it sounded as if a predator looking for easy prey was a great game. Something it wasn't.

"That's a horrible thing to say," Yvonne said, seated on the couch across from them. "I had no idea you considered humans so inferior."

"Not inferior. We have brains, and we can think. Reason. Act. Rationalized action. That's what saved us from extinction," he said.

Yvonne snorted. "Doesn't sound like what you were saying before."

"What?" he asked in an injured tone. "I didn't mean it in a bad way." He caught Stacy's gaze and rolled his eyes. In a low tone, he said, "See what I mean? Add a dead body and everyone has an issue with life and death."

She laughed. "Of course. It just reminds us that we can't escape death."

"Yep, today or tomorrow. Our time will come." In a dark, mocking voice, he added, "The question is, will we die by our own hand, old age, or will someone else help us along the way?"

"GEORGE," ROYCE CALLED out quietly to his friend, walking behind him. "Did you hear anyone leave the cabin in the night?

"Nope." George walked up beside Royce. "What time are we talking?"

"Between two and three."

George shook his head. "I was sound asleep. I had trouble going to sleep, but, once I made it there, I never woke up until this morning."

"I wish. I woke to something weird. Thought I heard someone walking around but couldn't see anyone. I realized it was the outside door I'd heard, at least I thought I'd heard, but again I never could confirm that."

"I wouldn't worry about it. Chances are it was the wind slamming the door closed. You know that outside door is always being left ajar." George shifted his pack to his other shoulder. "Besides, so what if someone was walking about? We've both done that many times ourselves."

"True. I don't know why it bugged me but it did. It seemed …" Royce thought about it, adding with a foolish grin, "Maybe sinister."

He expected George's laughter, but instead George nodded and said, "I can see that. I thought I heard someone the first night we were here. I didn't understand it at all. Why go out during the night?"

Royce stared at him. "Really? Two of three nights? That's odd."

"Unless someone is going out to have a smoke."

"Then they are keeping that habit a secret, as I don't know anyone here who smokes."

George plodded along, sinking into the deep snow with each step, both working harder than they had to, as the path was really only wide enough for one.

"I'm surprised you haven't mentioned the dead guy we found," George said in a low voice.

"I would have, but someone's always around." Royce glanced around to see Kathleen in a deep conversation with Yvonne over the latest boards. "I'm trying to figure out how the guy got out here."

"I know. If we'd seen any vehicles, it would make more sense. There was a mention of it on the news this morning, but they are withholding the guy's name at this time and haven't released much in the way of details." George glanced back at his girlfriend. "I wish it hadn't happened on this trip. I wanted to get Stacy away from death."

"I hear you. Unfortunately she's a magnet for death."

"Not intentionally."

"She's coming out today, isn't she?" Royce asked, hating that sense of wrongness he'd woken up with and hadn't been able to shake.

"Yes, why?" George asked.

"No reason." He paused, thought about it, then added, "Except something feels off."

"Yeah, glad you said that. I feel the same way." He waved to Kathleen. "Let's keep an especially close eye on the women."

"Definitely. I really don't want this vacation to involve a death again."

George, already walking back to Kathleen, turned, and, with a somber voice, said, "It already does, remember?"

Chapter 20

OUT IN THE sunshine, there was lots of laughter and teasing. Ten minutes into the trip, Stacy stopped, thinking she might have left her camera back in the cabin. She put her pack down and dug through it. After a frantic moment, she found it in the side pocket. "Well, thank heavens for that."

She stood back up again and realized that her group was slightly ahead. She took several pictures of them, loving the casualness of the scene. Friends walking, talking, laughing. Looking forward to the day ahead. She glanced around, as she settled her pack on her shoulders. The place was pristine white. It was beautiful. Clean. So innocent looking. Except for the treachery always underneath.

Speaking of which, … she lifted her camera again. *Click. Click.* Phenomenal icicles hung off the trees to the left. They were huge. And would give someone a severe blow if they came down on top of their head.

She had no illusions when it came to snow and ice conditions. They were here snowboarding and skiing, but there were no guides. No safety guardrails. They were all past that level. They had all helicopter skied and had done other equally demanding sports. They were all fit.

But shit happened.

"Stacy? Come on."

Damn, she'd gotten lost in her camera again.

She watched the group ahead of her stop and point out a snowcat slowly heading down the mountain. She'd heard the resort was opening up new runs on this side of the mountain but hadn't thought to see the equipment actually working on it right now. From that long ski run, they could ski into the village below and hook up with other runs. And that was a damn good idea. Except the snowcat was going down the hill and not up. So not the way she wanted to go.

In fact, right now she wasn't sure she wanted to go anywhere. She waved the other group off to go on ahead; then she found a spot to sit in the sun. She hated to admit it, but she was tired. Maybe this was as far as she would go today. She needed to tell the group her plans, so they wouldn't worry.

Just then her phone rang, Royce wanting to know where she was. Apparently the second group had said she wasn't with them. She turned to study the direction the other group had gone, and, sure enough, they were out of sight already.

She texted back, telling him exactly where she was and that she was in view of the cabin.

Shit.

She laughed at that succinct answer. He had such a mastery of words. **I'm fine. I'll just take a few pictures. Nothing wrong with me sitting here and enjoying life.**

Not alone.

Sigh. **Why not?**

Because I don't like what's going on.

She glanced back at the text to reread it several times. Cautiously she responded, **What is going on?**

There was such a long silence that she wondered if he'd planned on answering her. Then it came back.

I'm afraid that man was murdered.

ROYCE STARED DOWN at his phone, wondering if he should have sent that text. Still, he wanted her to stay safe. The one day that George wanted to keep an extra eye on the women, and Stacy chose this day to be on her own. Like really? Royce was already on the other side of the second mountain. He'd be almost an hour getting back to her.

I'm fine. I'll be careful.

That was so not his point. He loved that she didn't address his comment. Did that mean she agreed? Had considered it? Or thought he was making a big deal out of nothing? And maybe he was, but something was not right.

He carved left and then right. These runs were empty, as they so often were at this time of morning. They weren't the easiest to access and commanded skill to do well. George and Kathleen were closer to town. They'd decided to have lunch at the pub. Royce would have loved to join them but got the impression that they were looking for a few moments of private time.

He wished. Then he brightened. If Stacy was alone, he could get some private time with her. Hell, he could be there in less than an hour. He had to hit the bottom of the run, catch the lift going up the opposite side, come down the seven-mile run, and grab the trail leading to the cabin. He dropped lower and picked up speed.

At the bottom was a coffee shop. He bought two cups and hopped on the first lift up. With his hands full, he couldn't text her that he was coming. And boarding the lift with two hot cups was not the smartest move on his part. He could only hope that the coffee would still be hot by the time he reached her. It was tricky taking the corners he needed to take. A part of him was hoping she had her video camera running as he came around. What a classy shot that would make. He finally hit the homestretch and cut to the right hard and slowed. Ha, he made it.

He straightened up and searched the trees for her. Someone was up ahead on the left. He called out, "Stacy? You there?"

Nothing. He searched the trees and thought he saw someone moving past another pocket of greenery. A red stripe on the jacket. Stacy didn't have any red on hers. At least none that he remembered.

He came to a stop and studied the furtive figure. His hackles rose. Nothing special was wrong. Just nothing spectacularly right. People could be here for any number of reasons, but none good that he could think of. The area was only accessible if the person knew the area well. And that he was doubtful of.

It was off the beaten path.

"Stacy?" He called her name louder again and again. No answer. He slid forward another few feet, his gaze hard. His ears were tuned and his gaze intent on the area he'd last seen that person.

No sign of him.

Anywhere.

Worse, no sign of Stacy either.

Damn it.

Where was she?

IDIOT. SHOW OFF. Lovestruck fool. Did Royce really think it would be that easy? To see him? To understand he was there? To understand what he was doing? So not.

He wouldn't be stupid here—unlike Royce, who held two cold cups of coffee in his hands, searching the woods. Stacy wasn't here. At least not right here.

He thought she had been. He'd tracked her down to this area, but, when he finally picked out the perfect spot to watch her, she was gone. He kinda liked that. He had no problem with a game of hide-and-seek. Predator and prey. Winner and loser.

The outcome was inevitable.

This was fun but not challenging. It was better to drag it out. See the normal reactions change to that inner suspicion of needing to look over her shoulder—of not being sure why but unable to stop checking.

Because, of course, her instincts were there, just not as finely tuned as her ancestors of hundreds of years ago. Obviously Stacy's instincts were better than most, as she'd booked it out of here. Interesting. So where the hell was she?

Royce appeared to be searching for her himself.

Great. Now to see who would find her first.

Chapter 21

DAMN IT. STACY wished Royce would stop yelling long enough to hear her own calls. But she was keeping her voice hushed, whereas he was letting the entire world know she was missing.

Great. If the guy watching her from the crest above her didn't know she'd been down there before, he sure knew now. She didn't know whether that watcher was just an innocent bystander or not. She'd caught him in her camera view several times and had managed to get a couple pictures, but they were a long way away. She doubted there would be enough detail to identify him. But it would prove she hadn't imagined him.

She'd held back texting anyone about it. She didn't want them to think she'd crossed that fine line of paranoia, now being back on the mountain.

But maybe, after this, she shouldn't hold back. Or maybe, after this, it just proved she was nervous over nothing. Something she wouldn't have thought of herself. She wasn't scared to be here. Or of something happening to her. It was more that something might happen to her friends.

She wasn't sure what to say to Royce's earlier comment about the man being murdered. It wasn't for her to confirm. And it was too early to judge. But all the indications pointed to foul play. It was hard to argue away the marks on his wrists. He might not have been murdered, but that didn't mean he hadn't been running for his life to escape something horrible and had succumbed to the elements.

Silence had descended on the area. She peered through the boughs of the big fir tree she'd taken refuge behind to see Royce standing nearby, staring, such a horrible look of loss on his face. And she realized maybe the others were correct. Maybe he really did care.

And damn if that didn't make her feel terrible. She'd been keeping him at a distance. Thinking he'd been mocking her. Playing with her. Treating her like his other relationships. But what if he was trying to show her that he cared?

Trying to let her know she was different.

Or was that just wishful thinking on her part?

There. A shadow shifted on the ridge above them. Movement to the left. Royce spun and stared up behind, where Stacy had seen her stalker earlier. "Hello?" he called out.

No answer. There was a heavy rustling sound, but, if anyone was still up there, they were leaving or were already gone. She stepped out from behind her hiding place. "Royce," she hissed.

He spun back again, relief washing over his face. Followed by instant anger. "What the hell were you doing hiding back there? I almost had a heart attack thinking—"

"*Shh*," she snapped in a harsh whisper. "Someone was sitting up there for a really long time, staring at me. But they were hidden from view. It made me really uncomfortable, so, when I thought I could, I slipped out of sight and waited."

His gaze was intent, searching her face. And, damn, he saw a lot. "He really scared you, *huh*?"

Trying to keep her voice calm and logical, she said, "A

couple times these last few days I felt like I was being watched. I never could see anyone though."

"What?" He stared at her in shock, anger still burning bright in his eyes. "And you're just now telling me?"

"When was I supposed to mention it?" she asked in what she thought was a reasonable tone of voice. Apparently he didn't agree.

"Tell me all of it." When she didn't answer fast enough, he snapped, "Now."

Feeling a sense of déjà vu, she said, "It's not much …" Then gave him the little bit she knew.

"And last night? Were you awoken in the night for any reason?"

"Yes! Were you?"

He nodded. "I thought I heard the outside door open and close."

"Which isn't all that odd or alarming. People go outside sometime in the night."

"I know." He nodded. "That's part of the problem. It could be completely innocent."

"So why are you so worried? It sounds like everyone's imagination is going wild."

"And your stalker today? Was that also your imagination?" He held out a cup of coffee for her. "This is probably cold by now …"

"That's fine. I could use the caffeine hit." She accepted the cup gratefully, touched by his thoughtfulness. She had no idea how he managed to do it, but the cup was still full and lukewarm.

He took a drink from his cup and made a face.

She grinned at him and took a big drink. "It's not hot, but it's caffeine."

"And the stalker?" he asked, staying persistent.

She raised her free hand. "All right. So maybe that incident wasn't my imagination."

"And, if it wasn't, then likely the other incidents weren't either," he said thoughtfully. "Still, I don't understand who this person is and what they want."

"Neither do I." Of course the clouds moved in and changed the bright sunlight to overcast and cloudy. The cool coffee was also having an effect on her. She shivered. "I think I'll head back to the cabin."

"Then I'm coming with you." He bent down and picked up his board and motioned in front of him. "Shall we?"

She started off in the right direction. "You don't have to come with me, you know?"

He snorted. "We've just finished discussing a stalker is following you …"

"Right. Fair enough." She was happy to have the company.

The trip back was quiet and uneventful. By the time she made it inside, she hated to admit she needed a rest. She would love to lie down, but the cabin was too cold.

"Go sit down, and I'll get the fire going again."

She gave him a grateful smile of thanks and put her stuff away in the loft, grimacing at the mess she'd left in her panic to get down on time. When she returned downstairs, a bright blaze was going. She filled the coffeepot and put it on the heater stove, then went to work, making a few sandwiches for the two of them. That done, she walked through the cabin, poking her head into the different rooms. She wasn't sure what she was looking for, if anything, but she'd seen red on the jacket. If one was here, then she'd like to know. But chances were good the owner of the jacket with the red stripe was wearing it still. It wouldn't be here.

"The guy is still out there most likely."

She turned away from George's bed to look at Royce, standing behind her. "What do you think I was doing?"

He shrugged, but his gaze was shrewd. "You're going from room to room. So you tell me."

With a dark look, she brushed past him. "I was just checking to see if anyone was here or not."

"*Not* is my vote." He followed her back to the kitchen, where she quickly cut the sandwiches, placing them on two plates and handing them to him. "I'll bring the coffee," she said. "Take these over, please."

"Sure. They look great. Thanks."

She didn't respond. It was just a sandwich. As she sat down beside him in front of the fire, he took a bite, studied her, and then asked, "So did you see anything besides red?"

She shook her head. "I only saw a strip of red in the trees. Nothing of his face or other gear."

"If it was here, it wouldn't be on your stalker out there," he said.

"Yeah, unless they whipped home and changed their jacket, then went out again." She smiled grimly. "And came in with the groups, as they arrived home."

He swallowed the bite in his mouth, as if the food were drier than he'd like. "Is that your logical mind at work or is that a really nasty imagination conjuring up horror stories? Are you really suspecting one of us?"

"You forget my line of work."

"That is not a nice thought." He took a huge bite of a sandwich and stared thoughtfully into the fire, as he chewed. "I guess that would be the easy answer, but not the smartest, as there's a good chance he would be seen or his jacket found."

"And the difficult answer?"

"It's a large mountain. Any number of people could have seen you and decided to stalk you."

"And the other incidences?" she asked, before popping the last of her sandwich into her mouth. She stared down at her empty plate, then decided a second would be good and stood.

"Same thing."

"Maybe." She started in the direction of the kitchen. "I'm going to make another sandwich. Do you want more?"

"Yes, please." She started building a second sandwich for both of them, as he leaned against the doorjamb, finishing off the first one. She was just about done when he said, "I wonder."

"Wonder what?" She slapped the tops of the sandwiches, then cut them in half. She took his plate from him and filled it again. She picked up her plate and turned back to him. "Wonder what?"

"You searched the rooms to see if there was a jacket. As in you were looking for something that might have been left behind. Did you happen to consider that we should instead be looking for what might be missing?"

She stopped cold. There was a weird tingling inside her. Her mind cast through all he wasn't saying. "You think someone might have searched the cabin while we were gone?"

"A cabin inhabited by a large group of people here on a vacation? If I were a criminal or someone looking for a quick score, there would be easy money here, wouldn't there?"

His tone had darkened with an ugly overtone. She stayed quiet, thinking about it. "And?" she asked, when he didn't continue.

"And, if I saw a woman I really liked the look of, I'd be tempted to follow her back to where she was staying, so I could learn more about her."

Unbidden, her gaze went to the loft, where she'd dumped her camera bag. And the disarray she hadn't expected to see. She'd been in a rush this morning, but she hadn't been in that much of a rush—or had she? She found the days and mornings blending into each other. She couldn't remember.

"Do you think we should be checking to see if we've been robbed?" she asked in a low voice, studying his face carefully.

"I think I'll be taking a closer look at my stuff. I didn't bring much of value, but there is a different perspective on what that word means to people."

Stacy carefully set down her sandwich, her appetite suddenly gone. "I think I'll go up and check," she murmured. She walked past him to the stairs, feeling his gaze on her every step. Up in the loft, she stopped and looked around first. Her bed appeared to be as she had left it. Nothing was different on it or around it. She wanted to make sure, so she flipped back the covers and then quickly remade it.

Her camera bag was tossed. The contents haphazard on the bed. The lenses were worth a lot of money. Seeing them made her feel better. If their belongings had been searched, surely a thief would have snagged the high-priced lenses.

Next she turned to her bag. She lifted it up to rest on the bed. She slowly removed everything inside, her mind mentally ticking off the items as she did so. Two pairs of jeans, two sets of thermals, seven sets of underwear, and two heavy wool sweaters. She kept on until the bag was empty.

Then she turned to the side pockets. The first was packed with her toiletries. Normal. Everything was there, as far as she could tell. She opened up the other end of the bag and pulled out the few things she'd stuffed in there. Then sat back on her heels. She stared at the pile and wondered if she'd have missed anything. She stood up and flicked on the light switch. And studied the small space.

Several extra bedrolls were available, but she hadn't used any of them, just the one atop her bed. She hadn't even been over there to check any out. But one was disturbed. As if someone had sat on it, maybe. She frowned. To her knowledge, no one had been up here, but … here was proof that someone had been. Maybe. … Or maybe it was just her mind becoming overwrought. Damn.

She repacked her things carefully and realized something else. She packed the same way all the time, but that wasn't the way she'd unpacked. Someone had taken her stuff out of her bag and had carefully packed it, just not exactly the same way she had done so. She had to stop and wonder if she'd made the mistake. But she knew herself better than that.

She was a creature of habit. And a neat freak. A condition that had only gotten much worse, since so much in her world had gotten out of control; so she'd locked down on what she could control. She was only just now easing up some of those restrictions she'd put on herself. Coming here was one of them.

She walked back down slowly, her mind wondering at who and why, when she hit the bottom stair and saw Royce standing there, holding out her plate, with the sandwich.

"And?" he asked.

"I can't be sure, but I think someone went through my bag."

He scowled. "Anything missing?"

She shook her head. "I don't think so." She stared into his eyes, her mind racing through the items she brought. Finally she shook her head and repeated, "I don't think so."

ROYCE POLISHED OFF his second sandwich in a few bites. He got up and poked the fire, while she ate slowly. He understood. She was processing. There was a lot of information to sort through.

"You said you thought the man we found had been murdered. Do you have any evidence that points that way?"

He shook his head. "Proof? No."

She nodded, as if she had suspected as much.

He stood. "You must have your suspicions."

"Sure." She grabbed his plate and walked into the kitchen. "The circumstances were beyond odd. The marks on his wrists revealed he'd been tied up recently, and he wasn't dressed for the weather." She sighed. "But he's not on my table, and I can't know for sure." She glanced at him. "Without the details from the autopsy, I'd say Mother Nature killed him—it's just a question whether someone contributed in any way."

"Can you make a professional call and find out?"

She glanced over at him, as he came closer and leaned against the counter. "I was trying to avoid doing that. You know—that need for a vacation?"

"Yeah, *some* vacation." He looked at the fatigue lines on her face. She needed something to brighten her day. And he had just the answer. "Let's go sledding."

She looked at him in shock. "What?"

"I said, let's go sledding. There's a big run not far from

here. It's safe and long and a ton of fun."

An odd look entered her eyes. Then she shrugged. "Sure, why not?"

He grinned. "Let's go."

He tugged her toward the doorway. "Get your boots and coat on. I'll grab the magic carpets."

At that last bit, she turned to stare at him, then giggled. "Magic carpets? Really?"

His grin widened. "Really."

Warmly dressed, the two ran out the door. He led the way to the top of the hill he knew well. It led down to the parking lot. At the bottom of the run, they could board the tram up the other side. Then they would have fun on a few of the smaller runs. This area was well-known by the local sledders, and often the tourists joined in on the fun.

And that's exactly what Stacy needed. He was the perfect person to introduce her to a childhood favorite sport.

She was way too serious most of the time, and now she was wary to boot. There might or might not be a stalker, but, for the next few hours, it wouldn't matter. They'd have nothing but a great time.

He hoped.

WHAT THE HELL was Royce carrying—and why? He watched the two race to the top of the hill on the left, and damn if they didn't both get on something small and bright and slide down the long easy slope. From where he stood, he saw them bouncing and flying through the air, hitting a bank of snow and jumping forward into the suddenly raised cloud. He heard the shrieks of laughter, and something tightened inside him.

How dare they?

He didn't want them having fun like that.

He didn't want them laughing.

He definitely didn't want Royce getting any closer to Stacy.

With a snarl, he sat back on his haunches and stared at the two of them. They were almost at the bottom of the hill now, still laughing and cheering the ride on. Fear, anger, disgust, and so much more roiled through him. He wanted to hit something. Lash out at the two of them.

Make them pay.

And yet … why?

They were having fun—so what? At least if they became closer, they'd hurt that much more when one of them went missing.

He contemplated ruining two lives with one act. His hobby was definitely getting more complicated.

That worked.

As long as they didn't find anything important out there, he was good.

Actually he was great.

Chapter 22

S TACY COULDN'T REMEMBER ever having such fun. She felt like a kid. Like how cool was that? She sat on the sled, Royce's arms around her waist, and raced down hillside after hillside in complete abandon. The way the mountain had set up the sliding area allowed for both skiers and sliders to go up the chair lift, but, at the top, the paths split off, and both wound down in different directions. She had no idea this area was even here. She'd seen other sledders over the years, but being a die-hard skier, she'd relished every moment she had on the mountain, and that meant always with boards strapped to her feet. At least one, if not two.

It was great to switch that up—or down as the case may be. She loved this.

And the attentiveness Royce showered on her, the way he constantly held out his hand to help her up, always an eye out for her care, warmed her inside. She didn't remember ever seeing this side of him before. Surely it had been there but not directed her way. Probably at one of his gazillion girlfriends. And that was the difference. It also made him that much more attractive. She understood the women falling for him.

After all, she had too—once. That didn't mean she was willing to repeat it. But a part of her wanted to.

She shrieked as they hit a large bump, and the snow flew

in her face, the icy crystals biting into her skin. Then she laughed. For all the icy wind hitting her, the cold sting of the snow made her feel alive. Revitalized. For this, she thanked Royce. He'd shown her a good time these past few hours.

The sun was going down behind the mountains, casting long shadows on the trees and adding a chill to the day. Still, it had been a fantastic afternoon. Her morning had been good too. She'd gotten decent pictures earlier today.

From this happier position, she had a better perspective. She had some distance from the mess of her belongings and realized there could be any number of reasons why her bags might have been searched—either of the two women might have needed monthly supplies unexpectedly for one. As for the stalker? Maybe it was someone out for a hike, and he'd stopped to take a few pictures. As she had.

And the man they'd found? That had nothing to do with them. He'd had an unlucky death. Until she knew more, she couldn't say what had happened or why, and speculation was dangerous. As she knew all too well. "That was fun." She stood and brushed the snow off her coat.

"Do you want to go again?"

"Do we have time?" She turned to study the chair lift. It was still running, but there was no line. A single boarder stepped onto a chair as their turn came. She studied the clock. "We don't have time. Maybe we can go up one last time, but that's it."

He turned to look at her. "Let's grab this lift. We have to catch the Hummingbird lift to go even higher, then turn toward the cabin."

She frowned up at him. "Can we do that?"

He shrugged. "I have before, but it's a little touchy."

"Ya think?" She grinned. "As long as you know where

we're going, let's do it."

He grabbed her hand and raced to the chair. The lift operator was walking around, checking his watch, as if looking to see when he could shut it down. She screamed, "We're here. We're here."

The lift operator waved at her.

She laughed as she ran through the empty path leading to the chair. "Thanks!"

"No problem. You still had a few minutes. This is your last lift though."

"No problem. We need to catch the Hummingbird as well too."

He nodded. "I'll tag them that you two are coming."

"Thanks." She hopped up onto the chair, Royce taking the seat beside her, as the chair scooped them up and carried them uphill. "Glad we made that."

"It's a long hard walk if we hadn't," Royce agreed. "Too bad no coffee is at the top of Hummingbird."

"Oh, I could really use some hot coffee," she exclaimed, "but we could hardly sled home with our hands full of hot drinks."

He laughed. "We'd be wearing the coffees on the first bump."

"True. Besides, the rest of the group will have coffee made."

"Sounds good to me."

The chair rose up to another tower, weighed down by ice and snow. The beauty was incredible, the stark contrast between Mother Nature and the steel structure incredibly strong. She loved it. The trees stood tall under their white snowcaps, and some bowed under the weight of the world beside them. There was no sound but for the steady hum of the steel cable slowly climbing higher and higher.

The higher they climbed, the colder the air and the more biting the wind. She huddled deeper into her jacket, her collar pulled up over her ears. Damn, she'd forgotten this chill. They'd been racing into the wind as they streamed down the mountain, but sitting still like they were now, the cold was treacherous.

Royce reached out and wrapped an arm around her, pulling her close. She nestled in and closed her eyes, letting her breath warm up her face.

She was glad they were heading back. Honestly they should've gone back earlier, but, with the sun up and having so much fun, it had been easy to push away the idea.

Now she wished she'd thought to think ahead.

"You okay?" Royce's warm voice tickled her ear and heated up her neck.

She nodded but stayed quiet.

"Good. We're almost there."

In fact, the chair lift slowed, and the chair swung slightly, as it slowed its ascent. She got ready to jump off and get out of the way before it hit her.

As they landed, he grabbed her hand and raced her over to the sister lift.

Thankfully this one was short. At their landing on the top, she shivered. The wind was bitingly cold. "Wow, this is nasty up here."

He nodded. "Not to worry, we won't be here long." He motioned at a path going down the back. "We need to go down there." She nodded and sat down on the hard plastic. Instead of trying for a big running push, then hopping on, the way he always had before, he just sat down behind her and pushed them forward with his hand. The sled took off but at a slower pace.

It curved to the left, taking them toward the slash in the trees. She was grateful they weren't going at top speed. She couldn't imagine what would happen if they hit a tree.

Then she understood. The trees, although a long distance away, were up a small rise. If she'd been on skis, it wouldn't be noticeable, but on the magic carpet, with much of the momentum already running out, they barely crested it. At the top, he put his boots down and slowed them to a stop. He pointed to the right this time. Down below, a long way away, was the cabin.

"We could walk, or we could slide."

"And how do we stop when we get there?" she asked, worried.

"We'll have to crisscross our way down. A lot of deep snow is on the side of the hill, and that will bring us to a stop, at which point we turn and cross to the other side again."

"Oh, that makes so much sense." She laughed. "Let's slide then."

And that's what they did.

As they neared the cabin, someone from inside must have seen them because, before they came to a stop just in front, the rest of the group had all tumbled out to see them.

"Oh, man, if I'd known you were going sliding, I'd have come too!" complained Stevie.

"I had no plans to throw myself down the mountain on a little piece of plastic," Stacy said, with a laugh. "Boards, yes. Plastic, no."

George reached down and helped her to her feet. "You look like you had a blast."

"I did." She beamed up at him. "We had tons of fun."

She watched him nod at Royce behind her back, thankfulness in that glance. She reached out and hugged her brother. "I'm feeling much better."

"Good."

With his arm wrapped around her, George turned to look up the mountain. His forehead creased. He looked from her to Royce and back again. "You were with Yvonne, right?"

Stacy shook her head. "No, I haven't seen her. Why?"

"She hasn't come back, and no one remembers seeing her since last night. Possibly this morning."

"I saw her this morning," Stacy said, "but she wasn't here when we came back around lunchtime, nor have I seen her since." She turned to Royce and asked, "Have you?"

He shook his head. "She was with us until just before lunch. Then we split up, and I met up with you."

Stevie grabbed his coat and gloves and announced, "Therefore, she's gone missing. And that's not good."

ROYCE CONTACTED SEARCH and rescue and was one of the first to volunteer. They'd been to the resort enough over the years that their assistance had been requested in the past. Now hours later, he was cold and chilled, and bad weather was moving in quickly. All the public venues had been checked, the local runs searched, and her photograph shown to everyone. The initial hope that she'd stopped off at a pub for a beer waned, when all restaurants and pubs were checked, and there was still no sign of her. It was dark. The four of them that had been part of the search and rescue volunteer group drove up to the cabin. Lights blazed inside. Geoffrey had stayed behind with Kathleen and Stacy, in case Yvonne had returned on her own. They'd been in phone contact with each other all evening, but there'd been no sign of her.

Now with the search called off for the night because of encroaching bad weather, everyone was exhausted and somber on the truck ride back to the cabin. It would be a long night for Yvonne, if she were out there in the elements. It was only slightly reassuring that she was an old hand at winter sports.

"I can't believe, after all our efforts to keep the group together, that she's gone missing." George's voice was hard, angry, his grip on the wheel tightening. He couldn't hold back his frustration. He looked like he wanted to punch something.

"She could have picked up a stranger and planned a private evening with someone."

"You'd likely know about that, right?" George asked, staring at Royce. "Wasn't she after you?"

Royce winced. "Not really. I turned her down."

"Really?" Stevie leaned forward. In an aggrieved voice, he added, "Wow. You could have turned her my way."

Royce managed a smile, albeit a poor one. "Wish I could have, buddy."

"Why would you turn her down?" asked Mark.

"Ha." Stevie grinned. "His interests lie elsewhere."

An odd silence followed, as Mark considered the issue. He asked in a pensive voice, "So?"

Reaching the cabin, George parked, while Royce let out a bark of laughter and hopped out of the truck. He walked to the cabin door to find the rest of the group standing just inside the boot room, hope and fear on their faces. He shook his head.

Gasps filled the air, and tears immediately came to Kathleen's eyes. She ran past Royce and threw herself into George's arms.

Stacy walked forward and, in a low voice, asked him, "Nothing at all?"

He shook his head. "No one has seen her." He was so damn tired now. Inside and out. Dispirited, he took off his coat and hung it up on the hook. Then bent over to take off his snow-packed boots. When he straightened, he realized he was the last male in the room, … and Stacy still stood before him. He could smell the coffee behind her. He glanced at her curiously, wondering why she stood here, almost awkwardly in front. When he went to move around her, she put out an arm to stop him.

He stepped back slightly out of view of the others. "What?" he asked in a low voice.

"This," she said. And stepped forward to hug him.

His arms closed around her. Surprised but delighted, he held her against him. Something he'd wanted to do—and had been doing in a different way—all day. Just knowing she was here, safe, caring to be with him, offering him comfort, … it mattered. After a long moment, she stepped back, with a smile. "We need to join the others before they come looking for us."

He didn't give a damn if they did. He just wanted her back in his arms. "Stacy?"

She stopped at his voice and looked at him.

"Why?" he asked her.

Her eyebrows shot up. "You looked like you needed it." She turned and left him standing in the boot room.

He *had* needed it. Looking for Yvonne had been difficult. Deaths happened often on a mountain like this. It went with the territory. But he sure didn't want any to happen on his watch. No, he wasn't responsible for Yvonne having gone missing—but it felt like he was. At least partially. He knew they would all feel that way.

And, until they found her, there'd be no answers.

He walked toward his room and stopped at the doorway. Stacy was talking to Kathleen not far away. He called her over. "Stacy, when you took a look into the rooms earlier today, was Yvonne's stuff in here, like this?" He nodded to her bag, dumped upside down on her bed.

Stacy joined him at the doorway. "I don't know. I can't remember. Would she have done that herself?"

Kathleen stepped up and asked, "What's wrong?"

Royce called out to the group in general. "Did any of you notice Yvonne's bag earlier? Was it always dumped upside down like it is now? Did anyone here touch it?"

The others crowded around.

"It looked like that when I saw it."

"No, I didn't touch it."

"I looked in earlier," Kathleen said. "I wondered if she had taken her wallet. If she had money, then she could be in the pub."

"Good thought." Royce walked inside the room and gazed at the items on the bed. "I don't see it here, did you?"

Kathleen brushed forward and joined him. "It didn't look like this before. And her wallet was right here." She flipped the bag back on its proper end and shifted the items on Yvonne's bed. "It *was* here."

"So she might have come back and gotten it?" Royce asked. That would be good news. Maybe she'd been the one who rifled through Stacy's stuff. Or someone altogether different had, and, after finding Yvonne's wallet, had taken it. Shit.

"Stacy and I wondered if someone had searched our belongings today." He turned to the others. "I suggest you all check your own stuff and confirm nothing is missing. I have to pack up Yvonne's stuff for the police. They were supposed to be here tonight, but, given the storm that just moved in, it will likely be in the morning." The others scattered, as he unceremoniously stuffed all of Yvonne's belongings back inside her backpack.

A new face appeared in the doorway.

Royce startled. Shit, he'd forgotten that the other two would be joining them. "Kevin, I know you just got here today. Sorry, man."

Kevin stood awkwardly to the side. "Christine and I got in about an hour ago. I'm sorry about Yvonne. That sucks." He looked around the large cabin. "I left my gear outside in the boot room. Not sure where everyone has bunked down. Is there an empty bed, or do I join whoever is in the loft?"

A tiny gasp came from behind him, and Royce knew instinctively that having Kevin join Stacy up there would not be her choice.

"I'm moving anyway," Royce said, snagging up his gear and putting it all together. He left Yvonne's bed alone. "I'd like to keep her bed for her—just in case."

"Oh, absolutely, but I don't want to chase you away," Kevin protested.

"You're not." Royce grinned. "I've been planning this move all along." And he turned, brushed past a narrow-eyed Stacy, and walked up the stairs to the loft where he casually dropped his gear and returned to the living room and the waiting coffeepot.

She never said a word.

Damn right.

"SOUNDS LIKE A tough week for you guys," Kevin said to the room at large. "I'm sorry to hear that."

The room quieted down even further.

"We've done all we can do for now," Geoffrey said grimly. "Let's hope that Yvonne's tucked away, nice and warm somewhere, enjoying life so much that she never thought to check in."

"I hope so," Stacy said.

"I don't know Yvonne all that well." Kevin glanced over at Stacy, before his gaze continued to Kathleen. "Is she the kind to take off like this?" He settled back, trying to fit into the group that had been together for days already and feeling a bit like an outsider. He knew them all. Had gone on trips with them all, although not very often. And not with all of them in this same group.

"No. I wouldn't think so," Kathleen said, tucked up close to George. "She'd shown interest in Royce, so I would have thought she would work hard to get back to him."

Kevin looked over at Royce and hid his grin. Royce looked decidedly uncomfortable, as the guys chuckled and elbowed each other at his expense.

"Ah, well, maybe she's having dinner with someone who is more appreciative," Stevie said, grinning. He glanced at the kitchen, where Christine and Mark were working hard. "Is there food coming soon?"

"Yep. Be right there," Christine called back.

Someone's stomach growled loudly. Kevin shrugged, as everyone looked at him. "Sorry. Long drive here." He called out to Christine in the kitchen. "I'm surprised you're doing okay, Christine. You drove in with me."

"Ha, I've been snacking while I've been cooking."

"That was smart." He could have gone in and snacked too but felt odd with all the other males out searching for the missing woman. Thankfully it looked like dinner was just about ready.

"And food is here," Christine said, coming out with a huge cookie sheet full of nacho chips covered in ground beef and onions, topped with cheese, alongside big piles of guacamole and sour cream.

"Oh, yum."

"Yay, food."

Mark came up from behind with a second tray. Both trays were placed equidistant on the table, and, as soon as their hands were gone, the crowd dug in.

Christine and Mark came back with several bottles of wine and a third tray of more nachos.

After that, it was chaos. Kevin was glad he'd come in right now.

The only thing that bothered him was their ability to forget the missing woman. He could almost understand.

But, if he were missing, he'd sure be hoping they'd be looking for him all night.

THEY WERE ALL fools. If they were really friends, they'd have gone looking for Yvonne, even if the search had been called off until first light.

Idiots. They still had no clue. Of course that's how he wanted it, but it would be so much fun to add an element of suspense to this mess. But he wouldn't give himself away. This was too much fun to cut short.

Besides, he had worked hard. If he was the only one to appreciate his skills, then so be it.

Too bad though, he'd love to have someone show some appreciation.

He studied Stacy. Maybe if he kept her alive long enough, maybe she'd come to understand.

Maybe she'd see him for who he really was. Finally.

Chapter 23

THE EVENING WAS subdued, as everyone kept expecting the phone to ring or a vehicle to come up to the door and Yvonne to walk inside. It never happened. There was no word from her or about her. Neither did she come home. Stacy, already in her PJs, sat curled in the armchair all evening, sipping her wine. She'd hoped this wouldn't be a sleepless night, but, given the circumstances … When the wind picked up outside, screaming through the cabin, howling as it pounded on the door several times, she jumped, thinking it was Yvonne, trying to open the door against the wind.

Royce leaned over and patted her hand. "It's just the wind."

"I know." She gave him a small smile. "I just keep hoping it's her."

"We all are."

Stacy nodded. The long day was having an effect on her. Not to mention the warm fire and the several glasses of wine she'd had to help her relax. She couldn't get over the thought of Yvonne, injured, lying in the snow somewhere, wondering if she'd make it through the night. And damn if it didn't bring back all the old fears of her friends being buried alive in that damn avalanche. She hadn't slept for months after the accident, always waking up from the nightmare of seeing her friends waiting for rescue—a rescue that never came.

She stood slowly, feeling her muscles seize up. She gently stepped around the many legs stretched out in front of the fire.

"Are you heading to bed, Stacy?" George asked quietly.

She nodded. "That sledding wore me out today. I was laughing and screaming so much, my throat is feeling a little rough."

He frowned. "That's not good. Your immune system is already shot."

She would have hugged him if she could reach him, but he appeared to be cradling Kathleen in his arms, as she snored gently. "She needs to go to bed too," Stacy said, nodding toward Kathleen.

"I'm thinking we all do." Royce stood up. "I'm beat."

"Yeah, me too." Stevie rose as well. "Good night, all."

Stacy called out to him, as he started toward the bathroom. "Good night, Stevie. You worked hard today. You need some sleep."

"Ha, I work hard every day," he replied, but his words were slurred. His eyes dropped, and damn if he didn't sway in place. As Stacy watched in alarm, Royce walked over and led him down the hall to his room.

"Almost there." At the doorway, Royce gave him a gentle push. "Go lie down."

Stevie went like an obedient puppy.

Stacy stood on the bottom of the stairs and felt her heart melt a little. Royce had done just the right thing. Stevie was a big kid, but he'd had a tough day. To know Royce could take care of others like he did also said a lot about who he was on the inside.

And she found she liked that inside man more and more.

After brushing her teeth, the same lassitude that had overtaken Stevie filled her bones. Then he'd had more wine than she had. Chances were good the alcohol was stripping the energy from her bones.

Just moving up the stairs made her feel like she'd gained one hundred pounds. As she crested over the top step, Royce pounded up the stairs after her.

"Are you okay, Stacy?" he asked. "You are starting to scare me."

"I'm fine," she muttered, not even trying to hold back a yawn. "Just did too much today." She stumbled over to her bed, crawled in and pulled the covers up to her chin.

"Stacy?"

His voice sounded strange. "*Hmm?*" she mumbled, so grateful to be in her bed at this moment. It was cold, but her skin was colder, so even that little bit felt wonderful. She slowly relaxed.

"Stacy," Royce snapped sharply. "Look at me."

"Can't."

"Yes, you can."

He shook her shoulders hard, her head snapping back and forth.

"Ouch. Stop that. It hurts."

"Good. Open your eyes."

"No, go away." She wanted to be pissed, but there was no heat in her voice. She tried again. "Leave me alone. I just want to sleep."

"That's what I'm afraid of." Royce lowered his head. "Think, Stacy. You are too sleepy. Too tired. This isn't normal for you."

She struggled to think from behind the black fog in her mind. "No, been sick. Did too much."

"Maybe, but, if you'd open your eyes, you would see how dilated your pupils are."

Silly. "I've been drinking," she mumbled, trying and failing to open them. "'Course they're dilated."

Her eyelids were roughly opened, and a light flashed.

She wanted to cry out but couldn't. She sagged against him, heard the heartfelt "Shit" coming out of his mouth—then knew no more.

SHIT, SHIT, *SHIT*. Royce cradled Stacy's limp body in his arms for a long moment. He laid her back down on the bed and stared at her precious face. Stevie had been just as tired. Then he remembered Kathleen. He leaned over the railing and stared down into the darkness. The only light was coming from the fire. The flames flickered and danced, as if appreciating an audience—finally.

Royce raced down the stairs. George snored on the couch; Kathleen snored gently in his lap.

He raced to Stevie's room to find Mark already out cold, just like the others.

"Kevin?" He pushed open the door. The heavy rhythmic noise coming from Kevin's chest said much about the depth of his slumber. Christine slept in a tight ball above him in the bunk beds. Geoffrey snored loudly on the opposite set of bunks. They'd all helped kill several bottles of wine tonight.

Royce spun around and ran back to George. He lifted Kathleen and carried her to George's bed, then came back and shook George's shoulder hard. When that got no reaction but a disjointed movement of his head, Royce hauled back and smacked him across the face. George groaned. Royce repeated it.

George groaned again. "Wha—"

Royce smacked him a third time.

George's eyes popped open, and he glared at Royce. "You'd better have a hell of a reason for doing that."

"Everyone's been drugged."

George's eyes widened. His gaze was unfocused, but Royce could see the wheels attempting to turn behind them.

"What?" he choked out, as he tried to stand. Royce grabbed his arm and pulled him to his feet. He stood, swayed, and fell back down again. He looked around, then back at Royce. "Kathleen? Stacy?"

"They're both out of it. They're in their beds."

The relief in George's gaze made Royce realize just how much George cared for Kathleen. Like Royce, George had had many relationships in his active life. He loved women. And women loved George. But Kathleen appeared to be his sweet spot.

Royce was happy for his friend. Now if only Royce could get Stacy back in his life, he'd be happy for both of them.

"Help me up," George ordered, a little more grit in his voice than before. Royce hefted him back to his feet. "To the boot room," he ordered. "Maybe the cold will knock some sense back into my brain."

With Royce keeping a steady hand on his friend's arm, he led him out to the anteroom, where the gear and outerwear were stored. The bite of cold air hit their faces. "Take a few deep breaths," Royce said.

George walked back and forth in the small space, as he focused on getting fresh air into his system and clearing his head.

Then he turned and faced Royce.

"What the fuck is going on?"

RAGE SAT IN George's gut and festered. He stared down at Kathleen, seeing the drug-induced coma for himself. "I want to call the police. Right now. Have them sort this out."

Royce had already collected the wineglasses and empty bottles in a box for the police. Hopefully they'd test it all and find the drugs used. George wasn't showing too much reaction at this point, which was a damn good thing. Then again, he was a big guy and wasn't much of a wine drinker. But how else had the drugs gotten into their systems if not through the wine? It was the only thing everyone had shared—except for Royce. He'd just had soda pop in his glass. It could have easily looked like wine, particularly in the evening light.

He tasted wine in his glass at one point, as a bottle had been emptied, and another opened. Used to it, as often the others tried to trick him into drinking it, he'd just gotten up quietly and dumped it. Casting his mind back, he tried to remember who had opened the bottles. They needed to know that in order to determine if they'd been tampered with. And it was likely too late for that, given everyone's comatose state.

Royce spun. "Jesus. You're fine, but what about Kathleen? She's really tiny."

"I checked. She's definitely drugged, but, when I shook her, I did get a response." He glared at Royce. "I won't be smacking her around."

"I wouldn't either." Royce smacked him on the shoulder. "Just you."

"Next time, go a little lighter," George snapped.

As they walked into the kitchen and stared from the doorway, George wondered out loud, his voice hard. "Is it one of us?"

Silence.

He looked over at Royce to see his jaw muscle flickering in a staccato tempo. "What?"

"I'm wondering if it's related to Yvonne."

"Her disappearance? Or are you thinking she did this and booked it?" George laughed, his voice harsh. "How badly did you let her down? Would she have done this in revenge?"

Royce shook his head. "Honestly, not bad at all. I thought, at the time, she'd been joking the way she had said that it would be warmer for both of us if she joined me in my bed." He laughed ruefully. "She laughed. I laughed. I didn't think anything about it."

"And it might not be anything. It's hard to say at this point." George ran his hands down his face, as if that would help shake the last of the cobwebs from his brain. He wanted to hit something so badly. That someone had done this was unbelievable, but to all of them at the same time? Disgusting. Why had no one seen anything? Then he realized they might have, but he wouldn't know until they woke up.

"Who had access to the cabin today?" Royce asked.

"You mean, who didn't have access?" George responded. He walked into the main room of the cabin, crossing to the kitchen sink. He reached for a glass and turned on the tap. Water poured. He filled the glass and took a long drink. It felt good. His throat was parched. Dry. He emptied the glass, then refilled it for Royce. "Were you drugged?" George asked.

"Not really." But he stayed quiet, thoughtful.

"What does that mean?"

Royce turned to face him. "I hate wine," he said. "There was wine in my glass at one point in the evening. I tasted it, realized what it was, and dumped it down the sink. I refilled the glass with pop and sipped that all evening. But there was an odd taste to it."

"So you're thinking the wine was drugged, and some of it either stayed in your mouth after that one sip or in your glass because you didn't wash it clean?" He considered the several bottles of wine that had flowed freely. They'd each brought several, so they weren't all from the same store. "They must have been tampered with here."

"With all of us getting up and pouring drinks, it could have been anyone." Royce's voice hardened. "I've been trying to think of how it could be anyone other than one of us, and I can't."

"Anyone could have come in during the afternoon," George reminded him. "You yourself saw the rooms. Our belongings had been searched."

"But not just anyone could have known which bottles would be used or likely have had time to tamper with them, while they were still sealed." He stared at George, grim lines at the corner of his mouth. "This is no longer a random break-in."

"Shit."

Chapter 24

THE LIGHT HURT her eyes. Stacy slammed them shut and moaned. It shouldn't be like that. She tried to sort out where she was. And remembered. She was at the cabin. They'd been boarding and sledding. Then she remembered. *Yvonne.*

She bolted upright and gasped, both hands rushing to support her head. She fell back before the sledgehammer in her head succeeded in getting out. "What the hell?" she whispered. "How much did I drink?"

"Stacy?"

Suddenly Royce was there. His hand was gentle, soothing on her forehead. "You'll need a bit of time. Take it easy and just rest in place for a moment."

"What happened?" she tried to enunciate clearly, but her tongue felt swollen and awkward. Something was wrong.

"A hell of a hangover," Royce said.

But no laughter was in his voice. He sounded worried. She opened her eyes a slit and peered under her lashes. "I've had hangovers. This is not a hangover." She closed her eyes and took several deep breaths. "My stomach doesn't feel very good."

"Nope, and no one else's does either."

At that, she stilled. "Bad wine?"

"That's one way to look at it."

"We were drugged," she said softly. Her eyes flew open. "Was everyone affected?"

"I was the least," he said. "I did have a sip, then dumped it."

"Right." Now that her brain was waking up, she remembered how he hated wine. He drank most alcoholic drinks but not that. "But someone tried?"

He was slow to answer.

She studied his face, wishing things would stay in focus and not move back and forth, like they were currently doing. "Royce?" she prodded him.

"I think so."

She would have nodded, but she remembered at the last second that it would hurt to move. "Son of a bitch."

"Sorry about the head. You and Kathleen seem to be feeling the effects the strongest."

"Being smaller, the effect would be stronger and longer lasting." She rolled over slightly. "Would have been much better if I'd thrown it all up last night."

"We didn't figure it out until everyone was unconscious." His big hand slowly stroked her back and shoulder. "I'm just glad you're awake. You're the last one."

She smiled weakly. "I did enjoy the wine."

He laughed lightly. "I wonder if you will again."

"Not sure I'll ever drink again."

"Speaking of which, you need to sit up and get down some water." He helped her into a sitting position, then held up a glass of water for her to drink.

It took some effort, but she managed to get half of it down. Then he helped her lie back.

She sighed. "It feels better to be horizontal."

"How about we get you downstairs? You can wait there."

"Wait for what?" She groaned, as she sat up again. Only she already knew. She studied his grim expression, the gathering darkness in his eyes. "The cops?"

He nodded. "We called them early, and they've been here for the last hour." He motioned to the noise on the other side of the railing and down below. Now that it was pointed out to her, she heard the loud noises, the extra voices. The string of words floating up to her.

"You'll likely be last."

"Poison?"

"Hate."

"Angry."

"Jealous."

None of those words made any sense, not when said to the friends she'd known for years. "They think one of us did it?"

"It's the only real answer."

Stifling a groan, she pushed herself up again and sat with crossed legs. Her head hurt just from that movement. She couldn't imagine trying to go down the stairs and being nice while being questioned. But she'd do it. It was part of what she did anyway. "Can you help me up, please?" she asked in a shaky voice.

He grabbed her elbows and gently tugged her to her feet. Vertical, she swayed in place. The room spun around her. "I don't think I can make it downstairs."

"I'll help." He smiled, and, in an easy move, he carefully scooped her up into his arms, and, moving slowly, he walked over to the stairs and headed down. As he reached the bottom step, there were cries from the others.

"Yay, she's awake."

"Welcome to the land of dry throats and massive headaches, Stacy."

She groaned. "I hear you there. That's one club I could do without a membership to."

That elicited a few responding groans of laughter.

"How are you feeling, Miss Carter?" the uniformed police officer asked in concern.

"I'm okay. At least I hope I'll be okay." She wasn't so sure, but, if she looked like the rest of them, she was dead already.

Royce lowered her to the couch, where she sat in the middle, with Stevie on the left and Geoffrey on the right. Royce headed to the kitchen. He returned a moment later with a full glass of water for her. She thanked him and sipped it. It felt like she would never get enough, yet she was full. Or at least her stomach said she was too full. At the same time, she was desperate to have more.

She sighed and sank back.

Stevie muttered, "Yeah, you got the same problem." He held up the glass in his hand. "I want to drink. It tastes so great that I want to drain the glass over and over again. But, at the same time, I'm full. My stomach says it'll upchuck if I throw anything else down there."

"Me too," said Geoffrey. "Sucks."

"Have you all given statements?" the uniformed cop asked the two men beside Stacy.

They both nodded. "We have. I think you just have Stacy left."

"*Great,*" Stacy quipped. "Nice to know I'm on time for something."

The uniformed officer sat down in front of her on the coffee table. "I just need to ask you a few questions."

She nodded. "To be expected. Although I have no idea

how I can help."

"Did you open any of the wine bottles yourself?"

She frowned. "No, I don't think so."

"Did you watch anyone else open a bottle?"

She thought about it and said slowly, "I must have, but I can't say that I remember who or when or even what bottles." She looked over at Stevie. "You filled my glass last, as you said something about it helping me to sleep. Helping me to forget about Yvonne."

"Did I?" He dropped his head backward on the back of the couch. "I don't remember much about the end of the evening. I understand that Royce got me to my bed, and I crashed, fully dressed."

"Nice," Stacy said, with a grin. "At least I managed to get into my PJs before collapsing."

"On the other side of that coin," Stevie said, "I'm fully dressed now, but you, my dear, are *still* in your pajamas. And you'll have to make it back upstairs and get dressed." At her groan, he laughed. "See? There is a method to my madness."

"No," she said. "You're just lazy."

"Well, now that you two are working through the merits of sleeping in your clothes or having to get changed twice," Geoffrey snapped, "maybe we can get back to the questions for Stacy, so we can get to the bottom of this mess."

Hearing and echoing his frustration in her mind, Stacy turned back to the policeman. "Sorry," she said. "It helps to lighten the worry with humor."

"Understood. As long as we are joking around though, the longer this will take to get through."

That wiped the laughter off her face. "Sorry. Please continue."

He quickly ran through the questions. She answered the

best she could.

When he asked her about the afternoon and supposedly feeling as if her belongings had been disturbed, the others turned to her with interest.

"I can't really explain it, except that I noticed the clothing wasn't exactly as I'd left it. I'm a bit of a neat freak," she said apologetically. "My clothes weren't packed as I'd packed them."

"Do you know of any reason why anyone would do that?"

"I wondered if one of the women might have needed monthly supplies unexpectedly, and, not being here to ask, they just looked for themselves. Other than that, I can't imagine. Unless a stranger entered and was looking for money or other small valuables."

"But would a stranger who'd come into the cabin on the off chance that it was empty care about replacing the clothing in the same order? Wouldn't they have just dumped the bags and sorted through to find what they wanted? And was there anything missing?"

At the rush of questions, she had to stop, marshal her thoughts, then answer them in order. "I don't know. I imagine, and no."

By the time the police had finished questioning everyone, Stacy felt marginally better. The coffee helped, as did getting up and walking around, followed by a hot shower. When she came out dressed and feeling warm, her stomach gurgled loudly. Someone had made pancakes, and the group sat down at the table in silence to eat. She joined them, reaching for a stack to transfer to her plate. No one said a word. That usually meant there was no good news, but she needed to know.

Finally, after a few moments, she had to ask the one question that hadn't been brought up. "Has anyone heard anything of Yvonne?"

Silence.

They glanced around at each other, while she watched. She caught George's gaze, and he shook his head. She nodded. Search and rescue would have been back out at first light. That her group was not joining them said much about the shape they were in today after the drugs. And how impaired the drugs made them feel. She waited a few moments, before bringing it up again. After several bites of the light, fluffy treat, she asked, "Do you think it is related?"

Silence.

She kept eating, wishing she understood the undercurrents.

"Well, I highly doubt she'd have drugged the wine and then pulled a disappearing act," Geoffrey said. "Especially not because Royce here turned her down."

Stacy's head jerked up, her gaze going from Geoffrey to Royce's bent head.

"Oh, you missed that part," Geoffrey said. "Apparently that's the conclusion these two brilliant men came up with."

"No, not really," Royce said patiently, "but it's a possibility that we have to consider."

"Right." Geoffrey subsided into sullen silence. The only sounds were the occasional *clang* of cutlery against the plates.

"Or the same person drugged us and had something to do with Yvonne's disappearance," Stacy suggested. "Not that I am looking at a worst-case scenario but …"

Geoffrey stared at her. "You have a dark mind."

She shrugged. "Maybe."

How could she explain the stuff she saw and heard every

day? Cases that were the worst of what mankind could do to each other. "Or it was a prank," she suggested. "Maybe this was meant to be a joke, and the drugs were more powerful than they thought."

"You're reaching there, sis."

She nodded, as she ate another bite. "Occupational hazard." She had to think about the issue carefully. "Two issues here. My question is, are they related?"

"Three issues, if we're counting everyone's belongings were searched."

A few nods came around the table, but no one said much of anything. She lifted her cup of coffee to her mouth, when her phone went off. She pulled it out and read the text. It was from James, another coworker. He'd gotten the information for her on the male they'd found by contacting the RCMP here in Canada.

All indications said he'd been drugged before freezing to death. The drugs were still frozen in his bloodstream. Tox screen was in progress. She appreciated the professional courtesy.

Her heart sinking, she sat back slightly, so she could ask him to connect with the police here, explaining about the missing woman and the drugs in their wine.

She looked up, caught her brother's gaze, and gave a subtle head motion toward the other room. She stood and took her coffee with her. Thankfully she'd finished eating. "I'm going to sit by the fire." She turned her back and walked casually to the living room, where she chose a seat farthest away from the others. She heard footsteps and knew her brother was coming. She had her phone out and decided to give James a few other details and explained more about Yvonne's disappearance and their belongings being searched.

She knew he'd freak. That Stevie and Mark were being super quiet told her they already understood how big a mess they were mired in.

George sat down beside her. Royce came and sat on the other side. She should have known.

"What's up, Stacy?" her brother asked.

"The man we found?" She glanced between them to make sure, with all that had happened, that they remembered whom she spoke about.

They both nodded.

"He was drugged but ultimately died from exposure."

Royce sat back, a gentle "*Shit*" slipping from his lips.

George stared at her. "Drugged?" he asked softly. "Do we know what drugs?"

"Not yet. I've told James about what just happened to us. He's in contact with local law enforcement here. They'll try to see if the drugs were the same as the ones we were given. He's also limited to the goodwill of the local police. Remember. We're in a different country."

"So are we thinking that man was murdered?"

"Well, if he was drugged and then died, he sure as hell was," George said. "Yet that doesn't mean it was intentional. If any of us had gone outside last night, it could have ended up with the same result."

"Are we really thinking we have … what? … A serial drugging going on here?" Royce shook his head. "That sounds too bizarre."

"I suspect the drugging is just a means to an end," Stacy said quietly. "I just don't know what the end result is." But she was afraid she did. Kidnapping. But for what purpose, she had no clue.

"And Yvonne?"

She shook her head. "I don't know. Maybe she opened a bottle of wine and had several glasses before going back out for a few runs."

"Hell," Royce whispered. "That's all too possible."

"So what gives?" Geoffrey asked.

They'd been talking so low that she hadn't realized the rest of their friends had come to stand around them, worry on their faces.

George quickly filled them in.

Instead of surprised shock, there was mostly silence.

After a moment, Stevie said, "Not good."

"Are we thinking that the drugs were more of a prank then? With this dead guy just deciding to go for a walk in his drunken, drugged stupor? Neither scenario is likely, surely?" Kathleen asked, curling up close to George. She shuddered. George tugged her closer.

"I'm not sure yet," Stacy said seriously. "First, we're checking that the drugs used on him were the same that were used on us."

"That's horrible." Stevie threw himself onto the closest chair. "I came for a chance to rip down some runs, not get my ass drugged," he mumbled.

Stacy snorted. "And I came to finally get a vacation."

"A busman's vacation," Geoffrey said, with a snigger.

No arguing that.

ROYCE HATED THE thought of what was going on. They needed to shift the energy of the place, but, at the same time, he wanted to do a thorough search of everyone's stuff himself. He figured he might get a little resistance on that. George would agree with him. Unless they would all leave and not know any better. The cops were likely to come back here as well.

Then Stacy did it. "I'll take my camera outside and find something beautiful to photograph. Maybe that will make me feel better."

"Not alone," Royce snapped.

She glared at him. "I didn't get a chance to finish. I was going to suggest that we all get out. Go boarding. Catch a few runs. Something to change this depressed energy we are all feeling."

"If we have energy for that," Geoffrey said sharply, "then we have energy to rejoin the search for Yvonne."

"We aren't allowed to," George said quietly. "They don't know the effects of the drugs. They don't want us out there, in case they have to turn around and rescue us."

"Then, for the same reason, boarding and skiing are out."

Stevie looked at George for confirmation. At his nod, he groaned. "This is not the vacation I planned."

"It's not the vacation any of us planned," Kathleen said. "What about driving to the village and spending the afternoon walking around, have lunch out, do coffee? Something to get us out of here but not enough to zap our strength?"

"Another consideration," Christine said, "is the police. Are we allowed to go anywhere, or do we have to stay cooped up here?"

Silence.

"Damn if I know," Stacy said. "I'm presuming they got what they needed from us, so we can leave. If they need more, they'll come back or contact us at home. In the meantime, I need some fresh air." She got up and walked over to the boot room. "I know it would be foolish to go alone, so does anyone want to go with me?"

"I'm coming," Royce said in a hard voice.

She shrugged. "Fine, thank you."

"Aren't you going to bring your camera?" he asked curiously. "It's still upstairs, isn't it?"

She exhaled noisily. "Damn it."

He raised his eyebrows. "You might want to acknowledge that you aren't 100 percent yet."

"I know, but I need to get out. To get away." She motioned to the somber group sitting around the fire. "I don't want to do that all day."

"I'll go get your bag." He could get there easier than she could. He figured he'd take her out to the hillside, and they could sit in the sun and enjoy a few minutes respite. "Then we'll take a walk."

Up in the loft, he grabbed her stuff, took a quick look around to see if there was anything else she needed, and saw something odd sticking out from under Stacy's blankets. He bent down for a closer look.

A syringe. He pulled his sleeve down over his hand and picked it up. He sniffed the tip end but couldn't smell anything. He held it up to the tiny bit of light and realized there was still a little bit left inside. Stacy had a travel pack of tissues on her bed, and he carefully placed the syringe inside, then dumped her makeup bag and hid it all in there. He didn't want the others to know about it.

He knew Stacy wouldn't have been the one spiking the wine bottles, but that was likely to be the immediate reasoning of the rest of the group. She knew drugs. She'd been here all afternoon, so she had opportunity.

He did too, if he looked at it that way. Some could say he'd tucked it under Stacy's bed to throw suspicion on her, whereas sleeping up here, like he had last night, gave him access to her sleeping space. He hated to think of his friends turning on him, but no doubt he was questioning those he'd called a *friend* himself.

Except George. He would never hurt his sister, and he'd been furious that anyone might hurt Kathleen. Stevie and Mark on the other hand had just as much knowledge of drugs as Stacy did. They could have come back anytime and spiked the wine bottles themselves.

But why? The two men worked with Stacy every day. They would have had lots of opportunity to drug her.

Then he remembered the stalker that Stacy had felt in the bushes yesterday. What if that person was making sure she was out there and not in the cabin, so they could put the drugs in the wine? And through a syringe, no less. He slipped the makeup bag under his shirt and walked downstairs.

"Oh, Royce has it bad. Now he's even the gopher," Christine teased.

Royce laughed. "We won't be long, and we'll keep the cabin in sight the whole time we're out," he promised. "If anyone cares to join us, feel free."

"As if we'd be welcome," scoffed Stevie.

"Actually you would be," Stacy said, from the boot room doorway. "Especially if you come in an hour or so and bring coffee."

STUPID IDIOTS. LOOK at them, too scared to do anything. Looking sideways at each other, wondering if one of their friends had just fucked them over.

He smiled inside.

Oh happy days. This was an extra bit of fun he hadn't ex-

pected.

Well worth repeating though. Watching this close-knit group slowly fall apart. Soon they'd turn on each other, like rabid dogs, and start attacking.

He couldn't wait.

They had no idea what was coming.

But they would soon.

Fools.

Chapter 25

STACY STOPPED AT the crest of the hill and breathed deep. Then did it again. She couldn't believe how stifling the cabin had begun to feel. How difficult the atmosphere. She suspected that, with her and Royce gone, there'd be talk about them. As long as no one suspected them for this wine-doping scenario, she was fine with the talk. Expected it even. After all, humans loved to gossip.

"Feel better?" Royce asked quietly.

"Much." She tilted her head back and let the sun hit her face. "It was getting hard to take in there."

"I agree."

She stilled at an odd note in his tone. Without trying to make it obvious, she studied his face. Worry tensed his features, as he stared blankly ahead. Something was going on behind those magnetic eyes. "What's wrong?" she asked. He opened his mouth to say something, and she cut him off. "Don't lie."

The look on his face was both comical and affronted.

"Sorry," she rushed to assure him. "I didn't mean that quite the way it sounded. I would just prefer to know everything. I can't deal if I don't have all the facts."

In a subtle furtive movement, he checked around them to make sure they were alone.

She watched him curiously. "What is it?"

"When I went to get your camera bag," he said, pulling out her makeup bag from inside his coat, "I found this almost under your bed. As if you may have dropped it."

"My makeup bag?" She frowned. "I thought I left it on my bed."

"You did. I dumped the contents on the bed so I could use the bag." He motioned toward it. "Open carefully."

She unzipped the pouch, while he continued to watch the area. And saw the syringe stuffed into her Kleenex travel pack. "Oh my God." She blinked several times as she processed the implications. "Is it possible I was injected with the drugs?" she wondered.

"Possible, but, unless you can find an injection site, I doubt it. I figured it was likely the method of getting the drugs in the sealed wine bottles. People might have noticed an uncorked bottle or one that had been opened and recorked. However, with so many of us in the cabin, they would have assumed someone else opened it. But no one would have noticed a tiny pinprick through the cork."

She closed her eyes. "Shit. That took some planning. And do you think leaving this bit of evidence beside my bed was on purpose? Or did it fall from the perp's pocket while searching my room?"

With a shrug, he said, "Could be either."

Now it was her turn to look around the area to make sure they were alone. Yet she hoped the police were driving up to ask more questions. Instead the snowy area was calm, the air still. Nothing moved but the two of them. "We need to get this to the police."

"I know. I wasn't so sure I should let the others know what I found."

"Thank you for that." She smiled wryly. "And for trusting that I'm not the bad guy here."

"I never suspected you," he said. "It's not your way."

"Really? You don't think I could freeze someone to death?" she joked. "Look. He's even making it easy on them by drugging them first."

That gaze latched on to her face and narrowed. "Put that way, I wonder if that was the end that he hoped for the rest of us."

"On average, most poisoners are women."

"But we weren't poisoned," he corrected. "We were drugged."

"And, for some people, there is no difference."

He looked at her. "So do we have a woman then? Are we back to thinking it was Yvonne?"

"No." Stacy stared down at the cabin. "I actually don't."

"Why is that?"

Yeah, why did she think that? She studied the cabin, thinking about the sequence of events, even as she tucked the small bag into Royce's coat pocket. "I don't think she'd have left her gear behind like that. I can't see a motive for turning on everyone just because she was upset at you."

He protested. "She wasn't upset."

"Maybe she just didn't show it."

His hand whipped up and ran through his hair in a gesture she was starting to recognize as his instinctive reaction to stressful news. "She wasn't upset," he reiterated. "I do understand women, and she was not seriously coming on to me, and she was not feeling rejected."

"On the off chance you are correct, what do you think happened to her?"

He glared at her. "I am correct."

After studying the look in his eyes for a long moment

and wondering how any woman could not feel affected by a brush-off from him, Stacy willed it to the back of her mind and shifted her gaze away. "Fine. That doesn't change the fact that she is missing."

He took a step forward and grasped Stacy's face between his hands. "I need you to trust me."

Frowning, her gaze locked on to his. Searching. "I never said I didn't."

"No, you haven't." He stared at the sky over her head, as if wrestling with something. "But I don't hear that you do either."

That magnetic gaze of his locked onto hers again, willing her to give him what he wanted. Needed. She wanted to pull away but somehow found it impossible to break the hold he had on her. "I do trust you."

"Do you? You're out here in the woods with me, but do you trust that I wasn't the one to tamper with the wine? I had the opportunity. You did too. I trust you. But, if I did it, of course I would trust you. And you would never know."

Something hard was in his voice. Almost mean. As if she'd done something to piss him off. Instead of making her nervous by his harshness or the tension in his hands, her anger soared. She leaned forward and glared at him. "I wouldn't be out here if I didn't trust you."

The light in his eyes deepened. In a surprise move, he lowered his head and blocked the bright sun from her eyes. The cool touch of his lips surprised her. But the banked heat didn't. It had always been there. Barely leashed, sitting just under the surface. Waiting to ignite. She shivered. Her body remembered the touch of his hands, the tone of his muscles. The warmth of his breath.

He deepened the kiss, heat flaring between them, as he

bent her over his arm. Her arms clutched him tightly, as her world spun, inside and out. She moaned deep in the back of her throat.

Suddenly she was back on her feet and set apart from him. She struggled to keep her balance in the world suddenly gone awry. She gasped for breath.

"I'm sorry," he finally got out, his chest heaving, his breathing raspy and deep. He rubbed his face. "I shouldn't have done that."

She blinked, struggling to adjust to the sudden change in his manner. She'd have done a lot for him to grab her and kiss her again, but … he looked guilty. *Why?* "Why did you then?" she asked in what she thought was a reasonable voice.

"Because I wanted to, damn it."

Her mouth dropped open.

"Oh, for God's sake. You know how I feel about you." He raised his hands in frustration and turned away.

It was hard to know what to say. She decided the truth might be the best way forward. "I don't know how you feel about me."

He spun and glared. "Bullshit. Of course you do. Hell, everyone does."

"I'd heard something from a couple people, but more of a joke—"

"It is a big joke to them. They all know."

"Know what?" she asked, her voice steady, her gaze direct, questioning. She had to know. Had to get to the root of this. It was too important to just gloss over.

He snorted, shaking his head, glaring at her. "Never mind." He motioned to the gorgeous scenery around them. "Take your damn pictures. I'll stand guard."

Shit. She wanted to push the issue. Get him to open up

and to say exactly what he wanted from her. But a tiny part of her didn't really want to know. She'd kept him out of her life by pushing him away and by closing the door between them.

Because she didn't want to open it.

Hadn't wanted to open it.

Keeping it closed had been easier.

And slamming him for his behavior had given her some righteous logic for keeping the door closed. Excuses to not let him into her heart.

Because he'd break it.

And she was so weak that she didn't want to be hurt again. So she kept the door closed.

She was a coward.

REALLY? THEY WERE standing on the hillside in a lover's clench. For everyone to see. As if they were a couple. As if they had a right to such a relationship. Bull. They had the right to nothing.

Sunshine shone down on them, like a lover's kiss, and he hated it.

She was not for him. He was not for her. Neither should be allowed to live. That was obscene. Royce went with anyone. He was a rabid dog in heat. Everyone knew that. But even that bastard should have standards. Obviously he didn't.

Disgusting.

And out in the open like that.

Oh wait, what's this? Trouble in paradise. He watched as the two separated, as if Royce flung her away.

"Good boy, Royce. I knew you had more sense than that." *He chuckled at the temper showing in the line of Royce's shoulders and back, as he faced the cabin. Stacy stood behind him, her hand out toward him.*

And Royce ignored her. Good. He couldn't see them clear enough to see the expressions on their faces or to hear the words exchanged, but he could see their silhouettes, and that was enough. For the moment, that was enough.

This might be a winter paradise setting here, but there was no paradise on this mountain today. This week. This lifetime. At least not for them.

Only for him.

ROYCE REFUSED TO turn around. He locked down the emotions he'd stuffed inside a long time ago. He shouldn't have kissed her. Not because of her but because of him. The taste of such sweet honey, a passion so thick and wild—once tasted, it was hard to forget, and having stirred it all up again would make it that much harder to stomp back inside again.

Bitterness clawed at his throat. He wanted to make love to her until they were both stupid, but, since that wouldn't happen, no point in wishing things were different.

He'd tried so damn hard to be there for her. Now look. It was all gone again. Resolve stretched inside him. He needed to turn a new leaf after this nightmare. He needed to walk away forever. Be friends with her, sure, because he wouldn't forfeit his best friend, George. But it was time to grow up. Realize some dreams were hang-ups from previous days. Previous years. Previous lives.

No, it was time to move on.

And leave her behind.

He took a deep breath, feeling better as the cool air hit his lungs.

Bullshit. He felt worse. Fresh air wouldn't make any difference in his life. Only one thing would.

And that ain't happening.

Then he felt a hand slide into his and lace their fingers together.

His resolve, his anger, his bitterness evaporated in an instant, and he knew he could no more walk away from her than he could walk away from his heart.

It was impossible.

They were the same.

Chapter 26

STACY STARED DOWN at her hand. Had it actually crept out and done what she thought it might have done? Betrayed her? His hands squeezed over hers so tightly that she thought he'd surely break something. But it didn't hurt. Instead, it was as if, by that very pressure, something inside her was building, an inner tension that needed him to squeeze harder and harder. Maybe finally breaking through the barriers she'd erected against him so long ago. Against the world so long ago. Against fate so long ago.

He turned slowly, and she almost gasped at the pain in his gaze as he studied her. His eyes open, full of hope, and yet expecting so much less.

Damn, she was a fool. And a bitch to cause so much agony. "I'm sorry," she said.

He shuttered his gaze, his shoulders slumping slightly. He nodded. "Not to worry. I'm a big boy." He went to drop her hand, but she hung on.

"No," she cried. "You don't understand."

He stilled, then slowly turned back to face her. "What don't I understand?"

"Why I'm sorry."

A light opened in his gaze, letting her see inside for the first time. Not too far in. But maybe enough.

She dropped her gaze. "It was hard for me. That weekend. I was desperate to know there was a purpose to living. To have a reason to get up every day. When I lost my friends, well, my world collapsed. When I lost them, I was like a ship that had run aground. No way to float away."

She shivered against the chill inside.

"Nothing to do but be beaten by the times of change, and I felt like I couldn't move. When I saw you that weekend, something clicked. I needed to be held. Needed to be connected at least in some way to someone else. To the rest of the world."

She stopped, unsure of what to say next and a little embarrassed by the outpouring already. Yet she needed to get it all out. "I was looking to find a purpose to continue with life. I wasn't suicidal. I just didn't feel anything." She gave a small deprecating movement. "I don't mean to make so much about it, but I thought, if you understood how I felt, maybe you'd understand my reaction."

When she didn't continue for a long moment, he nudged her gently. "And your reaction afterward?" he asked cautiously. "I do understand your reasons for that weekend. We've all had that need to be close to someone. But afterward …" Sadness once again glanced off his tone. "What was that all about?"

Instinctively she tried to pull her hand away, only he held her fast, letting her know he wanted answers and he wanted them now.

She opened her mouth, then closed it. He narrowed his gaze at her. She gave him a lopsided smile and the truth. "I was scared."

That dark, mysterious gaze widened, and the light inside that she'd seen before slowly flared back into life.

"Scared?" He shook his head. "How the devil could you

be scared of me after that weekend? You had to know by then that I'd never hurt you."

"Not scared of you. Scared of getting hurt again. Scared of caring and losing again. Scared of falling so far off the grid that next time I might not survive. Scared of what could be—knowing I didn't deserve it. Or you."

His mouth dropped open.

She continued. "Scared of your lifestyle. It could kill you, you know? Scared of your quick and easy girlfriends because I didn't want to become one—and yet I just had been. I'd never done anything like that before. Promised myself I never would. I held myself accountable to a specific standard."

"And fell into the ghetto by spending that weekend with me?" This time, his tone was incredulous and so was the hurt.

Damn, all she seemed to do was hurt him.

But she had to get it all out. Then he'd realize that they wouldn't be any good together. That he could move on. That it was better that he did so.

"For having that weekend that I'd always wanted. I wasn't like you. I wasn't like your string of girlfriends, and I didn't want to be like them. I wanted to have longer than three-day relationships. To care about the people I went to bed with. Sex was never casual for me."

Her voice dropped. "That weekend I needed you. I wanted you. I took what you offered, and then I walked away." Her voice broke. "I'd always thought I was better than one of your weekend flings, only I ended up falling there anyway. Ended up worse than the other women. They'd at least been honest about why they were in your bed and what they wanted. Me? I just lied to you. To me.

Because I was where I'd always wanted to be," she admitted, "since forever. And I couldn't even be honest about it."

He stared at her in shocked silence, obviously not getting it.

"Don't you understand?" she cried out. "I'm not good enough. I don't deserve you or to be happy. I couldn't give you what you needed." She snorted in disgust. "I should have done more to stop Janice and Francine. More to warn them. Maybe if I'd gone with them, I might have been able to save them. I lost them, and I survived." Tears clouded her vision. "Why me? They were so full of life. They shouldn't have died."

"Ah hell," he snapped, exasperation in every line of his body. "Did you really put me through these last few years, *us* through these last few years, out of guilt? Survivor's guilt?"

Her gaze widened in response.

"Damn it." He reached out and snatched her into his arms. "To think of all the pain I've gone through—"

"Exactly," she cried out, trying to step back out of his arms. "I put you through all that—"

"For being one the smartest women I know, you are the st—"

"Don't say it," she warned.

"Ha. I know the answer to this problem." And he took her mouth with a force that surprised them both. The bite of pain, the hard pressure of his lips, the clamped arms around her back …

And she barely noticed. She kissed him back with all the longing she'd held inside for so long. Finally having the freedom to take a little and to give a lot, she tried to show him how sorry she was. How much she wanted this. How desperately glad she was to be back in his arms.

Until she tasted salt. As in salty tears.

Her own.

"Jesus." He pulled back slightly, his thumb reaching to stroke her swollen lips. The look on his face was one of dismay and shame. "I'm so sorry," he whispered, replacing his thumb with his lips, as he dropped delicate kisses along her mouth, her chin, and up to her nose and her drenched eyes. "I'm so sorry."

She shook her head. "I'm fine. You didn't hurt me."

"This"—he dropped a tender kiss on her lips, then at the corner of her eyes—"and this say otherwise."

She smiled through the tears. "No. It's an outpouring of emotions but not pain." Then she corrected herself immediately. "Outpouring of pain held in for too long."

"In that case …" He pulled her closer and cuddled her against his chest. "Cry away."

And damn if his permission didn't bring on the waterworks. And she bawled. With shaking shoulders, her face buried against his coat, she released the last few years of what she'd thought she'd been handling, only to now realize she'd avoided it and had instead stuffed the pain and hurt deep inside.

ROYCE HELD HER close, his heart full, his mind overwhelmed. Stacy was an incredibly strong woman. She lived in her head so much that she'd used that space to disconnect from her heart. And now that that bridge had been rebuilt, the floodgates opened up between them.

It might take her a bit to reconcile the new connection.

He'd be there to help her.

If she would let him.

He knew she'd take a huge step back if she could right now, just because it would be more comfortable for her. And she had to be feeling raw.

As he worked through his next step, he noted her shoulders were no longer shaking and her sobs had been reduced to sniffles. He couldn't help himself—he cuddled her even closer, his cheek resting on top of her head. She'd said a lot that he would have to consider, not the least about his own behavior. How it looked to others hadn't been a consideration before. From her perspective, he could understand her hesitancy to go in that direction. He'd had similar thoughts earlier. He didn't particularly like her assessment, but he understood it. By the same twisted measure, he was incredibly happy she hadn't led his same lifestyle. How did that work?

Except to make him not feel too good about his own standards.

"What are you thinking?" she asked, her voice low, hesitant.

He sighed. It would take her some time to feel secure at this new place in her life.

"I'm thinking that I'm guilty of the same judgment. I'm personally very happy that you've been more restrained with your relationships," he admitted. "And that's not something I expected to feel. It's never mattered before."

That startled a gurgle of laughter from her.

He grinned, loving the sound and loving her.

Loving her. He paused. Did he?

He hadn't quite taken the thought process that far. He'd been obsessed with her for a long time. Loved being with her. Loved making love to her. But did he love her? Hell, yes. And had probably spent more than half of his life in love with her.

A shout from behind had them both turning around.

Stevie. With two travel mugs full of coffee.

"Oops," Stacy said, "I guess our hour is up." She wiped the tears from her eyes and smiled at Stevie.

Royce? He just glared at his friend, who was giving them that all-too-knowing grin.

Damn friends.

Couldn't live with them and couldn't live without them.

Chapter 27

STACY SMILED AT Stevie, ignoring his wry grin. She knew her crying jag still showed on her face. There wasn't much she could do about it. Besides, Stevie was a romantic. He'd love to think of her and Royce settling their differences. There hadn't been an open war between them, but there'd been a definite cold front.

She accepted the cup of coffee with relief. "Thank you," she murmured. She twisted off the lid and breathed in the aromatic steam. "This smells divine."

"Nothing like a great cup of java to help you overcome all that relationship angst."

"What would you know?" she countered, with a smile. "Your relationships last all of ten minutes."

Royce gave a great shout of laughter at that, while Stevie gave her a wounded look, but, in the end, his eyes were twinkling. "And that's because you won't go out with me," he cried out in a piteous voice. "Now if you would …"

"Ha," she said, with a big grin, "Then what?"

"I might manage twenty!"

On that note of laughter, she turned to smile down at the cabin, knowing most of them had likely seen her and Royce make up. Oh well. Let them. She felt better. That's what counted. And that Royce should feel better. She slid a sideways glance his way and realized he was frowning.

She followed the direction of his gaze.

A person stumbled through the trees. Fell. Got up and stumbled forward, headed for the cabin.

"Good Lord. Who is that?" she cried out.

Stevie turned to stare. Then they all galvanized into action.

They raced across the hill, only to watch the person fall again, and this time he didn't get up.

Royce reached him first, Stevie and Stacy on his heels.

Royce picked up the stranger and ran to the cabin. Stacy pulled out her phone and called for medical assistance. She gave what little details she had, watching as Stevie peeled past Royce to get to the cabin in preparation.

She came barreling in to see Royce lay the stranger in front of the fire, everyone crowding around, as he tried to warm him up.

A scarf was wrapped around his head, and he wore a coat that appeared to be too big.

Royce gently undressed him.

And they all stopped in shock.

Stacy ran up to squeeze in between her brother and Kathleen.

"What's wrong?" she cried.

"It's Yvonne," Royce said, his voice grave. "Only this is not her coat."

Stacy came down beside Yvonne and picked up her icy hand. "I've called it in. Where could she have been all this time?"

"Given she's wearing someone else's coat, do we want to assume she was alone?" George asked in a hard voice, his gaze looking out the window and the mountain behind them. "I suggest a group search the direction she came from and make sure another person isn't in trouble."

Stacy nodded. "Please do. We'll try to get her warm, until the ambulance arrives."

She heard most of them splitting off and getting dressed to search. While Stevie and Royce worked on Yvonne, she stripped off the wet outer clothing and boots. Once Yvonne was wrapped up in blankets, Stacy carried the clothing to the kitchen table and carefully went through the pockets. It was a man's coat. She continued to work her way through the pockets and folds, looking for anything to indicate what had happened and who the other party was. Inside the breast pocket of the big coat was a business card. She pulled it out. "Brian Hennessey."

"What?"

"Inside the pocket is a business card with that name on it."

"Repeat the name," Royce said. She walked over and showed the card to him. He shrugged. "I've never heard it."

She turned it for Stevie to look at, and he shook his head. "Me neither." He turned his attention back to Yvonne.

Next Stacy returned to the boots that Yvonne wore and searched both, including lifting the sole of one and then the other. Nothing. However, they were an expensive leather brand by a high-end company. And new from the looks of them. The coat was 100 percent wool and looked more appropriate for a stroll around town than in a winter resort. However, it wasn't impossible.

She checked the pants and shirt next. Yvonne still had on her long underwear. And all four items were ones Stacy recognized. So she'd been in her own clothes but wearing a man's coat. That wasn't even all that odd.

"Did you find anything, Stacy?" Royce asked.

"No. Nothing useful." She kept the oddities out of the conversation for the moment. She turned back to the men. "How is she?"

"In bad shape."

In the background, she heard the sirens of an incoming emergency vehicle. She raced to the door.

The police SUV pulled up behind the first responder. Yvonne was quickly loaded up and taken away, leaving the three of them to face the police. When they explained who was in the emergency vehicle, Stacy was delighted to see the relief on the cops' faces. No one had expected her disappearance to turn out so well. Stacy showed them the clothing they'd taken off her and the business card.

At the card, the first officer asked, "Do you know this name?"

Stacy shook her head. "No."

"Are you sure?"

"Yes. I might know his face, but I don't know his name."

"He's the man you found frozen in the snow."

She stared at him in shock. "What? But that means Yvonne was possibly with him? As she's wearing his coat. Only ..."

Royce finished her thought. "Only he died before she went missing."

ROYCE DIDN'T LIKE this turn of events. Arms crossed, he stood in front of the fire, as he listened to Stacy and the cop work things back and forth. The problem was, there was no easy way to work it. They'd found a dead man. Two days later, a friend of theirs went missing and turned up the next day, wearing the dead man's coat.

That didn't make sense, not any way he tried to fit the pieces together. He'd also taken one of the policemen aside and handed over the syringe. The cop hadn't been impressed at not being called right away but asked a few more questions and packed up the syringe for testing.

As the cops made a move to leave, they looked up the hill to see the rest of his group coming back.

George reached them first. "No sign of anyone else," he said, gasping for breath. "We tracked her a long way up but need snowmobiles to go any farther."

"We have someone on the way already. Thanks for checking." The cop pulled out the business card found in Yvonne's coat. "Do you know this name?"

George read the card, a frown on his face, as he replied, "No, should I?"

"It was in the pocket of the man's coat Yvonne was wearing," Stacy said.

He looked over at her, a question in his eyes.

It was the cop who answered. "The card belongs to the dead man you found in the snow a few days ago."

"What?" George reacted in shock. "How is that possible she was wearing his coat then?" He frowned at the others. "Maybe he took it off in his confusion, and she found it while she was in trouble and put it on. It's the only thing that makes sense."

"We'll see," the cop said noncommittally. "There will be an answer."

"There always is," Royce said quietly, his gaze on Stacy, whose gaze hadn't left the business card in the cop's hand. What did she know?

Chapter 28

THE SNOWMOBILES ARRIVED before the police were out of sight. There were two. The drivers stopped, asked for what little information was available, then took off in a rush. There were still a few hours of daylight left.

Stacy turned to Royce. "I'd like to go up there and take a look for myself."

He frowned, instinctively shaking his head.

She nodded. "I know we can't go as fast or as far as the sled, but I'd like to see the trail she made to determine where she was coming from."

"The backside of the mountain."

"But she wasn't wearing her boarding gear, so why was she down there?" Stacy countered. "I'd just like to go."

Royce gave in. He knew she wouldn't give up. She wasn't considered hardheaded and stubborn for nothing. She geared up for a trek outdoors, then turned and said, "George, would you mind grabbing my camera bag, please?"

She waited while he fetched it for her, then, with that over her shoulder, Royce at her side, they headed out. As several snowmobiles had traveled the same track, the walking was easier now. Trudging uphill for the first part, she had a hard time holding back the knot of nervousness inside. She had a horrible feeling this was all connected to something so much bigger but knew they didn't have all the pieces yet. She didn't know if the snowmobile guys would find something, but she wanted to double-check that she hadn't missed something herself.

"So do you want to tell me what we're really doing?" Royce asked.

"I saw something the other day. It was stunning, eerie, and incredibly beautiful. Now I'm wondering if there wasn't something more sinister."

She felt his sharp gaze but didn't take her gaze off the hillside ahead of her.

"I want to know if the direction Yvonne came from was in the same area as what I photographed earlier. If it wasn't, that's great then, so what I saw before was Mother Nature at her best. If it is where Yvonne came from, however, then we need to inspect it closer."

"Do I get to know what 'it' is?" he asked calmly.

"I don't have a problem telling you, but I'd prefer to see your initial reaction, in case it's not the same as mine. I could be imagining this. I just can't be sure."

"Good enough. Where is this place?"

"Where we were the day we were late because I was taking pictures."

"I don't think she came from that direction," he said slowly.

"It depends how far away she might have been."

With that, she fell silent. She needed to save her energy. At the top, she took several deep breaths, as she regained her strength. Ahead, she noted the snowmobile tracks, heading to the right and up. She studied the ridge ahead.

The images she'd seen earlier were around the corner.

ROYCE STUDIED STACY'S face, as she looked at the snowy ridge ahead of them. Concentration glowed from those blue eyes, as she picked out one geographical marker, then zipped across, looking for another. She chewed on her bottom lip—an action guaranteed to drive him nuts. He wanted to tell her to stop it. That her lips were swollen from the abuse. But then he wanted to soothe them with his own lips.

And that she wasn't ready for. At least he didn't think so.

But he could hope.

Then she turned to face him, a question in her gaze. He smiled, shrugged, and turned to study the mountain. She so wasn't ready to know what he'd been thinking.

But that didn't mean he'd stop thinking about it.

Chapter 29

CRAZY THOUGHTS TWISTED inside Stacy's head. Could other cabins be in the backwoods? Could Yvonne have been trying to come home? Was there a cabin close by that they didn't know about? Just because she didn't know about such a place didn't mean it didn't exist. It was a huge resort. This area had been settled for over one hundred years, with many private lots. Cabins dotted the area—out of the way but close enough to all the amenities of the resort. Still, the authorities would know. The search and rescue team as well.

As they trudged forward, Stacy removed her camera from her bag and pulled up the pictures she'd taken the other day.

"What's going on?" Royce asked. "What are you looking for?"

"I thought I saw something the other day," she said, flicking through the strip of photos. "Remember when I was out here for so long?"

"Right, and you appeared to be fascinated with that waterfall?"

"Yes, I was, but what fascinates me now is what's beside it. There was opaqueness to the ice, as if a big black space were behind it."

"Like a cave or something?"

"*Hmm ...*" she murmured, carefully studying the image

in front of her. "I just wondered if maybe there was a cabin or a dwelling of some kind here, likely very old, that maybe Yvonne and whoever she was with—if she was with someone—tripped into and spent the night, then tried to find their way back out again in the morning."

"If they were snowmobiling and broke down, they might have taken refuge, but I can't imagine any other scenario where that would make sense."

"I know." She motioned at the image to the left of the hillside, where the shadow was. An odd-shaped shadow. "Doesn't that look different along there?"

He peered at it, shrugged, and said, "Honestly, not really."

She laughed. "Let's go take a closer look."

It took another ten minutes of slogging through the snow on the tracks that were just crusted enough to hold their weight, until they went to take the next step, at which point they broke through to the soft snow below.

By the time they got to where she had stood before, she was sweating freely and wondering just how healthy she truly was. She groaned, opening her jacket to let in some fresh air. "That's hard work today," she said.

"It is."

She stared up at the left side of the hill adjacent to the frozen waterfall.

She turned to study the scene.

The shadow was as high as the right side. The slope easier. There didn't appear to be any way up, but, of course, there never was, unless you knew the routes.

Royce headed over to the area she'd pointed out, and Stacy fell in behind him. They were halfway there when she heard the snowmobiles.

She couldn't see them yet, but their engines were loud enough to hear over the blanket of snow separating them. She understood they were coming farther off to the left. Renewing her excitement that maybe she was correct, she and Royce kept climbing, finally cresting the small rise, as the sleds bounded toward them.

Up top was a flat stretch of long pristine snow, marred by a set of tracks. The snowmobiles came to a stop. One of the search and rescue team noted that they'd followed the tracks to this area, but it had stopped in the trees. The snow had been trampled in many places, but they hadn't found anything or anyone else.

"Do you two want a lift back?" the first man asked.

Stacy did. Desperately. But she wanted to take a look around her first. Then hearing that the snowmobiles were going back now and not in fifteen minutes, she declined. She stood at the top of the hill and watched them slash their way across the hillside below, heading for the cabin and everyone who waited there. Resolutely she turned. Now that she was here, she had no idea what she expected to find. She was aware of Royce watching her.

Finally he said, "If you tell me what you're looking for, maybe I could help you look."

"It's kind of stupid. I was just thinking there might be a way inside."

"Inside?" he asked cautiously. "Inside what?"

"I think a big cavern is here. A cave. Something."

"And?"

"I was just wondering if that's where Yvonne had been all night."

"And why would she have?"

She could tell he was trying not to say she was being crazy.

"I don't know. But I thought I saw a person in the ice images when I had my camera out before. I had my zoom lens and could see so much but had trouble capturing it. Now it doesn't look the same," she cried out in frustration. "I can't find what I saw before."

"A man?"

She stopped, her temper igniting. "Yes. A man."

He threw up his hands. "Hey, that's fine. Maybe you did see someone here. But what difference does that make?"

She really hated having to tell him. It was her line of work that immediately saw all the good things in life and the bad that were right beside them. In this case, inside them. She refused to answer, instead walking to a small depression in the snow. A tree above them, with its overhung branches, kept them pretty well protected, but new snow had fallen from its boughs above. Hiding whatever was below. She walked closer.

And fell.

Through the snow.

Through the ice.

Through the air to the ground.

She screamed as her world flipped. Cold sharp shards of ice bit at her, and she flailed her arms and legs, trying to stop her fall. Her landing was fast and hard. Stars slammed into her mind.

Dimly in the background, she heard Royce yelling for her.

She groaned.

"Stacy? Don't move. I'm coming down."

She whispered, "Don't." Then realizing he couldn't hear her, she called out, "Don't, it's too dangerous."

"Right," he called out, humor in his voice. "So I'm supposed to just leave you?"

Of course he wouldn't. She knew that. Neither did she want him crashing down with her. They hadn't brought any rescue gear, so he'd need to go back and get some rope. She'd just lie here and rest until he returned.

In the back of her mind, she realized he was talking to someone. Good. Someone else to help. But she also realized that what she really wanted was to roll over and sleep. It would feel *sooo* good. She shifted, trying to get more comfortable, and moaned when she moved her head.

That shifted the sleepy cobwebs from her mind. She had to move. Had to get up. It was the head injury making her want to lie here. She reached up and checked the sore spot, but her fingers weren't sticky, so the wound hadn't broken through the skin. Good. It was just a stunner of a crack. She shifted gently onto her hands and knees and managed to sit on her haunches and look around. Fallen snow and ice were everywhere. She snatched up her camera, grateful to see it still in good working order. She glanced up at Royce, who slowly came down the snowslide, making a rough set of steps as he came.

"I'm okay," she said. "I just saw stars for a moment."

He kept working his way toward her, his gaze intent. "Even small cracks like that can kill you."

"I do know that," she said in a conversational tone. All too well. The last case on her table had been a woman who'd fallen while skiing and had refused medical attention. She'd not been wearing a helmet at the time of the accident, and she'd retreated to her hotel room. She was dead the next day from a small bleed in the brain.

"*Right.*"

She laughed. "I will get checked over. I won't be stupid about this. I'm just telling you that nothing is broken and that I'm feeling well. It was just a small tumble."

"Doesn't matter how small. In these conditions, it still counts."

He'd almost reached her by the time she'd decided to try standing up. That worked. She was a little shaky, but being on her feet felt much better. She checked herself over and shook out her arms and legs. "I'm actually quite fine," she said to him as he reached her.

"Better than fine." And he gently tugged her into his arms.

She relaxed against him, happy to know that she could now. Falling was scary, but knowing she wasn't alone and had someone responsible enough to help was even better. That it was Royce was perfect.

After a moment she pushed back slightly, looked up into his warm eyes, and saw the relief and care in his gaze. She reached up and kissed him gently. "Thank you."

"For what?" he asked, his gaze quizzical.

"For being here."

A beautiful light flickered to life in those beautiful brown eyes of his. He tugged her back into his arms and cuddled her close. "Thanks for letting me," he whispered against her hair.

She smiled. She couldn't see much of what they were standing on from where she was. She twisted, still in the circle of his arms, and tried to look around. "What is this place?"

"Likely just another trap waiting for an unsuspecting person to find it." He laughed. "Congratulations for being that lucky person."

"Ha, I should buy a lottery ticket." The walls were fallen snow that had tumbled in with her. With the sun shining down into her pit and reflecting on the snow, it was so blinding she had to use her hands to stop the glare. She slid her boot back and forth and looked down to see a hard sheet of ice under the fallen snow. At least the hollow was big enough to walk a few feet forward and back.

"Do you think you can try getting out," he asked, "or do you want me to call for help?"

She glanced back the way he'd come down. Coming down had been easy. She wasn't so sure she'd get up the same way. There were no visible steps as they'd crumbled under his weight. But she might still be able to climb up. Stepping carefully, as her balance still wasn't perfect, she made it to the bottom of where he'd half-climbed, half-slid down. Standing at the bottom looking up, it appeared much steeper—and much higher than she expected.

"We'll wait for the crew to come," Royce said cheerfully. "I'm not up to climbing that sucker."

"You would manage that easily," she said. "I don't think I can." She stepped up and tried to grab onto a boulder in front of her. It crumbled under the pressure. "There's nothing to grasp. Nothing to step on." As she said that, the first snow step under her boots sank, giving emphasis to her words.

"Exactly. So we wait."

"I wonder how far this fault goes." She took a few steps toward him.

He reached out to steady her, tucking her up closer. "I doubt very far. We could be at ground level where we're standing and the walls on either side of us are just a big snow dump from the cliff above."

"That's possible." She looked up and saw the top of the waterfall and the bare rock. She motioned in the direction where she'd originally fallen. "It looked like an opening was down there."

"Doesn't matter if there is," he said. "We're not exploring." He gave her a stern look. "We've had enough excitement for one day."

Under a hooded glance, she wondered what the chances were of changing his mind.

"No," he said sternly. "We're not looking."

Just then they heard shouts from the rescue team. Stevie's voice was the loudest, as he called out to them.

"See?" Royce smiled. "For once, he has perfect timing."

ROYCE LET OUT a sigh of relief when he and Stacy were back on top of the pit. He wasn't exactly sure what kind of fault had created that trap, but he was so glad Stacy hadn't been alone. Maybe that was what had happened to Yvonne. Except where would she have gotten the coat?

Stacy said, "A heartfelt *thank you* to everyone."

"Let's go," Royce said. "Hot rum toddies sound like the perfect end to a very rough day."

The group slowly trekked down the hillside, Stacy and Royce safely ensconced in the middle. Royce carried one of the ropes that had been used to help them climb back up, as the sides continuously caved in on them, hampering their efforts. Now all he wanted was to be home. Not back in the cabin, although that would be a good place to start, but home in Seattle and his cozy apartment—or in Stacy's cedar-and-glass converted loft would be much better. And her bed.

He wouldn't push her, but, once they were alone, the air

would spark and fire between them, with no help from him. They'd be tearing up the sheets in no time. He doubted she was ready for that at the cabin, due to a lack of privacy.

But, after all the accidents and weird events, he wouldn't let her sleep alone. Good thing he'd moved his stuff up there last night. They were supposed to stay a few more days, but he could see this curtailing the festivities. Personally he'd go home tomorrow, if he could get Stacy to go too.

Then again, if they could get a fun day out of this, it would end the vacation on a much better note, even if they did cut it short by a day or so.

Stacy's cheeks were bright red by the time they made it to the cabin, shedding their outerwear and their boots in the boot room first. Just one step inside the main cabin, and Royce smelled the wonderful aromas. Kathleen had stayed behind and had made coffee and had a thick beef stew simmering. Just the smell alone was heavenly. After standing in the cold as long as they had, Royce was chilled and starving. He doubted Stacy was feeling any differently.

She was likely worse. He could see the fatigue in her eyes again. Damn it, she was supposed to rest while here. Regain her strength.

"I'm fine. Stop worrying."

"Not going to happen," he muttered. "This vacation has been nothing but hell."

There was an odd silence beside him. He turned to look at her, wondering what he'd said or didn't say. "What?"

"It certainly has had some low points, but there have also been a few highlights." She squeezed his hand.

Damn. He lifted her hand and kissed the back of it. "That there has been," he whispered, hoping it was only loud enough for her to hear.

It wasn't.

"That's enough mushy stuff, you two. Keep walking."

Geoffrey and Stevie gave the two of them a gentle push deeper toward the living room. Stacy rubbed her hands together, appreciating the warmth of being inside and out of the elements. Standing in front of the fire was heavenly. Royce headed for the kitchen and got two big mugs. He made hot mochas and laced them with rum, before taking them back to Stacy. She sat on the couch, her feet in front of the fire.

He knew that, with a hot meal, a hot drink, and a hot fire, she'd be asleep in no time. He envied her.

She was talking to Stevie in a low voice, as Royce approached. "I know I saw something. I'll go back up there tomorrow."

He stopped in front of her. "You're not going anywhere near back there." His voice was hard, cold. Damn it. When would she quit?

She smiled sweetly and said nothing.

He didn't trust her. Taking the spot next to her, he leaned his head back and waited. But she surprised him by letting the subject drop.

She sipped her hot drink, stopped, and sipped again. "This is really good."

That was an understatement. But he sipped his, just glad to be under cover and safe. The wind was picking up, and, sure enough, there'd be a snowstorm again tonight. Then again, that's partly why they came here. Winter playtime.

Only, so far, there hadn't been much fun.

UNBELIEVABLE. HE COULDN'T *understand how he'd gotten so*

lucky. Unlucky to begin with, then lucky. And he'd stick with the lucky part. It was crazy good, but, at the same time, he couldn't hold his hot rum toddy in his hands, as they trembled so badly that it would be noticeable. And this wasn't the time for a show of nerves.

Unless they were nerves of steel. Odd that he was reacting to today's close call so badly. Why this time?

Because it was the closest anyone had come to his space. His private space. He had never shared that part of the mountain. Well, except for one other. That person understood a part of him. He loved to snowboard down that strip, climb the frozen waterfall, and enjoy his surroundings.

He had never intended to share that pristine wilderness.

If Stacy went back up—oh, yeah, he'd heard her talking about it—well, she may have gotten off lucky today, but she wouldn't have the same luck the second time.

He'd make sure of it.

Chapter 30

STACY TOOK HER bowl back to the kitchen and filled the sink with hot water. She'd do the dishes now, in case she crashed early. She could feel her energy disappearing with the tick of the clock. Too many shocks and adrenaline rushes today. Her system was on overload and would shut down soon.

She felt it draining with each dish she washed. Finally she was done. She needed to talk to Royce about what she'd seen and what she'd thought she'd opened up there, but she knew he wouldn't be receptive, and she wasn't up for the fight.

If she went to bed soon, she could review the pictures she'd taken, some from the other day and others from today.

She visited for a few minutes longer and then said good night. Within minutes, she was ready for bed and climbing the stairs to the loft. Alone, she pulled out her camera and flicked through to the set of images she took earlier. She wished she had her laptop or tablet, but she didn't, so she could only look on the small screen. Not ideal.

She shifted to the images she took today and went back and forth several times, trying to figure out what she'd seen. After a few moments, her eyelids started to droop.

With the images still up, she crawled into bed and studied them. When she couldn't hold the camera anymore, she closed her eyes and rested. Something was bugging her. Something she wished she could pull out from the back of her mind.

But she was too tired.

As she was drifted off to sleep, she heard someone climbing the stairs. Royce. Her eyes flew open. Or was it? Her muscles tensed as she waited.

He was so quiet, she wasn't sure. She rolled over, so she could look at him. And found Royce staring down at her.

"Hey." He sat down on the side of her bed. "I had hoped you would be asleep by now."

"I was looking at my pictures," she said sleepily. "Seeing if I could figure out what was bugging me."

"And did you?" He stroked his fingers down her cheeks, soothing, caressing.

She made a tiny shaking movement of her head.

"See? It's probably not there."

She gave a sleepy smile. "Maybe."

"So forget about it right now. And sleep."

"Can't. I keep seeing the image in my head."

He reached down and picked up the camera, flicking through the images one by one. He stopped at one, then another. He held up the one and turned it, so she could see what he was looking at. "This one?"

"No." She grabbed it and moved through the images again. "These."

He looked at the images and then down at her, before returning to study the images. He angled the camera slightly toward the light, frowned, went to the next one, and then the next one. Finally he sat back. "*Huh.*"

"Yeah. What do you see?"

"Maybe a cave behind a thin layer of ice. Maybe nothing. Maybe a person." He looked at her again. "What lens did you have for this? It's super close-up, but I've never seen anything this clear."

"I took those that day you were watching, waiting for me." She pushed herself up on one elbow and twisted so she could point out the first image. "I have a wonderful zoom that I used to get these. You can see magnification with each image."

"I can. And this last one is close but not enough to make anything out. This is why you wanted to go today and see that area again? Did you figure it out when you were there today?"

"No. I was hoping to, but then I fell."

"How close to this blackness were we when you fell?" he asked, studying the latest images with a frown on his face.

"Almost right on top."

ROYCE STUDIED THE pictures, his frown deepening. He wasn't sure he liked any of this. There was definitely a dark spot. It could be a woman. Why would anyone be there? It was likely just a trick of the light.

But he didn't like it.

If someone was hiding, why? Was she hurt? Or in trouble? Stacy had taken these days ago. Was it the man they'd found dead? Had he been caught there like that? Or was it someone with a cabin close by? This cabin was remote, so it was all too plausible that there were others around.

What was there at the frozen waterfall?

Now that he could see what Stacy had seen, he wanted to go back too.

He settled back slightly and couldn't take his gaze from

her. "Do you think this has something to do with Yvonne's disappearance?"

She winced. "I don't know. What I do know is that, if a space is there, if a person is there, maybe Yvonne was too."

"Honey, you can't save everyone." He reached down and pulled her into his arms. He held her close, cradled her in his arms, and held her tight. "We'll talk about it in the morning. And I don't want us going up there alone. There might be someone in trouble who needs our help or there might be someone causing trouble. We don't go alone. Got it?"

"Yes."

"Good." He lay her back down. "Now get some sleep. I'll keep watch to make sure that tumble didn't cause more damage than we suspect." He leaned over and kissed her. She threw her arms around his head and chest and pulled him closer.

Just like last time, heat flashed out of control, as she pressed herself against him, her hands hungry, as they held him close.

His lips plundered, and she was greedy in response.

God, he'd never gotten enough before. And he didn't think he could get enough now. She was dynamite. And, for once, she was his.

She heard snickers and laughter from the group below. She motioned with her head, her gaze regretful.

"I'm sorry," he whispered.

Her lips quirked. "Me too."

"Go back to sleep," he said quietly. "Tomorrow is a new day."

She shifted to the far side of her bed and threw back the covers, then patted the space beside her.

His eyes lit up. "Are you sure?" he asked, his voice low,

his gaze searching.

She nodded. "I'm so tired that you won't disturb me."

He stood and returned to his bed, where he quickly got changed. Leaving his clothes on his bed, he returned to her side of the loft and slid under the covers.

He tugged her up close to his chest and shifted them both, so they fit on the bed and with each other. She smiled, snuggled in, and closed her eyes.

Listening to her soft breathing, as it deepened and slowed, he realized he didn't want to sleep. His body needed it. His mind and heart, however, didn't want to miss this moment. He was afraid he'd wake up and find the previous day had been a dream, and she would still be holding him at arm's length.

Right now, with her in his arms, he was happy.

LOOK AT THEM. All of a sudden they were a couple. Just like that. From enemies to lovers. He couldn't hear anything from the loft at this point, but knowing they were up there together made his blood boil. He tossed back his laced hot chocolate and smiled at the others. "All right, I'm turning in. I'm tired myself."

"We all are," someone murmured from the corner.

He couldn't determine which of the three crashed males had spoken. They all were stretched over the furniture, as if the thought of getting up and shifting to their beds was the last thing on their minds.

"You all would get a better night if you slept in your beds and not on the couches."

"Mmm," came a mumble from the corner.

"Your loss." *He walked past a pair of splayed legs, and he wasn't sure, but that looked like Kathleen asleep on the floor.*

Whatever.

The more trusting they were, the easier it would be to set his plans in motion.

Except he needed sleep himself. Then he'd take the next step.

Chapter 31

SOMETIME IN THE middle of the night, Stacy woke to heat, fire, and ice. Warm hands inside the back of her shirt and a chill to the air.

She opened her eyes, shifting back slightly to look at Royce's face. And saw his heated gaze staring down at her. "About time you woke up," he murmured thickly and lowered his head.

With her arms around him, she abandoned herself to the moment and his embrace. He deepened the kiss. Her lips parted, letting him inside. She moaned, the tiny sound catching in the back of her throat.

"*Shh*," he whispered, his lips trailing down her cheek. "It's after midnight. The others are asleep."

Her gaze widened, and she froze. The heat from his breath bathed her neck and throat, sending shivers down her spine. She thought about protesting—until his wicked fingers slid around her ribs, before climbing a little higher. When his hand closed around her breast, she gasped and arched.

"*Shh*."

The effort to hold back, when her nerves were screaming into awareness, was excruciating. He bent his head and took her nipple into his mouth and suckled.

She whimpered once, twice, then again, her body twisting in the dark of the night. She couldn't hear anyone else up, but she couldn't really hear anything over the pounding of her heart and the rasp of her shirt, as he lifted it up and over her head. Cold air hit her fevered body. She wanted him. Oh God, she wanted him. She slid her hands down his hard body, realizing he'd already divested himself of all clothing.

She wanted to explore him, as his hands were making mincemeat of her. In front of her own eyes, she had turned into a mewling kitten, desperate for more. She stroked his back, his chest, and his long powerful arms, before sliding her hands down to his buttocks, where they rested for a long moment, loving the feel of the muscles, hard and hot, beneath her fingers. He shifted his attention from her breast, as his fingers slid down to the curls already damp with need, her pajama bottoms having somehow disappeared long ago. She parted her thighs, giving those devilish fingers access. And shuddered with the effort of holding back her cries, as he gently parted the folds and slid one finger in. She dug her nails into the taut muscles of his back, tugging him closer.

He shifted, settling himself between her legs.

She gasped, her back arching, his lips coming down on hers to hold in her cries. He settled in such a perfect spot and yet … not. She almost couldn't bear it.

Supported on his elbows, he slid his hands up to hold her head still, while he dropped kisses on her chin and nose, as she wiggled frantically beneath him. He kissed her again, but it was tiny teasing kisses, … so not what she wanted.

He held his hips back and away just enough …

Enough. Her hands, eager and hot, slipped between their bodies to stroke him.

"Oh no you don't," he whispered, reaching down to

grab her hand. Instantly she lifted up and kissed him with all the passion she'd kept pent-up.

He shuddered, pulled her hand up to rest on the pillow beside her head, and sank into her willing, waiting, wet body.

She opened her mouth to cry out her joy. Instantly he sealed her mouth with his own. He stroked in and out, slowly, lightly. Going a tiny bit deeper each time.

She lost track of time. She couldn't see anything. She could only feel, as her body raced to the end of the road. It knew what was coming, knew the end would be something glorious, and she couldn't hold it back. Couldn't prolong the moment. It. Had. To. Be. Now.

Her climax ripped through her. Silent. Powerful. Explosive.

She floated in the rainbow of sensations, dimly aware of Royce's own explosive release, right before he collapsed beside her. She slipped her arms around him, holding him close.

"Are you okay?" he asked a few moments later, worry in his voice. He kissed the corner of her eyes, and she realized that she was crying. Tears of release. Tears of relief. Tears of rejoicing.

Best thing ever.

SO GOOD. ROYCE lay in bed, listening to Stacy's heavy breathing, as she slipped back into dreamland. At least he hoped her dreams would be sweet and joyful. He knew his would be. He was so damn happy right now. Emotions swamped him, and he held back the sudden burning in the corner of his eyes. But damn it, he wanted to cry. For joy.

She'd never left his heart. He'd wanted her back in his arms for so long. Wanted her back in his bed for so long. His arms squeezed convulsively.

She murmured a gentle protest. He immediately relaxed and dropped kisses on her head, "It's fine—sleep," he whispered.

She snuggled closer and swelled his heart.

He had no idea what time it was. The cabin was dark. He couldn't see the top of the stairs from where he lay, and no light shone from the windows below. And he would have seen light in the room if dawn had arrived.

He heard a few sounds below. An odd rustle. Someone snoring. That made him grin. That would be Stevie. That guy could move mountains with the force of his snore.

There were a few other gentler noises, but nothing out of the ordinary.

With Stacy slumbering gently in his arms, he felt his own worries slip away. Surely they were all safe for the night?

THEY'D NEVER BE safe.

Or maybe it was more a case of some of them would rest forever. Soon. At least one of them.

It was all in the planning and in the execution. The reason he hadn't been caught? He was careful. Damn careful. And, no matter the temptation, he'd wait until the timing was right to make his move. In the meantime, he'd continue to imagine the possibilities.

After all, an artist was only as good as his or her imagination.

And he'd never come up short yet.

He wasn't about to start now.

Chapter 32

STACY COULDN'T KEEP the smile off her face the next morning. George teased her mercilessly. Thankfully he kept it generic, so not everyone would know, but, from others' hidden grins, most did. Stevie had given her a hug in the morning, an unusual thing for him to do.

He'd whispered in her hair, "Another one bites the dust."

She wasn't sure if he'd been referring to her or to Royce. She'd hoped Royce, considering the laments Stevie had poured out over the years, about losing his boarding buddies to women. More to the point, the women had usually added to the men's life, but, to Stevie, there was something completely male about going to the mountain and blasting down at psychotic speeds in conqueror mode.

Not that she saw Stevie as a conqueror type. But he did.

She could see Royce fitting that role. She perked up. That would be a good thing in her opinion. He was on his way to becoming a lawyer. Something he never advertised. It was seriously hard work, and few recognized it. He'd also had a later start than most.

Stacy understood. Getting her degrees had been nothing short of brutal—but with a difference. She'd at least enjoyed the knowledge, the learning, the problem solving. And the puzzles. She'd always loved puzzles as a kid. They'd been a highlight on her Saturday evenings to do one with her grandpa. Nostalgia hit, as she thought about those evenings so long ago.

Her gramps had died close to ten years ago now. His death had hit her harder than expected.

Then there'd been more deaths, like her aunt, followed by her grandmother. All older people, all dying well past the first bloom of life.

She shouldn't have been as distressed by those deaths as others, but they'd had an accumulated effect that had been blown out of proportion with the sudden and tragic loss of her two best friends.

Her job was separate from her personal life. She excelled in death at work and was terrified of it at home. She'd become a workaholic, burying herself in death to avoid the reality of what death really was. She was sure a shrink would have a heyday with her crazy mind-set. But death at work was fine. Death at home was not. She honored death at the one, so she didn't have to deal with it at the other.

It was as if she'd gone into this line of work, thinking that would garner her a special pass from death in her private life.

When it hadn't, she'd felt betrayed.

Stupid.

But enlightened. She'd have to ruminate on that a little longer. Maybe find another few truths that were a little too close to home for comfort but were the better for being brought into the light.

"Thoughts?" Royce asked beside her. She threw him a sunny smile. "Nothing special."

He quirked an eyebrow, but she turned away. Most of the others would try to find some sunshine and empty runs before the day became too busy. They'd all decided to stay for one more day, just to see if they could leave on a good note.

George had called the hospital to check on Yvonne, but she was in a coma. Still, she was alive. That's what counted at this stage. She'd pulled through the night, and every extra night gave her body a chance to heal.

"Okay, we're ready to head out. Everyone got cell phones? We've had enough problems this week, let's have no more." Geoffrey turned to look at Stacy, as if to say he knew she'd be the one to have problems.

She smiled and waved at him.

He sighed, turned, and headed out the door into the bright sunshine.

Stacy grabbed the pot of coffee and refilled her mug. Being up late meant most of the others had eaten and had their fill of coffee, long before she'd even made it down. Royce and George had been speaking quietly in the corner. She had a good idea about what. Now that George was walking out, she could relax alone with Royce. Although, as she turned to the bedrooms, she realized she hadn't seen Kevin. "Where is Kevin?" she asked Royce.

He looked at her and shrugged. "No idea. I didn't get downstairs much before you did, and he wasn't here."

"He must have gone out already then."

She turned to stare at the back bedrooms. "Unless he is still asleep?" She walked down the hallway, checking the doorways as she came to them. There was one closed door. She wondered about opening it. She turned back to Royce and motioned. "Do we open it? He could still be asleep."

"True." Royce grabbed the doorknob, turned it gently, peered inside, and then withdrew. Kevin was still sleeping.

"Oh good." Stacy stepped back, as he closed the door. "Kevin was pretty exhausted last night."

"Hell, we all were."

"True." She returned to the living room. "I need food. What about you?"

"Yes." Together, they made up a hearty bacon-and-egg breakfast. Happy in the glow of a new relationship, with the added warmth of knowing this was their time, Stacy fought back the worry that the bubble might burst.

She deserved happiness.

But it felt fleeting. As if it wouldn't last. She figured that her previous experience with Royce was behind it all and tried to toss away the feeling.

They polished off their breakfast and did the dishes.

"Do you want to go skiing?"

She smiled at him. "I want to go back to that corner."

"Well, as that's not happening, at least not right now, how about a few hours of skiing instead?"

She sighed and agreed. It took a short while to get dressed for the weather, to grab their gear, and make their way to the lifts.

The sun was shining. The sky was blue. The wait lines for the lift were short.

It was a perfect ski morning. They sat on the chair, climbing up the mountain, loving the moment. At the top, they slid off the chair, cut around the people standing at the top, and dove off the edge of the run. Royce was a scary boarder, and he loved to play in the parks, whereas Stacy was a great skier and loved doing runs through the trees.

Together they found a middle ground and raced, laughed, and raced some more. By the time they had several runs under their belt, Royce suggested they try a couple different ones. And for the next couple hours they skidded, swerved, and explored new terrain.

Her cheeks were cold and her lips chapped by the time they decided to take a break. She didn't want to go to a restaurant. Maybe the cabin was empty, and they could have it to themselves.

Royce pointed out the break in the trees. "Shall we go back for some food?"

She nodded. They cut into the side run and came to a peak. She recognized the area. She motioned toward where they'd been yesterday. He frowned, considered it, then shrugged his shoulders. They wouldn't get far because of the angle they were coming in from. She led the way, trying to stay high, and that also meant she couldn't ski fast. She was going almost uphill. Royce held his speed a little better. Finally they were across the top and could descend to the other side.

They were still not at the place where she'd fallen, when Royce pointed to the right. "Stacy," Royce called out. "Look."

She studied the area, the dark shadow that she had to consider was open space behind the rock face. But nothing was different about it today. Her gaze shifted higher to the area where she had fallen.

"Damn it," she whispered beside him. "Someone is up there."

ROYCE ADMITTED TO being curious about what they'd see today, when back at this spot. Especially after Stacy's images were caught on camera. But to see someone walking around up there was odd indeed. They were too far way to identify who it was, and he couldn't even be sure whether it was a man or a woman.

"Could it be the search and rescue team putting up warning barriers?" Stacy asked in a reasonable tone.

"Hell, this whole area is out-of-bounds." They only came this way because it led to the cabin, without having to drive around the roads.

He glanced over at her to see her frowning up at the ridge. He turned back to stare himself. And sucked in his breath. As he watched, the man disappeared from view.

"He's gone down that damn hole," she whispered. "If he's alone, he might get stuck."

"First, we can't see what he's done. Second, he's obviously brought gear and set it up to get out on his own if that's the case or ..." But he couldn't think of an *or.*

Stacy had. "Or he knows the area and has another way out."

They waited to see if the man would surface again.

He didn't.

The two returned to the cabin in silence. With their winter gear off and drying by the heater stove, Stacy rummaged in the kitchen to warm up leftover stew. It didn't take long. And that, with a couple buns and a fresh pot of coffee, was lunch.

They never said a word. They both sat down on the couch and ate in silence. When Royce finished his bowl, he set it down on the table and said, "We'd better go check."

He glanced over at Stacy, still eating her stew, the rosy flush on her cheeks calming down. He knew the combination of heavy activity in the cold, followed by a hot meal, would have a deadly effect on her energy. She'd likely need a nap. But he couldn't get what he'd seen out of his mind. He also didn't want to drag Stacy back up that hill. Not that she would allow herself to be left behind.

Leaving her alone here wasn't an option. He glanced down the hallway to where Kevin had been sleeping. The door was ajar. Good. So he'd gotten up and probably hit the slopes. It was a perfect day for it.

He turned his attention back to Stacy, her bowl now on the coffee table beside his. She was curled into a ball beside him. He wondered if he should go alone.

"I'm going to power nap for twenty minutes, then we'll go."

He glanced at his watch and considered that. It was just after one-thirty, so lots of daylight still left yet, and they'd be out in the better part of the afternoon. So that worked. While she slept, he got up and cleaned away the lunch mess.

They still had lots of food, particularly if they were cutting the trip short. There was talk of one or two people staying behind, if the others left early, but no decisions had been made, and the further away they were from the incidents, the more people were inclined to stay for the rest of the week.

For all the sadness and difficulties of these last few days, Royce couldn't regret coming. And, if he had to leave early, at least he knew he'd be leaving with Stacy. He could always come back another week.

When he was finished, he went up to the loft and removed his heavy sweater. He wouldn't need it this afternoon.

When he came down, Stacy was already sitting up and rubbing the sleep out of her eyes.

"Hey, how was your nap?" he asked, sitting down beside her and tugging her into his arms. He kissed her gently, wishing they hadn't seen that man earlier. Royce wouldn't be going anywhere but to bed right now otherwise. And that's so where he wanted to be.

She gave him a bright-eyed smile. "It was good. I'm ready to go." She motioned to the coffeepot on the stove. "Any left? We could take a thermos up with us."

"I'll get it," he volunteered, hopping to his feet. She was right. A thermos of coffee up there would be good. "Are you taking your camera?" he called back to her.

"Absolutely, the view of the cabin and the whole valley is spectacular from there."

"Too bad we don't have a snowmobile. It would make this trip a piece of cake."

"What's the matter, tired?" she teased from the doorway, a bright smile on her face.

"Ha. Tired of the problems, yes. Physically tired, no." And he waggled his eyebrows.

"Down, boy." She laughed. "Let's go. The others could come in at any time."

He stopped and considered her words. "That's actually a good idea. Then we'd have backup."

"No, we won't have enough time, if they don't get here soon enough," she said. "We'll text them all and leave a note behind." She turned around and headed to the living room, calling back, "George left his scratch pad here. I'll write him one on that."

Royce took the thermos out to the boot room, where he started getting dressed to go outside again. Stacy joined him, and, within minutes, they were fully dressed and back out in the winter wonderland.

Chapter 33

STACY LED THE way back to the frozen waterfall. With the sun melting the top layer, they still had an icy layer underneath to contend with, but, in her winter hikers, she had good traction. She wasn't as tired as she expected to be right now, and it was too beautiful out to be anything but amazed at Mother Nature's artwork.

With the bright sun twinkling off the white canvas, and the ice reflecting and refracting at will, the colors of the cold air could be glimpsed in some unexpected spots. It was amazing. She stopped to take several photographs as they walked.

Royce stood at her side. He never asked her to speed it up or what she was looking at, seemingly content to let her take her time.

Something she appreciated.

"That's probably good for here." She took several steps forward and exclaimed over a large snowflake pattern frozen into the top of a melted, then refrozen surface. "I can't resist." *Click. Click.* She sighed happily and turned to look at how far they'd come. As she studied the distance, something caught her attention from the corner of her eye. Stevie and Kevin were walking down the slope toward the cabin.

"Stevie!"

Sure enough, he turned, saw her, waved, and veered toward them.

"Where are you two heading at this hour?" he asked. He was covered in snow, as if he'd tumbled through a few snow banks, but he wore a big smile.

"We're going back up to where I fell in," Stacy said, holding up her camera. "I want to take a few shots."

Stevie rolled his eyes and grinned. "Figures. Please don't fall in again."

Royce shook the coil of rope he carried over one shoulder. "Just in case. She does seem to get into trouble a lot."

"Hey, that's not fair," she protested. "It's not my fault."

"It isn't, but it is," Royce said, by way of cryptic answer.

"As if that makes any sense," she scoffed. She turned back to the cabin and motioned at it to Stevie. "Are you cutting the day short? That's not like you."

"Yeah, I argued with a tree back there." He gave her a sheepish, lopsided grin. "Figured it might be a good time to call it quits for the day. I've been going strong since early morning. Besides"—he patted his stomach—"I'm starving."

"Me too," Kevin said, nudging Stevie down the hill. "I am not used to days like these. I didn't prepare enough."

"Prepare?" Royce asked, eyeing Kevin's big grin. "Prepare how?"

"I woke up and realized everyone had left, so I ran out the door, without eating breakfast," he said, laughing. "Time to fix that."

With that comment, the two took off down the mountain, creating a new path in the snow. Stacy couldn't resist. She pulled out her camera and took several shots of the two friends sauntering down to the cabin. She could just imagine all kinds of captions for these photos.

Still grinning, she turned back to find that Royce had

started to climb the slope, slashing across the hillside. "We're almost there," he called back.

"I'm coming."

The rest of the climb was harder work, but she made it to the top without too much effort. After a moment to catch her breath, she took off her jacket and cooled down.

Royce watched her. "Just be sure you don't catch a chill."

She nodded. "I won't, but walking into the sun was harder than I expected today."

"We've also put in a good day's work already. You should be tired." He walked a couple steps toward the crevasse, stopping a safe distance away. "Good. No one is here. Take your look, snap a few photos, then let's head back."

It was a good idea. Now that they were here, it was hard to see anything menacing in the area—except for the pit itself. Since no one was lying unconscious or injured below, the man they'd seen had to have left safely. He probably worked for the resort. Snowmobile tracks were around, but it was hard to tell how old they were.

She took several pictures, careful to stand back. If she were higher, looking down, she could take better shots, but there wasn't much option to do that. She gave the pit a wide berth, as she walked around. "Do you see tracks from whomever we saw earlier?" she asked.

"There were lots of people here yesterday," Royce said, looking at the trampled snow. "Who can tell?"

She walked farther out, looking for any sign that someone had approached from a different direction. The two snowmobiles had raced over the top of some tracks, almost obliterating them. "True enough. It's hard to see anything anymore."

"Not to mention the temperatures today were much warmer, with some melting going on."

She nodded. Still, she couldn't help take a few photographs of the snowmobiles' tracks and the trampled ground around the hole. "It's deeper than I remember."

"No wonder. You fell in and didn't really get a good look at it afterward. You were hustled down to the cabin to warm up."

She stared down the crevasse and wondered why it bothered her so badly. She glanced up at the frozen waterfall then back down at the deep slice in the snow pack. She'd come here to solve one problem, and instead she'd opened up another. Loathe to leave just yet, but knowing Royce was getting impatient, she walked for a last time to the far side.

And saw the blackness behind the fallen snow. She'd had to see it just right. The stack of snow hid the shadow. Even if they didn't explore what was behind it, that snow should be collapsed, so that someone else didn't fall in. "Royce, we need to do something about this."

He walked over to stand at her side. She studied his face to see if he saw what she saw and noted his narrowed gaze, as he caught sight of the blackness. A long tree branch lay to the side. She dimly remembered seeing someone using it to test the edges of the fault line.

Royce picked it up and knocked down the tower of fallen snow protecting the space behind. He frowned. He tried knocking more snow off the top so the space would open up, but instead his branch hit something hard. They rushed over and approached from the side, his stick carefully brushing the snow of the side. It was an overhang made of rock. But what was under it?

"I want to see what's down there."

Royce glanced over at her. "It's likely nothing."

"Likely, yes," she admitted. "That, however, isn't the same thing as knowing for sure. We saw someone jump down here. There's no sign of anyone. Where did he go?"

They both studied the darkness. "He probably used a rope and climbed back out. I'll go," Royce said. "I'll set up the ropes first, then I can climb back out, if need be."

He attached the one end to the big tree standing guard for so many years, then threw the rest over the edge.

He'd brought a rope ladder.

She hadn't seen one in ages. "I didn't realize that's what you were carrying."

"I figured it was the easiest way to get out, when the sides keep crumbling in on us here."

"Good thinking," she said. And it was. It was brilliant. Then Royce thrived on this kind of thing. He was a definite Boy Scout and followed the *be prepared for anything* motto very well. She'd always been amazed at the things he'd pulled off with her brother. Some were stupid, and some were damn good. Now he carefully skittered down the slope into the narrow ravine and called back. "I'm down."

"Test your ladder first," she said.

"A little late to test if I'm already here," he teased. "But I will, if it makes you feel better."

Under her watchful gaze, he climbed up several rungs easily. "See?"

"Good. Then I'll come down too."

"No need. You stay up and keep watch. I'll check out this cave, and then we can leave."

"I want to see too," she complained.

"You do realize that you could be making a big deal out

of nothing. I'll see a rock wall and turn around and come right back up there." He glared at her. "Stay where you are, and I'll check. If there's anything to find, you'll see it when I knock back the snow."

He turned his back on her and started doing just that. It was evident very quickly that he would need a couple minutes to clear a path.

She watched and waited from up above. Every once in a while she turned around to find the pristine countryside empty and untouched. No one was out here but the two of them. It should have made her feel better, but instead it was too empty. No bird flew past, no songs or warbles sounded on the air. It was still, watchful. Waiting.

She hated that her imagination was on overdrive, but it didn't seem fanciful that Royce just might find something that the birds already knew about.

ROYCE WORKED STEADILY to drop the snow to a reasonable-size pile that he could get around and see what was behind the mass. He'd seen many different footprints, which made no sense. After all, there wasn't—or shouldn't have been—anyone down here. Except for the man they'd seen.

Maybe it was just curiosity, but …

Stacy didn't believe it, and her nervousness made him question his own assumptions. The footprints added to his concern.

After a moment, he peered in. All he could see was black. He pulled out his flashlight and turned it on. The light shone deep into the cavern. And it was huge. And there were more footprints.

Damn.

He puzzled over it.

It wasn't criminal to have come in here. It wasn't even abnormal. This was a hugely popular resort for skiing, snowboarding, snowmobiling, spelunkers, and climbers of all kinds every month of the year.

Yet why the secrecy?

Or was anything secret about it? He backed up slightly, so that he could turn to talk to Stacy, only to rear back as she stood right beside him. In exasperation, he asked, "Do you do anything that you are told to do?"

"Sure," she said, with a big grin. "Lots. But only the ones I like."

"Really?" He shook his head. "I doubt it."

"Wow." She bent forward and peered into the blackness. "What is this?"

"It's a cavern of some kind." He turned the flashlight to cast the flare of light across the darkness.

"It's huge," she cried out.

"It does appear to be."

He looked at her and then stepped around the snow pile inside the cavern.

"What an amazing space." She quickly followed him. "Footprints."

He stopped in front of her and shone the light down on it. "It's just one set, I think."

"One set in and one set out," she said. "Or is he still in here? We saw him jump down a few hours ago, if you remember."

"True. But remember that stack of snow I had to knock down to get in here?"

She didn't note that the stranger could have stacked this pile up to hide his tracks in or out regardless of which way he went. "*Hmm*. Maybe not. Maybe he found another exit."

"Maybe," Royce said. "We don't know enough at this point. No way to sort out the tracks." Particularly as they'd just stomped over them too.

"True. The ground is a bit of a mess."

Taking a step forward, she realized they would lose all the natural daylight from outside if they carried on any farther.

And she wasn't sure she wanted to do that.

"Are we going in or going back?" Royce asked.

She winced. "I guess we have to check." She turned to look back the way they'd come. "We should make sure that others know we are here."

"Good point." Royce walked back a couple steps and kicked the rest of the snow away from the entrance so that it would be open and clean. Then he made an arrow in the snow pointing to the cavern. And a big *R*.

She laughed. "Well, if this opening isn't enough of a message, that should do it. We'll have to remember to remove that, just so someone doesn't come upon it later and think we or some other poor person whose name starts with an *R* is in there."

He grinned. "Good point."

As he walked past, she turned to follow him.

Chapter 34

STACY WAS DAMN glad she wasn't alone.

She followed Royce deeper into the cavern. An eerie silence surrounded them, punctuated by the crisp, staccato noise of Royce's footsteps on the icy ground. It was creepy. And scary. She'd seen some rough places in her time, but she'd never done any caving. She didn't like dark places. Or confined spaces. Again she reminded herself of the joy of having Royce with her. He stopped suddenly, and she bumped into him. "What is it?"

"The pathway splits here."

"Where do the footprints lead?"

"Both directions." An odd tone filled his words.

There wasn't room to get past him. She tried to peer around his shoulder but couldn't see much. "Is there a path more traveled?"

"No. I'm thinking they're both well used."

"Recently?" she asked incredulously. "Really? How is that possible?" She slipped closer to him. "That is so bizarre."

"I know." He hesitated. "I don't like it."

Relief flooded her. "Neither do I. I'm just not sure what to do about it."

The silence lengthened, as they considered the ramification of going deeper.

"Leave?" she suggested. "Come back with more people?

It just seems a little …" She couldn't find the word she wanted. "I don't know how to describe it. But I don't like it. At all."

"Back up then, be careful of your steps, and just turn around."

"I am." And she was. "Maybe we should tell the others?"

"I'm not sure which of them to talk to."

She put out her hand to use the wall for support. And heard something behind her. She spun around. "What was that?"

Royce was already walking toward the noise they'd both heard. "No idea." He walked forward with purpose.

She followed, her heart in her throat and her pulse pounding. She knew she'd been the one who had pushed to come here, but, at this point, she'd give a lot to just turn around and go home.

Still, if anyone injured was in here, crying out for help, then they needed to render aid. She'd been in trouble herself more than once, and she couldn't walk away.

But, damn, she wanted to.

Royce turned to the left. She winced. She was thinking turning right was the best bet. But he was closer and might have heard the noise better.

He paused and cocked an ear and listened intently.

She followed but heard nothing. She waited to see what Royce would do.

At first it seemed like he did nothing, but then he crept forward.

Crap. She followed close on his heels. As she took the next step, her foot slipped, and she flailed before going down. "*Ohm*," she cried out.

Royce spun around, his arm out to catch her, but it was

too late. She fell to the ground, her elbow cracking hard on the rock. She sat on the cold floor and held her arm against her chest.

Crouching in front of her, Royce whispered, "Are you okay?"

"Yes, I'm fine." She winced, as she tried to straighten her arm. "It hurts, but I don't think it's broken."

"Here. Grab my hand," he said. With his help, she stood up slowly. There she made a slow check of the rest of her. Everything was fine. Sore, but not too bad. "I'm fine."

"Good. Do you want to go onward or shall I take you back outside?"

"You're not going in any farther alone," she said. "I'll keep going."

He stood, undecided, in front of her. Then he pulled out his cell phone and typed on it. "I'm texting George. And Stevie."

She brightened. "You might as well text them all." That was the best idea yet. Then she heard another noise, this time from behind her to the right.

"What is that?"

"I don't know." Royce stood still, then groaned. "If it weren't for the footprints, I'd be concerned it was bears."

She gasped. "And it still might be."

"Not likely at this point." He nudged her toward the cave entrance. "But we're not taking the chance."

"Ok—"

And then came a louder noise, and, damn it, something that almost sounded like a human moan. But on the right.

"Shit." She looked at Royce's undecided expression and said, "The others are coming, but we need to see what or who that is. Someone might need our help." She walked forward confidently, trying to not nurse her arm. She'd be fine. Someone else wasn't.

There were no more noises to follow, but she kept stepping forward. "Royce, have you heard from anyone yet? We don't want to be sending texts and not have the messages go anywhere."

"I heard from Stevie. Kevin went back boarding, so Stevie is contacting the others and coming up alone. Maybe a half hour."

"Good." Feeling more confident, she turned to go down the right-hand path this time, walking carefully as she went. Royce kept a hand on her shoulder.

"Take it easy."

She stopped. "Shine your light up ahead, will you?"

He obliged and lit up the pathway a little farther down the darkness. She couldn't see anything up ahead. Taking a chance, she said, "Hello? Is anyone there?"

Silence.

She cast a worried look at Royce but kept on going. "Surely someone would have responded."

"Unless they can't."

She twisted her lips and remembered the footprints that came in but didn't leave, and she took another step. The ice was treacherous.

"Go slow." At her look, he grinned. "I know you are. We can also wait for the others to get here."

At that, she turned away and kept moving forward. And heard the noise from straight ahead. She had no idea what it was, but she was determined to find out. She turned another corner, amazed and worried at the depth they were traveling into this cavern.

Royce grabbed her shoulder and pulled her to a stop.

"Wait."

She stopped in place. He shone the light ahead again, from one side to the other, revealing an antechamber of some kind. She marveled at the beauty of what she could see. And the chill that had settled into her bones. It was so damn cold in here. The natural light couldn't reach this far, and there didn't appear to be any opening up top. Although there likely were some—but covered in ice.

She walked up to the entrance to the larger room and stopped. In front of her, lying on the ground …

Kathleen.

"Oh my God! Royce, look." She ran forward and dropped to Kathleen's side. "Oh no. She's in rough shape."

Royce was already taking off his coat and wrapping it around the injured woman's shoulders. "She needs medical help and fast."

"I'll make the calls." Taking the flashlight, she returned as close to the entrance as she could go, mindful of the treacherous footing, making sure she went far enough to get through on her phone.

"Emergency, we've found an injured woman. She's in rough shape. We'll need a rescue team here immediately." She quickly explained the location, adding, "The others from our group are supposed to be on their way up here too."

After hanging up, she looked for Stevie, but, since she was under the rock overhang, there was no way to know how close he was. She returned to Royce's side, as carefully as she could. Stacy couldn't begin to understand how or why Kathleen was here. She was also damn lucky to be found.

Back at Royce's side, she dropped to her knees. "I got through. They are sending a team."

"Good. Let's hope they get here soon."

He was busy rubbing Kathleen's arms and legs, trying to get the circulation going. Stacy took off her coat, and they rolled her on top of it. Kathleen opened her eyes and tried to open her mouth.

Stacy said, "*Shh*. We've found you now. A team is coming to help. Stay strong. Keep fighting." She rubbed Kathleen's cheeks. "Don't give up."

Her head rolled to the side, and she closed her eyes.

"No!" snapped Stacy.

Kathleen opened her eyes and tried to focus on Stacy's face. Then struggled to move.

"Good, she's still got some movement," Stacy said. "Don't try to move. You'll burn through too much energy. You need to conserve your strength and try to warm up."

Her mind churned. Why was Kathleen here? There was no reason for it. She and George had headed out early this morning to go boarding. That they hadn't returned yet was no biggie. They were still well within normal times. She hadn't texted or spoken to her brother at all today, but again that was not unusual.

Besides, she'd been with Royce. She hadn't wanted anyone—or anything—to intrude on their private time.

Now she stared down at the one girlfriend she thought her brother loved, a woman Stacy admired and liked and would be quite happy to have in the family. She couldn't help but worry that something had happened to her brother.

She looked over at Royce. In a low voice, she asked, "Any idea what happened to her? Why she'd be here?"

Royce shook his head. "Tuck up against her back, will you?" He'd pulled Kathleen close to his body, but the opposite side of Kathleen was open to the cold. Stacy sat down on the ground and wrapped her arms around them both. "Did you bring a thermal blanket in that pocket of yours?" she asked. "I left my pack behind." Of course it had emergency weather gear, but they'd only planned to be out for an hour or so.

Best laid plans and all those other mistakes people made on a regular basis.

"And where's George?" she asked fiercely.

"No idea," Royce whispered quietly, letting his warm breath bathe Kathleen's icy face. "He hasn't answered my text."

"Oh God." Stacy was torn between trying to help save Kathleen and going to search for her brother. It was likely that, if one was here, then the other was as well. She glanced into the dark shadows around them.

"You aren't leaving," Royce said in a low voice. "We don't know what happened to Kathleen. If she was attacked, then he could still be here."

"Does she have any injuries?"

"Head wound."

Stacy frowned. "I need to see it."

He shifted slightly and turned on the flashlight. Stacy moved so she could examine the injury. No longer bleeding, but it had bled originally. She explored the injury carefully. A definite skull fracture. She studied the angle and depression. "From what I can see, she was hit from behind by someone taller than her," she said quietly, her stomach knotting and her heart sinking. "This is so not good."

"There's no chance she could have fallen and hit a rock on her way down?"

"I'd have to see in better light, but the blow came from above. If a rock came down from the ceiling, then maybe."

"It only matters in that we might be looking for someone who wanted her dead."

"You think this was deliberate?" She kept her voice light. She couldn't see any other scenario herself but hoped there was one. "Her attacker might not have known the damage the blow caused."

"Or he might be coming back to make sure it had done exactly what he'd planned."

"Good," Stacy said in a hard voice. "Let him. We have lots of people coming too." There was a long silence. She sighed. "What now?"

She stared at him in the gloomy darkness, the flashlight pointed toward the entrance to help guide the others to the right place. He wrapped an arm around her, pulling her close, Kathleen sandwiched between them. After a moment he said, "You do realize that we may have sent out the SOS call to the very person who attacked her in the first place?"

She hesitated, hating the suspicion. The doubts. She knew everyone in their group. They were close to Royce as well. It was tough to glance at people—many you've known for a long time—and wonder if they were trying to kill you.

She whispered, "I know."

ROYCE WATCHED STACY carefully. The last thing he wanted was to have Stacy go off half-cocked and decide she wanted to search for her brother.

His phone jangled in his pocket. He reached down and pulled it out. "Stevie is at the top of the pit."

"Maybe I should guide him down here," she said quietly, staring in the direction where the light shone toward the entrance.

"He should be able to find the rope down." Royce was

busy texting him directions. The next text came in. "He found the rope, and he heard from Geoffrey. He and George are boarding together."

"Thank God." Stacy could feel some of the tension in her shoulders ease back now that she knew her brother was okay. "Stevie should be here in no time."

Royce studied Kathleen's face, hating the pallor. "Damn it, I wish I'd just picked her up and carried her out of here."

"She's better off here and being taken out on a stretcher. We're doing the best we can do for her. The rescuers will be here in minutes."

"We could have her halfway down to the cabin by now."

"And cause her more harm in the process. Here we're warming her as much as we can."

He knew she was right. The cavalry was on its way. He needed to keep Kathleen still and warm. And safe.

The icy floor was starting to creep into his bones. He welcomed it. It kept in check the raging anger that had heated his blood to the boiling point.

No point in losing his head. He had to figure this out. It occurred to him that someone just might be picking them off one by one.

He knew that the biggest group of suspects was his own friend group. That choked him, but he was trying to stay cool and collected. Many other people knew the group was staying here. And many more were finding out every day. That opened up the suspect pool.

"What are you thinking?" Stacy asked.

"Trying to figure out who did this. And why."

"The *why* is particularly disturbing," Stacy said. "I can't see that all of us could possibly have done something to piss off one person."

He gazed at her. "It wouldn't have to be all of us involved. I'm not sure this person cares about there being roadkill. People who got in the way would be secondary. Like in the drugging."

"You think it was the same person?"

His lopsided grin slipped out. "Could you imagine that we've pissed off more than one person during the last while?"

"Not likely."

"Then again …" Royce frowned. "I'm trying to remember if there were any major dissensions about this trip. Some people weren't impressed that you were coming. The timing was also an issue."

Stacy gasped. "Really? I could have stayed behind."

"No," he said sharply. "Don't ever think that. The concerns were more that you might be depressing to the group, if you weren't handling life well on your first time back."

Even in the dim light, he saw the wince ripple across her face. He was sorry for that, but they needed to get to the bottom of the truth here.

"That's fair," she said quietly. "Was anyone very upset?"

"No. Not at all."

"What about ex-girlfriends?" she asked, her voice hesitant.

"None serious for a very long time. None casual for awhile," he said, not even attempting to hold back the humor. "After tasting moonlight, there was no going back to the regular fare."

And her smile lit up the cavern.

He opened his mouth to say something when a shout sounded at the mouth of the tunnel.

"We're here," Royce called out.

Stacy hopped to her feet and ran in the direction of the

noise, before Royce had a chance to stop her.

Then he heard Stevie's voice and knew it was all fine.

REALLY? MORE SHIT happening that wasn't supposed to happen. Jesus. His heart pounded, his hands were sweaty, and he knew he was in serious danger of spending the rest of his life behind bars.

Shit. Shit. Shit.

He couldn't think.

He had to act. Had to find a way out.

Kathleen was to blame. First, she saw him in the kitchen; then she said something to George in front of him about him playing with the wine bottles. Like what the hell? Now he had to deal with both of them. They'd found Kathleen already. Unbelievable. That wasn't supposed to happen. She was supposed to be dead.

Dead people don't talk.

He'd gone to find George. Make sure he plugged that hole. Surely Kathleen would have been fine here for a few moments. Like how long had he been gone? Forty minutes max? He swore it wasn't longer. Surely not.

Just long enough for that meddling bitch and her stud to get in the way. How the hell had they found his secret place? What could he have possibly done wrong?

Now it didn't matter, damn it. Unless Kathleen died. He brightened. That was the trick. She needed to die. For real this time.

Except considering the number of people here trying to help her, he wouldn't get close enough to finish the job. He had to hope that Mother Nature had already done the damage for him.

Chapter 35

STACY RUSHED TOWARD the voice. "Hello? Hello?" she cried out. There was Stevie. "There you are."

She rushed into his arms, so damn happy that help had arrived.

"Easy, easy. I'm here."

"Oh thank God." She stepped back and smiled up at him. "Where are the others? She needs to get to the hospital now."

"Is she hurt?" he asked, splaying the flashlight behind her.

"A head wound," she said. Looking behind Stevie, she frowned and repeated, "Where are the others?"

"I couldn't find anyone else," he said. "I came and hoped the others would follow as they came in."

"Oh no." She ran out to the crevasse and stared up at the waning sun. "Surely they'd be at the cabin by now?"

"They should be there soon," he said, worry in his tone. "But even Kevin went back for a couple more runs."

"Hell." She turned. "Come on. She's not doing well at all." She led the way back to Royce. "Where is the search and rescue team?" she fretted. "I called it in myself."

"They'll be here," Stevie said. "You know they are relia-ble."

"Unless someone called it off," she snapped darkly.

"Kathleen has been hit in the head. She didn't do it to herself."

"Whoa, what?"

She spun around, slipped, and almost went down. Stevie reached out and caught her before she hit the ground, but her knee still wrenched, as she tried to save herself.

"Take it easy. We don't need another accident."

"No." She straightened slowly and winced. "I twisted my knee."

"Badly?"

"No." She tested her weight, limping forward gingerly. "I think it will be fine, but Kathleen is unconscious."

"What is she doing in here?" He looked around, as they slowly made their way forward. "And what is this place?"

"No idea. I thought I saw something like this in the waterfall pictures I took. As we're beside the same area, maybe a series of tunnels are connected inside."

"Good Lord. If it weren't for the circumstances, this would be a really cool find."

"*Cool* is not the word I'd use," she muttered. "But the temperature is definitely working against us at the moment." She pulled out her phone and turned it on, hoping to see a text from someone. There was nothing. "Damn it, where is everyone?" She called out, "Royce, you there?"

There was a faint echo all around them. She hated the fear sitting on the edge of her nerves. She didn't dare move faster.

"Are you lost?" Stevie asked. "Surely you didn't go too deep into this place on the off chance someone was in here."

So much disapproval filled his tone that she sighed. "I thought I heard something, so we ventured inside." She headed down the right-hand passageway. "Royce?"

She wanted to run, but her knee was hurting and complaining. She made it another twenty steps forward and called out again. "Royce."

This time she thought she heard something. She moved faster. And, sure enough, there was Royce, seated on the ground ahead of her.

She dropped to the ground beside him. "How is she?"

He shook his head. "Worse. We need her out of here."

Stevie took one look and opened his bag, tossing down thermal heater blankets. Stacy opened it up, and, with Royce's help, they removed their coats and bundled Kathleen into the first blanket. With the second blanket he'd brought, they repeated the action. Stacy snagged her coat and put it on. Instantly her body warmed. Royce put his on, then bent and lifted Kathleen into his arms.

"Are you su—"

"We must move her. If nobody else is here, we have to get her there ourselves. Lead the way, Stacy," Royce said.

She snorted. "Really? I almost got us lost finding you."

He grinned. "I wondered what took you so long."

She smiled and headed back toward the front entrance.

The light changed the closer they got to the outside. Instead of a bright light, there was only a muted glow. "Shit." She ran to the edge to find a wall of snow piled in front.

As the three stared, they realized what had happened. And that this was likely why the others hadn't come inside. "The snow from that tree must have fallen," she exclaimed. "And remember the pile on the ledge?"

"Yeah. Shitty timing."

While Royce held Kathleen in his arms, Stevie and Stacy kicked away at the snow. Stevie had his little shovel out now, and they managed to punch through enough for them to see outside where the search and rescue team waited, having no idea where they were supposed to be.

Stacy called out, "We're here."

A round of cheers went up.

ROYCE HANDED OVER his burden to the paramedics and stepped back. The men surrounded Kathleen and quickly had her vitals checked and monitored, before packing her up in the sled. They were on their way in minutes. There were two other snowmobiles. Royce insisted that Stacy catch a ride down to the cabin. He'd walk with Stevie. It wasn't far, and there wasn't room for all three of them to ride back. The sun was low and getting lower behind the mountain. The shadowy long fingers stretched across the pristine white snow.

They started down the slope. Royce lifted his face to the cool air and took several deep breaths. "It's good to be alive."

"It is at that." Stevie walked a few more steps, then the words exploded from him. "What the hell is going on?"

"I don't know," Royce admitted. "I think one of us is hunting either all of us or one or two of us."

"Shit." Stevie glared at him. "You think one of us is killing people in our group?"

"I think so. I can't imagine a stranger drugging our wine. It just doesn't fit."

"But anyone could have had access. We don't leave a guard on watch."

"True, but they'd have to know where the wine was and who'd be drinking it."

"Or they didn't care. Maybe they were after the women. One went missing, and one is injured."

"Maybe." Royce pondered that. "But why?"

"The oldest reason in the world maybe."

"Sex? Rape? I didn't see any evidence of a sexual attack on Kathleen." Royce came to a dead stop. "Shit. What about George? He doesn't know yet. What if he's in that damn cave?"

"I saw them both together earlier. They were heading to the peak," Stevie said, staring up at the hillside and the fading light.

Royce stopped and stared. "He left Kathleen to go home on her own? I find that hard to believe."

"She wasn't with him there. And he wouldn't have let her leave alone. She must have come with someone from our group. Someone George trusted. No way he would let her go off alone otherwise." Stevie frowned. "Are you thinking that the person she came back to the cabin with is the one who attacked her?"

"I don't know what else to think," Royce admitted. "I doubt that she went in that cavern on her own. She hates dark spaces. She wanted to go home yesterday, but George wanted to stay."

"Shit." Stevie groaned. "And, if she doesn't wake up, no way to know why she came here."

"George might know. Maybe?"

"And maybe not. In which case no way to know who in our group is doing this, allowing him to sit among us."

"I know. Interesting dilemma, isn't it?"

"No, it's bloody awful."

HE COULD ONLY hope Kathleen died instead of waking up. Damn bitch. Damn interfering bitch. Now what the hell was he

to do?

Part of him knew he needed to just pack in his plan this time around and play it safe. Just walk away. And yet … he couldn't quite do that.

He'd waited years for this. And, after this week, he had no idea when he'd get such a chance again.

It was risky.

Shitty odds.

But he couldn't let it pass by.

He'd just have to figure out a way to make this work.

Chapter 36

STACY CLIMBED OFF the snowmobile and thanked the rescue team.

"Are you sure you'll be okay?"

"I'm fine now that I'm back here, safe and sound," she said, with a reassuring smile. "If no one is here, I'll get the fire going and get a meal together. Thank you so much for coming to the aid of my friend."

"Glad we got to her on time."

"Me too," she said, heartfelt relief in her voice. With a wave, the two snowmobiles took off.

She watched them go. The chill she'd never quite rid herself of flared into an icy awareness again. She turned to look up the hillside, delighted to see that both Stevie and Royce were in sight. She waved up at them and smiled when they both waved back; then she headed inside. The cabin was empty.

And cold.

She'd had enough of being cold. The heater stove had been turned down, but there were still embers. She opened it up and had a roaring fire in no time. It immediately chased the chill from the cabin, adding cheery comfort. She filled the coffeepot and put it on the stove to warm up. Then she wandered into the kitchen to see what food was left to put a meal together. They'd lost track of the menu days ago, and, with the odd schedule and problems, bits and pieces of different food items were left.

The big kielbasa sausages fired her culinary imagination, and she quickly started a Hungarian stew. With lots of peppers, onions, and tomatoes, she could make this happen in time for dinner. She found a partial package of uncooked pasta to use up as well.

Working and happy to be doing so, she chopped, diced, and stirred the basics together. When she heard the men at the outside door, she started in on the smoked sausages. They'd add a major boost to the dish. Actually they were an integral part. A few potatoes sat off to the side. She had to wonder whether they were needed for breakfast or she could add them as substance to the stew. Making an executive decision, she snatched them up.

"Something smells good, Stacy," Royce said, coming into the kitchen.

"Food," Stevie cried out. "Is that cooked?" He reached out and nicked a chunk of sausage and chewed on it, before she had a chance to answer.

"These are smoked." She reached for another one to cut up and found those pieces disappearing from her board faster than she could cut. She held up her knife in a mocking, threatening motion. "Go check on the coffee," she snapped lightly. "And let me get this on to cook."

"The others should be here soon." Royce sat at the table beside her. "Can I help?"

"No, I've got this," she said, happy to be doing something. "It just needs to simmer for an hour, if we can."

"An hour is likely fine," Royce said. "Everyone will have coffee, when they get here. They might need a snack though."

She pointed to the box of food off to the side. "Check in there. Likely to be chips still, maybe bagels that could be toasted. Possibly some crackers and cheese."

He hopped up and started digging through the box. He pulled out everything that appealed to him.

"If you open packages and set out the food onto platters, then we can hand them out when everyone gets in."

He nodded.

She felt his gaze on her, but she kept her head down and on her work.

She didn't want to talk about what was going on. The danger they were all in. She knew a killer was among them. Maybe Kathleen would survive, but maybe she wouldn't. Stacy had to consider that Kathleen's attacker hadn't expected her to. At the very least, he would not be pleased to find out that Kathleen had been found.

Stacy couldn't deal with it all at the moment. She was focusing on what she could do right now. The rest was too much.

"Stacy?"

The warm, caring concern in Royce's voice made her stop, and she realized she'd taken the first pepper and had basically diced it into nothing.

She bowed her head. "I want to go home."

Warm hands slid around her shoulders and tugged her backward.

The tears burned the back of her eyes.

"Understood," he said against her ear.

And damn if that didn't start the tears flowing. "And," she said, her voice choked up as she fought the emotions clogging her throat and heart, "I know that I came to face the mountain, the loss of my friends, my fears, grief, you, any number of other issues, but I don't think I want to come back. *Ever.*"

He tightened his arms around her. She dropped the knife, turned into his arms, and let a damn hiccough escape.

God, she was tired. She didn't know what the hell was going on here, but it was scary and deadly. When would this stop? And would it stop before anyone else got hurt?

She didn't want that to be Royce. Or anyone else she knew.

It hurt to consider one of the people she'd known for years was doing this.

And made her wonder just how well she knew any of them.

A heavy pounding came on the cabin door. Royce released her. "I'll get it."

She brushed her eyes and turned back to finish what she was doing. All the pieces could join the pot on the stove and just simmer.

She heard voices in the living room, as she dumped in the last of the ingredients. She grabbed a cloth to clean up, then poured two cups of coffee and carried them out to see who was there.

She stopped in the doorway.

It was the police. One cop stationed himself at the doorway and watched the proceedings. The second cop was the same man she'd spoken to earlier. He looked over at her. The serious look in his eyes had her nerves jangling. "Do you have news about Kathleen?" Her lips trembled. In a faint voice, she asked, "Is she dead?"

The cop shook his head. "She's still fighting. They took her to Vancouver General. Your other friend is there too."

"Oh thank God." Stacy walked forward and handed the

coffee to Royce and Stevie. She asked the two policemen if they wanted some, but both shook their heads. She rushed back into the kitchen to get herself a cup.

Royce patted the couch beside him for her to sit.

"Now. Please tell us how you happened to find her."

"There's so little to tell, it's scary," Stacy said. "I'm going to have nightmares for years worrying about the 'what ifs.'"

"Explain," the cop asked, his gaze intent.

She sighed. She rubbed her forehead as she tried to figure out how to best say this. "I'm …" And she stopped.

Royce reached out a hand and squeezed hers.

"Okay, let's go back a bit." She glanced over at Stevie and Royce, saw the compassion in their faces, and took a deep breath.

"Three years ago, I came here with two best friends and many others. A group similar to the one here today. We were all excellent boarders and skiers, young and stupid."

"Stupid?"

Of course the cop picked up on that word. "The other two were more reckless, had little respect for rules, and felt that they could do what they wanted, if it wouldn't affect anyone else."

God, this was hard. She hated to say anything negative about the dead, but, dammit, that's what they'd been like. She swallowed a sip of coffee. "They wanted me to go on the backside of Gopher Run one morning, and I said hell no. The avalanche risk was high, and it was out-of-bounds, and I'm a much more cautious skier. I talked them out of it. I hadn't been feeling all that great and wanted to cut the afternoon short." She stared at the cop but saw instead the young adventurous faces of her friends. "I left."

And she saw the understanding in the cop's face. "I went

into the village and did a bit of shopping, then thought maybe I'd meet up with them again. I went up the lift to midstation and texted my girlfriends to meet me. We met up, talked for a few moments, then my brother and his friends joined us. My brother and his friends took off downhill, and I went to follow him, thinking the women were behind me. They weren't."

She gripped her cup, the whites of her knuckles showing. But all she could see was the white from that day. "I turned back to find them …"

She faltered. Stevie came and sat down beside her and held her other hand. She gave him a grateful smile and returned to her story. "I crested over the top of the mountain, and, by that time, I knew where they were. I was on top, looking down, and I could see them way below, having a wonderful time." She smiled wistfully. Then her smile fell away, and she gazed at the man waiting, memories haunting her. "Then an avalanche started."

She stopped and swallowed. "I screamed at them. Of course they couldn't hear me." She turned to stare at the cabin walls. The same cabin they'd stayed at during that vacation. A cabin she'd sworn never to return to. "It hit them hard. They were picked up and swallowed like tiny krill eaten by a blue whale." She sighed and fell silent a moment. "The avalanche went over a cliff and just kept going. Their bodies were never recovered."

There was an odd silence, as the cops digested that. Heavy in the air was the hanging question of how anything that happened a few years ago connected to the series of bizarre events now.

Her smile was crooked, when she answered that unspoken question. "So you see? The reason that I went in that cave is because I'm obsessed. I see those women's faces everywhere on this mountain. I saw a spectacular series of light refracting into women's faces on the frozen waterfall when we were at the other day, and I took a lot of pictures of it." She felt more than saw Royce stand up and return with her camera.

"I hated to come back here again, but, at the same time, I can't get rid of the feeling that I might be able to find my friends and to bring them home." Her voice faltered. "I feel compelled to search everywhere, under every rock, inside every hollow. Even though I know I'm nowhere near where they fell, I can't let go of that little bit of hope."

"You were very close to these friends, I presume?" the cop asked.

She nodded, wiping the tears from her eyes. "Very. It was always the three of us. We were a matched set. Just very different personalities. Janice was the daredevil, and I was the opposite, while Francine was in the middle, but she could be persuaded to go either way."

She paused, and the room was silent, as if they were all waiting for her to say more. When she spoke again, her voice cracked. "I've been lost since."

"Here are the images she saw on the waterfall," Royce said, holding out the camera. Everyone crowded around. There were a few exclamations at the beauty in the ice.

"Wow."

The second cop stepped forward. "I know you. You're the artist who photographs the faces of Mother Nature."

Stacy nodded. "Yes, that's me. Now you know why faces are my focus."

He nodded, staring at the images. The cop clicked through them, until Royce said, "Stop." He pointed at the image. "This is the one that had us going back to look."

In the image was an eerie blackness in the ice, as if a cave were behind it.

"Then she fell in the crevasse yesterday and thought she'd seen something more." He looked over at Stacy for confirmation, then continued. "After we saw what appeared to be a man jump into the same crevasse, we went back and found that cavern opening."

"Did you know that it opened up, Stacy?" the cop asked.

"The geographical layout said it *could* connect to the cave behind the waterfall, and, once I saw that dark shadow at the end of the pit I'd fallen into, I couldn't get it out of my mind." She shrugged. "I insisted on going back."

"Damn good thing," the cop said. "Kathleen would be dead by now if you hadn't."

She knew that. "But why was she there in the first place?"

Royce piped up, "And how much does this have to do with the drugged wine and Yvonne?"

As the second cop returned to his position at the door, the other cop looked from one to the other. "They have to be connected. Too much going on with the ten of you for it not to be connected."

"Eight," Stacy corrected sadly. "There are only eight of us here in the cabin now."

ROYCE LISTENED TO Stacy and her teary explanation. He had known she'd been badly affected by the loss of her friends, but he hadn't *really* known. How could he? She hadn't shared very much with him. Then again, he sat back thinking, three years ago he'd just come out of a short-term relationship with Janice. And likely Janice had told Stacy. Royce should have too. No wonder she refused to see him. To go out with him. Every time she'd looked at him, she would've felt the loss of her friends all over again.

He damned himself for that weekend. He'd often wondered why bright, vivacious, man-eater Janice had come on to him at that time. Just after he'd asked Stacy out and had been laughingly told off as not being serious. Only he had been serious. And the rejection hadn't been easy.

Accepting Janice's offer had been easier, had filled a need to be wanted after too many rejections that had driven down his self-esteem. Part of his pattern back then. After that fateful weekend three years ago, he knew he'd have to change to make something long-lasting with Stacy. They'd both taken years to get to this point. And now it was all rearing its ugly head yet again.

He could only hope she wouldn't push him away. He squeezed her hand, unable to break contact with her, just in case.

The first cop spoke in a quiet voice, "So you saw someone up there, and he disappeared into the same crevasse that you fell into?"

"As far as I could see."

She looked up at Royce, and he nodded. "I saw him too."

"Him? For sure? Not Kathleen?"

"Oh." Stacy shook her head. "No, it wasn't Kathleen I saw up there. At least, I don't think so."

The cop nodded and wrote down a few more notes. "What are everyone's plans at the moment?"

"I'd like to go home," Stacy said. "But, given the time of day, the weather, that won't likely be until morning, and that was our original plan." And she was worried about George. Very worried. Usually he was with Kathleen.

"A storm is coming in tonight, so, if you are leaving, you need to leave now, but not before we have all your contact information."

"We can't leave now. Half our group isn't back yet." Royce checked his watch. "They should be soon though."

Stevie's cell phone went off at that point. "That's George. He and Geoffrey are on the way back."

"No one has told him about Kathleen, have they?" Stacy asked. "He'll want to leave immediately to be at her side."

"If they don't get back soon …" Royce noted, "he may not be able to."

"Speaking of which," the cop said, "we're heading back to the station. If you leave, let us know who and when, so we can keep track of you. And please stick together. Let's have no one else go missing."

Royce stood. "We'll let you know what we decide."

The cop nodded and walked to his partner's side at the door. He turned back once he reached the doorway and gave them a stern look. "Stay safe."

It was a grim warning in light of what was going on. But a sensible one. Royce shook his hand. "Are you sure it's safe for us to stay here?"

The cop stared at him. "I'm not sure it's safe for any of you anywhere. If you split up and head off to separate homes, you won't know who's been attacked, who's gone missing, or who is doing these attacks. If you stay here together, maybe someone will show their hand."

And, with that, they left.

Chapter 37

S TACY SAT IN front of the fire, using the hot mug of coffee to warm her cold hands. The conversation ranged from anger to disbelief. And her brother had yet to make it back. He'd texted several times to say they were coming. The weather had shifted, and high winds were slowing their return trip.

She'd held back telling him anything. She wanted him here, safe and sound. Royce had called the hospital to find that Kathleen had made it there safely, and they were slowly raising her body temperature and were optimistic about her chances. There was no change in Yvonne's condition.

For Stacy, that wasn't good enough. She knew the worst would be telling her brother what had happened. She stood up and stirred the stew, then added the prepped potatoes and some more seasoning. Somehow the dish had grown large enough to feed a dozen, so she hoped the men were all hungry. She was anything but.

Of course, her stomach was still nursing the caffeine she'd poured down to keep her going.

Royce sat on the couch and waited for her to join him. "Are you okay to stay the night?"

She nodded. "I am." She glanced over at him. "As long as I'm not sleeping alone."

"Not going to happen." He slid an arm around her

shoulders. "We need to keep an eye on everyone tonight."

"In more ways than one," she added in a low voice. He hugged her gently. Outside, she heard noises over the wind. "Hopefully that's George and Geoffrey."

"I'll go see." Royce stood, handed her his coffee, and stepped out to the boot room area. She hears the raised voices, as the men came in. Relief flooded her heart. Her brother was home safe. She felt so sorry for him for what she knew was to come.

She waited, her body tense. The loud voices shut off to almost complete silence, followed by yelling like she hadn't heard before. Then a hard bounce, as if her brother had picked up Royce and slammed him against a wall. Her brother was quite capable of that. And, given the circumstances, Royce would likely take it as well.

More shouting and more pounding shook the whole cabin.

When the silence hit again, she got up and walked over. Her brother sat on the bench, his head bowed and his shoulders shaking. Mark and Kevin stood there, looking at the ground, shaking their heads in disbelief. Geoffrey sat in stunned silence.

She didn't hesitate. She walked up to George and wrapped her arms around her brother. Immediately he buried his head against her and held her tight. She held on, until the storm of George's rage had passed. When he was calmer, she sat down beside him and gave him the update that she'd gotten from the hospital. "She's going to pull through, George."

He nodded, his face in his hands. When he looked up at her, she saw the ravaged soul of a guilty conscience.

She reached out and grabbed his hand. "Tell me."

"She wanted to go home today. Get away from here. I wanted to stay one more day. Enjoy the mountain. Make something good to take away."

"I wanted to go too, but, at the same time, I didn't need more bad memories to overcome the good," Stacy replied. "So I stayed for the same reason you did."

"Except she wouldn't have been hurt if we'd left," he said bitterly. "If I'd listened to her, she'd—we'd be safe at home and thankful to be there."

"And now she's safe in the hospital, with staff who know what they are doing."

He gazed at her sorrowfully. "Did she say anything?"

Stacy shook her head. "No. Not that I could hear." She looked over at Royce, who shook his head as well. "Come inside, get warm, and grab some coffee. Dinner is almost ready. We can discuss what to do then."

George let Stacy lead him into the other room, where everyone watched his slow, unsteady steps. Learning of Kathleen's attack had hit him at a level she'd never seen before. And she didn't want to see it ever again.

The blow was too much even for a strong man.

She served him coffee, before returning to the kitchen to stir the pot, simmering away. Then she realized something else. She turned and faced the others. Where was Christine?

"It smells good, Stacy," Royce said.

"Who cares about food?" Kevin said. "I just want to go home." He held up his phone. "I can't raise Christine on the phone. She has friends here, but she should have checked in by now."

"Oh no. Not again," Stacy said. "I was just going to ask where she was."

Kevin shrugged. "But I don't know that it is a problem.

Her phone could have just died. She was really upset at what was going on. Said it was bad voodoo or something and planned to find another place to stay. I didn't say anything to you guys, figured you'd be pissed."

"But we'd understand," Stacy said. "I sure do."

"I think that goes for most of us," Royce said. "We'll have to pack and clean up tonight to leave in the morning. If anyone wants to put in a few runs tomorrow, we can discuss it then."

"I don't," George snapped. "Maybe never again."

Stacy felt the same way, but she wasn't about to join this discussion. She had more reason to never want to return than anyone. Yet, for some reason, she wasn't having the same reaction the others were.

Odd.

Well, not really. She knew why. It had come up when she'd been talking to the cop. About the *what ifs* that plagued her. "For the moment, I presume she's found some place to stay. Keep trying to reach her and get confirmation."

Kevin nodded. "Will do."

"What are the police doing about that hazard?" Stevie asked.

"Good point." Kevin leaned forward.

"What can they do?" Mark asked. "The area is riddled with them."

"I think they are looking to check it out early tomorrow, if they haven't already," Stacy said. "We gave them all the information we knew about it today."

Mark nodded. "Interesting."

"I did tell them that I took a look around but didn't see anything or anyone else up there." Royce lifted his coffee cup and took a sip. "I don't think that space went anywhere."

"These mountains are riddled with caves," Stevie said. "It's not unusual to see something like this. It's only because we found it that makes it unusual. If it had been mapped, then we'd have thought nothing of it."

True enough, and something Stacy hadn't thought about.

"Dinner is ready," she said. "Royce, can you please carry it to the table?"

He hopped up and carried over the large pot. The others, appetites returning, crowded around, dishing up full bowls. She walked into the kitchen and pulled out the last of the French bread, sliced it up, and took it out to the table. Everyone grabbed a slice, and silence prevailed.

But it was a good sound. Stacy ate slowly, enjoying the hot meal. Just being inside, safe, was a comfort. Knowing that she would be leaving tomorrow was another comfort. And, as much as she didn't want to look at everyone around this table with suspicion, she didn't know how not to.

After dinner, the group slowly did dishes together, no one moving quickly or happily. The conversation stayed muted and centered around generic issues. Stacy stood in the kitchen and wondered what to do with all the food. Was it worth packing up tonight or should she wait until the morning, after they'd all eaten?

"Leave it for now, Stacy." Royce stood in the doorway. "Everyone is likely to want a snack later tonight, and we still need a meal in the morning."

"I'd just decided on that too." She filled the teakettle and put it on the stove. "I'd like a cup of tea."

"You could have a drink," he said. "There'll be a lot of that flowing this evening."

She shuddered. "No thanks. And I wouldn't trust any of

those bottles, and neither would I want to lose my wits to any degree tonight."

"I should have said that"—he walked closer—"if you wanted a drink, I'd watch over you."

She smiled up at him. "You aren't going to drink?"

He shook his head. "No."

Clear. Firm. Decisive. She liked that. But she still wouldn't have a drink from anything.

ROYCE HELD OUT his arms, smiling when she stepped into them. He hugged her close. The two of them stayed quiet until the teakettle whistled. She stepped back and walked over to the stove and the kettle.

"Do you want a cup of tea?" Stacy asked him.

"No thanks." He waited for her to make tea, then stayed behind her, until she walked out to the main living room, where the rest of them sat.

She might not have connected the dots. He wondered how long before she realized that she was the last woman left in the group, although Christine had disappeared on her own—at least as far as anyone could figure.

Only Stacy was left, and he planned on watching over her like a hawk. He wouldn't drink or eat anything, unless Stacy or he had made it. That wouldn't guarantee his safety, but it would give him a better chance. He wondered about the Hungarian stew, but the only time Stacy had left it unguarded was when they were in the boot room with George, and Royce had stood in the doorway to keep an eye on the others.

Now it was late but not late enough for bed. They had a few hours to kill.

He winced at that phrase. So not what he needed to think about right now.

Standing beside the fire, he studied the others around the room. He couldn't believe any were cold-blooded killers. Still, maybe Kathleen's had been an accident. Yvonne? Well, who knew? Christine? No one had heard from her, but hopefully she'd found a safer place to stay.

Kathleen's attacker could have been anyone. A stranger.

Not one of his friends. They'd never shown any tendency toward violence. A few had tempers, but then so did he. A few got mouthy when drunk, while others were adrenaline junkies. He used to be one of them.

No, he couldn't believe it of his group. Someone else had to be responsible.

His mind worked the issues. What if this friend of Kathleen's had been responsible for her accident? Maybe they'd had a falling out. It could even have been Christine. She was conveniently missing. Maybe she'd lured Kathleen to the cave. They fought. Then Christine had run.

Possibly getting revenge on something Kathleen had said or done. He glanced over at George. Had George ever had an affair with Christine? If so, could that be why? Not that such a thing warranted killing the woman.

He sat down beside George and asked him in a low voice.

George stared at him in confusion, before a tinge of anger flared in his gaze.

"I'm just wondering if she'd be holding a grudge against Kathleen." George still stared at him, but at least there was spark of awareness.

"What if Christine isn't missing? What if she planned this? Then found a chance to get her revenge on Kathleen and took it?"

George shook his head. "Christine isn't like that."

Royce shrugged. "Maybe not, but I'd have sworn none of us were."

"Kevin came in late," George muttered in a barely there whisper. "Maybe it was him."

"But why?"

"For the same reason I have to consider Stevie." At that, George stared at Royce hard, as if willing him to understand his reasoning.

Royce sat back and stared at Kevin and Stevie, without trying to make it look like he was. They'd both been friends with the group for years. So had Mark for that matter. Mark sat in the corner and nursed a bottle of whiskey. Royce wondered. Had Kevin or Mark ever made a play for Kathleen? He dimly remembered that Stevie had. Somehow he felt he could discount that. Stevie made a play for every woman.

Had Christine, though, made a play for George? His friend hadn't answered that query. He repeated his question and watched George's gaze slide away.

Ah, shit. "How long ago?"

George sighed and sat back, his shoulders slumped. "A month before I hooked up with Kathleen. Christine came on to me, but I said no. I was into Kathleen by then."

ALL HIS PLANS were falling to pieces. He couldn't have that. Not at this stage. He'd wanted this for so long that he wanted to cry. Like a baby, with a long-promised treat snatched out from under him, he wanted to scream and rage.

But he'd grown up a long time ago.

And this? Well, this was something he needed. What the other two needed. It was completing the circle. Something that had to happen this time around.

Who knew when he'd get another chance? No, he couldn't let this time slip away. They had no idea. A weird save on Kathleen, but, other than that, no one had any reason to suspect him. At all.

That Irish luck of his grandmother's was still holding.

Nice timing with Christine gone missing to mix up the issue too.

He felt his nerves jangling. His heart racing. Damn it. How could he make this happen and in such a short time?

Everyone was leaving tomorrow … or maybe not. An idea sparked in the back of his worried mind. An idea that just might be doable.

But he might need help. Only asking for that help might cause him to lose the prize. He knew where Stacy belonged but knew his buddy wanted her too. And his plans were different. Ugly.

That couldn't happen.

His own vision was beautiful. So how could he make this work?

Chapter 38

STACY WANTED TO go to bed and sleep, but she knew she'd never close her eyes long enough to get there. Who could? Too much was unknown, and too much was suspected. She knew Royce and her brother couldn't have had anything to do with this. But, in the back of her mind, she could see file upon file of morgue cases, where men and women had said the same thing about their loved ones. Did you ever really know someone?

She didn't want Royce to have anything to do with them. She trusted him.

And many a woman had lost their lives doing the same thing, trusting the wrong person.

She tried to look at this scientifically. Who had the opportunity? As Royce had been with her all day, neither of them had attacked Kathleen. George had left Kathleen to go to the peak with Geoffrey. That should then clear both of them.

According to Kevin, the rest of them were going to the village for lunch, when Kathleen got a text. She said she would stay, until a friend caught up with her. Then they'd both come to find him for a cup of coffee. She'd been standing in the middle of the crowd, texting away. He hadn't caught the name of the person she was meeting. And he hadn't thought to ask.

Her cell phone wasn't with Kathleen when she was found. It was easy to assume that her friend was the attacker and had removed the evidence of the meeting.

No one had seen her again. And, they admitted, they hadn't worried about it or her. She'd met a friend. They were all on vacation, so who knew how long the two had gotten to talking? Maybe they'd decided to go to a restaurant, or, if they were both into snowboarding, maybe do a couple runs. If it was George she was meeting, they were likely coming to the cabin for a few moments of privacy. They hadn't seriously thought anything of it.

Until they'd found her, George hadn't even known she'd been missing. Mark and Stevie were together boarding until Stevie hit the tree. Kevin joined Mark for a couple runs, before going off on his own, then back for more runs. They confirmed that George and Geoffrey were together, up to where they split with Kathleen. Then Kevin had joined them, and he and Kathleen went for coffee. George and Geoffrey had gone out boarding again. They may have lost sight of each other on the runs, but they'd always met up at the bottom. And, yes, they were boarding on this side of the mountain.

Stevie frowned. "This sucks. I hate to think we are all sitting here, wondering if one of us attacked Kathleen."

"I'm not worried," Geoffrey said. "I was boarding with George all afternoon."

"And you never once lost sight of him? You never did runs in different directions or lost each other only to meet up on the top of the mountain again, where you both laughed and took off down one more time?" Stevie sneered, more than a little bitterness in his voice.

Stacy studied Geoffrey's face as he reacted to Stevie's

accusation.

"No, we did not," he snapped. "We did all the runs together. You know what the peak is like. That's not a place to go alone or to lose sight of your buddy."

"Hell, we've all done that peak on our own," argued Stevie. "And we've all pulled stunts where we ditched our buddy to go left and take a series of jumps."

"Regardless of small things like that, we weren't out of each other's sight for more than a few minutes." George glared at Stevie. "To get to where Kathleen was found and to come back would have taken thirty minutes at least. More likely forty minutes."

Geoffrey subsided into his chair, anger vibrating through his long lanky frame. "I had nothing to do with her attack." He stared at the shot of scotch in his hand and refused to say any more.

Stacy looked over at Royce. She knew this was important. They needed to know where everyone was, but, at the same time, it was damn scary.

Just when she thought the conversation would die down, Mark piped up, "You know, just because Stacy and Royce found her, that doesn't mean they weren't the ones who knocked her out."

Stacy stared at someone she'd known and worked with for years and felt that inside center that kept her stable and calm start to crumble. Could they really be accusing her?

Royce, as if knowing how the comment had unsettled her, said calmly, "But it's not likely, is it?"

"You could have had an argument and pushed her. The crack in her head from the fall was worse than Stacy realized. When she never showed up, you knew exactly where to go and find her. Nice and easy."

Stacy stayed still, waiting to see if anyone else would jump on that bandwagon. She could have said the evidence would say Kathleen had been lying in the cold for a couple hours, but, since she and Royce had been together all day and mostly alone, Mark's theory was plausible.

"Motive?" Royce asked, curiosity in his voice. "What could we possibly have fought about?"

"Well, let's look at this rationally. Honestly, the best people to figure this out is us. We don't need the police poking into our lives any more than they are already," George said quietly. "We'll all analytically dissect everyone here and what motive or where they were at the time Kathleen was attacked. We know she was with me until twelve-thirty, and, no, I wasn't alone with her. There were a good half-dozen witnesses."

"Then, as you've already started on Royce and me," Stacy said, "let's finish and move on to each of you."

The others nodded.

"So motive for me to have attacked Kathleen?" Stacy asked, her voice steady, feeling an unreal sensation at what was happening.

"Maybe you were jealous?" Stevie said, shrugging. "Maybe it was an argument over George?"

"Why would there be an argument over George?"

Stevie looked at George and then away. He stayed silent. Stacy contemplated Stevie's face, then turned to look at her brother. "George, what don't I know?"

"Nothing much."

"Much?" She pounced on that word. "But there is something?"

"I just wanted you to come on this trip to help you move past your grief. She thought I spent too much time and effort on it."

"But you've only been together for what, six, seven months? I've been dealing with this for three years. Why would that cause her any jealousy?"

"She felt that because she was related to the winter sport side of my life that you weren't being accepting of her. We've talked marriage, and that was an issue for her. That I felt you still needed me so much and that she felt like you didn't want anything to do with her."

"Good Lord." Stacy sat back in shock. "First, I like Kathleen. Then I also really liked Anna, Sarah, and Jessica." At that comment, the place erupted in laughter. "If I'm not all over her, it's more a case of I'm afraid she'll go by the wayside, as all the others have. It's hard on me too when you break up with them, you know? I make friends with your partners, and the partners disappear, and I'm on the receiving end of that loss too."

George stared at her, his mouth open. With difficulty, he closed it. "I never thought of that."

"No, of course not," she muttered. "And, for the record, you don't need to hover over me, nor do I resent her because she's associated with winter sports ..." She rolled her eyes at that one. "But you and I are close. I expect to be close with your partner. I'd just not like to make and lose a dozen friends before you decide on the right one."

More laughter broke through the crowd, and even George grinned at her. "But trying out that dozen is so much fun," he said, laughing.

The humor helped ease the tension in the room.

"Anyone else got any reason why there'd be a problem that would cause me to attack Kathleen and then leave her? Only to turn around, presumably out of remorse, to save her?"

One by one, they all shook their heads. She sighed with relief. "Well, that's good to know. I was with Royce all day, so he's my alibi."

"Which," Royce pointed out, "just means we can alibi each other."

She nodded. "Also problematic." She smiled. "So let's analyze Royce next."

Now the group, feeling a little more at ease, fell into the game. For Royce, all they could determine was a potential prior relationship with Kathleen or an argument where she'd determined to cause problems with him and Stacy.

As nothing made any sense there, they moved on around the circle.

When they fell silent, Stevie said, "That didn't help."

"Yes, it did," Stacy said. "Now we aren't looking at each other as if we'll try to murder each other while we sleep."

He grinned. "So true. Besides, if you were going to kill me, it would be at work. There you threaten me all the time."

"And me," Mark said, laughing.

She smiled at him. He'd been snowboarding with Stevie all morning, and they'd done a few runs on their own on the other mountain, but he'd seen George at lunchtime too. It appeared, if he were telling the truth, he was off the hook at this point. Then again, they all were.

"One person we aren't mentioning is Christine," Royce said. "She's unaccounted for right now. Had she fallen down a crevasse like Stacy and had no one to help her? Was she attacked and is lying lost for someone to find down the road? Did she find a place to stay and would like to not know us this trip?"

"Wasn't she good friends with Kathleen?" Stevie asked. "I thought that's how she came to be here this weekend?" He glanced from one blank face to the other. "If so, what if they had an argument, and it was Christine who left Kathleen in there?"

There was a moment of heavy silence, as if the thought of the two women fighting could end up in one of them almost dying.

Stacy knew it happened all the time.

But no one ever wanted to consider it happening to two women they knew. Kevin had called the police and had let them know she hadn't checked in. They were trying to locate Christine, but they were overwhelmed with the weather causing trouble and hampering their efforts. Given it was one of the members of their group, the police were taking her disappearance seriously.

George suggested, "Maybe the same person who attacked Kathleen also took out Christine?"

"Why though?" Stacy asked, her heart shuddering at the thought.

"And Christine is probably sitting in someone's private pool, grateful to have found a spot for the weekend," Kevin snapped. "She'd really not like us discussing her this way."

"If something happened to both women, and if they were both in the same location," Stacy said quietly, "then I'd say the two women either saw something, overheard something, or found something that someone wanted to protect."

Silence.

ROYCE WATCHED STACY'S bomb drop into the vast well of silence. She could be right. But there was one thing that no one was bringing up. He would in a moment, if no one else did, but he was wondering if it had occurred to anyone else. All of them had been together for a long time. They'd gone on trips at various times through the years, with various group configurations, depending on who could come. They often had people come and go in between, as work schedules allowed people to get away. But, in three years, there was only one change this time.

Kevin shook his head. "Don't go there. Christine is fine. Let's keep her out of this."

"I think it all centers around Stacy," Stevie said. "Regardless of what the two women may or may not have seen, Stacy's the common denominator."

Stacy stared at her coworker in shock. "I'm what?"

Royce sat back to listen. This was what he'd been expecting.

"We've never had a problem before this trip. We've done many similar trips with no problem." Stevie leaned forward, his hands clasped in front of him, as if trying to straighten out his thoughts. "Now three women have been attacked or have gone missing, Stacy is the fourth and last one standing. We've found a missing man no one knows anything about. And we've been drugged." He looked from one curious face to the other, finally landing on Stacy. "So what's different this time? Stacy is here."

Her gaze widened, and Royce could see her mind spinning. "Glad you brought that up," Royce said. "The question here is really about whether she made this happen or if her presence acted as a catalyst to make this happen."

"That's such a fine difference, isn't it?" George asked. "How are they any different?"

"Did the trouble come *with* me? Or did it happen because I'm actually here?" Stacy leaned back. "That really sucks. Thanks for that, Stevie."

"Not trying to make you feel bad. I'm just saying that your presence is about the only difference that I can see from all the other trips in recent years."

"Not quite true," George said. "There is a shortage of women this time, and one of them is in a more committed relationship this time around."

"So sex being a motive then?" Kevin shrugged. "Women have never been an issue. We're all well-known for picking up someone for a night or two."

"And yet we haven't done that in years," Stevie pointed out. "In fact, I can't remember the last time I did."

Stacy smirked.

He caught sight of it and narrowed his gaze at her. "I haven't since Janice and Francine. I loved them as much as any friend, and losing them changed my attitude."

Royce felt her gasp of pain. He was already holding her hand but needed to do more. He reached his arm around her shoulders and tugged her up against him. She came, ever-so-slightly stiff, as if from a blow, but she relaxed into his arms. "It was a tough time back then," she said. "We were all such great friends. Their loss was difficult to get over."

"I certainly changed."

"So did I," Mark said quietly. "It took a long time to not expect them to be around every corner, pranking us at every opportunity."

Stacy smiled, her eyes overly bright. "They were always so vivacious."

Geoffrey said, "I understand that you've all lost someone important to you, but exactly what does that have to do with the scenario right now?"

"Maybe it doesn't," Stevie said, "but we lost two women that week. And now we came here this week—the first time Stacy is actually back with us—and two more women are also taken out."

"Oh God." Stacy slid down on the couch and burst into tears.

Chapter 39

STACY TRIED TO rally from the emotional blows, but the last comparison was stunning and painful.

In the background, she heard George protest. "Surely that's just a coincidence. Besides, if Christine is missing, then the numbers don't work. That's just stupid. There's no connection to what happened on that trip and this time."

"Just Stacy," repeated Stevie in a subdued voice. "God, I'm sorry for bringing it up, Stacy."

She nodded, but the motion made the nausea rise in the back of her throat. She shifted to drop her head between her knees, while she fought to not lose her dinner.

"That's gross," Kevin said. "I'm going to be really glad when this trip is over with."

"Same here," Stevie said, standing up. He walked to where the open bottle of scotch stood and filled his glass. "I'm tempted to drive out of here tonight. Except Mother Nature is making sure we can't do that."

"Easy, Stevie," Royce said.

"I am taking it easy." Stevie gave a broken laugh. "What the hell is wrong with me?"

"Nothing," Stacy said loyally. "Nothing at all."

He snorted. "Really? Well, you wouldn't go out with me, so there must be something." He threw back half the glass of scotch in his hand and wheezed as the hot liquor burned its way down his throat.

The others waited for him to stop coughing, keeping a careful eye on him. Stacy had forgotten this part. The maudlin side to Stevie's character that always came out when he got drunk. Something he didn't do often. Considering the circumstances, she'd love to find oblivion herself.

But she didn't dare. She stayed quiet, hating that anything of this trip would be connected to her last trip here. She'd come to honor her friends and the memories they'd had together and to get past it, so they would not hold her back from enjoying the rest of her life.

To a certain extent, she'd done that. She would feel much better if their bodies were found, but, at the same time, she could deal with the reality of their grave. To think that someone had somehow connected the two trips in their mind was incredibly unsettling.

If it were true, if her brother and her friends had been worried about Stacy's mind-set these last few years, had they all missed someone else's deteriorating mind-set as well? Someone maybe who'd been alone through tough times? She'd been blessed to have her brother watching over her.

She had no idea who it could be. Stevie had been devastated. Mark less so. George had felt guilty. She herself had gone to pieces.

She knew now that there was no saving Janice or Francine. And, if it hadn't been the avalanche, it would have likely been something else. Those two were hotheaded, rash, and careless. Stacy doubted either would have reached their thirties.

She'd often wondered why the three had been such great friends. Stacy had been the staid, safe, shy contrast to their bubbling, outgoing adventurousness.

God, she missed them.

"Stacy?"

She glanced over at Royce. He nodded toward Stevie, who tossed back another hefty slug of scotch, while she watched. Time to put aside her own grief. She stood and walked over to Stevie and took away the bottle of scotch. "Bedtime, buddy."

He glared at her. "Not ready to sleep."

She smirked. "Lie down, and you'll be out like a light in no time."

A heavy sigh slid from his chest. "I hurt, Stacy," he muttered. "I miss them."

She knew how he felt. She wrapped her arm around him. "Come on. Let's get you to your room."

With stumbling steps, she walked him down the hallway to his bed. He stared at it and took a couple steps forward. She turned him around, gave him a little push, and he sat down with a heavy sigh.

"I miss them so much," he said again, as he flopped sideways, his head hitting the pillow. She bent down and lifted his feet, until he was stretched out. He never was one to make his bed, and this morning was no different. That was a good thing, as his covers—an open sleeping bag—had been shoved along the back wall. She reached over and dragged it forward, covering him up.

She started to walk away, when he reached out and grabbed her hand. "Don't you miss them too, Stacy?"

"I do, Stevie. So much." She bent down, gave him a goodnight kiss on his cheek, and said, "Now sleep. We'll go home in the morning, so we have to be up in good time to pack."

"Don't wanna," he whined, but it was more of a whisper. He followed that with a huge jaw-cracking yawn. "So tired."

"Then sleep."

She watched him for a long moment, as he fell deeper and deeper into a nice peaceful slumber. "At least you'll sleep tonight, buddy."

Royce spoke from the doorway. "The others are heading to bed too."

"Good." She walked toward him, her hand out for his. "How is George?"

"He's sitting beside the fire."

"Then that's where I'm going first." Still holding hands, she walked over to her brother and sat down beside him. "Will you sleep tonight?"

He shook his head. "Not likely. I should be at the hospital."

"And that can't happen, so you might as well get some sleep so you're in decent shape to watch over her tomorrow."

"A good idea in theory, but the last thing I feel like doing is putting myself at risk here," he said in a low voice. "I don't know if we're in danger, but what if one of us did attack those women?"

Royce sat down beside her. "I understand, but I'm not sure how we're supposed to solve that issue."

"I want to solve it. I figure, if I beat everyone up, at least I'll be assured of getting the right guy in the mix."

She snorted. "Thanks, but no thanks."

"You're exempt," George said. He ran his hand over his weary face. "I feel like shit. I keep thinking that, if I hadn't gone up to the peak, she'd be sitting beside me right now. But no—I had to do one last run. Damn it." He glared at the two of them, as if they could turn back time and give him a chance to make the right decision. "Why do I always have to push it? She was tired. I was tired. I knew that. But I also knew that our time was coming to an end and that I still had enough energy for a couple last runs. Plus, she doesn't like the peak, and I wanted to hit that run at least once."

"So what? There's no way to know that you could have stopped this anyway. You didn't have a crystal ball to say this would happen," Stacy said. "You can't know everything."

"But we all knew it could happen." He curled his hands into fists, as his voice broke. "And I ignored it."

Stacy didn't know how to help him. He needed rest. They had a lot to do in the morning to get ready to leave, and she knew he'd want to go at the first break in the weather. Hell, if it wasn't for that storm out there, they'd be driving toward Kathleen right now.

"I know your emotions are all over the place," she said quietly, "but you need to be wide awake and alert to help us in the morning. Plus, it's a long drive."

"I'll be fine." He brushed off her concerns with a wave of his hands. "Go to bed. I'll stay here for a while and doze if I need to."

She reached over and kissed his cheek. "Okay, but if you can sleep, please do."

He looked over at her and smiled. "Go and rest."

She rolled her eyes at him and got up. With her brother still up to watch the fire, she checked that all the food had been put away, then carried on to the stairs. The others had gone to their rooms. As she passed the room George had been sleeping in with Kathleen, her footsteps slowed. That's why he didn't want to go to bed. He'd be surrounded with reminders of her.

Royce nudged her forward again. "Let him stay up. He'll

be fine."

She nodded and kept moving up the stairs to the loft. She was too keyed up to sleep, yet, at the same time, she was exhausted. So much going on. So much turmoil. And the grief, … the fear, … it was all so crippling.

And it made her tired. A bone-deep weariness that she couldn't recharge because that same tension sat inside, nagging at her. Not allowing her to ever let her guard down. How could she? Someone had attacked her friends. Was maybe still looking to assault her. None of it made sense. And her head ached, trying to figure it out.

"Stop thinking about it," Royce said. "Get into bed and at least rest."

She nodded and quickly changed her clothing. She wanted to lie down before she dropped. She tugged on her long johns and crawled up to her pillow and crashed.

ROYCE WATCHED HER settle down on top of the blankets. "Hey, Stacy," he said quietly, trying to roll her over so he could tug the blankets free. She murmured and rolled where he wanted, but it was like rolling a sleeping child, only much larger. Finally he had the covers out from under her and could cover her up.

He hadn't realized she was so tired, but she'd hit that bed and was out like a light. He sat protectively at her side and stared over the railing. He saw George nursing a beer on the couch, where they'd left him. It would be a while before he forgot his role or lack of role in today's events. Royce knew Kathleen had a good chance of recovering, but if they'd been any later … The medical center at the resort was top-notch and knew how to handle cases like hers. That she'd been flown out to the closest hospital meant they were doing the best for her. It was up to her to fight for survival now. She'd done that in the cave; he just hoped she still had a little more fight left in her.

For George's sake too.

Royce was tired but had no plans to sleep. Someone had to watch over Stacy. She was the only female left. And he had a bad feeling about why that was. He could well believe Christine wanted nothing to do with them now. Royce wanted to go home and to spend his life becoming reacquainted with Stacy. Not regretting that he hadn't done enough.

He heard no movements from the others below him. He didn't know whether they were lying wide-eyed in bed or sleeping. He hoped sleeping. Stevie needed to sleep off the booze. But, if it gave him a good night's rest, then so be it. There were worse things one could do. Royce stared down at his empty hands, thinking he should have brought up a bottle himself. But he wouldn't want to lose control.

God, what a nightmare.

He shifted to lean back against the railing. Stacy slumbered gently beside him. Lord, it would be a long night.

WHAT A SILLY air-clearing bonding session. Did anyone believe the lies they'd all told? Stacy and Royce might have been together the whole time—except for when Stacy left Royce alone with Kathleen to go to the front of the cavern for help. He smiled, his teeth flashing in the darkness. He'd seriously considered taking out Royce right then and there. Yet he had nothing against the guy. Royce was good people, and the world needed more like him.

But the opportunity to finish off that nosy bitch Kathleen would have been perfect. He could only hope the cold did the job for him. Then Royce had been rejoined by Stacy and Stevie, and he'd lost his opportunity. How damn wrong.

So close and yet so far.

Still, it was what it was.

He was in the clear and still moving forward to his goal.

But he was running out of time. Or was he?

He thought about the vehicle configurations as to who was leaving with whom, wondering if he could change the seating arrangements. Isolate the one person he needed to isolate—and preferably in a place where there were lots of people to confuse the issue again. He needed suspects. Lots and lots of suspects.

He fell into a deep sleep, as his mind worked on options.

It was all good.

Chapter 40

STACY WOKE THE next morning, tears clogging her throat and burning her eyes. She'd dreamed of her beautiful friends all night. Painful memories. Emotional memories. She wiped away the tears and sniffled. Instantly a warm hand landed on her shoulder and tugged her close.

Damn if that didn't turn on the waterworks. No, she was stronger than this. She'd never had anyone to hold her close before and was scared to come to rely on it now. She couldn't stand it if that was pulled away from her. The loss would be so difficult.

"Wake up, Stacy," Royce's sleepy voice murmured in her ear. "You're having another bad dream."

She smiled through her tears and nestled against his bare chest. Another bad dream? Had he been watching over her all night? Of course he had. That was Royce. Why had she pushed him away for so long? All the reasons seemed so frivolous right now. So not important. His history was his alone, and his behavior? Well, she wasn't sure it was ever as bad as she'd made it out to be.

She'd believed it to keep him at a distance and hadn't yet updated her vision of the old Royce to the new Royce. He'd lost that big playboy act years ago, but she wouldn't let herself acknowledge it. If she did, she wouldn't have a reason to keep pushing him away. And without that, she'd have to acknowledge the feelings she'd kept locked down inside since forever. To let those feelings out meant to actually honor them and to feel them, and that would mean being vulnerable. A possibility of getting hurt. If she lost him, that would be something she might never recover from. Look how she'd gone off the deep end with losing her friends.

To have Royce in a relationship where she gave everything was frightening to her. To lose him would be to lose herself.

And that couldn't happen. Not again.

She lay here, tears gathering in the back of her eyes. God, she was such a coward.

How had that happened? She'd always been the cautious one, but she'd assumed that was because she was the sensible one. Now, as she looked at her brother's wild lifestyle, her friends' crazy lifestyles, and what she'd assumed Royce's to be back then, it wasn't the commonsense side of her that drove her actions; it was the cowardly side. She could lose so many people she cared about because of their lifestyle choices that she'd put up walls, had locked herself down, and had refused to let them in any further.

After losing her two girlfriends, well, she'd damn-near slammed the door to her heart closed forever.

Maybe George was right. Maybe Kathleen had felt a wall up between her and Stacy. It was also true that Kathleen was like the twelfth girlfriend in that long string of George's girlfriends, but, at the same time, Stacy had shut the door to letting her in, fearing she would lose Kathleen too. As Stacy had all of George's other girlfriends. As she thought deeper and deeper about it, she realized she hadn't let anyone new into her life in these last few years at all.

At work, she was polite and professional. Mark and Stevie were there, and they'd known her since before the accident and had refused to be kicked out of her inner circle. But it had closed around them, not letting anyone else in. Royce was someone who had managed to get in, and she could see that, over time, Kathleen would make it too, but she hadn't yet because dear, safe, cowardly Stacy was still protecting her heart.

Fool.

She wondered how many times Royce had woken her up last night to calm her down, as her subconscious worked on her grief and fears. She wished she'd woken up with energy and a sense of closure, and, maybe for her two friends, she had. She knew she'd never see them again. That they would never walk into her room, regaling her with tales of their colorful evenings and the games the two of them had gotten up to. There'd been no malice to either of them, but there'd not been much substance either, as her father would have said. "Flighty, frippery women" he would have called them. And maybe he had been correct, but that in no way devalued who they were. The world was a big place and had space for people of all kinds—even fireflies.

As she lay here, it slowly dawned on her that it was almost light in the cabin. Noises were happening downstairs, and she should get up. She wanted to leave, but, safe in Royce's arms, she didn't want to move.

She slowly disentangled herself from his arms and sat up.

He shifted beside her. "Is it time to get up?"

She looked down at the sprawled conqueror in her bed and thought, *What a waste.* "Someone else is up too."

He sighed. "Well, the sooner we get moving, the faster we can get home."

"I hear you there." Whoever was moving around downstairs hadn't been up long, as the fire crackled cheerfully, but the warmth hadn't reached the loft yet. Moving quickly against the bite of cold air, she pulled on her wool socks, pants, and a heavy sweater. Her eyes had a gritty feel to them. A combination of a lack of sleep, too many tears, and dry air.

She turned back to Royce, who hadn't moved, bent to kiss him, and found herself tugged down on top of his broad chest. She laughed.

"You could stay here for a little bit," he murmured against her lips.

Her own curved in response. "It wouldn't be a 'little bit,' as you know. Wait until we're home. Then we'll have all the time in the world. I don't go back to work until Monday."

"So the rest of today and tomorrow is mine, right?"

"It's a date. But I get a hot bubble bath when I get home first."

He looked interested in that concept, then said with a wicked grin, "Is the tub big enough for the two of us?" His gaze heated as he stared at her, waiting for her answer.

Images of the two of them flooded her mind, making it hard to breathe. "Deadly. You are so deadly."

She got up, plucking her sweater away from her chest, as if to cool herself off, and walked to the stairway.

"Wait," he called softly, "you didn't answer my question."

She smirked. "That's because I don't know. I guess we'll find out though."

And she headed downstairs.

ROYCE LAY BACK down. He couldn't stop grinning. Despite

everything that had happened, life was damn good. Now to pack up and get home. That hot bath for two sounded pretty damn fine.

Checking the time, he sat up and quickly got dressed. It was damn cold, but he couldn't hear the wind outside anymore. That was a good thing. There were no windows in the loft, so he couldn't see out, and what he could see from the downstairs windows was nothing but sheer white. He realized they would likely have to shovel the vehicles out this morning.

Given that, he quickly packed up his gear and left his single bag beside Stacy's unpacked belongings. She wouldn't need more than a few minutes to collect her stuff. He walked downstairs and lifted his nose appreciatively. Nothing like the heady aroma of coffee on a chilly morning in the mountains. And, from the intensity of that smell, it was almost ready to drink. He wandered into the kitchen to find Stacy already pouring.

"Hey, sleepyhead," she said, as she handed him a mug. "Just in time."

"As you only came down five minutes ago, it's hard to call me a sleepyhead," he protested.

"Ha, it wasn't hard at all." She grinned and walked past him toward the fireplace.

She sat down in the living room on the couch where she usually sat; he took up the spot beside her.

"So who's already up?"

She looked down the hallway. "No idea. The fire was lit and the coffee on when I came down. I presume that person is packing up right now to leave."

That made sense. "I'm packed. I put my bag beside yours."

She nodded. "Okay, after this cup, I'll go collect my stuff, and both bags can go into the vehicle right away. Then we have to sort out the winter gear."

"I'll do that. I'm more concerned with how much work there will be to dig out the vehicles."

"I've already been outside shoveling," George said, walking down the hallway, carrying his and Kathleen's bags. "And Kathleen is responding well. The doctors are optimistic. They also suspect she might have drugs in her system. The tox screen is pending."

Royce stared. "What?"

George nodded. "That's actually good news, as some of her symptoms were due to drugs and not to the severity of her condition."

Stacy leaned forward, her gaze intent. "Really? But that changes everything."

Royce stared at her. "How? Nothing has changed. Someone drugged her. And attacked her and left her for dead."

Stacy was shaking her head at them, her hair sliding from side to side. "No. He likely drugged her. She realized something was wrong, fought to get away, and was struck from behind. Left there because Mother Nature would finish the job after the drugs and the blow to the head."

HE LISTENED TO the three of them talk. Shit. Shit. Shit. He shouldn't have waited. Shouldn't have let events develop to this point.

Who could have foreseen that Kathleen would be found in time to be saved? Or that the damn doctors would consider checking for drugs? Shit. When they realized the drugs were the same as in the wine, they'd connect her attacker to this group.

Their lives would be torn apart by the cops at that point.

His mind raced. What options did he have? He considered saving his ass and giving up on his plan, only to realize that the plan dominated. His matched set had to be complete. That was his goal. His purpose. If he got to continue his life as before with that goal complete, then it would be a perfect finish.

So how could he get Stacy away from the others?

Chapter 41

STACY PACKED UP the kitchen. She'd done it many times before, but she wasn't sure she'd ever done it alone. There were mostly empty coolers, lots of opened packages, and a shortage of tie clips to keep them closed. Breakfast had been a hodgepodge of leftovers that needed to be eaten. She'd had leftover Hungarian stew herself. A hot meal, although spicy, had seemed to fit the bill for the long drive ahead. She washed up the dishes, hearing sounds of the others packing and putting the cabin back to the way it was. It was a process they'd all done many times over.

"Okay, that's our bags in the boot room with our gear." Royce walked to where she was stacking up the last of the dishes. She would have to rinse any coffee cups, once they were done packing up. Usually everyone sat, had a last mug of coffee, and ran through the checklist a final time.

"Are you sure you don't want to do a few runs before we head out?" Royce asked.

She turned to look at him, surprise lighting her face. "I actually hadn't considered that. Is someone staying here?"

"Both Stevie and Mark are going to. We could go back with them."

She frowned, thinking about it. She wanted to go home but—and she knew he'd be frustrated at this—she also kind of wanted to go back to where they'd found Kathleen. She couldn't get it out of her mind that she'd been in that location for a reason. Besides, it would be completely safe, now with all the mountain crews out posting warning signs and with all the officials involved.

George walked in. "Stacy, you two do what you want to do. I'm going straight to the hospital to see Kathleen."

She nodded. "Understood. I presume you'll be staying there with her for a while."

He nodded. "I won't stay all day, but it could be a good couple hours."

She'd expected no less. She pulled the plug in the sink, letting the soapy water drain. "Royce, as we don't have our own wheels, we have three choices, I presume."

"Right. Ride with George and stay at the hospital, until he's ready to go home." He ticked off his fingers. "Stay with Stevie and Mark and either board with them for a couple hours or go into the town and just walk around and have coffee."

"That's possible." She was here, and, as much as she wanted to go straight home, that wasn't an option. She had a few hours to kill no matter what.

"And third is to go with Geoffrey and Kevin."

"I don't see them here. Do we know what their plans are?" she asked, hoping that maybe they'd be heading straight back and wishing she'd brought her own transportation. "And did Kevin hear from Christine?"

"Geoffrey is getting a few runs in while Kevin is heading to the search and rescue office first to find out more about Christine. I doubt he'll leave without knowing something." George's grin slid out sideways, and he shrugged. "If he gets answers, he's likely to meet up with Geoffrey for a run or two. After all, our passes are still good for today."

She nodded in understanding. And these guys lived for this. "Okay, so a few hours to kill no matter what. Sit at a hospital, ski, or walk the town."

"If you're coming with me, you need to be ready to leave in a few minutes," George said, filling his travel mug. "I've got the SUV dug out and warming up."

Stacy looked over at Royce. He gazed back at her. She dropped her gaze. She knew what she wanted to do, but, hell, it's not likely that it would happen. But she would always wonder. And the part of her that was so good at her job was rearing its ugly head.

"I guess another choice is to stay in the cabin or to grab my camera and wait for the first group to come back and leave with them," she said, raising an eyebrow at Royce.

He nodded in surprise. "That can happen too."

She turned to her brother. "Go. I know you're rushing to get away. Please drive carefully and let me know when you get there."

He grabbed her in a big hug. "Will do." He turned to Royce, slapped him on the back, and said, "Keep her safe."

"You know it," Royce said quietly.

And, with that, George was gone.

ROYCE WATCHED GEORGE leave with misgivings. He couldn't help but feel that Stacy should have gone with him. She'd be out of this mess then. Safe. She, for some reason, hadn't chosen that option.

Likely it was knowing that the trip would stall at the hospital—possibly for the rest of the day or even overnight. That did not hold any appeal for him either.

What was it about the bright light of day that made everything seem less sinister and more positive? Then he glanced at her staring down at the floor and realized she had something else on her mind. His stomach sank. Damn that woman. He had a bad feeling that she would want to go back to the cave, where they'd found Kathleen.

Even though the search and rescue people were doing their jobs, it wouldn't likely be enough for Stacy. Although, with so many people around the area, it should be safe enough.

He sighed.

As the others got ready to put on their outdoor gear, he leaned against the kitchen counter and asked in a low voice, so the others couldn't hear, "You want to go back up there and look around, don't you?"

She glanced under her lashes at him, as if trying to gauge his reaction, but she made no attempt to not understand his meaning. "I can't get rid of the feeling that there is something more to this. Why would Kathleen have been there in the first place? It makes no sense. And Christine hasn't checked in. Maybe she's avoiding us, and maybe she truly is missing. Kathleen either walked in there on her own or had been carried. And, yes"—she held up a hand to forestall his response—"maybe that was just to keep her out of sight."

He nodded and stayed quiet, waiting.

She returned to staring at the floor. Then, with a little sigh, she said, "I could never go back to where I lost my friends. I almost lost this one because we weren't going in any deeper. Now I just need to confirm that we checked everything and know that Christine isn't in there too. That no one else is either."

"It's not good enough that we found Kathleen? That search and rescue have been notified that Christine didn't check in with us?" he asked, a thin thread of humor in his voice.

"Yes and no." Then she shrugged. "I can't explain it. But I need to go back."

She motioned outside. "The others are boarding. George is gone. We have a couple hours to kill, and I have my camera on a bright sunny day. Is it so wrong to go in, take a moment to walk the space, then leave so I really know for sure that all is well?" Her smile turned up a notch. "It should be safe with the officials all over the area now."

He studied her earnest face for a long moment. "Will you leave it alone after this?"

She smiled a bright, glorious smile and said, "Yes, I will."

Chapter 42

KEVIN AND GEOFFREY packed their vehicle up fully and drove into the village and parked at the main gondola. They would snowboard from that location, then head home when they were ready, further reducing Stacy's options.

Emotional goodbyes were par for the course—especially this time. With words of warning to be careful and to let them know if they heard from Christine, Stacy waved them off. She hoped they had a fantastic day. Now that she was alone with Royce, there was a keyed-up restlessness inside. She wanted to go to the cavern, then leave—and leave it all behind. Stevie and Mark had gone snowboarding, promising to be back by noon, so they could leave and get home in good time. She looked down at her watch. It was almost nine. They had three hours. Not tons of time, but enough. She looked up at Royce. "Ready?"

He nodded. They lifted their packs and ropes, determined to not get into any trouble on this quick trip, then back to the cabin to be ready when the guys returned. She had enough food to create some hefty sandwiches for while they were on the road. She couldn't wait to get back home. She planned on convincing Royce to stay at her place for the rest of the weekend. Monday, and their jobs would come soon enough. So be it. Her world was rosy again. And she loved it.

They walked quickly in the well-packed snow. A light dusting was on top from last night's storm, but as much as had blown in appeared to have been picked up and blown out again. They created new steps as they traveled. It was a gorgeous day out.

"I'm glad the weather will be nice for the drive home," she said, as they walked at a steady pace. Royce appeared to be deep in thought, his gaze on the path ahead but his attention elsewhere.

She waited a moment, then asked, "What are you thinking?"

He glanced down at her, then gave a noncommittal shrug. "Just thinking timelines. Now knowing that Kathleen had been drugged, it means she hadn't been in that place very long, so I'm rethinking everyone's alibi based on the new information."

Ugh. She walked beside him, her mind going over what Stevie had said he'd been doing. And Mark. Then Geoffrey and George. She couldn't remember what Kevin had said. "It would still take a good half hour to get to this place, deal with Kathleen, then another half hour to get back, all without being seen," she said. "That's a big chunk of time to be missing."

"I know. But someone attacked her." He turned to study her. "And Christine hasn't turned up."

"I know," she said quietly. "And that's just one of the issues bugging me. If Kathleen had already been drugged, why attack her?"

"The most likely reason is the drugs weren't taking effect fast enough, and she was fighting her attacker."

The hill was just up ahead. It was a little harder to climb with the loose snow under her feet, but they were at the top before long. She wandered closer to the out-of-bounds tape and saw a churning up of the snow below. There might have been some fresh snow, but, with the blowing and lifting in the wind, very little had landed down below. Myriad prints remained from yesterday. And the snowmobile tracks were all over the top of the pit. "Looks like some of the team came back and checked on the place," she said, pointing to the newer tracks.

"They said they would."

She caught the hint of long-suffering patience in his voice and had to grin. "Did I say *thank you* for coming with me today?"

"You did. Let's get on with it."

He dropped the rope ladder over the ledge, tied it off around a tree, and went down first. She scurried after him. Down in the darker depths, she remembered the eerie chill she'd felt last time. "It's like something old and dark is about this place."

"It *is* old. I doubt this ice has ever seen the sun's warming rays."

The trail to the cave was completely flattened now. Good. It was less scary as when it had seemed to have been deliberately hidden.

He walked inside first, ducking to go under the overhang. He turned on his strong flashlight, the bright beam casting a long shadow over the exterior. "Interesting place," he said, studying the icy walls and bits of rock showing through. He walked in deeper, Stacy following.

Suddenly they were at the place where they'd found Kathleen.

She turned around slowly. Now that it was early in the day, and, with the beam of the flashlight, she could see that they weren't actually far from the entrance. Kathleen might have stumbled in here on her own, if she were trying to get way from someone, or someone could have easily carried her that short distance.

Grimly, she looked at the blood on the ground. Given these temperatures, it would be here forever. Royce carefully searched the small space. She walked to the closest wall, and, with him pointing the flashlight so she could see, she put out her hand to touch the wall and walked the room, just so she didn't miss anything.

Ice was like a mirror and was equally deceptive. She walked all the way around and realized nothing was here. Her heart bloomed with relief. "Oh thank heavens," she murmured. "I was so afraid."

"Afraid of what?" Royce asked.

"That I'd find something much worse." But she refused to elaborate. She returned to where the corridor split and stared down the left-hand path, then realized she had to know. She motioned him ahead of her. "Let's check this one out."

"Stacy—"

"Please," she said, desperation in her voice. "I have to know."

He strode forward silently. There was another room, bigger and higher here. She did the same thing. She put her hand on the left side and proceeded to walk the chamber, the light leading the way and letting her ensure nothing was here to be worried about.

On the left side, she stopped. There was another cut in the wall, almost like a hallway. "Royce, come look."

He walked closer. "Damn it."

His flashlight shone on the smooth icy sides and the

rock ceiling. Stacy grabbed his arm and lowered the blaze of light to the ground, she saw the bits of fresh snow on the path that had fallen from someone's boots. It was likely from this morning.

She froze. Her mind instantly went on alert. It could have been one of the search and rescue team making sure the cavern was empty—but it didn't feel like it.

Stacy deliberately and very quietly said, "Let's go."

And she walked forward, silently following whoever had come before them into this icy place this morning.

"WAIT," ROYCE SAID, his voice low. He had his cell phone out and texted George, even though he knew he'd be driving. He wasn't sure who else he could trust at this point. **In the cavern. Found something odd. If you don't hear from us every ten minutes for the next hour, we are in trouble and need help. Send the cavalry. Hell, send everyone anyway. This is bad.**

Then he put away his phone, stepped in front of her, and walked down the corridor. They came to another widening in the chamber, and they both came to a sudden stop.

Stevie sat in the middle of the room, huge fat tears falling down his cheeks. He looked over at them, his face a complete wreck.

Whatever was going on here had finished him. He pointed to the wall to the right of them. "I can't believe it. I just found them. They can't be here. It's too grotesque. It's so wrong."

Royce shone the light on the wall.

Stacy cried and ran forward.

There, suspended by wires, holding the two women in a pseudo graceful midair display, as delicate as multiple broken bones and torn clothing could make them, were the two women who had been killed by an avalanche—her best friends—Janice and Francine.

They'd been hung in place, forever on display in their icy art museum.

Chapter 43

S TACY VOMITED.

She dropped to her knees, as projectile vomit leaped from her throat to hurl onto the icy ground. She heard sounds dimly in the background, but she was too busy shaking and trembling on her knees. Her mind screamed against the abomination, the grotesqueness of what she could see in front of her.

Her friends—real-life dolls.

Frozen for eternity.

So lifelike that she wanted them to jump down—to rush over and to give her a hug and an explanation for why'd they'd been hiding for so long.

Until she saw the dead eyes. The hard marble flesh. The broken teeth in the grimace of a smile.

The only consolation was that her friends weren't alive when this had been done to them. Determined to take a closer look and to know the worst, she stood up shakily, Royce's firm hand on her elbow.

Or maybe not so firm, as she sensed the tremors running through him. He had his phone out; he'd taken several pictures and was sending them somewhere. Hopefully to get help for her friends.

She took a deep breath, dug deep, and tried to get into professional mode and do what she did naturally. Now that she was a little calmer, or maybe just frozen, she analyzed the scene. Both women had sustained multiple broken bones. Janice's knee was twisted, the kneecap not quite right. Some attempts had been made to straighten it the way it would be normally. Stacy noted in a dispassionate way that the tiny wires were used to hold her leg in a close approximation to the right location and position.

She studied the twisted ends of the wire that had been fashioned into locking closures.

An elaborate setup held the women in the most natural positions possible, as if they were flying down the mountain on snowboards—just as they'd been before the avalanche had wiped them out. Their frozen knees bent, their arms out for balance, their bodies showing a natural grace of movement. Both women had been gifted snowboarders, taking to the sport easily.

This macabre display puzzled Stacy. Although broken, so many attempts had been made to place them in a natural position. A display of some kind. An artist's rendering? A memorial?

The person who'd done this had tried to reenact that wonderful free spirit both women had in life. She felt her tears sliding down her face, as she stepped in front of Janice. Her face had a dead flat-white look of having been frozen for a long time.

With a start, she realized a layer of color had been applied over her icy complexion, as if someone had used blush and possibly eyeliner to give the woman a more alive look.

Well, it was beyond anything Stacy had seen before. She walked over to Francine, noting the same attempts with the makeup, the broken arm wired together, the tear in her snow pants that had been crudely mended, and something was off in the neck and head alignment.

To see what her friends had suffered through with their deaths. The fear. The pain. The awareness at the last moment ... Stacy bowed her head, struggling to hold back the waves of emotions threatening to send her in a tailspin. After a long moment, the icy silence around her filtered into her mind. She shook her head and stepped back, distancing herself.

With a heavy sigh, she turned back to Royce—and Stevie, the blubbering ball of emotional distress on the floor. She walked over to him, compassion and sadness filling her head. Was he distressed at having just seen this, or had he done this and was now overwrought at being caught? She remembered him talking about the two missing friends and how he missed them. A mantra he'd said over and over again these last few years. She bent down and wrapped her arms around him, holding him tight. He hung on and cried and cried. "Easy, Stevie."

He shook his head. "It's not right."

"I know."

She really hoped he'd had nothing to do with this.

"They look so beautiful," he whispered, staring in agony at the two women, poised on a snow bank in mid-dash down the mountain. "And so wrong."

She nodded, agreeing silently. She glanced over at Royce, but he stood staring at something beside the two women, a muscle in his jaw twitching in a hard staccato manner. He was furious. She knew he would have already sent out a distress call, and it was only a matter of time before the place was overrun with police and crime scene people. In this case, she could easily pinpoint the time of death. That horrific avalanche off the cliff face three years ago.

Still, someone had gone to a lot of time and trouble to find these women and to bring them here.

"Stacy." Royce's voice was cold, clear, direct. A command. Not a request. She patted Stevie on the shoulders and tried to stand up.

"No, don't go over there," Stevie said, clutching at her.

"It's okay, Stevie. Royce needs to show me something."

Stevie hung on harder, but she managed to step out of his grasp, and, as if understanding he'd lost the chance to stop her, he collapsed into a pile of weeping jelly again.

Concerned, she stared down at her friend, wondering if he'd done this.

"Stacy."

She turned and walked over to where Royce stood. She stepped to his side and asked, "What?"

He pointed to the spot higher up on the small hill of snow the artist had created as part of the slope the women were snowboarding on. He then pointed to the spot above the two women. Janice's name was on a large card. Beside her was a card bearing Francine's name.

Stacy sighed. Then realized he was pointing to a third and empty spot. A spot waiting for another model—a third art piece to be put into position.

There was a name on that last label too.

Stacy.

AS SAD AND so psychologically heartbreaking as the display in front of him was, Royce's stomach had wanted to follow Stacy's massive upchuck when he saw the third name card. He barely managed to hold it back.

He'd known both women. Just not as well as the others in their group. They'd been Stacy's best friends. And Stevie's very close friends. He glanced over at Stevie, wondering what the hell his role in this was.

God, what a sick thought.

They'd never thought to find the women's bodies after the massive search had been called off. The whole area had been too dangerous, as more avalanches had threatened to go off.

Obviously someone hadn't been able to let them go. Royce couldn't imagine the effort required to reclaim the bodies from the mountain. Someone must have seen the two women as they were tossed in the avalanche or maybe caught sight of one of them as the storm of snow had finally abated. Maybe that had given him a starting place, and he'd lucked into actually finding the one, then had persevered to find the second one. There was no doubt the women had died that day, but to do this to them …

Royce shook his head. He couldn't imagine the mind-set of the person who couldn't let them go.

And then he'd seen the name cards. And found Stacy's over the empty spot. Was she supposed to have died that day? Had someone set off that avalanche on purpose? It could happen, but it wasn't all that easy to do. Or had someone decided that the three women belonged together?

"What was it Mark, or had that been Geoffrey, who'd said something about matched sets?" Royce asked in a low voice. He frowned. What else had he said? Something about *The three women had done everything together.*

Did either of those men have the expertise to pull this off? Then he realized the expertise would have been in recovering the bodies, but the rest was all about muscle and rope knowledge. So both did. Actually they'd all done courses in search and rescue work. The wire was crude but effective. All the men in their group were big enough to manhandle the bodies onto sleds and into this space. He had to wonder if there wasn't another entrance, as Stacy had suggested early on. This display would never have been found, if Stacy hadn't fallen down that crevasse in the first place.

Stacy, pale and shaky looking, hovered protectively over a distraught Stevie. She would recover now. She'd been looking for her friends, but he doubted she'd expected to find them and had certainly never expected to find them like this.

He glanced at his watch. He was loathe to leave the two of them, but surely there should be a rescue team here by now? The police? Their friends? He'd texted damn-near everyone he knew. Had this person despaired of Stacy ever joining the other two and had decided that Kathleen fit the bill as well, or had Kathleen stumbled onto this by accident and had been taken out?

He kept watch, knowing all too well that this was not over. Not until they were surrounded by the police and the "artist" caught.

And where was Christine? He'd wondered if she could be here as well. It didn't necessarily fit, but no normal mind would say this was logical either. Christine and Kathleen to join Janice and Francine. Then Stacy for a perfect set?

He had to wonder just how far over the edge this person had actually gone. Was he even now murdering women to add to his collection?

Royce, now thoroughly chilled by death, returned to the other entrance and cocked an ear, listening for the others.

Surely they should be here by now?

Chapter 44

STACY STEPPED BACK from Stevie, her heart sore, her mind almost numb. She didn't know if Stevie had done this, but he was in no shape to be questioned about it now. The police would take care of it. Although she had no idea what the charges would be in this case—if any. Had he attacked Kathleen as well?

If so, then everything changed. She got up and walked closer to her friends, unable to leave them alone like this. Her body fought the chill that had settled deep inside. She'd wanted to find her friends since forever. Have their bodies sent home for burial. Find closure. Obviously someone else had needed closure as well. She shook her head at the enormity of this.

Did the person come back and forth all the time and visit with the women?

She spotted a box to one side. She walked over and opened the lid, making sure to use her gloves. Inside were candles and flashlights. Emergency rations. If Kathleen had found these, she would have been a little better off, but nothing would have staved off that mind-numbing cold for long. Stacy studied the items, wondering what they said about the person who owned it. Could she identify the owner of the box by the contents?

Every one of the men she'd come to the cabin with

would have kept candles and matches in here. A few would have put in a small something for warmth as well. She dug into the box farther and, sure enough, found a couple emergency blankets and even several granola bars. Just in case. She sat back on her heels. Just in case, what? That they got caught out here in the cold? Chose to stay beside her friends? To watch over them? To be with them? Were they lost without them?

"Stacy? What did you find?" Royce called out.

"A box with supplies," she called back. They weren't far away from each other, but the sound of their voices echoed weirdly in the small chamber.

With the flashlight she found in the box, she turned it on and used it to search further. There was an odd travel bag to the one side. She frowned, recognizing it. She turned around. "I think Christine's bag is here," she said, her voice rising.

"What? Just her bag?"

"I don't know. I can't see anything else." She already had the bag open. "Makeup, a hairbrush, her wallet."

No response from Royce.

"Royce?" she called back. Where the hell was he? This was too important. Still crouched, she spun around, shining her flashlight across the darkened room. Royce's flashlight wasn't on. Shit. She turned hers off and moved quickly to the side. She could dimly see Stevie in the center of the room, still crying. But it was more of a deep wrenching sob. She knew he'd loved the two women but had no idea they'd been this close. Then again, Stevie had always been a big teddy bear.

Unlike Mark, who had always worshipped them from a distance. Lusting after women he couldn't have. Adoring models and movie starlets with a passion. He almost set up a shrine to each and every one, as they shifted through his consciousness and his life. He was fickle too. He adored one woman, then moved on. Even though he never knew them personally, it was as if they didn't measure up, and he had to go look for another one to idolize.

He'd always been like that. He'd wanted Stacy for a while, but she'd made it clear that it wasn't in the cards. As she remembered, he'd been after Janice. She thought Janice had spent a weekend with him for fun, then no more. It was so Janice's style. Francine had been the same. When Janice had been done with him, then Francine had stepped in. Hell, they'd both done the rounds with every male in the group. Including Royce and her brother, for sure. It had been part of the lifestyle. One Stacy hadn't been a part of.

She took another step back, her heart in her throat, and fear started to cut off her ability to think. There was no sign of Royce. No sound to say he was anywhere close.

And yet she heard heavy breathing. Heavy breathing she recognized.

And she thought she knew.

Please not.

Please let her be wrong.

She swallowed and closed her eyes. Her heart pounded, as her blood rushed through her body. She could barely breathe.

Where the hell was Royce?

ROYCE COULDN'T CATCH his breath. He'd been sucker punched from behind so fast that he not only hadn't seen it, he hadn't felt it, until his ribs could no longer expand to gasp for air. He couldn't groan. He couldn't move. Someone had snuck up on him and taken him out so damn easily.

Anger filled his brain, and the rest of him was so full of pain.

Physical pain. He had to move. If he'd been taken out that fast, not even leaving him a clue as to who had done him in or his intentions, then what would they do to Stevie and Stacy?

He could still hear Stevie sobbing. Had he been the one to rig up the women? He'd been completely devastated when they'd gone missing. He'd come here for several vacations to be close to them. In a twisted way, Royce could understand Stevie keeping the women here like this. But he couldn't see Stevie attacking Kathleen or Yvonne. And Christine? That made no sense.

So who else?

He rolled over and gasped, willing himself to get to his knees. The shards of pain almost dropped him. Black mist filled his eyes, and his head dropped. Christ.

Stacy. He had to keep going for her.

He used the wall to stand upright. He hit vertical. Dizziness took over, and he sagged. He had no idea what the guy had done to him, but it was lethal.

Lethal? He frowned, considering what he was up against. Who he was up against? Did he know anyone with that kind of training? The man had moved too smoothly. Too quickly. It was a practiced move. He'd known what to do and where to hit. Royce had to consider that there might be a few other people hanging here than just the two women. He would hate to think so, but, if he'd been dropped so easily, his attacker could pick off any of the winter enthusiasts without much trouble.

Although there weren't many missing people from the area.

But they'd found a dead man, who hadn't been reported missing too.

Royce took a deep breath, straightened his shoulders, and hobbled a couple steps forward. Only darkness surrounded him. He didn't dare turn on the flashlight. He searched the shadows. Where was Stacy?

Silently huddling close to the wall, he sent a message, screaming for help to George, the only one not here and the only one he could then trust. George would help. And fast.

As soon as he was finished, he crouched and waited. Up ahead in the deep darkness in front of him, an odd sound tinkled through the space. An odd sound, discordant to the surroundings. And too damn perfect in timing. He froze.

It was a cell phone.

And it played George's favorite ringtone.

OH, WHAT FUN. Now the cat was out of the bag. Or was it? They had no idea whose phone went off. Ringtones were fun and easy to change. He smiled. He didn't even bother looking at the text—but he'd have to remember to thank the sender. It was a great time to get a text.

He wasn't nuts, although more than a few people might think so.

He wondered if Stacy recognized the ringtone. She was incredibly brilliant in one way but in others? ... Not so much. Still, she was about to take a very different career path.

One she'd been destined for a long time ago. He felt that sense of accomplishment well up inside him.

This was working out perfectly.

They were all here. He had no idea what to do with the sniveling Stevie. God, the man was a mess. A coward and just a wimp.

Not like him. He wasn't a wimp himself. He'd never been one. He loved women. Of all kinds. Some men kept mementos. So what if he kept the women? He'd been hearing news stories of all kinds of men out there keeping women as sex slaves in their basements. He wasn't that bad. Geesh. He did love to look at them though.

He knew where they all were. They hadn't found his collection yet. The matched set was front and center. And that one wasn't even his.

He'd been forced to find another stage to play on. A happy sigh slipped out.

Creativity was inspiring. He could do so much. None of these women would mind. Even if they were still alive, they wouldn't. He knew them. Knew what they were like under the skin. The two showcase specimens took the highest position, and that's where both of them would say they deserved to be. They'd also put Stacy slightly below them both, whether she'd understood that about her friends or not.

They considered her an oddity, someone below them in life. Not as good as they were.

And her place was ready and waiting for her.

At least for a little while.

Chapter 45

THAT RINGTONE.

Stacy's heart froze. Then shattered. Blow after blow. How many more could she take and still stay upright? This wasn't right. This couldn't be. There had to be another explanation. Her mind struggled to grasp any logical reason her brother's ringtone should have sounded in the dark space. She'd curled up tight against the corner, beside her friends. Hoping, praying she was wrong. Maybe whoever it was had changed his ringtone, so that he'd be mistaken for George. Or, and her heart seized at the idea, maybe George didn't have his phone because this asshole had taken him out and retrieved the phone. Maybe George had left it behind.

She knew she was grasping at straws. Only so many options were ahead of her, and none of them looked good.

And none of them addressed why Royce wasn't responding.

Her mind kept asking, *Was she sure it wasn't Royce?* He could have taken George's phone before George pulled out this morning. It's not like her brother had been organized or collected. No, it had to be someone else. Royce would never do that. Janice's snowboard was only inches away from her hand. She wanted to reach out and touch it, to ensure it was real, to confirm she wasn't caught in some psychotic drug-induced nightmare.

But the thought of touching her friend—board, boot, clothing—three years dead, was too much, even for her. On her table? Yes. In the field to get the answers needed? Yes. Here and now? No.

She dropped her head to her knees. There had to be a way out of this. *Think, damn it. Think, before there'd be no thinking left.* She could just imagine this asshole taking out Stevie and Royce. No one would ever find them. No one would ever find her best friends. Or find her.

She'd not believed in God in a very long time. Now she couldn't help but hope she'd been wrong. Only she suspected He helped those who helped themselves, rather than stepping into a scenario like this at the last moment.

A scrape rasped across the ice on her left. Shit. She had no weapon. Nothing.

And, for all she knew, she was the last one capable of saving anyone.

Then she heard something that made the hairs on the back of her neck stand up.

Heavy raspy breathing, … from the right …

She tried to shrink smaller.

A flashlight turned on, blinding her. "There you are."

She stared. In shock.

Stevie. She scrambled to her feet in relief. "Oh, thank God. I got so turned around, I didn't know who was here and who wasn't. Who was the good guy and who wasn't." She threw herself into his arms and hung on.

"Stacy?"

She paused, turned. "Royce! Oh, I'm so glad to see you." She slipped away from Stevie and gave him a huge smile. "I was so scared."

"Uh, Stacy," Royce said, "come here, please."

She took a step toward him, a little puzzled at the odd tone to his voice.

"Ac—" She choked back a scream, as an arm came around her throat and locked across her windpipe. She was dragged backward, her chest screaming for air, red swimming before her eyes. She couldn't focus. Everything was focused on the pain in her throat—the air her lungs were struggling to lock onto.

Her feet slid out from under her, as she was dragged farther backward.

And she finally heard the words being exchanged.

"Don't hurt her, Stevie." Royce's voice broke. "Please don't hurt her."

"I'm not going to hurt her," Stevie said, his voice a chilling singsong tone. "She's finally going to be with her friends. They're best friends, you know? Stacy has been lost without them. She's going to love being with them again."

Stacy tried to say no, tried to tell him that she didn't want to be with them. But he wasn't listening. As she heard the weird pitch in his voice, she realized that he would likely not hear her anyway. He was in his own world.

She tried to cry out for help. Tried to let Royce know she was choking to death.

"Stevie," she choked out. "I can't breathe."

Instantly the choke hold around her neck eased up, but he still held her tight, so she couldn't get free. She gasped, gulping madly for air.

"There. See? She's fine, Royce." Stevie turned Stacy to face Janice. "See, Stacy? They are waiting for you. All this time. They will be so happy to have you with them. I'll just put you up into the right position, so you can look at each other for eternity. You'll look perfect again."

"Is that what you're trying to do, Stevie?" Stacy asked, feeling hot tears in her eyes. She coughed, still trying to get air back into her lungs. "Give the three of us a chance to be together again?"

"Of course. They've been waiting for you. I tried to make them look right as they were …" He looked at Janice, frustration and worry on his pale features. "But they never looked right. Something was missing. Incomplete. And I finally knew why." A beatific smile shone from his face. "They were missing you, Stacy."

He pinned her in place with his arms. "And Stacy was missing the women. You've been missing them so much, haven't you, Stacy?"

"I do miss …" Her voice came out like a frog. She cleared her throat and tried again. "I do miss them, Stevie, but I don't want to join them."

With a wary glance at where she'd last seen Royce, she tried to shuffle slightly away from Stevie, but, backed up as she was to where Janice hung in the macabre horror show, she had nowhere to go.

"Yes, you do," he crooned in a soft voice. "I'll let you visit with them, until the cold puts you to sleep permanently." He looked at the hooks and wires he had waiting. "You'll like that. But I have to get you into position before you freeze." Frustration entered his voice. "It's really difficult to fix the position after you're frozen."

Oh God. "Stevie, don't you want to visit with me over the next many years? We've had such fun together."

"Oh, I will be here a lot. Now that I have you to visit too," he exclaimed lovingly.

His voice sent shivers through her. She hurt for him. She understood that, as much as she'd retreated from life for a while to deal with her losses, he hadn't been able to. He'd become obsessed with finding the women, and, once he had, he couldn't let them go.

She understood.

But she didn't want to join them in this sad gallery. She didn't know how all this worked with the other crap that had been going on, but she needed to find that out if she could. If she was lucky, someone was listening in. Even if they couldn't protect her, maybe the truth would come out.

"Stevie, did you drug everyone?"

"Me? No." He looked so outraged at her, she was taken aback. "Why would you think I'd do that? I'd never hurt you."

She blinked but managed to not look at her hanging friends. He hadn't killed them. He just couldn't let them go. "I didn't think so," she said in a soft voice. "I know that's not you." When he appeared to relax, slightly mollified, she added, "Do you know who would have done it?"

He shook his head. "Damn asshole. My head was killing me for days."

She nodded, as if she understood. And really she did. She'd suffered from that as well. But, if he hadn't drugged everyone, then who had?

"Have you had anyone else here to admire your work?" she asked, trying to keep her voice light and interested.

"Just one."

Oh no. She so needed to know who that was.

"But he told me that you wouldn't appreciate it. That I shouldn't show you." He looked at her brokenly. "But you understand, don't you? You miss them as much as I do."

Oh dear God. "I do." She hesitated, struggling to keep her voice calm. "Did someone help you do this?" She couldn't stop the hysteria rising in her tone.

"Do this?" His voice rose. "What do you mean by *this?*"

She fought for control. "Did someone help you create this display?" She didn't know what else to call it.

"Ah, yes, but just a little bit. He said I inspired him to try something similar."

There was almost disgust in his voice. She wondered what the hell she'd missed. "You don't like his work?"

"It's all right, but mine has heart. I'm doing something that *needs* to happen. Something that completes these lost souls."

"And what is his?" She was trying to keep him talking. To pretend interest in his work. He loved his work because he loved his subjects—literally. But who else was here? And how dangerous was he?

If he was here with Stevie and knew about her friends, then he was no friend to her. She had to expect him to be dangerous. More so than Stevie. He wanted her to hang to complete the matched set, as they'd always been called, but this other guy? … What was he up to?

Royce had to be here somewhere. But maybe so was someone else.

ROYCE FROZE AS he heard Stevie's words. Someone else who knew about this nightmare? And he hadn't turned Stevie in? *Shit.*

He looked around the darkness, grateful his eyes had adjusted. Not enough to see clearly, but with Stevie swinging around the flashlight, Royce was getting an idea of the room. There appeared to be another room off the far side.

Was that where the other person kept his work? And, if

it was, did Royce really want to see it? Or would it be just as gruesome as this nightmare?

He heard a sound coming around the corner toward Stevie. He shrank back out of sight.

There might be a way to come around behind these two. Now if only he had a weapon. He didn't want to think of going hand-to-hand against the man who'd already taken him down once. However, they'd used tools to do this work, so what were the chances they'd left something behind?

Trying to keep an eye on the newcomer and Stacy, Royce crawled along the outside edge of the floor.

And heard a voice that made his blood curdle.

AH, LOOK AT this. His little boy Stevie was moving up in life. He had Stacy, and she was still alive. For Stevie, that was big.

It was also likely to make him cross that fine line into insanity. Stevie didn't do this work because he was compelled to find pure expression of his art form. He did it because he was lost. Lost in his love of the friends who he'd cared for so deeply.

See? That was just the wrong reason.

He, on the other hand, loved this work. He operated on a completely different motivational level because of it. As Stevie became weaker and more mentally unbalanced, he himself got stronger. Too bad for Stevie. Good job for him.

Now wait until Stacy got a good look at him. She'd never believe it.

He couldn't wait.

And he stepped into the limelight, where every great achiever deserved to be.

And heard her gasp.

Only it wasn't as big a one as he'd hoped. It wasn't as

shocked as he'd hoped. In fact, it was more of an element in proving her theory correct.

And that just pissed him off. If she'd guessed it had been him, then she was damn wrong.

No one knew him that well. He made sure they didn't. In fact, he made dead *sure.*

Chapter 46

STACY LOOKED INTO Mark's eyes, and what she saw was scarier than Stevie's blind and misguided devotion. His actions were understandable, if you saw the fractured mind behind it all.

Mark's eyes, on the other hand, were the opposite. This was fun for him. This was something he planned, looked forward to, and didn't give a damn about the outcome—because he was sure he'd be the winner. This wasn't a game. Couldn't be one—there couldn't be anyone out there that was strong enough, good enough to beat him.

Because he was better than everyone. He'd always had that superior arrogance. It had gotten him in trouble several times at work, but he'd always skimmed past the trouble, just shy of any of it sticking to him.

Now as she stared at the two best friends, the two men she'd worked with for close to eight years, she wondered if she'd ever really known them. She hadn't seen Stevie's decline, and she should have. She hadn't seen the psychopath in Mark, and she should have.

She collapsed to the cold floor at Stevie's feet, her butt numb, but her head on fire, as she realized the number of times the two men had alibied each other. "Why the drugs, Mark?"

He laughed. "Why not? It was fun watching you bump

around in the dark, trying to figure it out. And getting nowhere. I had to throw things into confusion. Make Yvonne play into the mess. God, I hated her. As much as I wanted her to suffer, I didn't want her here forever with the others." He shrugged. "I drugged her and kept her here just long enough for her to wake up and to try to escape. Should have given her more drugs apparently. Still, I got what I wanted."

Stacy frowned. "What you wanted or who?"

"Oh, very good." He grinned and walked closer, pulling her to her feet. "Come and see for yourself."

She really didn't want to, but he dragged her forward regardless, Stevie trailing behind, crying out, "Don't hurt her."

"I'm not going to hurt her, Stevie, but, since you got to show her your work, I get to show her mine." And he thrust her forward, turning the commercial flashlight in his hands on full beam.

The sight slammed into her brain, and she squeezed her eyes closed in horror, her breath catching in her chest. She shuddered and opened her eyes to stare at the macabre scene. Poor Christine hung in an awkward angle, her neck obviously broken. Instead of trying to make his victims look alive and in action, like Stevie had managed, Mark's victims looked terrified and bore the marks of multiple injuries with bruising, indicating they'd been inflicted while they were still alive.

Stacy's hope that they would find Christine alive, as they had Kathleen, just died. Christine had most likely been killed soon after she hadn't checked in the first time. Likely when Kathleen had been attacked. Damn it. They hadn't even known. No one had gone to look for her. Had Mark been in this room the whole time—with Christine? While they were trying to save Kathleen?

Had she been alive long? Hoping someone would come and save her, as they had Kathleen?

Grief choked Stacy. And anger. And hatred.

He shone the light around to show her several other women in unfortunate positions, as he arranged them to suit him. Some were dressed, one was not. She didn't recognize the woman, but she'd been arranged in a sexually explicit manner.

"How many?" she asked in a hoarse voice, her eyes burning with unshed tears. So many women. They couldn't have all come from here. No way. He must have been picking them up from other locations and driving them here. Those poor women.

"I'm up to eleven now," he said casually. "I planned several more for this piece. Of course a couple weren't quite right." He shrugged. "I'd have kept Kathleen though. I had to do something when she saw me with the wine bottles. She wasn't sure what she'd seen, but, once she mentioned it to George, I knew she had to go."

Stacy closed her eyes, not wanting to know what he'd done with those discards.

Then she remembered the man they'd found. The one with the cowboy boots.

"Don't tell me. The cowboy boots didn't fit?"

Mark gave a bark of laughter. "Actually I was considering another sculpture with men, but it didn't feel right. I let him escape weeks ago. Figured he wouldn't get far. His girlfriend now though …" He shone his light on a stunning redhead on the left, a very broken doll-like redhead.

Stacy choked back the questions bubbling up. So many

victims. She didn't want to know what this scene in front of her was supposed to represent—but knew it would have special meaning to Mark. It always did. She couldn't see any theme or reason why the women were in these positions. And she didn't want to know. All she wanted was to get the hell out of here and never come back. Ever.

"Even then," Mark added, "I haven't kept all the women. I let Yvonne go too. I hadn't expected her to survive though." He smirked. "Too bad she's still alive. Although, from what I hear, she's not likely to make it anyway."

Stacy's stomach heaved. There shouldn't have been anything left inside to eject, but her body was proving her wrong. She bent over, collapsing to her knees, as she vomited again.

"Oh gross. Not again." Stevie danced backward. "I'll get the shovel again and clean up."

He disappeared, and she was grateful. She didn't think she had much chance of getting out of here alive, but, if she messed up their display, she would at least have accomplished something. Gasping for breath, she asked in a low voice, "Is there water?"

A bottle was thrust into her hand, and she took a drink, then rinsed her mouth.

"I gather you don't appreciate our work," Mark said, a rough edge to his voice.

"It's a bit much to take in all at once."

"Isn't it though?" He kicked some snow over her acidic spewing. "Stevie? Where the hell are you with that damn shovel?"

"I guess it made it more fun to have a partner for all this."

"Ha, it certainly made it easier," Mark said in a conversational tone. "I saw what he'd done and couldn't believe what our Stevie boy had accomplished all on his own. It was like a challenge to try my hand."

She nodded, as if she understood. Like hell. Who could?

Her gaze landed on several tools tossed on the ground ahead of her. As if they'd been working and had just dropped them when they heard sounds. She didn't know what he expected from her, but she wasn't going down without a fight.

"Get up. I have to find Stevie."

She shifted forward, getting hold of a hammer and sliding it along her grip.

He glared in the direction Stevie had gone. She must hurry. She swung, aiming for his temple. Hard. And danced back. Then flew forward and smashed him in the same spot again. And again.

He yelled, his one hand going for her throat, his other hand going to the side of his head that gushed blood. She danced out of his way, shifted to his other side, and, with both hands, she used the hammer like a baseball bat and took out his knee.

He went down screaming. One of his hands was splayed out flat on the ice, trying to support himself. She danced in and smashed his fingers as hard as she could. With his martial arts skills, she'd be lucky to get away from him, even if he had only one hand and one knee. She dared not let him get his hands on her.

Hammer ready, she danced just out of reach, her breathing panicked. She wanted to go in and hit him over and over again, until he was nothing but hamburger, but she didn't kill people. She wasn't him. She refused to become him.

"Stacy?"

Royce. "Oh my God." She threw the hammer down and ran into his arms. "Are you okay? I was so afraid they'd gotten to you."

"Mark here did. But I managed to recover long enough to hear what was going on. Stevie is out cold and …" He motioned toward where Mark had crumpled on the ground. "Apparently you handled this guy all by yourself."

"Nothing like knowing you were the next specimen to be put on display to give you strength and courage," she said, with a grimace. She pointed to the wall of women. "He's killed eleven."

Royce stared in grim horror at the room of his victims. "I'd like to hit him eleven times just for these poor souls."

Noises behind them had them both spinning around, expecting the worst, only to have the room fill with cops and rescue personnel. As one, they came to a sudden stop inside the big cavern and stared.

"Oh dear God. Those poor women."

"A serial killer?"

"He killed all of them? There must be a dozen women here."

"He …" Stacy pointed out Mark, where he lay moaning on the ground. "He has killed eleven. But they are not all here in this room."

"And that horrific snowboarding scene we just walked past?" one of the men asked incredulously. "What about those two?"

Stacy looked at him sadly. "They both died in an avalanche three years ago." She ran her hand down the side of her head, not surprised to see her hand shaking badly. "Stevie, the man Royce knocked out cold here, he's responsible for finding their bodies and arranging them in that display. They were our best friends," she said gently, sadly. "He couldn't handle losing them."

"So he found them and kept them here as what? Mementos that he could come and visit?" one of the men asked, staring at the room of horror, his voice trembling and thin. "I can't believe this has been going on for so long."

"A memorial, I think. The two women died three years ago, so they weren't here longer than that. The other women less so, as Mark started his collection after he saw Stevie's work."

"Stevie had to finish the job he started—for the women's sake. So they could be together again," Mark defended his friend. "Can't you appreciate that?"

Stacy could. But she had no idea how to even contemplate Mark's actions. And she didn't want to.

The authorities stared at Mark, then at each other.

They turned their backs on him and started to process the scene. Two cops were in the mix. One walked over and grabbed Mark's arms and tugged them behind his back, ignoring his screams as they handcuffed him. In a smooth movement, the cops lifted him to his feet. He continued to scream that he was injured. "Stacy beat me with a hammer," he said, crying out. "I wasn't doing anything to her."

One of the men turned and asked her, "Did you?"

She nodded faintly. "I did. Several times. Self-defense. He was trying to make me his twelfth victim."

"Too bad you didn't hit him some more. Then he'd be dead, and we wouldn't have the problem of a trial."

She searched his gaze, then admitted softly, "I hit him several times in the temple. I'm not sure he'll survive anyway."

The guy's eyes widened. He grinned. "You're Stacy

Carter, aren't you? I attended a talk you gave last year in Vancouver."

"I love Vancouver." She gave him a wan smile. "I hope I acquitted myself well."

"That talk was great." He turned to look at the chaos around him. "I'm glad to see you can handle yourself in the field too." He nodded and moved on.

She turned to Royce. "Are you ready to leave?"

His lopsided smile slipped out. "If you remember, I never wanted to come here."

Teary-eyed, she stepped into his arms. "That may be true, but I am very glad to finally have this at rest."

Burrowing his head against hers, he hugged her tight. Then he turned in the direction of the exit. "Let's get going."

They walked back out to the crevasse, walking around a dozen people. "This place will be a busy hub for days," she said.

"And our ride is now gone too. I presume they will take Mark's truck and impound it?"

She sighed. "They will. We'll have to find a ride home on our own."

"Or not." Royce pointed up to the top of the hill.

George, a worried frown on his face, stood waiting for them. As soon as they reached him, he grabbed Stacy and hugged her tight. "I went in and saw," he said, "then came right back out and puked." He shook his head. "Jesus. Stevie and Mark?"

"Yeah, but we've got them now," Stacy said. "Unfortunately Christine is dead."

Holding her tight, George kept repeating, "Dear God. I almost lost you too."

"I'm safe." She pulled back slightly, her exhausted gaze

going from one man to the other. "However, I don't think I'll ever let you talk me into another winter vacation here again."

"You?" Royce said, "Hell, I won't ever come back myself."

"Ditto."

The three hooked arms and carefully made their way back to the cabin and George's waiting Land Rover.

"Can we leave?" Royce asked, as they loaded up their bags.

"Yes, they'll get a hold of us tomorrow for full statements," George said. "I was going through Squamish when I started getting your texts, so I still haven't seen Kathleen, but she's awake and talking. Maybe she can leave today too. Yvonne has woken from the coma, but she'll be a couple days yet."

"Good, then home it is. There's a bathtub with my name on it," he said, with a big grin on his face. "At Stacy's place."

"A bathtub, *huh*?" George turned to look at his sister. "Is that okay with you?"

"Oh yeah," she said. "It's got my name on it too."

And she couldn't wait. Her future looked the best she'd ever seen it.

This concludes Book 3 of By Death: *Chilled by Death*.

Read the first chapter of Tuesday's Child: Psychic Visions, Book 1

Psychic Visions: Tuesday's Child (Book #1)
Chapter 1

March 18 at 2:35 a.m.

SAMANTHA BLAIR STRUGGLED against phantom restraints. *No, not again.*

This wasn't her room or her bed, and it sure as hell wasn't her body. Tears welled and trickled slowly from eyes not her own. Then the pain started. Still she couldn't move. She could only endure. Terror clawed at her soul, while dying nerves screamed.

The attack became a frenzy of stabs and slices, snatching away all thought. Her body jerked and arched in a macabre dance. Black spots blurred her vision, and still the slaughter continued.

Sam screamed. The terror was hers, but the cracked, broken voice was not.

Confusion reigned, as her mind grappled with reality. What was going on?

Understanding crashed in on her. With it came despair and horror.

She'd become a visitor in someone else's nightmare. Locked inside a horrifying energy warp, she'd linked to this poor woman, whose life dripped away from multiple gashes.

Another psychic vision.

The knife slashed down, impaling the woman's abdomen, splitting her wide from rib cage to pelvis. Her agonized scream echoed on forever in Sam's mind. She cringed.

The other woman slipped into unconsciousness. Sam wasn't offered the same gift. Now the pain was Sam's alone. The stab wounds and broken bones became Sam's to experience, even though they weren't hers.

The woman's head cocked to one side, her cheek resting on the blood-soaked bedding. From the new vantage point, Sam's horrified gaze locked on a bloody knife, held high by a man dressed in black from the top of his head down. Only his eyes showed, glowing with feverish delight. She shuddered. *Please, dear God, let it end soon.*

The attacker's fury died suddenly. A fine tremor shook his arm, as fatigue set in. "Shit." He removed his glove and scratched the exposed skin.

In the waning moonlight, from the corner of her eye, Sam caught the metallic glint of a ring on his finger. It mattered. She knew it did. She struggled to imprint the image before the opportunity was lost. Her eyes drifted closed. In the darkness of her mind, the wait for Death was endless.

Sam's soul wept. Oh, God, she hated this. Why? Why was she here? She couldn't help the woman. She couldn't even help herself.

Sam welcomed the next blow—so light, only a minor flinch undulated through the dreadfully damaged body of this woman. Maybe the poor woman had passed on. Sam's tortured spirit stirred deep within the rolling waves of blackness, struggling for freedom from this nightmare.

With one last surge of energy, the woman opened her

eyes and locked on to the killer's gaze staring back from within the mask. In ever-slowing heartbeats, her—and Sam's—circle of vision narrowed, until the two soulless orbs blended into one small band, before it blinked out altogether. The silence, when it came, was absolute.

Gratefully Sam relaxed into the woman's death.

Twenty minutes later, Sam bolted upright in her own bed. Survival instincts screamed at her to run. White agony dropped her in place.

"*Ooooh,*" she cried out. Fearing more pain, she slid her hands over her belly. Her fingers slipped along the raw edges of a deep slash. Searing pain made her gasp and twist away. Hot tears poured. Warm sticky fluid coated her fingers. "Oh, God. Oh, God. Oh, God," she chanted.

Staring in confusion around her, fear, panic, and finally recognition seeped into her dazed mind. Early morning rays highlighted the water stains on the ceiling, shining through the slapdash coat of whitewash on there, and Sam's banged-up suitcases, open on the floor. An empty room—an empty life. A remnant of a foster-care childhood.

She was home.

Memories swamped her, flooding her senses with yet more hurt. Sam broke down. Like an animal, she tried to curl into a tiny ball, only to scream again as pain jackknifed through her. Torn edges of muscle tissue and flesh rubbed against each other, and broken ribs creaked with her slightest movement. Blood slipped over her torn breasts to soak the sheets below.

The smell. Wet wool fought with the unique and unforgettable smell of fresh blood.

Sam caught her breath and froze, her face hot, tight with agony. "Shit, shit, and shit!" She swore under her breath, like a mantra.

Tremors wracked her tiny frame, keeping the pain alive, as she morphed through realities. *Transition time.* What a joke. That always brought images of New Age mumbo jumbo to mind. Nothing light and airy could describe this. Each blow leveled at the victim had manifested in Sam's own body. This was hard-core healing time for Sam—time when bones knitted, sliced ligaments and muscle tissue grew back together, and skin stitched itself closed.

Sam understood her injuries had something to do with her imperfect control, paired with her inability to accept her gifts. Apparently, if she could surmount the latter, the first would diminish. She didn't quite understand how or why. Or what to do about it. Her body somehow always healed; the physical and mental scars always remained. She was a mess.

The physical process usually took anywhere from ten to twenty minutes—depending on the injuries. The mental confusion, disconnectedness, sense of isolation took longer to disappear. She paid a high price for moving too soon. Shuddering, Sam reached for the frayed edges of her control. It wouldn't be much longer. She hoped.

Nothing could stop the hot tears, leaking from her closed eyelids.

This session had been bad. Apart from the broken ribs, there were so many stab wounds. She'd never experienced one death so physically damaging. Nervously she wondered at the extent of her blood loss. If she didn't learn how to disconnect, these visions could be the end of her—literally.

Just like that poor woman.

Sam hated that these episodes were changing, growing, developing. So powerful and so ugly, they made her sick to her soul.

Several minutes later, Sam raised her head to survey the bed. The pain was manageable, although she wouldn't move her limbs yet. Blood had soaked the top of the many Thrift Store blankets piled high on the bed. Her hollowed belly had become a vessel for the cooling puddle of blood. Shit. The stuff was everywhere.

The metallic taste clung to her lips and teeth. She rolled the disgusting spit around the inside of her mouth, waiting. She wanted to run away—from the memories, the visions, her life. But knowing that pain simmered beneath the surface, waiting to rip her apart, stopped her. Weary, ageless patience added to the bleakness in her heart.

Ten more minutes passed. Now she should be good to go. Lifting her head, she spat the bloody gob onto the waiting wad of tissue and noted the time.

Transition had taken fifteen minutes this morning.

She was improving.

Oh, God. Sam broke into sobs again. When would this end? Other psychics found things or heard things. Many of them saw events before they happened. She saw violence— not only saw it but experienced it too.

Occasional shudders racked her frame from the coldness that seemed destined to live in her veins. The odd straggling sniffle escaped. She couldn't remember when she'd last been warm. Dropping the top blood-soaked blanket to the floor, Sam tugged the motley collection of covers tighter around her skinny frame. Warmth was a comfort that belonged to others.

She wasn't so lucky.

She walked with one foot on the dark side—whether she liked it or not. And that was the problem. She'd been running for a long time. Then she'd landed at this cabin and had been hiding ever since. That was no answer either.

Her resolve firmed. Enough was enough. It was time to gain control of her *gift*. Time to do something, even if just reading more books on psychics, maybe finding one she could talk to. This monster had to be stopped.

Plus, Christ, she was tired of waking up dead.

Book 1 is available now!
To find out more visit Dale Mayer's website.
https://geni.us/Dmtuesdayuniversal

Simon Says... HIDE: Kate Morgan (Book #1)

Welcome to a new thriller series from *USA Today* Best-Selling Author Dale Mayer. Set in Vancouver, BC, the team of Detective Kate Morgan and Simon St. Laurant, an unwilling psychic, marries all the elements of Dale's work that you've come to love, plus so much more.

Detective Kate Morgan, newly promoted to the Vancouver PD Homicide Department, stands for the victims in her world. She was once a victim herself, just as her mother had been a victim, and then her brother—an unsolved missing child's case—was yet another victim. She can't stand those who take advantage of others, and the worst ones are those who prey on the hopes of desperate people to line their own pockets.

So, when she finds a connection between a current case and more than a half-dozen cold cases, where a child's life hangs in the balance, Kate would make a deal with the devil himself to find the culprit and to save the child.

Simon St. Laurant's grandmother had the Sight and had

warned him that, once he used it, he could never walk away. Until now, her caution had made it easy to avoid that first step. But, when nightmares of his own past are triggered, Simon can't stand back and watch child after child be abused. Not without offering his help to those chasing the monsters.

Even if it means dealing with the cranky and critical Detective Kate Morgan …

Find Simon Says… Hide here!
To find out more visit Dale Mayer's website.
https://geni.us/DMSSHideUniversal

Simon Says... HIDE: Kate Morgan (Book #1)
Chapter 1

Vancouver, First Monday in June ...

NEWLY MINTED HOMICIDE detective Kate Morgan sat on one of the many benches positioned in this child-friendly park, watching the kids play on the swings in downtown Vancouver. She'd passed her first three months in her new position amid the craziness of too many murder cases to count. Vancouver, BC, was like any big city around the world and had its share of criminal activity. The city had its issues—just being on the coast and blending many different nationalities—yet somehow it all worked. Plus it was home for her. Always had been.

Because of those life-and-death issues, Vancouver had three homicide units, usually with six or seven detectives in each unit. She chuckled. At one time, the two other units called themselves Team Canuck or Team Flames, showing how hockey crazy Canada got. She didn't know what her unit used to call themselves, as she was the odd-one-out still. New enough to know her place and not so new to misunderstand the team needed time to meld.

Her ever-assessing gaze watched two men on a bench on the far side of the park. One got up, tossed a bright yellow ball at the other and then, with a raised hand, turned and walked away.

Her focus flitted to the storm approaching in the distance, assessed its threat, and dismissed it. Rain was part of the reality when living on the coast. The more pressing threats in her world were the two-legged predators. She'd known the dangers ever since her younger brother had disappeared, even now, twenty-five years later with still no trace of him. She kept a copy of his file on her desk, as a reminder of the work she'd dedicated herself to. Timmy was always close to her heart. She could only hope to get closure, as she worked to give closure to others.

Sudden movement on her left had her watching a lean man of average height, walking into the park and staring at the kids on the swing. Something about his gaze set her nerves on edge. He was slightly turned away from her, only letting her see his jeans and well-worn jacket with the upturned collar. He perched on a nearby bench seat, seemingly fascinated by the boys' antics.

The single male on the far side stood suddenly and strode her way, tossing the yellow ball and catching it smoothly with every step. He gazed at the street beside her, unconcerned for the kids or other adults. His focus was internal. From the power suit he wore, business deals most likely.

As she turned back to the other man, he'd disappeared. Her gaze zipped to the boys at the swings. They were still there. Relaxing slightly, she studied the park exits. Both men had left at the same time. From opposite sides of the park.

It shouldn't have meant anything.

But it felt like it did.

Her phone rang just then. Rodney, one of her team.

"We found another one. Prepare yourself. It's a little boy."

Tuesday

SIMON ST. LAURANT had had a bad week. He twisted in bed, kicking off the blanket. His body shimmered with sweat. He drifted in and out of sleep. He'd been up until two in the morning in one of his friendlier gambling games and had crashed soon afterward. Now it was five in the morning, and the last thing he wanted was to be awake. He rolled over, pulled the sheet over his sweating body, and closed his eyes.

As he tried to fall asleep again, he drifted down the same godforsaken dark street, just a halo of light coming from the streetlamps across on the other side. A small man, holding the hand of a very young boy at his side, walked quietly down the street. The little boy asked, "When will we be there?"

"We'll be there soon," the older man promised.

Something was just so damn wrong about that picture that Simon kept telling the little boy to run, wanting to reach out and drag him to safety. But, even as Simon reached out a hand, he saw that it wasn't real, that he wasn't there, that he couldn't grab that little boy and escape. As the older man walked under the streetlamp, Simon caught the hungry look on the man's face. A predator's look. Yet not clear enough to identify him.

Simon woke immediately, sat up, and groaned in frustration. "Why that same goddamn freaking nightmare?" he cried out, before flopping to his back yet again.

He was exhausted, his mind overwhelmed, as he drifted once again into the deepness of sleep. This time he landed in a small room, with lots of toys on the bed and on the floor.

A bed that broke his heart because it had a plastic sheet for the little kids who might wet themselves. A blanket was atop the bed but was otherwise empty. Simon's mind knew that a light was on the side of the room and that Simon would see the child soon, but he didn't want to go there. He kicked himself out of the dream, sitting up again, shuddering in the dark. "Damn it," he muttered, rubbing his eyes. "What fresh hell is this?"

Almost as if by asking that question, his body stiffened. He fell backward again, and this time he was in a different room, and the bed was bigger. It had little pink roses around the base and unicorns across the headboard. A little girl sobbed her eyes out, curled up into a tiny ball, hugging a teddy bear. The problem was that fancy little bed was completely out of place, surrounded by bare concrete walls and old cracked floors. The lack of carpet or any other niceties suggested this would not be a nice little home for her.

Instead Simon saw the bloodstains on the mattress around her, the pain and the terror in her heart, and the loneliness in her soul. He wanted to hold her and to tell her that it would be okay. But the same words rippled through his mind: *Hide. He's coming.*

Then everything went dark …

When he woke again, he lay in his bed, staring at the ceiling, dry-eyed, but felt as if he'd bawled his entire life away. Every part of his body hurt, especially his soul. He sat up, felt like he was thirty years older than his thirty-seven years on this planet. Thirty-seven years of pain and fighting to get the upper hand, trying to ensure that he wouldn't be a victim in this world again.

Years ago he'd sworn to be a victor instead. He played

the game, but he didn't let others play him. That wasn't part of his new reality. Not anymore—not for a long time. He looked down at his bed, the bottom sheet literally pulled off the mattress and twisted beneath him, while the top sheet was crumpled on the floor beside him.

"Looks like I had a party—and not the fun kind," he muttered, as he slowly straightened. He stretched, turned to get the kinks out of his neck and his back. A bad night had the effect of turning his spine into a pretzel that he could spend hours trying to untwist. He needed a hot shower to complete the job. Yet every time he went under the water, he kept seeing images of the boy that he'd seen in the first nightmare this morning.

It made no sense, when he'd seen many other children throughout his lifetime of nightmares, but, for some reason, he identified with that one. That night terror always upset him because he didn't know that child. It wasn't Simon as a child, and he didn't understand the dialogue, didn't remember it from his own life. What he did know was that these nightmares had to stop.

If he had a friend who was a doctor, he might have talked to him or her, but unfortunately he didn't even have that. In truth, speaking out loud of this weakness, … in the wrong hands, that knowledge could crush Simon. As he walked naked to the shower, he knew something had to change; he couldn't keep going on this way. The nightmares had restarted suddenly, for no current reason, and they were getting stronger, clearer, and more traumatic to view.

He should get away for a few days. Book a gambling cruise to take his mind off this mess. Maybe see Yale there. Simon's gaze caught sight of the yellow child's ball that Yale had tossed to Simon, the two men out of the blue both at the park yesterday.

Simon often walked that corridor and had come upon his old friend, looking sad and depressed. It had been nice to see Yale unexpectedly. Normally they'd be in on the same poker games or cruises, but he hadn't seen his old college friend in over six months.

Much happier after their visit, Yale had laughed, as he'd tossed him the ball, and said, "For old times' sake."

With a shrug, Simon stepped under the rain showerhead and let the hot water slosh over his head and down his back to the tiles below.

As soon as he was dry and dressed in lightweight pants with a linen shirt, perfect for summers in Vancouver, he picked up his blazer, flipped it over his shoulder, and headed out. He needed coffee in a big way, but he also had to escape the solitude of his own thoughts, preferably out in public, where he could disappear into the crowds. He walked off the elevator, crossed the lobby, and headed toward the front door, held open by the doorman.

Once outside, he stopped for a long moment, lifted his head, and sniffed the early morning Vancouver air. The nearby harbor, with that scent of salt, plus the noise and the bustle of city life, all of it melded together beautifully. With a smile he turned and headed toward his favorite coffee shop.

Find Simon Says... Hide here!
To find out more visit Dale Mayer's website.
https://geni.us/DMSSHideUniversal

Author's Note

Thank you for reading Chilled by Death! If you enjoyed my book, I'd appreciate it if you'd leave a review.

Dear reader,

I love to hear from readers, and you can contact me at my website: www.dalemayer.com or at my Facebook author page. To be informed of new releases and special offers, sign up for my newsletter or follow me on BookBub. And if you are interested in joining Dale Mayer's Reader Group, here is the Facebook sign up page.
http://geni.us/DaleMayerFBGroup

Cheers,
Dale Mayer

About the Author

Dale Mayer is a *USA Today* best-selling author, best known for her SEALs military romances, her Psychic Visions series, and her Lovely Lethal Garden cozy series. Her contemporary romances are raw and full of passion and emotion (Broken But … Mending, Hathaway House series). Her thrillers will keep you guessing (Kate Morgan, By Death series), and her romantic comedies will keep you giggling (*It's a Dog's Life*, a stand-alone novella; and the Broken Protocols series, starring Charming Marvin, the cat).

Dale honors the stories that come to her—and some of them are crazy, break all the rules and cross multiple genres!

To go with her fiction, she also writes nonfiction in many different fields, with books available on résumé writing, companion gardening, and the US mortgage system. All her books are available in print and ebook format.

Connect with Dale Mayer Online

Dale's Website – www.dalemayer.com
Twitter – @DaleMayer
Facebook Page – geni.us/DaleMayerFBFanPage
Facebook Group – geni.us/DaleMayerFBGroup
BookBub – geni.us/DaleMayerBookbub
Instagram – geni.us/DaleMayerInstagram
Goodreads – geni.us/DaleMayerGoodreads
Newsletter – geni.us/DaleNews

Also by Dale Mayer

Published Adult Books:

Shadow Recon

Magnus, Book 1

Bullard's Battle

Ryland's Reach, Book 1

Cain's Cross, Book 2

Eton's Escape, Book 3

Garret's Gambit, Book 4

Kano's Keep, Book 5

Fallon's Flaw, Book 6

Quinn's Quest, Book 7

Bullard's Beauty, Book 8

Bullard's Best, Book 9

Bullard's Battle, Books 1–2

Bullard's Battle, Books 3–4

Bullard's Battle, Books 5–6

Bullard's Battle, Books 7–8

Terkel's Team

Damon's Deal, Book 1

Wade's War, Book 2

Gage's Goal, Book 3

Calum's Contact, Book 4

Rick's Road, Book 5

Scott's Summit, Book 6

Brody's Beast, Book 7

Terkel's Twist, Book 8

Terkel's Triumph, Book 9

Terkel's Guardian

Radar, Book 1

Kate Morgan

Simon Says… Hide, Book 1

Simon Says… Jump, Book 2

Simon Says… Ride, Book 3

Simon Says… Scream, Book 4

Simon Says… Run, Book 5

Simon Says… Walk, Book 6

Hathaway House

Aaron, Book 1

Brock, Book 2

Cole, Book 3

Denton, Book 4

Elliot, Book 5

Finn, Book 6

Gregory, Book 7

Heath, Book 8

Iain, Book 9

Jaden, Book 10

Jenner, Book 16

Rhys, Book 17

Landon, Book 18

Harper, Book 19

Kascius, Book 20

The K9 Files, Books 1–2

The K9 Files, Books 3–4

The K9 Files, Books 5–6

The K9 Files, Books 7–8

The K9 Files, Books 9–10

The K9 Files, Books 11–12

Lovely Lethal Gardens

Arsenic in the Azaleas, Book 1

Bones in the Begonias, Book 2

Corpse in the Carnations, Book 3

Daggers in the Dahlias, Book 4

Evidence in the Echinacea, Book 5

Footprints in the Ferns, Book 6

Gun in the Gardenias, Book 7

Handcuffs in the Heather, Book 8

Ice Pick in the Ivy, Book 9

Jewels in the Juniper, Book 10

Killer in the Kiwis, Book 11

Lifeless in the Lilies, Book 12

Murder in the Marigolds, Book 13

Nabbed in the Nasturtiums, Book 14

Offed in the Orchids, Book 15

Poison in the Pansies, Book 16

Quarry in the Quince, Book 17

Revenge in the Roses, Book 18

Silenced in the Sunflowers, Book 19

Toes in the Tulips, Book 20

Lovely Lethal Gardens, Books 1–2

Lovely Lethal Gardens, Books 3–4

Lovely Lethal Gardens, Books 5–6

Lovely Lethal Gardens, Books 7–8

Lovely Lethal Gardens, Books 9–10

Psychic Vision Series

Tuesday's Child

Hide 'n Go Seek

Maddy's Floor

Garden of Sorrow

Knock Knock…

Rare Find

Eyes to the Soul

Now You See Her

Shattered

Into the Abyss

Seeds of Malice

Eye of the Falcon

Itsy-Bitsy Spider

Unmasked

Deep Beneath

From the Ashes

Stroke of Death

Ice Maiden

Snap, Crackle…

What If…

Talking Bones

String of Tears

Inked Forever

Psychic Visions Books 1–3

Psychic Visions Books 4–6

Psychic Visions Books 7–9

By Death Series

Touched by Death

Haunted by Death

Chilled by Death

By Death Books 1–3

Broken Protocols – Romantic Comedy Series

Cat's Meow

Cat's Pajamas

Cat's Cradle

Cat's Claus

Broken Protocols 1-4

Broken and… Mending

Skin

Scars

Scales (of Justice)

Broken but… Mending 1-3

Glory

Genesis

Tori

Celeste

Glory Trilogy

Biker Blues

Morgan: Biker Blues, Volume 1

Cash: Biker Blues, Volume 2

SEALs of Honor

Mason: SEALs of Honor, Book 1

Hawk: SEALs of Honor, Book 2

Dane: SEALs of Honor, Book 3

Swede: SEALs of Honor, Book 4

Shadow: SEALs of Honor, Book 5

Cooper: SEALs of Honor, Book 6

Markus: SEALs of Honor, Book 7

Evan: SEALs of Honor, Book 8

Mason's Wish: SEALs of Honor, Book 9

Chase: SEALs of Honor, Book 10

Brett: SEALs of Honor, Book 11

Devlin: SEALs of Honor, Book 12

Easton: SEALs of Honor, Book 13

Ryder: SEALs of Honor, Book 14

Macklin: SEALs of Honor, Book 15

Corey: SEALs of Honor, Book 16

Warrick: SEALs of Honor, Book 17

Tanner: SEALs of Honor, Book 18

Jackson: SEALs of Honor, Book 19

Kanen: SEALs of Honor, Book 20

Nelson: SEALs of Honor, Book 21

Taylor: SEALs of Honor, Book 22

Colton: SEALs of Honor, Book 23

Troy: SEALs of Honor, Book 24

Axel: SEALs of Honor, Book 25

Baylor: SEALs of Honor, Book 26

Hudson: SEALs of Honor, Book 27

Lachlan: SEALs of Honor, Book 28

Paxton: SEALs of Honor, Book 29

Bronson: SEALs of Honor, Book 30

Hale: SEALs of Honor, Book 31

SEALs of Honor, Books 1–3

SEALs of Honor, Books 4–6

SEALs of Honor, Books 7–10

SEALs of Honor, Books 11–13

SEALs of Honor, Books 14–16

SEALs of Honor, Books 17–19

SEALs of Honor, Books 20–22

SEALs of Honor, Books 23–25

Heroes for Hire

Levi's Legend: Heroes for Hire, Book 1

Stone's Surrender: Heroes for Hire, Book 2

Merk's Mistake: Heroes for Hire, Book 3

Rhodes's Reward: Heroes for Hire, Book 4

Flynn's Firecracker: Heroes for Hire, Book 5

Logan's Light: Heroes for Hire, Book 6

Harrison's Heart: Heroes for Hire, Book 7

Saul's Sweetheart: Heroes for Hire, Book 8

SEALs of Steel

Badger: SEALs of Steel, Book 1

Erick: SEALs of Steel, Book 2

Cade: SEALs of Steel, Book 3

Talon: SEALs of Steel, Book 4

Laszlo: SEALs of Steel, Book 5

Geir: SEALs of Steel, Book 6

Jager: SEALs of Steel, Book 7

The Final Reveal: SEALs of Steel, Book 8

SEALs of Steel, Books 1–4

SEALs of Steel, Books 5–8

SEALs of Steel, Books 1–8

The Mavericks

Kerrick, Book 1

Griffin, Book 2

Jax, Book 3

Beau, Book 4

Asher, Book 5

Ryker, Book 6

Miles, Book 7

Nico, Book 8

Keane, Book 9

Lennox, Book 10

Gavin, Book 11

Shane, Book 12

Diesel, Book 13

Jerricho, Book 14

Killian, Book 15

Hatch, Book 16

Corbin, Book 17

Aiden, Book 18

The Mavericks, Books 1–2

The Mavericks, Books 3–4

The Mavericks, Books 5–6

The Mavericks, Books 7–8

The Mavericks, Books 9–10

The Mavericks, Books 11–12

Standalone Novellas

It's a Dog's Life

Riana's Revenge

Second Chances

Published Young Adult Books:

Family Blood Ties Series

Vampire in Denial

Vampire in Distress

Vampire in Design

Vampire in Deceit

Vampire in Defiance

Vampire in Conflict

Vampire in Chaos

Vampire in Crisis

Vampire in Control

Vampire in Charge

Family Blood Ties Set 1–3

Family Blood Ties Set 1–5

Family Blood Ties Set 4–6

Family Blood Ties Set 7–9

Sian's Solution, A Family Blood Ties Series Prequel
Novelette

Design series

Dangerous Designs

Deadly Designs

Darkest Designs

Design Series Trilogy

Standalone

In Cassie's Corner

Gem Stone (a Gemma Stone Mystery)

Time Thieves

Published Non-Fiction Books:

Career Essentials

Career Essentials: The Résumé

Career Essentials: The Cover Letter

Career Essentials: The Interview

Career Essentials: 3 in 1